The Casebook of Inspector Armstrong Volume IV

THE BOOK CLUB

Martin Daley

Paperback ISBN 978-1-78705-642-8
ePub ISBN 978-1-78705-643-5
PDF ISBN 978-1-78705-644-2

Published in the UK by MX Publishing
335 Princess Park Manor, Royal Drive,
London, N11 3GX
www.mxpublishing.com

For my parents Paul and Noeline in their 60th year together

ONE

This was the day Miss Ester Sanderson had been looking forward to throughout the Christmas holidays. It was the day upon which she was to buy a pair of shoes that she had stared longingly at on several occasions since October, when they first started calling to her from the window of Gowan's Emporium on English Street.

Ester had dropped plenty of hints to her parents as Christmas approached, secretly hoping that her father would treat her to them as her present. But the subtleties of commenting on the latest fashions in London and Paris, the need to have decent footwear in the wintertime – not that these fashionable items were particularly practical, but she didn't need to elaborate on that too much – and the considerable discounts offered by Gowan's lately, had all failed to land as she intended.

Ester had then resorted to asking her father outright if he would buy her the shoes for Christmas. In response, he had made it quite clear that – despite his considerable wealth – he felt such a purchase was profligate and undisciplined. Instead, whilst accompanying his wife as she was doing some shopping for the holidays, he spotted what he believed was the perfect gift for his nineteen-year-old daughter: a little sequined box that, when opened revealed a tiny ballerina who rotated to a high-pitched tinkling of *The Dance of the Sugar Plum Fairy*.

Fortunately for Ester her mother was a little more in tune with what her daughter actually wanted and when a great aunt asked her what she could purchase for her favourite niece, Ester's mother told her about the shoes that her daughter coveted.

So on Christmas morning when they were opening their presents, the challenge for the young woman was to moderate her reactions to first, the feigning of enthusiasm and gratitude for a box that would have given only mild amusement to an eight-year-old; and secondly, the joy at the discovery of an envelope, inside of which contained a card that, when opened, revealed a coupon with the unmistakable

1

lettering of Gowan's Emporium emblazoned across it. Ester managed to disguise her squeak of delight as a suppressed sneeze and exchanged a knowing glance with her smiling mother.

The rest of the holidays were spent performing family duties and fulfilling social obligations, all the while wishing for the day to come where she could meet her friend Matilda Chambers and spend the morning relaxing, gossiping and most importantly of all, shopping.

When the day arrived, it was in keeping with the previous weeks; it had been the bitterest of winters with the city seemingly encased in an enormous white container since late November. The River Eden had become a patchwork of cracking ice and in the thinner parts; the water meandered slowly, dark and menacing. Parklands and pavements had all succumbed to a giant blanket of snow that had repeated a process of laying, freezing and snowing again for several weeks. Whether it was sunny mornings that revealed shiny spiders' webs draped over branches and hedges like crystal lace; or icy winds blowing in from the east taking the temperatures well below freezing, the net result was the same for all the citizens of Carlisle. Regardless of class or status, keeping warm and well-nourished was the main priority.

Ester – with her father's permission – and Matilda had arranged to meet at the southern terminus at ten o'clock and take the horse-drawn omnibus into town. At the appointed hour the two embraced, neither attempting to hide their delight at seeing their best friend for the first time since before the holidays; there was much catching up to do.

The two never knew what it was like to be without the other. Ester was an only child and whereas Matilda had an older brother, the two were as close as any two sisters could be. Their respective mothers originally knew each other when they sang in the church choir together. Coincidentally, they were expecting at the same time and Ester and Matilda therefore appeared within a week of one another; they had virtually been inseparable ever since. They enjoyed the sort of relationship that, despite growing up and going through school together, and spending as much time as possible during the summer holidays together, there was always plenty to catch up on: from boys to allowances; from grumpy fathers to the weather they would talk endlessly. And ever since Ester had seen her must-have items three months ago, the conversation had usually gravitated towards shoes and Gowan's.

On this bitterly cold morning, both wore long coats and had matching neck and hand mufflers. Although they had only been outside for a few minutes, the colour had already been whipped into their cheeks by the cold temperature. The omnibus was ready, waiting and already crowded by the time they arrived. The hot breath of the panting horses created a cloud around their ears and Ester and Matilda giggled to one another as one casually lifted its tale and defecated onto the glistening cobbles.

The two young women initially entered the lower deck: it was full of the usual assortment of old women in shawls and wicker baskets, top-hatted gentlemen and flat-capped artisans. They either read their newspapers, glanced at the advertisements posted above the heads of the passengers sitting opposite, or simply adopted the thousand-mile stare so many do when surrounded by their fellow travellers.

With no seats together – and knowing there was therefore no way of making fun of the other passengers – the two exchanged a quick glance and decided to climb the rear stairs that spiralled upwards towards the open, and not surprisingly empty, top deck.

"At least it will knock the cobwebs off us, as my dad would say," Matilda said over her shoulder. "Did you see the advertisement on the side of the bus?"

As she followed her friend upwards, Ester leaned over the side of the rail to see one of the many advertising hoardings that bedecked the omnibus: *Gowan's Emporium* it read, *for all of your household needs.* "If I could only receive some form of indication!" Ester called to her friend, giddy with excitement.

The ding-ding-ding of the bell signified the imminent departure and the bus finally lurched into movement rocking its passengers back and forward again, and they were underway. As it picked its way gingerly northwards towards the city centre, the two girls cheekily waved at the odd pedestrian, who dared to break off from their deliberate shuffling on the icy pavement, to glance up at the two figures who were the only ones who were apparently brave – or silly – enough to be riding up top, exposed to the elements. Ester and Matilda didn't care however; they were free from the conformities and expectations of young middle-class ladies for the morning and had instinctively reverted to their fun-loving and mischievous selves, developed in childhood, yet so repressed in adulthood.

Traffic thickened as journey's end approached; hansom carriages and large dray wagons, carts and four-wheelers, barrow-boys and bell-ringing buses all jostled for space on the slippery cobbles of Botchergate and then English Street, while pedestrians took their lives in their hands by skipping between vehicles to get from one side of the road to the other. There was even a man inappropriately dressed in a short jacket and a straw boater, sitting bolt upright as he rode his bicycle around the Crescent and through the twin rotundas onto English Street, the sight of which caused the two girls much amusement, so incongruous was he with his surroundings.

Upon alighting the omnibus the two rosy-cheeked friends joined the bustling throng in the market square. Men with sandwich boards, advertising everything from the latest offers in the city centre shops to the imminent end of the world, jostled for prime positions around the square, while businessmen and shoppers tottered from one destination to another, trying to keep their footing in the process on the treacherous surface. The sound from an old soldier's hurdy-gurdy drifted around the square while a man sold mugs of soup from a large steaming urn in front of the Town Hall.

Barely able to move or be heard amidst the noise and movement of the crowd, the two friends decided to warm themselves up by visiting Mrs. Morris's Coffee Shop that was adjacent to the Guild Hall. Inside, the rich aroma of the coffee was welcoming and the establishment was crowded with people from all different classes, united as one in trying to find respite from the harsh weather conditions.

"Over there!" shouted Ester to her friend, as she pointed across the hubbub towards a couple at the back of the shop who were preparing to vacate their table. The two young women skipped and hopped hastily through the crowd; in doing so, Matilda gave a coquettish smile to a man and his friend who had also seen the soon-to-be-vacated table. The man read the young woman's intention, smiled and touched the brim of his hat, thus allowing the lady and her companion to occupy the sought-after space.

After a short wait, the two ordered a pot of coffee; after a slightly longer wait, the waitress returned with the steaming pot that looked so inviting, and two cups.

Matilda took the long handle of the pot and poured the aromatic refreshment, "So, where to first then?" she asked.

Ester didn't say anything but simply smiled, almost guiltily at her friend.

"You want those shoes, don't you?" exclaimed Matilda, giddily.

Again Ester, didn't say anything; after a few seconds, the two friends burst into laughter at the thought of her decadence. Ester had told Matilda about the shoes on a few occasions when the two had met leading up to Christmas.

"Did your father finally relent?" asked Matilda.

"Good heavens, no," replied Ester, "it was my darling Aunt Rose who gave me a coupon for the cost of the shoes." Ester had also shared with Matilda the not-too-subtle approaches she had made to her father over the previous weeks and his criticisms of his daughter's wastefulness and her *"…silly womanly ways!"* Ester – the great mimic – had the two of them howling with laughter at her father's expense.

The two were in high spirits as it seemed they rarely had the chance to spend such time alone together these days – only half a dozen times in the last three months, as Matilda pointed out to her friend on the journey into town. Parental pressures, crushingly boring formal occasions – when pretty young ladies were expected to be seen and not heard – and limited opportunities to decide for themselves how to spend their time and who to spend it with, all combined to limit their chances of being together and being themselves: gossiping, teasing, laughing and relaxing.

The other issue that had taken much of Ester's time over the past twelve months was the match arranged with the son of a business colleague of her father. Whereas her father had ensured his daughter received the best education money could buy during the final decade of the nineteenth century, he failed to foresee that by doing so, Ester entered the adult world as the new kind of woman ready for the first decade of the twentieth. Not only well educated, she was well informed about national and local issues; she showed an interest in politics and social causes; and like many women entering the new century, she wanted enfranchisement for all.

The different outlooks of father and daughter were to be brought into sharp focus shortly after Ester's eighteenth birthday. Her father asked Ester to accompany him and her mother to a seemingly innocent 'Ladies Night' at his club; she attended only to find that the purpose of the evening was to introduce her to – and pair her with – Gerald Whitlock, the son of one of her father's associates, Ester was both inwardly furious and crestfallen in equal measure.

At the appointed hour during the evening's festivities, the ladies were ushered to one end of the long room in which the function was taking place while the men enjoyed their brandy and cigars at the other. Ester watched the scene from afar with revulsion as her father, his associates and, most depressing of all, her intended snorted and guffawed over subjects ranging from the working classes to women's suffrage.

With no income of her own, apart from her allowance, it appeared to Ester from that very evening, that she was destined to spend the rest of her adult life as her mother and her contemporaries had: oppressed and looked down upon by an overbearing, boorish husband.

Matilda was aware of Ester's predicament; her friend having confided in her shortly after the dreadful event. Matilda had been concerned for Ester following her disclosure as subsequently, it had been apparent that it was one subject her friend had always shied away from on the rare occasions the two met. On this occasion, they chatted desultorily for a while over their coffee before Matilda broached the subject. "How are things with Gerald," she asked.

The expression on Ester's face visibly altered and her eyes lowered, as if to study the steam from the cup in front of her, "Intolerable," she said simply, before immediately changing the subject.

Matilda inwardly noted her friend's reticence for the umpteenth time on the subject and sensed that continuing with her enquiry – however genuine her concern was – would potentially ruin their morning together. The sensible course of action would be to return to the main purpose of their trip. "Let's go shopping!" she announced and was pleased to see the smile return to the face of her friend.

The two women left the hostelry and walked across the market square where they stopped outside the window of Gowan's. The grandly named Gowan's Emporium was the largest store in the centre of the city and boasted that it catered for everything in the home, from food to clothes, to furniture. One of the highlights for the people of the city leading up to the festive season was to see the Christmas display in the window of the giant store. Children would stare in wonderment at toys their parents could never afford; adults would admire the displays, hoping that one day, their home could look just like that; and young women like Ester Sanderson would look at the latest fashions.

The window had frozen over, obscuring the view of any prospective customer, but like any treasure-hunter intent on finding the prize, Ester knew exactly where her prize was hidden along the shop frontage. A little rubbing of the window in the appropriate place with the side of her gloved hand and sure enough, slowly revealed were the shoes Ester had told her friend about: black sued with a slight heel and buttoned up the outside above the ankle.

"Aren't they gorgeous?" asked Ester, as much to herself as to her friend.

"They are," agreed Matilda, peering through the frost-marked glass at the price ticket before adding, "and expensive!" The two again gave each other a should-we-or-shouldn't-we look before going inside without another word.

The shoes fit perfectly as Ester knew they would and so, walking back and forth, occasionally hitching her skirts above the ankle to view them in the mirror, it didn't take much to persuade herself that she should take them.

"They are beautiful Ester, are you going to buy them?" asked her companion. Both women knew the answer without need for a reply.

The shop assistant boxed the shoes up and placed them in a paper carrier. Matilda discretely averted her eyes as her friend handed across the coupon given to her by her aunt. Ester was beside herself with joy as the two browsed around the rest of the shop. Not to be outdone, Matilda treated herself to a new petticoat and beautiful cream blouse that would look lovely when the warmer weather came.

In high spirits the two left the shop and almost immediately bumped into a young well-dressed rotund man who just happened to be passing. Keeping his feet on the slippery surface, the man moved to apologise to the ladies by touching the brim of his hat, when, looking up, he recognised Ester.

"Why, Miss Sanderson, what a pleasant surprise! And your lovely companion," he added looking at Matilda.

Ester was taken aback by the happenstance and her demeanour seemed to change as she, in turn, recognised the man. "Mr. Baldwin, good morning."

"Oh please, as I've told you before call me Stephen."

Ester smiled uncomfortably, before introducing Matilda, more as a matter of common courtesy than a desire to prolong the meeting.

"Miss Chambers, I'm charmed," said Baldwin, touching the brim of his hat again, "just doing a little shopping I see," he added pointing to the packages the two women carried.

"Yes," said Ester.

An uncomfortable silence followed until Baldwin put them all out of their misery, "Well ladies, it was lovely to see you but I really should be running along. There was something I was wanting to talk to you about Miss Sanderson but I'm sure it can wait until another more appropriate time. I'll bid you good morning." He touched the brim of his hat once more and made on his way.

"Who was that?" asked Matilda, sensing her friend's discomfort.

"He is a friend of Gerald's," said Ester.

Baldwin was another who was present at that dreadful evening and Ester was sickened to see him and Gerald behaving as boorishly as the older men. She also observed him through the cloud of cigar smoke intermittently nudging his friend Whitlock and cocking his head in the general direction of Ester. She was sickened by the thought of what they were discussing.

Ester's eyes followed Baldwin, as if in a trance, as he picked his way through the crowd of black-clad figures that went about their business in the bustling, frost-coated Market Cross. Matilda sensed an element of unease about her friend and as she watched her – Ester's eyes fixed on the man as he disappeared into the crowd.

"Where to next then?" she asked, breaking her friend's reverie.

"Ugh, oh yes," said Ester, recovering her composure and sense of excitement, "I saw a beautiful camisole in Turnbull's Ladies' Store the other day. Would it be terribly extravagant?"

Both knew the question needed no audible answer; they laughed at each other's mischief, linked arms and headed in the direction of Fisher Street. Despite their good spirits, Matilda observed her friend out of the corner of her eye as Ester involuntarily glanced back over her shoulder as the two crossed the square.

TWO

'The Queen is Dead!' proclaimed the *Carlisle Journal,* 'Long live the King!'

Cornelius Armstrong was in his sitting room eating his breakfast, one of over four hundred million of Victoria's subjects throughout the Empire wondering what the new era would bring. Like the vast majority of those subjects, she had been the only monarch he had ever known. Politicians had come and gone; great innovation had revolutionised industries and society; and wars had been fought and lands had been conquered. The one constant had been Queen Victoria.

Cornelius's eyes drifted from the page as the newspaper coverage prompted him to recall some of the events of his own life, most notably losing his own father in one of Victoria's Wars over twenty years earlier. Having gone through the brutality of Crimea and India without a scratch, to be killed in what was due to be his final posting was doubly cruel.

His thoughts then drifted to his best friend and cousin George who was fighting against the Boers in the current conflict in South Africa. *Would he have been there with George had his father come home?* he thought to himself. He was seventeen and ready to join the army himself upon his dad's return but Cornelius remembers the day those plans changed when there was that dreadful knock on the door. He and his mother exchanged looks of foreboding, somehow knowing what was coming.

From then on, it had been civilian life for Cornelius, carrying out various jobs and looking after his mother and widowed grandmother until his grandma passed away and his mam decided to move in with her older sister. Cornelius was earning enough at this point to find his own digs and his determination to better himself eventually led him to join the City Police Force in '88 and ultimately become the youngest member of the force to reach the rank of inspector five years' later.

He sat back in his chair and looked out of the window at Abbey Street towards the gardens of the Tullie House Library and Art

Gallery opposite. Tweaking the horns of his moustache he contemplated the triumphs and tragedies suffered by him and others. He smiled to himself and inwardly gave thanks for his own achievements – successes that many peers from his humble background in Caldewgate would have believed were unobtainable for someone of their class.

His reverie was broken by a knock on the sitting room door; the daughter of Mrs. Wheeler entered, "Can I take your tray, Mr. Armstrong?"

"Certainly Emma, thank you very much. It's time I was at work anyway," he added with a smile. Cornelius carefully wiped his mouth with the corner of his napkin and passed the tray to Emma.

"Mam also sent this up sir." Emma handed Cornelius a black armband.

Armstrong smiled at his housekeeper's thoughtfulness. Whatever the circumstance or event, she always succeeded in producing the appropriate item or making the suitable arrangement.

It was yet another morning in this seemingly endless winter that saw temperatures drop well below freezing and Armstrong was thankful that his lodgings were just a few minutes' walk to the police station on West Walls. The dark-clad figures who were out and about, set against the white streets, created a picture worthy of one of the canvasses hanging in the art gallery a few yards away.

No sooner had Inspector Armstrong entered the station when he was accosted by the Desk Sergeant Bill Townsend.

"Ah sir, I've just had a message arrive from Mr. Underwood of the Watch Committee. He was actually asking for Inspector Parker but he isn't here. Apparently, there has been a serious incident at the bottom of London Road. I've sent a couple of men down there but it will require a senior officer's attention."

Cornelius was puzzled by the message.

Herbert Underwood was a magistrate of long-time standing in the city as well as being chairman of the committee for overseeing the activity of the City Police Force. He was a figure who Armstrong viewed with some uncertainty having endured a few difficult encounters with him in the past. However, knowing that Chief Constable Henry Baker was away in Penrith meeting his counterparts from around Cumberland and Westmorland, perhaps it wasn't too unusual that he would seek to approach Baker's subordinates personally, although why Underwood would be reporting incidents at all was a bit of a mystery.

"What sort of incident," the detective asked his sergeant, "and why is it being reported by the Chairman of the Watch Committee?"

"He didn't say sir. He did mention a body being found. Here is the address." Townsend handed Armstrong his hand-written note.

"Why did he ask for Inspector Parker?"

"Again, he didn't say sir."

"Do we know where Parker is?"

Townsend hesitated; both men knew that the elderly Parker had his limitations, to put it mildly. "I think he is following up a line of enquiry regarding the recent burglaries, sir," said Townsend at last.

Both men held each other's expressionless gaze for a few moments. They wanted to afford their absent colleague the appropriate respect deserving of someone his age and rank and yet their silence conveyed their mutual judgement of Parker's hapless attempts to solve the spate of thefts that had gone on for months; collectively, they were a case for which he seemed no nearer to cracking.

"Very well," said Armstrong finally, "I'll go down there. Did you say there were a couple of lads down there?"

"Yes sir, I sent Tommy Gibson and Eddie Kirk about twenty minutes ago."

Armstrong took the scrap of paper from Townsend, "Can you get an ambulance down there – and arrange for Doctor Bell to attend.

"Will do, sir," said Townsend with a nod.

Armstrong left the station, never having made it to his office.

The address in question turned out to be a beautiful detached property that was the last one within the city boundary and was set back slightly from the main road that led south into the countryside. PC Eddie Kirk was standing guard on the few steps that led to up to the front door, signifying that all was not well inside. He broke off from stamping his feet on the iced concrete in a futile effort to keep warm and saluted Inspector Armstrong as he approached.

"Morning sir," he said opening the door behind him, "straight up the stairs – Gibson is up there now."

"Thank you, Kirk," said Armstrong as he passed the uniformed officer, "Sergeant Townsend is arranging for Doctor Bell and a vehicle to be brought down. Let me know when they arrive."

"Will do, sir."

The interior of the house was as elegant and as impressive as its exterior. The oak panels in the vestibule had a beautiful ruddy lustre; it then opened into a wide hall, decorated tastefully in dark red wallpaper and dominated by a huge crystal chandelier. There were four doors, all of which were closed, which presumably led to the various downstairs accommodation. Armstrong ignored them however and strode across to the stunning Regency staircase that had various portraits looking down on the policeman as he swept upwards towards the first floor.

Tommy Gibson had been sitting in one of the two Queen Ann chairs, positioned on the landing, when he heard his superior officer arrive downstairs. Leaning over the highly polished wooden rail to confirm Armstrong's arrival, he straightened his tunic and waited for the Inspector to appear at the top of the stairs.

"In here, sir." Gibson indicated the open door opposite. He handed his superior a piece of paper containing the few details he had managed to gather.

Armstrong entered silently and – never having had any indication of what he was attending – gave a start at the grisly sight. He stared at a limp body that hung from the high light fitting. He glanced at the large window in the room: one of the curtains was secured with a heavy silken rope, which created an elegant swirl of the material; the other hung free. Cornelius glanced back at the light fitting; the missing curtain tie had been used to fashion a makeshift noose. The victim's hands were untied.

After looking at the poor creature for a few minutes, the detective started to pick his way carefully round the room. The carpet, curtains and bed linen were of the finest quality; the two large teak wardrobes were full of beautiful clothes; and the free-standing furniture – full length mirror, chaise longue and dressing table – gave the room an eclectic, yet stylish appearance.

There was no sign of any struggle; the window was locked and there were no scuff marks on the sill. The only sign of movement was on the dark patterned carpet: four deep indentations were visible due to a large ottoman sitting under the window for a long period of time; there were then drag marks on the carpet indicating that it had been dragged to the centre of the room, presumably to be used as a make-shift scaffold.

On the dressing table was an assortment of items: circular baskets that overflowed with ribbons and hairpins, bottles of perfume, a jewellery box that sat open, a few family photographs and a hair brush, the white bristles of which were intertwined with long chestnut coloured hairs.

A gauzy nightgown was draped over the full- length mirror and a camisole had been laid out on the chair beside it. Armstrong spotted something on the floor underneath the chair and reached down to see what it was. It looked like a child's toy – a tiny ballerina that had been broken at its feet. Cornelius glanced back to the dressing table and to the jewellery box in particular. Upon closer inspection he saw the feet of the little figure protruding from a small plinth on the base of the box.

He looked at the piece of paper handed to him by Gibson and turned again to look at the body. He was drawn to the shoes of the deceased that were virtually in his eye-line. They were of the finest quality; black suede with a slight heel and buttoned up the outside above the ankle. They were also brand new, no scuff marks on the heel or the soles; no disturbing of the immaculately brushed suede; no sign at all that they had been worn outdoors. They were elegant and expensive, and in keeping with the rest of the clothes worn by the limp body of Miss Ester Sanderson as it hung from the light fitting above his head.

The detective's concentration was disturbed by PC Gibson who appeared in the doorway of the bedroom. "Doctor Bell is here, sir."

"Thank you, Tommy," said Armstrong.

He took one last look up at the young woman who must have been so beautiful in life; and who now hung by the neck from the elaborate light fitting in her bedroom.

"As soon as the doctor has finished, arrange to have her removed; the ambulance should be here shortly. I want nothing disturbed in the room and make sure we don't lose that curtain tie that's been used as a noose."

Cornelius met Doctor Bell on the landing. "Good morning James."

"Inspector," replied the doctor; he was the pathologist at the Cumberland Infirmary. It wasn't unheard of for him to be called by the police to inspect a body at its place of death, but it was rare, and this was the first time he had been asked to inspect the deceased in their own home. "A nasty business. I met the young woman's distraught parents on the way up."

"Parents?" questioned the policeman. He turned around to address the uniformed officer, "Gibson, you never told me that the girl's parents were in the house. Have you spoken to them?"

"Err, not really sir, we were waiting for you to arrive. We left them downstairs with Mr. Underwood."

"Underwood? What is he doing here?"

"Err, I don't know sir, he was here when we arrived. We thought you knew."

When Armstrong crossed the hallway half an hour earlier, there was no sound and no indication that anyone was in the house. The parents of the victim must obviously have been behind one of the closed doors in one of the various reception rooms. The detective suppressed whatever anger he had with Gibson and Kirk, neither of whom had informed him of their presence, and decided now wasn't the time for displays of admonishment. Instead he turned back to the pathologist.

15

"I'll leave you to it James while I speak with Mr. and Mrs. Sanderson."

The two nodded and went about their respective, unenviable tasks.

As he arrived at the foot of the stairs, he was met by Herbert Underwood Chairman of the Watch Committee. Armstrong was never a clubbable type and this non-conformity, coupled with his relatively young age when he was appointed, caused Underwood to view him with a certain amount of suspicion. The feeling was mutual as Armstrong had performed some sterling work since his promotion, yet there had never been any acknowledgement of this from Underwood and his colleagues. Fortunately Chief Constable Henry Baker considered Armstrong his best man and protected him from any unjustified criticism. But Baker was unavailable today and Cornelius was left to face Underwood head on.

"Inspector Armstrong, I asked for Mr. Parker to attend."

"Yes, I'm afraid Inspector Parker is unavailable this morning, sir." Cornelius's piercing blue eyes held the stare of the magistrate, "So I'm here."

"So I see," replied the haughty Underwood.

"May I ask what you are doing here sir?" asked the policeman.

"Edward and Edith are dear friends of mine. When the tragedy was discovered Edward called me in. They are through here."

Underwood ushered Armstrong through into a front parlour where Mr. and Mrs. Sanderson were perched on the edge of an elaborately patterned sofa. The two just stared at the opposite wall in silence, Mrs. Sanderson's eyes reduced to red rings, presumably with the constant crying for the past few hours.

"My condolences Mr. and Mrs. Sanderson," said Armstrong. It was the worst job of a policeman to speak to bereaved family members and something that Cornelius was convinced he would never get used to, nor master. "I'm afraid I need to ask you some questions."

Both parents looked blankly at the policeman, unable to comprehend the reality of this strange man in their home asking them questions about the death of their beloved daughter.

16

As gently as he could, Cornelius drew out of Mrs. Sanderson the timeline of events as she could recall them. Ester had gone to her room as usual around ten o'clock the previous evening. It was unlike her to sleep long so Mrs. Sanderson went to wake her at a little before eight o'clock this morning when she made the horrifying discovery.

"It was a scream that I will never forget as long as I live," mumbled her husband to himself as he struggled to keep his composure synonymous with a man of his position.

"Did you daughter receive any visitors yesterday?"

"I think she did answer the door to someone at one point but they weren't on the step for very long," said Sanderson, "I assume it was one of those blasted salesmen."

"Forgive me for asking," said the inspector, "but it obviously appears at this stage as though your daughter took her own life. Have you any idea what would drive her to such an action."

Sanderson looked at Armstrong, expressionless. If Ester didn't take her own life then it would mean that someone actually broke into their home and murdered her. It was a thought too abhorrent to consider; but then the alternative – as the policeman was suggesting – was also impossible to comprehend. It would appear that the same dichotomic thoughts passed through his wife's mind simultaneously as she once again burst into tears.

"I think that is enough Inspector," said a voice from behind.

Herbert Underwood had stood silently in the doorway the whole time and just as Armstrong looked towards him, he saw in the background, two of his men carrying the covered stretcher through the hall. He sensed that Doctor Bell was waiting for him outside. He returned his attention to Mr. Underwood who had disturbed his questioning. Part of him wanted to spell out to the magistrate that he himself would decide when he would cease to question witnesses, but in this case, he knew Underwood was correct and decided it was appropriate to leave the Sandersons to their grief.

"Once again, I am so sorry for your loss," he said as he stood to leave. "Ester will be taken to the Infirmary where Doctor Bell will carry out a post mortem. I will need to come back and see you in a few days but in the meantime, if you need anything, don't hesitate to make contact with me." He gave Mr. Sanderson a card with his details on and took his leave.

As he crossed the threshold of the room into the hall, Underwood closed the door behind him, creating the same silence in the hallway that Cornelius had experienced when he first arrived in the house over an hour earlier.

James Bell was waiting for Armstrong as he had expected. "A nasty business indeed Doctor. There was no sign of any intrusion."

"Yes, looks like a straight suicide but we'll get her up to the morgue and have a closer look. I should be back in touch within a day or two."

The two men were disturbed by a commotion outside. As they descended the steps onto the garden path, it was apparent that a young woman who seemed to be a similar age to the deceased, was clawing at the stretcher, such was her hysteria. She was dressed modestly and wholly inappropriately considering the bitter conditions: no hat or coat, just a thin woollen shawl that threatened to fall from her shoulders such was her frenzy.

"No, no!" she screeched, *"What have they done? What have they done?"*

Half an hour earlier, with the arrival of the police vehicle and with it, the increased uniformed presence, a combination of intrigue and prurience had pervaded the surrounding areas: curtains twitched and the more brazen stood outside the house, craning their necks over the railings to see what was going on. But it was the young woman's actions that had now drawn attention away from the house.

As three of his colleagues were trying to place the body into the ambulance, PC Kirk was trying to restrain the woman as best he could without manhandling her unnecessarily.

Inspector Armstrong approached at a hurry and sought to assist Kirk. "Miss, Miss, you must not interfere here."

The hysterical young woman looked at Armstrong but didn't see him, her eyes, nose and mouth running uncontrollably; the very picture of pain. His intervention appeared to defuse the incident and

18

the uniformed officers were allowed to complete their grim task. Doctor Bell climbed into the ambulance with the two hospital orderlies, while PCs Kirk and Gibson resumed their duties in securing the house. With the excitement now over and the make-shift ambulance turning to start its uncomfortable journey back into the city, the crowd gradually dispersed.

Armstrong meanwhile gently ushered the young woman into the hallway of the Sandersons' villa, to allow her to regain some composure and ask her about her connection to the victim.

THREE

When Matilda Chambers received a message from her friend Ester Sanderson between Christmas and New Year, inviting her to go shopping after the holidays, she was delighted. She hadn't seen Ester for at least three weeks; in fact, when she thought about it, she hadn't seen much of her friend at all during the last year. And during that first half of the year, Ester had appeared somewhat withdrawn and almost morose at times, but from around October onwards, she seemed to have perked up somewhat and Matilda was delighted to see that when the two met shortly after the holidays, Ester appeared to be back to her old self.

"Would you like to speak with Ester's parents," asked Cornelius, as the two sat in the hallway of the Sandersons' house.

"No, I think I should just go home; it's not far." Matilda's initial hysteria had changed into an exhausted sob as she looked down at her lap where she continued to twist the handkerchief Armstrong had given her.

"Very well, let me escort you there," said the policeman, taking off his overcoat and draping it round the young woman's shoulders.

As Matilda had indicated, her home was barely half a mile from Ester's, but Armstrong was struck by the modesty of the Chambers' house compared with that of the Sandersons. The dwelling itself was actually attached to a corner shop that took up a large part of the ground floor, although the shop itself was nothing to do with Matilda and her family. With one reception room beside the kitchen, a passageway led to the stairs and the first floor, and attic a room beyond.

Matilda took Cornelius into the kitchen to meet her widowed mother who, when she realised they had company, hastily wiped her floured hands on her apron before gesturing a greeting. "I'm terribly sorry," she said, "I had no idea Matilda was bringing someone back."

"Please don't apologise Mrs. Chambers, I hope I am not imposing. My name is Cornelius Armstrong, I am a policeman."

"A policeman?" cried Matilda's mother. She had heard the knock on the door earlier, followed by her daughter shutting it behind her, but assumed that on a morning like this, she was just popping next door. She now looked at Matilda, who had no outdoor clothes on and realised something was terribly wrong.

Matilda told her mother to sit down as she broke the news, she herself could still barely believe.

"Good heavens!" said Mrs. Chambers putting her hand to her forehead in disbelief, "there must be some mistake?" she asked in futility.

"I'm afraid not," said the inspector, "Ester is being taken to the Infirmary as we speak where a post mortem will be done shortly."

"Her poor mother," said Mrs. Chambers staring into the middle distance. The two were not as close as their daughters but had known each other for years and had always enjoyed a cordial relationship.

Between mother and daughter, they managed to compose themselves sufficiently to make some tea.

"I'm sorry but the bread won't be ready for a while yet," said Mrs. Chambers, embarrassed by her lack of preparedness, "If I'd known we were to have guests…"

"Please don't apologies," replied Cornelius with a kind wave of the hand; he was extremely grateful at the thought of a cup of tea, given that he hadn't had anything since breakfast, "you are being more than hospitable, especially in the circumstances."

The policeman in him also knew that the refreshment would also afford him an opportunity to ask Matilda a little more about Ester.

Matilda explained to Cornelius that the two had been close since childhood. It was clear that Ester was talented and charismatic, even at that young age; her confidence, ability and mischief always caused her to stand out from her peers. For her part, Ester loved Matilda's genuineness – not one of the fair weather, obsequious friends who sought popularity for themselves through their association with the popular girl.

Both went through primary school, Sunday school and ultimately Grammar School together. Ester was always going to achieve a place at the prestigious High School through a combination of her ability and her father's wealth. For Matilda's part, she was of equal academic ability but having lost her father at a young age, and her mother not having the financial resource to facilitate a private education, she was reliant on winning one of the scholarships offered by the school, which she duly did much to her and Ester's delight.

The two had left school two years earlier and Matilda had secured a position as a trainee clerk in the City Bank. Ester on the other hand was frustrated by her father's refusal to allow her to pursue a working career.

Matilda told Armstrong about the last time she had seen her friend, two weeks' earlier when they had met for an all-too-rare shopping trip into the city. "Ester was full of excitement as she had had her eye on a pair of shoes in Gowan's for some time. She had received a coupon from an aunt and was determined to buy them."

Cornelius nodded to himself and remembered the new shoes he had observed on Ester's body earlier.

One regret Matilda had regarding the trip was that she never got the chance to tell her friend about her own big news.

She explained that her mother worked four days' a week as a seamstress in the tailoring department of the large Cooperative store on Botchergate and one day in October of the previous year, Mr. Scott the Head Tailor had sent his apprentice Danny Corcoran round to the house with a message. Like all of the women in the department, Mary Chambers was fond of Danny and introduced him to Matilda. The two struck up friendship as a result and romance had since blossomed. Danny had even joined Matilda and her mother for Christmas lunch.

But such was the delicacy of Ester's courtship – which appeared to Matilda to be anything but romantic – she had shied away from raising the subject with her. It was something that saddened her, as she knew that ordinarily, it would have been a subject that two would have giggled and teased each other about.

Whether she knew it or not, Matilda was painting quite a depressing picture of her friend's life. It prompted Armstrong to probe a little further.

"Tell me Miss Chambers, when you saw Ester being taken away you yelled, 'what have they done.' What did you mean by that?"

Matilda thought for a while, not having realised what she had said. She thought of Ester's father and his antiquated view that young ladies should remain inside, protected from the glare of the sun and the pollution and vulgarity of the outside world. Whatever his intentions were, such a philosophy was crushing the life out of his daughter. She explained this to Armstrong.

"Then there was this strange relationship with this Gerald character," she continued; someone who Matilda had never actually met. "I can't actually remember saying that, but if I did, I suppose subconsciously, it was prompted by the little that Ester had shared with me about some of the people she was surrounded by."

She thought for a while longer, "I remember her telling me once about her 'companion'. When I asked her to whom she was referring to, she said 'not who but what.' She explained that she kept a journal that gave her some comfort. I'm ashamed to say I didn't take it too seriously at the time but she was clearly very sad."

Before Cornelius could ask the most delicate of questions, something else sprung to Matilda's mind.

"I've just remembered something...it's probably nothing but there was a strange occurrence when we were out shopping that morning." Matilda recalled the chance encounter the two had with Gerald's friend, Stephen somebody-or-other outside Gowan's. "It was as though poor Ester went into some sort of trance when she bumped into this man. I was quite disturbed by her reaction."

"Did she say why this man had such an effect on her?" asked the policeman.

"No, he disappeared and we carried on about our business. It was just such a strange encounter."

Cornelius wanted to ask the standard question: if Matilda was aware of anyone who might want to cause her friend harm. In the circumstances, he felt the time wasn't right to torment Ester's friend still further and whereas he may need to interview her again, it was probably sensible to wait until after he received the post mortem results before continuing with any difficult lines of enquiry.

Instead – as he had with Ester's parents – he indicated that he would probably need to speak with Matilda again in the future, but decided it was an appropriate time to leave the young woman and her mother with their grief.

On the way back to the station he wondered – assuming that it *was* suicide – if it would be more appropriate for old Parker to revisit the questioning in a few days' time; his kindly inoffensive manner would probably help with such a delicate situation. And come to think of it, Underwood had specifically asked for the senior detective, although Armstrong doubted if the Chairman of the Watch Committee was being so thoughtful in his request. He smiled to himself playfully at the name of Godfrey Parker and the word *detective* being thought of in the same context.

No sooner had he walked through the door of the station, when the first person he saw was none other than Inspector Parker.

"Morning Godfrey."

"Ah, good morning Cornelius," replied the elderly man. It was always difficult to age Godfrey Parker, with his high forehead that led to a few wisps of white hair which Godfrey seemed to continuously run his fingers through nervously. "Bill told me there was a message for me earlier?"

Cornelius recalled that Underwood had originally asked the desk sergeant for Godfrey earlier that morning. "Yes, let's go into my office and I'll brief you on what happened."

The two levered themselves out of their coats and hung them on the stand behind the door. Parker looked around Armstrong's office and commented how tidy and organised his colleague was. Rarely did Armstrong – nor anyone else for that matter – have the need to be in Godfrey's tiny office two doors down the corridor which led to the back of the building; he always naturally assumed that it would be as disorganised and as its occupant. He accepted the compliment however and offered Parker a seat. In one corner of his office was a small cast iron stove that had an open pipe running up through the

24

ceiling; on top of the stove stood a copper kettle. He was pleased Bill Townsend had filled both the stove – which gave his office a welcoming, cosy ambience on such a bitter day – and the kettle, in anticipation of his superior's return.

Cornelius retrieved his own tin mug from his desk draw, and unhooked another from a row of three that hung above the stove. "Do you know a family called Sanderson on London Road, Godfrey?" he asked his colleague as he went over to his desk with the tea.

"Oh, bless you Cornelius, thank you very much," said the gentle Parker, taking one of the mugs. He thought for a while, "Sanderson...Sanderson...no I don't think so?"

"Herbert Underwood asked for you attendance at their house this morning."

"Mr. Underwood? From the Watch Committee?" Godfrey had to put his mug on Armstrong's desk to stop himself from spilling the contents in his lap. He could not remember anyone asking for him personally to attend anything, let alone such a senior official.

"The daughter of Mr. and Mrs. Sanderson was found hanged in her bedroom this morning. Apparently, Mr. Underwood knows the family and asked that you attend."

"Good heavens!"

Cornelius was unsure as to whether Godfrey was more shocked about the apparent suicide or the fact that Underwood had asked for him.

Parker completed his thought process, "How awful! The poor young woman. I've no idea why Mr. Underwood would ask for me though." He felt compelled to explain his absence, "I was looking into those recent burglaries."

"Yes, Townsend informed me, that's why I attended. Did you have any luck incidentally?"

"With what?" asked the dateless Parker.

"The burglaries," replied Armstrong, suppressing a sigh.

"Oh no, I'm afraid not. Although there does seem to be a slight change on this occasion."

Cornelius raised his eyebrows in an effort to encourage his colleague to complete his comment. It took a few seconds for Godfrey to take the hint.

"Oh, yes I see," he said at last. "Well the others have been from shops and commercial premises, whereas the break-in yesterday was made at a solicitor's office."

The burglaries had begun about six months earlier with what appeared at the time to have been a random break-in at Ismay's Wine and Spirit Merchant on Scotch Street. As it seemed to be an isolated occurrence, Chief Constable Henry Baker gave the incident a low priority and assigned Parker to the case. The aging inspector failed to shed any light on the matter however, and when further similar incidents followed at three pawn broker shops around the city, Turnbull's Haberdashers and Rattigan's Musical Instrument Shop on Botchergate – and with Parker failing miserably to obtain the merest hint of a lead – Baker found himself being put under increasing pressure from the local Chamber of Commerce.

On each occasion, the thieves had gained access through the rear entrance and managed to get into the strong rooms of the respective shops where each kept their safes. What the burglaries also had in common was that they occurred over a quiet weekend period, before the previous week's takings were due to be taken to the bank as they were each Monday morning. This latest crime however was committed on a Tuesday and was the first to target a professional office. What was consistent was the gaining of entry into the building and the thieves' apparent awareness of where the business's safe was kept.

For once Cornelius was impressed by his colleague's ability to make the link yet differentiate between the crimes and his commenting on the possible significance of the change in pattern.

"Which solicitor was it?" he asked.

"Morley, Freeman and Whitlock on Fisher Street".

"And was there anything that might lead us in a particular area?" Armstrong inwardly chastised himself for asking a question that couldn't fail to embarrass both men.

"No, I'm afraid not," said Godfrey, seemingly missing the point that he hadn't made any progress whatsoever in months.

"Do we know how much was taken on this occasion?"

"No, Mr. Whitlock did not say."

Why would a solicitor's office be targeted by thieves on a Tuesday night in January? How would they know there would be any money kept in the offices? Could the attack be an unconnected act of retribution aimed at the solicitor in question who could possibly have been involved in prosecuting the perpetrator during a previous matter?

Armstrong knew there was little point in asking Parker these and other questions he would not know the answers to; or would not have had the whit or the wherewithal to ask himself. He also knew their superior Henry Baker would be annoyed by the latest incident and Parker's response to it, so he offered to help. "Perhaps I could give the matter a fresh perspective?" he suggested.

"But what about the matter you are dealing with Cornelius?"

Armstrong wasn't sure if there was much to investigate concerning Ester Sanderson's apparent suicide; and besides there was bound to be a delay with any further enquiries until he received the post mortem report from Doctor Bell.

"I'm sure I can spare a little time," he told Parker. "What details do you have?"

"Well the man I spoke to this morning was one of the partners," Parker hesitated and had to reach for his notebook, "a Mr. William Whitlock."

"Where were the other two?"

"The other two what?"

Armstrong clenched his teeth together causing his cheek to concave, "The other two partners. You said the firm was Morley, Freeman and Whitlock – where were Morley and Freeman?"

"Oh, I see what you mean. Apparently, Mr. Morley is no longer with us and Mr. Whitlock bought out the share of Mr. Freeman. He now runs the business with his son."

"Perhaps I could go around and speak to them again and see if I can glean anything else from them. If there is time, I could then revisit the other premises that have been burgled."

"Oh, that would be useful," said Parker, "I did say I would re-visit them some time to update them but I simply haven't had time."

Armstrong let his colleague's words hang in the air for a few moments but like most things, Parker did not see the significance of the hesitation, nor of what he had said.

"I'll go and visit Mr. Whitlock this afternoon then," said Armstrong at last, drawing their meeting to a close.

"Oh that would be splendid Cornelius, thank you," said Godfrey, rising to leave, "I'm sure Henry will be pleased with our progress when he returns from Kendal."

The reason Chief Constable Baker was in Kendal was that he had called a meeting of his counterparts around the two counties to discuss his concerns about the apparent increase in crime in Carlisle over the past twelve months. He wanted to gauge the feelings of his colleagues and compare their situation with his. Armstrong knew that this latest development would do nothing to assuage his frustration. He paused again, fixing his piercing blue eyes on his colleague. "Yes," he said slowly, "I'm sure he will."

Cornelius sat back, leant on one of the arms of his chair and absentmindedly twisted the horns of his moustache – a unknowing habit he adopted whenever he was contemplating an issue. In this case, he was contemplating the events of the last twenty-four hours.

First, there was a burglary he sensed would now take up more of his time once Henry Baker returned from Kendal to discover the hapless Parker was no further forward with his investigation.

Then there were the deaths of two women he had learned about earlier that day; one an elderly monarch, whose empire stretched across a fifth of the globe; the other, a young woman from Carlisle whose life should still have been ahead of her. He wondered how the immediate future would be influenced by each woman's passing.

FOUR

Billy Grant had grown to enjoy – even look forward to – his trips to Whitehaven. When he was first instructed to make the journey eight months earlier, he viewed the errand as an inconvenience – trailing down to some unknown place he knew nothing about and had never previously visited. He was far more comfortable in the back alleys of Carlisle but he dutifully did as his brother told him and after a dozen or more ventures, he now saw the benefits of the journey: good money, low risk and best of all, visiting *The Albion* on Swampmarsh Lane near the harbour.

On this occasion he was actually looking forward to getting away from Carlisle, troubled as he was after the events of the previous week. The trains had been slowed somewhat by the bitter January weather. But given that Billy had developed a habit over the past twelve months of travelling the day before his scheduled meeting anyway, he wasn't particularly concerned about missing the emissary whose ship wouldn't arrive until the following afternoon. He was more concerned about reducing his time at *The Albion,* for travelling a day early wasn't the only habit he had developed.

Whitehaven was one of the key harbours along the west coast of the country and, like many of its kind, provided an incongruous mix of humanity: local seaman and dock workers, laboured cheek by jowl with Chinese and lascars, while Persian merchants mixed with European passengers. The shouts and cries of different tongues were enhanced by the continuous squawking of gulls, indiscriminately scavenging for food.

On the dockside were piled large crates, giant ropes, barrels and sacks, while on the water tiny launches and tugs rocked gently, buffeted by tall merchant vessels and passenger liners.

The paradox was that the noisy multitude guaranteed any visitor complete anonymity. For amidst the hubbub, no one noticed anyone's face; no one paid any attention to anyone else unless they were conducting a business transaction or buying a ticket at the office.

And like any port of its kind there were plenty of temptations close by in the shape of clubs and dancing saloons that could relieve any man, whether he be visitor or worker, of his hard-earned money.

All of this suited Billy Grant nicely; the little anyone knew about his movements the better, for it wasn't the taverns and saloons that attracted Billy, it was another staple of any port that took *his* full attention: the opium den on Swampmarsh Lane.

He got down from the train and picked his way down the slippery cobbles through the harbour area, oblivious to the noise and activity that was going on around him. Two young women – barely in their twenties – huddled together over an open brazier. One looked up from the flames as Billy walked by.

"Want some company luv?"

He ignored her invitation – probably didn't even hear her – pulled his collar up and tottered on his way, picking his way through the melee towards his prize.

Billy Grant had discovered *The Albion* by chance twelve months earlier when, on one occasion, the carrier's schedule had been altered at the last minute and he was forced to drop off in Whitehaven a day before he was originally due. The network he worked for had many far-reaching tentacles which included knowledge of virtually every den and safe-point in every port around the country.

Whereas the delivery had previously been made in *The Duke of Cumberland* tavern on the quayside, on this occasion, arrangements were made to leave the contraband at *The Albion* from where young Grant would collect it. This communication was ultimately passed to Billy by his elder brother Freddie.

The two brothers had started as orphaned street urchins, discarded by society, kicked out of the Workhouse and forced to live on their wits hour by hour. If childhood was dominated by petty theft and pickpocketing, adulthood inevitably saw them descend into burglary and threatening behaviour. The stakes were raised still further however when Freddie encountered Jack Roberts in *The Goliah Inn* one night.

Roberts had arrived in the city some months earlier. He was a hardened criminal from Manchester with a long career on the wrong side of the law after having been involved in most things from extortion to violent assault.

With strong links to establishment figures in the city, he was encouraged to leave Manchester when he involved himself in one violent encounter too many which ended up with a body floating face down in the ship canal. Travelling north to Carlisle provided him with both a convenient escape and an opportunity to develop a similar enterprise to the one he had run so successfully in Manchester. Moreover there was more chance of keeping a low profile in such a quiet backwater – what could possibly go wrong?

In order to develop his activities, Roberts needed a small group of confederates and after meeting Freddie Grant that night in the *Goliah*, he was satisfied that he and his brother Billy would fit the roles nicely.

Over the following months, led by Roberts, the two brothers gradually increased their low-level nefarious activity to threatening tenants who were struggling to pay their rent and demanding protection money from back-street shop and pub owners. All the while, victims of the Roberts gang were warned against reporting their particular grievances. Brian Kyle, owner of *The Goliah* was used as an example after he suggested he would go to the police – he received a severe beating for his trouble.

Among Roberts's previous activity in Manchester was the receipt of opium into the port of Liverpool; distributed by a network of criminals in London who had the drugs trafficked from around the Empire. Roberts would organise the collection of the drugs and have them transported to Manchester. When the Manchester Ship Canal opened in the final decade of the century, Roberts's job became even easier when he found the contraband could be transported straight into its destination.

After he had fled to Carlisle, he wasted no time in replicating the process by utilising the rail links with the large port of Whitehaven to the west. The drug was no respecter of social standing and money

31

could be made from its sale; and once its addictive compounds have snared its victims, there would be a constant requirement. Supply and demand would in time guarantee increased prices which would naturally generate more income. He had the contacts that shipped drugs from all over the Empire to Bristol, Manchester and Glasgow on the west, and Hull, Newcastle and Edinburgh on the east. It would be no problem to add the port of Whitehaven to the network.

Not surprisingly, there were no dissenting voices to Roberts's proposal and he himself agreed to oversee the first shipment before handing the task over to Freddie and Billy Grant. When the two became involved in the scheme, they had mischievously sampled the contraband they were collecting and distributing. Unfortunately in the younger brother's case, idle curiosity had led to addiction, which in turn put at risk the operation Freddie had worked hard to put in place. He had warned Billy about the risks involved but once the younger Grant discovered *The Albion* on that fateful occasion, he found temptation too great.

Like all addicts, he was confident he could control his indulgence without compromising his primary mission, but he had already arrived back in Carlisle a day late on his previous visit to the west of the county. Billy's sloppiness was communicated through the network and it was the elder brother who was called in and warned against any repeat in future. It was stressed to him that any broken link in the chain of dishonesty could jeopardize the whole operation. He passed this message on to Billy in no uncertain terms.

This all raced through Billy's mind as he followed his well-trodden route through the quayside towards Swampmarsh Lane. He wasn't put off by Freddie's warnings; besides he wasn't actually addicted – he could handle it.

The most treacherous part of his journey was navigating the steep flight of steps that led down from the grubby lane. Thousands of boots had scuffed and scraped the surface of each concrete tread until they were smooth and worn away at their centre – the precarious condition of the steps was compounded, not only by the bitter January frost, but by the condition of the clientele who attempted to negotiate them.

As Billy picked his way gingerly down them, he glanced through the ragged window-curtain and saw the mulatto, whose name he had learned was Jethro, smiling back at him. He entered the murky establishment; the light and the noise from the street outside instantly died away.

It was twelve months ago when Billy first paid Jethro a tanner for a brown pellet of wax to be drawn from a dirty old gallipot. The rush of enjoyment was something he had never experienced before; from that moment, he was hooked, whether he cared to admit it or not. Jethro rarely spoke but had the sweetest smile that gave every visitor the impression that he knew them all. The truth was that they were all blank faces to him. They were all visiting the den to satisfy their indulgences – that is what made Jethro smile.

He offered Billy a pipe with a small supply of the drug. Young Grant thought of his brother and hesitated momentarily, biting his bottom lip. His hesitation was only momentary however and he stared from the pipe into the mesmeric eyes of Jethro; they both knew what his decision would be. Billy dropped some coins into the mulatto's open hand and took the pipe.

The Albion was basically the squalid basement of what was once an ornate hotel, but was now a run-down hostelry. It consisted of one large room and was dotted with gloomy stalls and benches that doubled as beds, many of which had collapsed under the weight of hundreds of occupants who had frequented – and continued to frequent – the establishment.

The air was permanently thick with cigarette and pipe smoke, combined with the dry burning smell of opium. If any visitor was not used to such an assault on the senses, their eyes and throat would be instantly irritated. But to the vulnerable regulars of such haunts, the thick brown heavy air itself was bliss, as it cast its spell on them and engulfed them like a giant comfort blanket.

Peering through the gloom and beyond the usual mix of bodies strewn across the floor and propped up against the flaking walls, Billy spotted a vacant stool beside the battered cast iron stove in the far corner of the room, whose warm glow seemed to beckon the newcomer. He picked his way carefully through the splayed limbs of those lying in front of him and eased a giggling idiot out of the way in order to sit on the vacated stool. Lighting his pipe he breathed deeply. And so it began.

The following day, the man he was supposed to meet descended the gangplank of the *Great Britain.* Billy Grant was nowhere to be seen. McVey had couriered for the best part of ten years. He himself was a tiny cog in the network; he had no idea where his contraband he carried came from, he simply dealt with his own contact at a clearing house in Rotherhithe. Originally the booty was transported by train but when the bags carrying the drugs were mistaken for mail bags and their contents ultimately seized, his predecessor in the role was arrested and the countrywide operation was moved from the land to the sea, with McVey appointed to operate it.

The change of approach proved perfect for the illegal process, as the anonymity afforded by the busy ports allowed McVey to go about his business unsuspected and therefore unmolested. He had in turn developed a tried and trusted relationship with his contacts around the country and from the dockside, the regular supply of opium which started its journey in the far east, would end its journey in the towns and cities of Britain, lining the pockets of those in the long chain, in the process.

When it was suggested to him that the port in West Cumberland should be added to the illegal trade route, the London villain expressed his reservations about disturbing what had become an almost fool-proof operation. But when the suggestion became an instruction, he had no choice but to carry it out. The *Great Britain* was a merchant vessel that made the domestic journey around the mainland once a week and, as Whitehaven was one of its scheduled stops, it should not have caused a major problem.

But McVey's reservations were to be proved well founded when he discovered his contact was unreliable, which led to him feeling nervous every time he descended the wooden gangway of the clipper.

The plan was always to meet in *The Duke of Cumberland*, a tavern on the quayside, but on the last two occasions Grant had failed to appear and McVey, had followed his instincts and found him in the opium den on Swampmarsh Lane.

On this occasion the courier waited in the *Duke* for a nervous twenty minutes. The hot coffee was welcome on such a bitter afternoon but when his constant head-turning towards the door proved fruitless, and with the *Great Britain* upping anchor in another hour for its onward journey to Glasgow, he slapped down his tin mug on the bar in annoyance and headed for the exit. It was now obvious where Grant was.

He hurried along towards Swampmarsh Lane with the large Seaman's sack that was to be handed over to this unreliable idiot who would probably be dipping into the contents before he made it back to Carlisle. That wasn't his problem; his job was to ensure the contraband was handed over safely.

But McVey liked to be in control of every situation; he had spent years developing this courier system that had worked liked clockwork to this point. This was the first time he was dealing with someone unreliable and it put him on edge. He had left several other similar sacks to the one he was carrying on board ship unattended, while he wandered away from the quayside. Although he was only a few streets away from the Wharf, he was breaking with his routine. In the dock area no one took any notice of the hundreds of people coming and going; as the traveller wandered further into the town, the chances of drawing attention to himself increased; this in turn could cause further delay and endanger the whole national operation.

With every step his mood worsened, until he arrived at *The Albion* ten minutes later. This was not assuaged when he almost lost his footing on the slippery steps and stumbled into the doorway.

Inside he was greeted by the familiar smile of Jethro who offered him a pipe.

"I'm not here for that," snapped McVey, "I'm looking for-"

He broke off, realising that Jethro probably didn't know the name of any of his clientele, and it probably wasn't wise to use

35

anyone's name anyway with regard to their subversive activity. He pushed passed the Mulatto and disappeared into the gloom. Picking his way through mumbling imbeciles, he wrestled with the heavy sailor's sack as he turned the limp bodies over to see their faces. Finally he saw Billy Grant, slumped by the battered stove in the far corner of the room. As he reached across to pick him up, he kicked over a tin bowl, spilling its contents which caused great consternation to its owner. He put his hand on Billy's shoulder who looked up at him with the same bloodshot eyes, sickly pallor and imbecilic grim worn by the others.

McVey grabbed him by the scruff of the neck, "What are you doing here?" he hissed, "You were supposed to meet me on the dockside."

"Hello mate," slurred Grant, "I thought you weren't coming till tomorrow."

"It *is* tomorrow, you idiot!"

McVey dragged Grant towards the doorway causing all sorts of disruption amongst the other intoxicated customers as he did so. Ignoring the smiling Jethro he bundled Grant out of the door and into the ice-cold air. The shock to the system forced Billy to gasp for breath and blink hard in order to focus. McVey pushed him against one of the chipped and worn pillars that flanked the once ornate entrance.

"This is the third time I've found you 'ere. You might not give a toss about this operation but I do and I'm not gonna let you ruin it. You're gonna bring us all down if you're not careful."

Grant was recovering his senses by the second. He realised that he must have been in the den for over twenty-four hours; he also remembered the reason for his trip to Whitehaven in the first place as he focused on the large sack carried by McVey. Freddie would not be happy if he found out about this.

"Here put your name on this," McVey produced a makeshift docket to prove to his masters that he delivered the contraband.

Grant took the pencil and paper thrust at him and scribbled something undecipherable on the bottom. McVey took it back and studied it.

"That'll have to do I suppose," he mumbled.

He pushed the large sack into the chest of Grant and scuttled up the steps back onto the lane and headed back towards the dockside. Billy sat in the well of the doorway clutching the sack, ashamed of himself.

His head was thumping but at least now he was thinking clearly. He had to get back to Carlisle; if he could do that with the opium undisturbed no one need know about this. He also swore to himself that he would learn the lesson from this near-miss.

The journey back was uncomfortable, with Billy feeling every jolt and rock of the train. He arrived back in the tenement where he lived with his brother around six o'clock.

Freddie smiled when he saw the large sack his brother carried, "Everything go all right?" he asked.

"Yeah, no problem," lied Billy.

"You learned from that carry on, last time then?"

"Yeah, no problem," he repeated.

FIVE

William Whitlock and George Freeman had acquired positions as apprentice solicitors with Josiah Morley thirty years earlier, at his modest office on St Mary's Gate, just across from the Cathedral. When the two young men became qualified, the business started to expand and they eventually became equal partners with Morley. The business moved offices to a larger premise on Fisher Street in the late eighties and two years later Josiah retired. He was only to enjoy eighteen months however before passing away and it was at this point that Whitlock bought out the founder's share from his widow. After much consideration George Freeman also agreed to sell his third of the partnership, leaving Whitlock as the sole owner. He therefore ran the business with the assistance of his son.

It was shortly after two o'clock when Inspector Armstrong visited Whitlock's offices to enquire about the burglary. He found the solicitor in an irritable mood – perhaps not surprising in the circumstances.

"I assume you have you brought the necessary paperwork?" he asked when Armstrong was introduced.

"Paperwork, sir?" questioned the policeman.

"Yes, the police report I require to make the insurance claim for the loss."

"No sir, I'm just here to ask you a few questions."

"I spoke to your colleague Parker this morning," he snapped, "I don't understand the need for further enquiries."

Cornelius wondered if Godfrey's hapless approach may have compounded Whitlock's ill-temper. He decided to steer the conversation away from that of his colleague, just in case.

"I'm visiting as part of the wider investigation, sir. As you may know, there have been other burglaries over the past few months and-"

"How would I know that?" interrupted Whitlock, seemingly quite affronted.

"Well, you may not," replied the policeman, "but there have been a number of burglaries and we are looking for patterns; clues that may link them. Hopefully I won't take too much of your time."

The solicitor's whiskers twitched as he pursed his lips in reluctant compliance, "Very well," he mumbled.

"I believe they gained entry from the rear yard; may I see it please?"

"Very well," said Whitlock, again making no attempt to disguise his annoyance.

He took the policeman from his office, along a corridor and down two steps into a kitchen. Above the Belfast sink was a grubby window through which Armstrong could see the rear yard, which led onto Spinners Lane.

"Can I see outside please?" asked the inspector.

Whitlock took a ring of keys from his pocket and opened the door. Armstrong stepped into the yard and walked towards the lane door, which was hanging limply with its lock broken and frame splintered. Looking up Spinners Lane itself, Cornelius could see back towards the bustling Fisher Street. He looked at the damaged door once more before returning to Whitlock who had remained standing in the entrance to the rear kitchen.

"Can I see this door please sir?" asked the policeman. Whitlock stood aside and Armstrong inspected the lock on the rear door. "They've kicked the lane door in but this lock is undamaged," he said to the solicitor.

"How very observant," said the solicitor, dismissively, "they must have picked the lock."

Armstrong stepped inside and swung the door in his hand in order to see the inside; there were two large bolts at the top and the bottom of the door, "Why was the door not bolted?" he asked.

The solicitor hesitated slightly, his haughty demeanour seemingly checked, "I'm not sure."

"Is the door usually bolted?"

"I assume so."

"Whose responsibility is it to lock up on an evening?"

"My son is often the last to leave, I'm sure he will have checked the building."

"But not last night it would seem."

"Damn your impertinence man!" shouted Whitlock.

One of Armstrong's character traits was that he treated people the way they treated him: if someone was a kindly soul, he would mirror their kindness; if someone was a no-nonsense character, he would not hesitate in getting straight to the point. In Whitlock's case, he found the solicitor to be an arrogant, disrespectful individual who he took an instant dislike to. Although such prejudice would never prevent him from doing his job, it would neither see him kowtow to the man's belief of superiority. He fixed his piercing blue eyes on the solicitor and ignored his outburst.

"Where *is* your son incidentally?" he asked.

"He has been called away."

"Last night?"

"No, I think it was this morning."

"I would like to speak with him when he returns." Armstrong was starting to indulge a guilty pleasure – that of enjoying his opponent's discomfort.

"I'm not sure when he will be back." Whitlock's cheeks and bald head were getting evermore red and his whiskers were twitching uncontrollably as he fought to retain any form of composure. "I might remind you Inspector, that we are the victims of this crime and I don't take kindly to being spoken to in this way."

"I do apologise Mr. Whitlock," said Armstrong – only he knew how sincere his act of contrition was – "it is not our intention to cause offence, we are only trying to establish the facts to give us the best possible chance of apprehending the perpetrators.

"Can I ask how much was actually taken from the safe?"

"Five thousand pounds."

"Where is the safe held?"

"In the strong room."

Whitlock escorted Armstrong back down the short corridor and down a second hallway that was at right angles to the first and opposite the solicitor's personal office. At the furthest point of the corridor was a large door that Whitlock unlocked with a large key from his ring and heaved open. Inside the musty, windowless room were shelves that rose from floor to ceiling; there was a ladder on wheels that was obviously used around the room to reach the high shelves. Against the furthest wall stood the large safe that was now closed and locked.

"Is it usual that you would hold such an amount in the building?" asked Cornelius.

"It can vary, depending on the clients' needs." Whitlock explained, "We could be carrying out some conveyancing work and could be therefore holding money for a property exchange; we could be holding the value of someone's estate following their death and pending the reading of their Will; there could be any number of reasons for having such an amount."

"Do you have any idea of who may have committed such a crime? A disgruntled former client perhaps?"

"No," replied the solicitor curtly, apparently keen to draw the meeting to a close.

"I see," said Armstrong, "well thank you for your time Mr. Whitlock, I'll speak with Inspector Parker again and get back to you. One of us will return and speak with your son at a convenient time."

The two bid each other a courteous, if reserved, good afternoon and Armstrong left Whitlock to go about his business. For his own part – knowing that Parker had not followed up on his promise to re-visit some of the other victims – he decided to visit a couple of the previous locations where burglaries took place.

One of the policeman's interests away from his work was music and some years earlier he had learned to play the piano. Having bought a beautiful Broadwood upright from Rattigan's Musical Instrument Shop on Botchergate at the time, he occasionally returned to the shop to buy sheet music. Michael Rattigan himself had also intermittently visited Cornelius at his lodgings to re-tune the instrument. Knowing that Rattigan's was one of the premises to be

41

broken into, and having had a particular piece in mind for the past several weeks, Armstrong decided it was an obvious port of call.

Although the January afternoons were bitterly cold, the days were getting slightly longer, so there was still two hours' light left as he made his way through the city centre and down Botchergate.

Rattingan's was the sort of shop where someone interested in that particular pastime could indulge themselves – a toy shop for adults. All kinds of musical instruments were available and if a customer ever asked for a particular instrument that was not on display, Rattigan would almost inevitably say, "I think I've got one in the back." He would then disappear through a rear curtain and – following a period of cacophonous symbol-crashing and piano-plinking – reappear with the requested item. Customers could never quite establish how big "the back" was but it was regularly the cause of both amusement and satisfaction in equal measure among the shop owner's clientele.

As Cornelius entered, the door disturbed the bell that hung down from the top of the inside frame. Within a few seconds the shop keeper appeared from behind the curtain.

"Mr. Armstrong sir, what a pleasant surprise."

"Good afternoon Michael, how's life treating you?"

"Oh, not bad sir, not bad, mustn't grumble. Are you here to extend your repertoire sir?" He indicated to a wall that was given over completely to stringed instruments, "I've just got some beautiful violins in from London before Christmas."

Cornelius smiled, "No, much as I enjoy my piano, I find that to be challenging enough."

"Some more sheet music then perhaps?"

"Yes that is a good idea, I quite fancy having a go at Beethoven's piano sonatas if you've got any."

"Yes, I'm sure I have," said Rattigan pulling open the top drawer to a cabinet that was presumably full of sheet music. After a little harrumphing under his breath, he said the words, that his customers longed to hear, "I'll just have a look in the back."

42

Emerging some minutes later the triumphant Rattigan announced, "Here we are sir, I have them all here."

"It was actually *Moonlight* I was interested in," said Cornelius.

Rattigan leafed through the selection of papers, "Yes, I have it here Mr. Armstrong."

"That's great," said the policeman reaching in his pocket for some change. As the shop keeper was putting the sheet music into a paper bag, Armstrong added, "It's not the only reason I was visiting today Michael. I wanted to ask you about the burglary you suffered a few months ago."

"Oh yes," said Rattigan, handing the bag to his customer, "that was a nasty business. That other policeman said he would come back to do some further enquiries but I never heard anything else from him."

"Yes, sorry about that," Cornelius was both embarrassed and annoyed by Parker's ineptitude.

"Never mind, we got things sorted pretty quick after that. There wasn't much damage and we got the money back."

"How do you mean you got the money back?"

"Well the solicitors sorted it all out for me. I have the shop and all the instruments insured and they managed to sort things out with the insurance company."

"Was any of your stock taken?"

"No, just money from the safe. I remember it was over a weekend when it was full of the week's takings. I got the back door repaired, received recompense for the losses and because there was no major damage, just put it down to experience. When the other inspector never returned, I just forgot about it."

Cornelius stared thoughtfully past Rattigan into the middle distance before the shop keeper broke the silence, "Sir?"

"Yes, sorry," replied Armstrong breaking his reverie. "Who are you insured with?"

Rattigan felt a little wrong-footed by the random question, "Erm, someone at Lloyds of London I think it is. The solicitors sort it all out for me."

"Which solicitors are they?"

"Erm, that lot on Fisher Street, Freeman, Whatsit and Somebody-or-other."

"Morley, Freeman and Whitlock?"

"Yes, that's them. They do all of my stuff for me. They're very good I must say."

"Thank you for that Michael, and for the music, that's my homework for tonight."

"You're very welcome Mr. Armstrong, nice to see you again, and good luck with Beethoven!"

With a ring of the bell and swish of the curtain, they both went their separate ways.

Knowing that Turnbull's Haberdashers close by had suffered a similar fate, Armstrong decided to call in before returning to the station and ask the manager about his experience. His narrative was almost identical to that of Michael Rattigan: weekend break-in when the safe was full, no other stock disturbed, no follow-up enquiry by Inspector Parker – much to Armstrong's annoyance – and a quick resolution to his insurance claim.

"Can I ask who you are insured with?" Armstrong asked Mr. Howard.

"Lloyd's of London," replied the manager.

"And your solicitor?"

"Morley, Freeman and Whitlock on Fisher Street."

"Thank you, sir, I won't disturb you further."

Cornelius took a slow walk back to the station pondering the days' events. When he arrived Sergeant Townsend informed him that Chief Constable Henry Baker was back in his office and was waiting for him.

"Thank you, Bill," said the Inspector, "I will speak to Godfrey first, is he in his office?"

"Yes sir."

Armstrong went into his own office and hung up his hat and coat before knocking on Inspector Parker's door. Inside, Parker was sitting at his desk with papers strewn everywhere, including on the two chairs that sat in front of his desk.

"Oh, Cornelius, how are you?"

"Good afternoon, Godfrey. Yes, I've had an interesting day, I visited William Whitlock and looked in on a couple of other shops that were burgled. I would like you to visit Ismay's on Scotch Street and the pawn brokers who were broken into."

Although Armstrong and Parker were both inspectors – in fact Parker was considerably senior to Armstrong in terms of years in post – there was no sense from either man that Armstrong's instruction was in any way disrespectful or unreasonable.

"Certainly," replied Godfrey.

"I am interested in exactly when the robberies took place, if anything other than money was taken, who their insurance company was and who their solicitor is."

"I will visit them all in the morning and speak with you then," said Parker, apparently re-invigorated by his colleague's input.

Armstrong then went further down the hall to his superior's office; he knocked and entered.

Baker was sitting at his desk reading a document. When the door opened, he looked up, "Ah, Inspector Armstrong."

Cornelius knew that Baker was in a serious mood when there were no informalities and he was using his professional title.

"Afternoon sir."

Opposite Baker sat a middle-aged man with a decidedly concerned look on his face. Baker introduced him.

"This is Mr. Benjamin Woodward, owner of the Iredale Brewery on Currock Street. Mr. Woodward, this is Cornelius Armstrong, my finest detective."

Cornelius was both flattered and proud, following his superior's compliment. He offered a hand, "Pleased to meet you Mr. Woodward."

Woodward replied with a weak smile and a nod.

Baker continued, "Mr. Woodward here has brought to my attention this letter he received this morning."

45

Baker indicated to Armstrong the vacant chair opposite Woodward and handed him the letter he had been reading moments earlier. Cornelius sat down and took a few minutes to read it.

"Blackmail," he said, as much to himself as anyone else.

The letter was scrawled in an almost illegible hand and threatened Woodward that his beer would be contaminated if he didn't pay £5,000 by the end of the month. The letter concluded:

...further instructions to follow, do not go to the police.

"When did you receive this, Mr. Woodward?" asked Armstrong.

"Last week," replied the brewery owner. I didn't know what to do. My dear wife was adamant that I should come and see you straight away; after much consideration I decided that this was the best course of action."

"I think that's right, sir," said the inspector, "I remember reading about problems with contaminated beer in the Manchester area last year."

Woodward recalled, "Yes, that is what ultimately influenced my decision to come and see you. It caused havoc in the industry. It turned out to be arsenic poisoning; deaths, illness amongst customers, and put some breweries out of business. I just couldn't take the chance."

"Are there any signs yet of problems with your operation?" asked Armstrong.

"No, thankfully not," replied Woodward, "I have had my managers running tests of all of our equipment, as well as the grain, hops and yeast. We've then tested samples of our beer itself and thankfully, everything is clear. I haven't told my staff why we have been doing this for fear of causing a panic."

The Chief Constable interrupted, "I agree with Armstrong Mr. Woodward. I suggest you continue your vigilance and keep us informed if there are any further developments."

"Thank you, gentlemen," said the brewery owner, "I'm pleased I have raised the matter."

"I'll show you out," said Baker.

The Chief Constable was a gentle man but like many in positions of authority, he could be irritable and impatient when put under excessive stress. He had called the meeting in Penrith earlier in the day to sound out his colleagues from around the county, about the rise in crime over the past twelve months or so. Returning to his office a few minutes later after escorting Woodward out, Cornelius could see that the façade of politeness had dissipated. He waited for his superior to speak.

"I was talking to Parker when he arrived," said Baker by way of an explanation. "It was useful that you arrived when you did; then you could hear this latest problem for yourself. I don't know what's going on recently, Cornelius."

"How did the meeting go?"

"It was a waste of time," said Baker, slumping into his chair, "none of the other Cumberland and Westmorland forces are experiencing the same level of crime."

"Well they are not as big as we are, Henry," offered Armstrong.

"Yes but even so." Baker thought for a while, "Parker said something about a breakthrough with the shop burglaries?"

"Well, I think 'breakthrough' is overstating it a little. I visited some of the premises this afternoon and there are a few areas we can look into."

Baker sighed, "Thank you Cornelius, we would be in a predicament without you." The tacit meaning regarding the abilities of his other senior officer needing no further elaboration.

Cornelius braced himself as he raised a different subject, "There was another incident this morning that you probably don't know about."

He told his Chief Constable about Ester Sanderson's apparent suicide and the events of that morning. Baker listened open-mouthed.

"How was Herbert Underwood involved?" he asked referring to the Chair of the Watch Committee.

"I don't know, he just told me he was a friend of the family. Doctor Bell took the body away and will report back after the post mortem."

Baker shook his head, "Again, Cornelius, what on earth is going on?"

SIX

Cornelius Armstrong got back to his lodgings shortly after six o'clock. Mrs. Wheeler had made the fire in time for his arrival and he smiled to himself at once more returning to his cosy sanctuary; his own little enclave that seemed to be a world away from the problems of the day.

The paper he was reading that morning reporting on the death of Queen Victoria was still lying on his desk in the corner of the sitting room. He picked it up briefly and thought about the state of the world: there was a piece on the newly Federated Australia; other articles on problems in India and Russia, as well as updates on the war in South Africa which raged on without any apparent end in sight. He then related the eclectic mixture of international problems to his own domestic duties: suicides, burglaries, threatening behaviour and blackmail. "Life's rich tapestry," he mumbled to himself tossing the paper back on the desk and levering himself out of his hat and coat.

There was a knock on the door and Mrs. Wheeler entered with a tray, on top of which was a pot of a tea and a large silver dome.

"Evening Mr. Armstrong, I've just got your tea for you. Mince and dumplings to warm you up on such a night, sir."

"Thank you, Mrs. Wheeler, you're an angel. And thanks as always for the fire."

"You're very welcome, sir," said the housekeeper, "have you had a good day?"

"Very busy, Mrs. Wheeler, very busy. I sometimes wonder what is wrong with the world today."

"Oh yes, and that terrible news about the queen God rest her soul. You never know what's around the corner."

"No you don't," agreed Cornelius.

"Anyway sir, I'll leave you in peace. Enjoy your meal and I'll send up Emma later to collect your tray."

"Thanks again Mrs. Wheeler."

Armstrong again smiled to himself. 'You never know what's around the corner,' was one of his housekeeper's favourite phrases. "Never a truer word spoken," said Cornelius to his empty room.

He took off his collar and freshened up before enjoying Mrs. Wheeler's cooking. As his mind wandered, he realised that he had left the sheet music purchased from Rattigan's on his desk at work.

Beethoven will have to wait for another night, he thought. Instead he poured himself a glass of rum and lit a pipe. He was not a heavy smoker, but occasionally Cornelius enjoyed a mild tobacco, thumbed into the elegant cherrywood pipe that was a present from his cousin George some years earlier. He took a final look out, down on to the glistening cobbles of Abbey Street. It was starting to snow again. Picking up the paper again, he sat down in his leather rocking chair by the fire. That was him for the night.

*

A few hours earlier, less than a mile away as the crow flew, Billy Grant had climbed the steps to the tenement he shared with his brother Freddie in Caldewgate. He fumbled for a key and opened the door; almost instantaneously he was greeted by a fist powering into his face, knocking him off his feet and back onto the open landing.

"Ugh, wha'?" Billy tried to compose himself and come to terms with what had just happened. He looked up at his brother who had some angry bruising on his face.

"You weren't there to meet the boat!"

"I saw the bloke," protested the younger brother, "I got the bag." He indicated towards the large canvass sack that he could see through the doorway.

"I've been told that he had to come looking for you. You were in that bloody drug den again."

"Who told you that?"

"I had a visit from Roberts – he'd been told in no uncertain terms that we're risking the whole thing." He pointed to his own face, indicating Roberts's handywork and dragged his brother to his feet by the scruff of his neck. "I'm telling you, Billy, don't mess this up for us. We've got a good thing going here."

Billy knew there was no point in denying his own carelessness. Instead he sat there on the landing nodding, silently accepting what his brother was saying.

"Good," said Freddie. "Now Roberts wants to see you tonight."

Billy's face flashed with terror, as he wondered what fate was to befall him.

"No, it's nothing like that," said his older brother, reading his mind, "I've already taken the brunt of that lunatic's anger for one day. No, he said he needs a hand with something tonight. I've got to sort this lot out for distribution" – he indicated towards the drugs – "so you need to go and meet him at the Irish Gate at nine o'clock."

"I don't want to see that bloke, Freddie, not after what happened last week.

Billy was referring to a summons the two had from Roberts who "…wanted a hand with a little problem."

The two brothers were no shrinking violets but they had become increasingly worried about some of the tasks they were being ordered to do by the Manchester criminal, but at the same time they were unwilling to upset the man who was bringing them income they had never dreamed about previously. They shared an unspoken, yet growing feeling that they were now into something that they couldn't get out of.

The Irish Gate pub, near the castle had become a regular meeting place for the brothers and the Manchester villain. When the appropriate time came on that third-week-in-January meeting, the two brothers saw their man in the far corner of the crowded, noisy hostelry. Freddie signalled to him asking if he wanted a drink; Roberts shook his head and gestured for them both to join him.

"All right Jack," said the older brother sitting down.

Roberts did not respond. He was a stocky man with a hardened, leathery face; his appearance put fear into most people who met him and the Grant brothers were no exception.

"I need to meet someone and I could do with a hand," said Roberts.

The two brothers looked at one another puzzled.

"Is he coming here?" asked Freddie.

"That's the plan." Roberts took out a grubby piece of paper from his pocket and smoothed it out on the trestle table in front of him with the side of his hand. "He lives at Globe Lane; do you know where that is?"

"Yeah," said Freddie, still a little uncertain, "it's within walking distance. Who is this bloke? Why do you want to see him? And what do you need us for?"

"He's a business acquaintance of a friend of mine who asked me to have a word with him." Roberts smirked, as if enjoying a private joke.

"What about?"

"You don't need to concern yourself with that."

"I need you to go around to the yard in the abattoir and wait for me there," said Roberts.

The abattoir was at the bottom of Devonshire Walk, a narrow road adjacent to the castle and just a few hundred yards from the pub where the three were meeting. The road led down to the wooded parkland and the River Eden beyond it.

"The abattoir?" cried the brothers almost in unison.

Roberts snarled at them both, "Yeah, the abattoir. Now get yourselves round there and I'll be there in a few minutes."

The brothers were increasingly uncomfortable about what they were being told – or not being told – but felt they had no choice; Freddie and Billy were not sure where the boundaries were with this man but they were sure that they didn't want to test them.

They trudged through the snow past the row of terraced houses on Devonshire Walk towards the slaughter house and waited in the yard. The constant traffic of vehicles and animals – dead and alive – in and out of the building had turned the cobbles a deep brown colour. It was virtually impossible for snow to settle on such a surface that was permanently wet and slimy. Along one wall of the yard were a dozen or more wooden carts and barrows. Although there was a night shift working inside, the building was locked up against the cold weather outside.

"I don't like the sound of this," Billy said to his brother as the two of them stood trying to warm themselves in the shadow of the giant building.

While they were exchanging their reservations about the current predicament they found themselves in, Jack Roberts left his table and made his way to the entrance of the pub. He looked at the large clock above the bar; it was a minute before nine o'clock and the Manchester man stepped outside. Fortunately, there was no one around. Within seconds he saw the man he was waiting for, approaching. He was in a long black coat and wore a wide-brimmed hat. Roberts had been advised of his victim's movements the previous day and had familiarised himself with what he looked like in preparation for this evening. As the man approached, the light from the hostelry confirmed the man's identity to Roberts; he saw the distinctive full black beard and thick matching hair under his hat.

"Do you have a light mate?" asked Roberts as the man walked by towards the door of the pub.

"Yes, certainly," replied the stranger, stopping and reaching in his pocket for some matches.

"Are you Dominic James by any chance?" asked Roberts

"Yes," said the man with some uncertainty.

In a flash, Roberts produced a thick cudgel from behind his back and crashed down a blow on the man's head, instantly rendering him unconscious. He collapsed into the villain's arms and Roberts adeptly slung one of the limp arms over his own shoulder, managed to secure the man's hat to his head, and headed off in the direction the meeting point with the Grant brothers. To any casual observer the two simply looked like a couple of drunks staggering home.

Roberts guided his victim down the slight decline of Devonshire Walk towards the entrance of the slaughter house yard. Both brothers were startled at the sight.

"'Ere, give me a hand," hissed Roberts as he approached.

Freddie and Billy took the man from him and laid him on the ground just inside the gate.

"What's going on?" asked Freddie.

"He's the bloke I was waiting for," Roberts stared at the unconscious man with contempt.

"Who is he? What's he done?"

"He's an enemy, that's all you need to know."

It was as though Roberts was possessed by another being – he talked in monotone and continued to stare.

"Is he dead?" asked Billy.

To the brothers' horror, Roberts produced a cudgel and thundered a blow into the man's head, splitting it open with a sickening crunch. Within seconds, a slither of blood became a gushing torrent, while the blackened cobbles onto which it fell instantly gave it the impression of engine oil. The blood of the two brothers meanwhile ran cold at the sight of what they had just witnessed.

"He is now," whispered the murderer. As Freddie and Billy stood wide-eyed and open-mouthed in disbelief, Roberts snapped out of his reverie, "Now you two, get rid of it."

Billy continued to stare in disbelief, while Freddie looked at Roberts, "What do you mean, get rid of it?"

"I mean get rid of it," snarled Roberts.

"Where?"

"I don't know where, you're from round here. Fire him in the river," he gestured towards the parkland, knowing that the Eden was beyond it. He was in no mood to argue, "Get one of those barrows and cart him down there."

Freddie was silent for a moment, just looking at Roberts, still in shock and unsure how to respond. His brother was rooted to the spot, unable to comprehend what he had just witnessed: the violence, the matter-of-factness, the recklessness, given that it was in the yard of a working building and within a few hundred yards of many pubs, not to mention the castle where a battalion of the local regiment were garrisoned.

Roberts spotted a pile of hessian sacks tied with string, beside some heavy-duty brushes, presumably used to sweep and swill the yard clean. He knocked the snow off the top of the sacks with his forearm and took out a knife – something Freddie saw glinting when it caught the light – and cut the string. The sacks were old and stained with the dried blood of hundreds of animals.

"Here," said Roberts, "wrap him in these and load him onto one of them barrows. I'll sweep the blood away." It was an order, not a suggestion.

Freddie, nudged Billy out of his funk and indicated towards one of the barrows that were lined up against the wall of the yard. The younger brother went to get one, while Freddie started to wrap the corpse, as best he could, into the dirty old sacks. Billy wheeled the large wooden barrow across towards them, and Freddie and Roberts lifted the victim up and unceremoniously dumped him on the flat surface.

Just then, there was the sound of a door opening to the side of the slaughter house. The three stopped and stood in silence. From where they were standing, they could see some rubbish bins running parallel to the side of the building. From the angle they were at, they saw someone's arms hurl some rubbish into one of the bins and then heard the slamming of the door shut. They never saw his face and more importantly, he never saw them.

Roberts thought this was all very amusing, "You better get on with it," he said, "before someone else comes out."

Freddie nudged his brother once more and the two started to lug the heavy barrow through the snow in the direction of the parkland. He looked back at Roberts who was sweeping the blood into the cobbles and towards the drain, as if it were the most natural thing in the world to bludgeon a man to death in cold blood. Such was Freddie Grant's upbringing that he wasn't easily scared, but this psychopath terrified him. He knew now that there was no going back for him and Billy; Roberts wouldn't hesitate to give them the same treatment if they tried to cross him.

The Grant brothers heaved the barrow through the trees. The whiteness of the snow afforded the only visibility on such a black night but made their task twice as hard as it would have been if the conditions were dry. The only consolation was that in such conditions, at this time of night, the whole area was now deserted; the chances of anyone seeing them therefore was virtually impossible.

Despite the freezing cold temperature, the two began to sweat profusely as their task became harder and harder. The other paradox was that, despite their disgust at what they were now accessories to, there was a relief to be away from Roberts – the man was completely out of control.

It must have taken half an hour to drag the barrow the half mile or so through the trees and down towards the river.

"What do we do now?" asked the panting Billy.

Freddie thought for a while, still struggling to comprehend what he and his brother were now involved with, "I suppose we'll have to tip the body into the river."

It was obvious to both of them that this is what they intended to do, but it was though one of them had to say the words before it became a reality. The brothers shuffled the barrow to the edge of a steep section of the bank and tipped it up, causing the body to fall off the back and down the slope. They stood in silence. It started to snow heavily yet again.

"Come on," said Freddie, let's get this back and go home."

He and Billy dragged the barrow back through the snow. Freddie was relieved to see that there were no signs of any blood visible as they re-traced their steps: a combination of the victim's body losing the majority of blood in the yard, and whatever remnants there were being covered by the new snow, appeared to have covered their tracks.

By the time they got back to the yard of the slaughter house, there was no sign of Roberts and inspecting the cobbles, little sign of the violence that had taken place less than an hour earlier. They quickly returned the barrow to its parking spot against the far wall, did a final check that no one had seen them and hurried home.

Freddie was relieved that he hadn't seen Roberts for almost a week following the murder but when the Manchester criminal did appear at his door, he knew something was wrong. The elder Grant had been determined to keep his head down but his younger brother had failed to stick to his planned task of collecting and bringing the shipment of opium from Whitehaven on time. The courier McVey had reported as much to his paymasters and word had quickly got through to Roberts in Carlisle. While Billy was amusing himself at the opium den in Whitehaven, his brother was being roughed up on his behalf in Carlisle.

"I don't care if you don't want to see him Billy," said Freddie, after informing him of Roberts's visit and his summons, "we haven't got much choice in the matter anymore."

On his way to the Irish Gate, Billy recalled the same journey he had made with his brother the previous week and what it had led to. He was now completely sober and it was with some trepidation that he entered and saw Roberts sitting in the far corner at the same table.

"Hello, Billy boy!" Roberts's greeting was sinister.

"Hello Jack, I'm sorry about the delay in Whitehaven."

"Well, it's sorted now," said Roberts looking into his tankard. Without moving his head, he raised his eyes to look at Billy, "but if it ever happens again...well, I'm sure you can imagine what might happen." His eyeballs darted to the right, indicating the direction of the abattoir.

"It won't Jack, it won't," stammered Billy in his terror.

"Good lad. Now, we have to collect some rent and you've got a chance to redeem yourself. I want you to go round the boss's houses and business and collect what's owing. Then you need to tell them that the rent is going up as from next month."

"Going up? Some of them can't afford it as it is, how can they afford more?"

"There's always a way Billy boy. We've got to squeeze them." Roberts slowly closed his fist as if ringing out an imaginary cloth, "we've got to squeeze them hard. You can get on with it tomorrow."

With that, he drained his tankard and left Billy sitting at the table to contemplate his situation.

SEVEN

Billy Grant had spent a restless night, unable as he was to erase the snarling features of Jack Roberts from his mind. In truth he hadn't slept properly since the events of the previous week when he and his brother had been accessories to the murder of the man in the slaughter house yard. The only respite he enjoyed was the twenty-four-hour stupor in the opium den near Whitehaven docks a couple of days ago, and even that had ended up causing trouble for him and Freddie.

His brother's task this day was to take the drugs Billy had brought from the courier to where they would be distributed around the city. Pubs owners, street corner peddlers and runners had all been drawn into the illegal web to the point where supply was struggling to keep up with the addictive demand.

Billy meanwhile, dare not deviate from his instructions from the night before, however unpleasant and unjust they were. He had a list of businesses and tenements in the Caldewgate, Shaddongate and Wapping areas of the city from where he was to collect rent, and then inform the owners and occupiers that more would be collected from the following month.

Since Roberts's arrival in Carlisle, those businesses that were not actually renting premises from his paymasters became susceptible to threats of vandalism and fire unless they paid what the villain called 'protection money'. When Billy had naively asked Roberts what the money was protecting them from, Roberts flashed an evil smile his way before turning to Freddie, "Not very bright your boy, is he?" It was now Billy's unenviable job of carrying out Roberts's threats and demands.

It was Market Day in the city and Paddy's Market in particular was a popular event in Caldewgate, the Irish quarter of Carlisle. Caldewgate consisted of a wide main road – Bridge Street – on which either side were hundreds of tiny houses and commercial premises crammed into the labyrinthine alleys and courts that seemed to go on forever.

It was yet another raw day in this seemingly merciless winter. An icy fog had now compounded the uncomfortable overnight temperature and it had weaved its way through the narrow lanes of Caldewgate – barely wide enough for two people to pass in places – and mingled with the steam and smoke being generated from laundry rooms, smithy's shops and open street braziers. In these conditions people going about their normal business would startle each other as they suddenly appeared from nowhere like phantoms.

By the time Billy left his own tenement just off Byron Street and made it through the misty maze and onto Bridge Street, the pavements were crowded and shoppers jostled each other as they searched for produce amid the awninged stalls.

"Nice goose for you here luv!" shouted a voice as Billy picked his way through the crowd. He looked over to see a woman standing behind her poultry stall, inadequately dressed in a woollen shawl, fingerless gloves and a straw boater. Beside her was a steaming urn, "Or a nice bowl of soup?"

The thought of a bowl of soup on such a morning sounded particularly appetizing but he knew that stopping would only delay the unenviable tasks he had to do and therefore, would make them even harder to perform. He smiled and gave a negative acknowledgement without breaking stride. His first port of call was to be residents of the tiny Lowes Court on the south side of Bridge Street.

Billy entered the labyrinth of lanes that virtually mirrored those on the north side of the street. He walked twenty yards along Rigg Lane and made a left turn only to quickly dart back around the corner and plant himself against the brick wall. His mind began to race as he fought to control his already fragile nerves. He removed his cap with a grab and gently moved to peek around the corner to confirm what he had seen. Less than ten yards away, two men were standing talking, silhouetted under a brick arch, as a wintery sun fought to illuminate the gloomy alley. Billy thought he recognised both men.

One was well dressed and dapper: he wore a homburg and had a long overcoat; he also sported a distinctive moustache with sharp points that Billy could just about see given he and his companion were so close. The other man was stoutly built and wore an old tattered frock-coat that had long seen better days. Baggy trousers hung over his scuffed boots and covering his tousled hair was an old flat top bowler hat. At the man's feet sat an obedient bulldog.

The vapour from their warm breath dissipated into the mist under the arch as they engaged in their deep conversation. They were close enough for Billy to hear their voices, but not close enough to make out what they were saying. He eased himself back around the corner to his position of hiding; fortunately they hadn't seen him, so engrossed were they in their conversation.

His brief glance had confirmed his initial thought: the first bloke was that copper Inspector Armstrong while the other was Reuben Hanks.

Although he personally had never had any run-ins with the policeman, his brother Freddie encountered him a year or two back when he was picked up for organising an illegal cock fight in Wapping. The gathering had ended up, not only with dead animals but it had descended into a mass brawl amongst those present. The elder brother had always found his encounters with the police to be an occupational hazard over the years and paid little attention to them. On that particular occasion however, he found Inspector Armstrong to be very different in his approach to some of the others: far more thorough and professional, and not someone who could be fobbed off like the rest. Billy remembered Freddie telling him, "He's not someone you want to get on the wrong side of."

Reuben Hanks meanwhile was a working-class character from Caldewgate, like the two Grant brothers. Ordinarily, if someone like Armstrong was engaging with someone like Hanks, it would usually mean that one was arresting the other for some misdemeanour. But on this occasion, there was no sense of confrontation between the two.

As Grant was contemplating the situation, a washerwoman with a basket of clothes appeared from around the corner and gave a start at the man who was just standing there with his back against the wall. She gave him a look of admonishment and walked on, as Billy gave an apologetic smile.

He wondered what was best to do: sneak back out and disappear into the crowds on Bridge Street; go back and speak with Freddie; perhaps even confront Hanks and ask him what he was doing. Maybe the last one wasn't a sensible option – Reuben Hanks was another hard man who wouldn't take lightly to being questioned by someone like Billy Grant. Thinking of hard men, Billy suddenly remembered what Roberts had tasked him with this morning; whatever Hanks and Armstrong were talking about, he couldn't allow them to distract him from his primary mission.

He went to sneak a further peek around the corner to see if he could hear anything but as he did so, it became apparent that the meeting between the two was coming to an end; both men were on the half-turn as they prepared to part. Hanks turned away and walked in the opposite direction from Grant's vantage point, disappearing under the arch and being engulfed by the fog as he did so. To Billy's horror, Armstrong turned the opposite way and headed for where he was standing. He quickly scampered a few yards back down the alley and darted into a doorway, where he pressed his back as hard as he could into the shadows and held his breath, for fear of the vapour from him exhaling betraying his hiding place. Sure enough, seconds later he saw the copper walk past – he hadn't seen him.

Billy emerged from the dark doorway and gave a relieved sigh; he looked at Inspector Armstrong as he too vanished into the fog. Standing for a moment, he considered the oddity of a policeman like Armstrong talking to a character like Reuben Hanks. *What were they talking about?* he wondered.

*

Cornelius Armstrong and Reuben Hanks were themselves both from Caldewgate, having lived most of their childhood not far from where Billy Grant and his brother now stayed. The particular group of lanes, streets and courts were colloquially known as Poet's Corner. The desperate conditions endured by the residents there were completely at odds with the impression given by the names of Byron, Milton and Shakespeare, all of whom had streets named after them.

Cornelius was slightly older than Hanks, lived on Henderson Square, just off Byron Street with his mother. Reuben meanwhile was part of the large family of nine who were crammed into a one-bedroom tenement on Johns Court, a small alleyway at the bottom of Shakespeare Street. The two knew each other as children – everyone knew everyone else in such a tight-knit community – but were not necessarily friends. Cornelius always harboured ambitions to educate and better himself, while Reuben – like many of their contemporaries – was happy to job and labour in order to scrape a living, and if there were unconventional gains to be had at any point, well they were very welcome too.

When Cornelius joined the City Police Force in '88, it didn't take long before their paths crossed again. Armstrong stumbled on an illegal sweep being run in one of the pubs local to Poet's Corner. It wasn't long before PC Armstrong found out that it was Reuben Hanks that was behind the activity. When he brought his suspect back to the police station, the desk sergeant of the time showed little enthusiasm for processing an issue that he saw as relatively harmless. Once the matter had been dealt with Sergeant Carruthers – a grizzled army veteran of campaigns in India and Africa – gave the young constable a piece of advice.

"Don't waste your time on nonsense like this, son, we've got bigger fish to fry than wastrels like him."

The words of wisdom stayed with Armstrong, and so the next time he found Reuben bending the rules of law – illegally pawning goods – he decided to take him to one side and have a chat about how he could be of use to the policeman. Thereafter, the two developed an understanding whereby the rogue would keep his questionable activity to a minimum and the policeman would not actively look into any misdemeanours. In return, Armstrong's childhood neighbour, who still moved in the lower social circles, would provide him with important information whenever he had a problem.

Cornelius was always keen to ensure that he did not overuse this unconventional resource – after all, he realised it was incumbent on the official police force themselves to prevent and solve crimes; it was not the responsibility of the general public. But the arrangement proved beneficial for both parties and it was something that developed further when Armstrong became a detective inspector, something Hanks was happy with. The only stipulation he made was that the two met discretely, out of the sight of his friends and associates. On this occasion, the two arranged to meet in a quiet lane, while the rest of Caldewgate was occupied with Paddy's Market.

Several issues were wrestling for attention in Armstrong's mind: the spate burglaries, the marked increase in opium-related activity and now the blackmail threat to Iredale's Brewery. He wanted to know if Reuben Hanks could offer any leads.

Referring to the first issue, Hanks said, "The robberies could be anybody, sir. There's many a scallywag knocking about as you well know."

"I'm not so sure, Reuben," replied Armstrong, "they are just stealing cash only; ignoring goods that could presumably be sold on for more profit. The burglars know exactly who to target and when, and perhaps most significantly, they can crack the combinations of safes and strong rooms. It's as though they are stealing to order."

As he was speaking, a washerwoman carrying a basket of clothes appeared out of the gloom; the two men stood aside – Cornelius touching the brim of his hat as they did so – and allowed her to ease between them and carry on her journey down the narrow lane, her footsteps crunching on the frosty walkway. A few seconds later, Cornelius heard a shuffling noise and muffled voice from the direction in which the woman walked and thought initially that she had lost her footing on the slippery surface. As he moved to go and help her, he instantly heard her footsteps again and presumed she had simply skidded slightly as she turned the corner onto Rigg Lane. He looked down the lane but could see nothing in the misty conditions. He turned back to Reuben.

"Whoever is doing this is a cut above your average sneak-thief."

"I can't think of anyone round here with those skills Mr. Armstrong."

"No, I've had a quick glance through the records of people we've picked up on burglary charges over the past three or four years and nobody stands out."

Reuben changed the subject to that of the seemingly copious amounts of opium in the city over the past few months. "One o' the lads in Blue Lugs the other night was telling me about a dosshouse on Robert Street where they've got their fair share of drugs. I think he said it was number seven. Never been myself but apparently it's getting quite popular."

"Robert Street," repeated Armstrong, "that's fairly near Iredale's Brewery on Currock Street, I suppose. I might be clutching at straws but I wonder if they are connected in some way?"

"Maybe," said Reuben, although it was apparent that Armstrong was talking to himself as much as he was to him at that point. "Like the thieving," said Hanks, "blackmail doesn't sound like anything anybody round here would be involved in."

"How about someone who might work there?" asked Cornelius, "if someone is threatening to poison the beer, they would have to have access to the factory. Do you know of anybody who might fit the bill?"

"I know of a few blokes who work there and another who delivers barley but it wouldn't be any of them – none of them have got the brains!"

Cornelius knew he was clutching at straws if he thought Reuben could shed enough light on the confused matters to allow him to solve the various cases; but he believed that he should leave no stone unturned and therefore, it was useful to plant the seed with his informant. With nothing further to be discussed, he called their unorthodox meeting to a close.

"Thanks for your help Reuben, if you could keep your ear to the ground for me it would be appreciated. In the meantime, I'll pay that house on Robert Street a visit and see what's going on there."

"No problem, Mr. Armstrong, if I hear anything else, I'll be in touch. C'mon Boris." The bulldog that had sat at his feet looking up at the two men quizzically during their conversation, got to his feet and waddled off into the fog after his master.

Cornelius meanwhile, headed off in the other direction towards Bridge Street with the intention of returning to the station before visiting the house on Robert Street.

*

Billy Grant watched the policeman disappear down the lane. What he had just witnessed unnerved him somewhat but he had work to do and, as unpleasant as that work was, the consequences of not doing it and having to inform Roberts, didn't bear thinking about. He would get on with it and report his concerns back to Freddie later.

The task in hand was a grim one. His first port of call was a row of tatty terraced houses in Millers Court

"RENT...RENT DAY!" he yelled, as he banged on the near-rotten front door with the flat of his hand.

A young woman came to the door, carrying an infant, while a toddler tugged at her skirts. Billy could hear the voices of more children in the background. Her tired face spoke volumes.

"I'm 'ere for the rent luv," said Grant, almost apologetically. He wasn't a very imposing figure himself but they both knew it was the message he was carrying that was significant, not the person who was delivering it.

"I won't have it till Friday, when my husband gets paid," said the woman, "that's if I can catch him before he gets to the pub."

There was an uncomfortable silence between the two.

"Listen..." Billy referred to his book, "Mary – it's really important you get the rent, for both our sakes, and that of your husband."

Mary hadn't experienced the consequences of not paying on time herself, but she had heard from Peggy Sidebottom, two doors down, that her man got a good hiding from some bloke who found him drinking the rent money away in *The Duke of York* last month. She therefore understood Billy's cryptic message.

"There's something else," said Billy, "it's going up a shilling from next month."

Mary looked, expressionless, at the rent collector, "I'll tell Frank when he gets home." With that, she shut the door.

Billy thought about shouting a reminder about Friday but his heart wasn't in it. Instead he got on with repeating the message to the poor unfortunates, who were at the mercy of landlords, intent on squeezing them dry and a psychopath who took great delight in terrorising anyone who he encountered.

Of the dozens of calls he made that morning – from Millers Court in Caldewgate, to Johnson's Pawn Brokers on Water Street – Billy saw the same resigned expression on the faces of the tenants: bled dry of whatever funds they had and uncertain as to what the future held.

The younger Grant returned home with what money he had collected. By the time he got there his brother Freddie was gone, on his own mission of distributing the opium Billy had collected in Whitehaven. It was probably just as well his brother had taken all of the drugs away; the younger Grant didn't trust himself. He looked round the small room in their tenement flat, beset by a combination of depression on behalf of the people he knew couldn't afford anything further and frightened on his own behalf, as he now had to find a way of telling Roberts that he didn't have all the money. He slumped down in a chair, wishing that he and his brother had never become involved in such an enterprise.

EIGHT

The inquest into the death of Ester Sanderson was opened and immediately adjourned to allow for reports to be submitted to the coroner, one of which was the post mortem, to be carried out by Doctor James Bell.

Doctor Bell had worked at the Cumberland Infirmary for a number of years and was a highly respected pathologist within the medical community throughout the north of England. He had also gained the respect of the local police force, with whom he had worked with on three occasions during the previous five years. The feeling was mutual, as Bell was impressed with the competence and compassion shown by Chief Constable Henry Baker and his Inspector, Cornelius Armstrong.

Bell had been at home reading about the passing of the Queen when a courier sent from Sergeant Townsend asked him to attend 'an incident' at the bottom of London Road. Bell smiled at Townsend's discretion, but he knew if he was being called for it could only mean one thing: there was a dead body – or dead bodies – to examine.

PC Eddie Kirk was standing guard at the house on London Road when Doctor Bell arrived. As he did so, a black four-wheeled ambulance also pulled up – confirmation, if it were needed that a body needed be moved from the premises.

"Sergeant Townsend also sent word to the hospital, sir," said Kirk nodding towards the ambulance, "if you'd like to step inside, I'll let Inspector Armstrong know you're here."

"What has happened here, constable?" asked Bell, "The note I received gave no details?"

"Sorry about that, sir," replied Kirk. "A young woman's been found hanging in her bedroom."

He escorted the doctor inside and bounded up the elegant staircase at the top of which Bell could see a second uniformed officer sitting outside one of the bedroom doors.

As Bell was waiting to be summoned, one of the four doors that were accessed from the hallway opened and Herbert Underwood, Chairman of the Watch Committee appeared.

"Good morning, Doctor Bell," he said, "the victim's parents are in here, "I don't suppose Inspector Parker has arrived yet?"

Bell knew who Underwood was but had never been formally introduced to him. He was a little surprised by his manner, or what he was even doing here but replied anyway, "I believe Inspector Armstrong is upstairs now."

"Armstrong?" repeated Underwood, "I asked for Parker to attend."

Bell didn't really understand the comment. "Presumably, you know the family?"

His question took a few seconds to register with Underwood, "Ugh? Oh yes," he said, almost to himself, "I'm a friend of the family."

"May I offer my condolences before I go up?" asked Bell.

"Yes, yes, of course," said Underwood standing aside to allow the doctor into the room.

Inside were a couple in late middle-age, sitting huddled together on a sofa, sobbing.

"Good morning, my name is James Bell. I am the doctor who…" he suddenly realised that he neither knew the name of the victim or that of her parents, "…who will be attending this morning."

The two barely looked up but the man gave a curt nod of acknowledgement.

"Please accept my heartfelt condolences," said Bell and took his leave.

As he re-entered the hallway PC Kirk was coming back down the stairs, "You can go up there now," he said, "my colleague PC Gibson will meet you up there and show you in."

Bell climbed the stairs and was actually met by Cornelius Armstrong on the landing.

"Good morning James."

"Inspector," he replied, "a nasty business. I met the young woman's distraught parents on the way up."

"Parents?" questioned the policeman. He turned around to address the uniformed officer, "Gibson, you never told me that the girl's parents were in the house. Have you spoken to them?"

"Err, not really sir, we were waiting for you to arrive. We left them downstairs with Mr. Underwood."

"Underwood? What is he doing here?"

"Err, I don't know sir, he was here when we arrived. We thought you knew."

Bell and Armstrong nodded to one another in a tacit understanding that their meeting was over and they were now to go about their respective, difficult tasks.

Doctor Bell entered the bedroom of the young woman; PC Gibson followed him in.

"A Miss Ester Sanderson," said Gibson, "found this morning by her mother apparently."

Bell was struck by how immaculately attired the victim was. After a few moments he said, "I think we'll take her down, constable, if you could give me a hand."

The pathologist took the weight of the body while Tommy Gibson climbed up onto the ottoman that had been dragged into the middle of the room, and untied the ligature that had been wrapped tightly round the victim's neck. The two men then gently laid the rigid body on the bed. The dress the young woman wore had a high collar and it had been unbuttoned to ensure the ligature was tight against the neck. Bell eased the collar back to inspect the neck more closely: what was soft and elegant in life now bore dark black and red marks all around it. The rope had broken the skin in certain places causing a slight weeping of blood, while one side of the neck was more heavily marked than the other.

"When you untied the noose, constable, it had been secured on one side of the neck, is that correct?" Bell's comment was more of a statement than a question, having observed the body himself when he entered the room.

"That's right, doctor," confirmed Tommy Gibson.

If it wasn't obvious beforehand, the pathologist's preliminary examination confirmed that the victim had been hanging there for several hours. The more severe injuries on one side of the neck were consistent with someone forming a ligature themselves and being unable to reach round the back of their own neck to secure it in the centre of the nape.

"There is not much more I can do here, constable," said Doctor Bell at last, "perhaps you could arrange for a stretcher to have the deceased moved to the ambulance."

"Very good, sir," said the constable with a salute.

Bell meanwhile went downstairs to wait for Inspector Armstrong who appeared from the sitting room in which Bell himself had met the bereaved parents earlier.

The two men exchanged initial thoughts before they were disturbed by a commotion outside. It seems that a young woman had broken from the burgeoning crowd and was hindering Gibson, Kirk and the two hospital orderlies from loading the stretcher into the vehicle. She was clearly distressed.

"No, no!" she screamed, *"What have they done? What have they done?"*

Inspector Armstrong moved to placate the young woman, who was obviously a friend of the victim. He escorted her back inside while Doctor Bell climbed onto the ambulance with the two orderlies.

The uncomfortable journey across the city took the best part of an hour, what with the weather, the traffic and the respectful pace the driver adopted, given his sensitive cargo. Every pedestrian and passer-by stopped to observe the sad sight of the black vehicle with the red cross carrying a covered stretcher, as it slowly walked past.

After the best part of an hour, the ambulance finally pulled into the yard of the west wing of the Cumberland Infirmary which contained the City Morgue. The two orderlies gently manhandled the stretcher out of the vehicle and Doctor Bell awkwardly held the door for them as the carried Ester's body inside.

As they were doing so Bell heard the scurrying footsteps of someone hurrying along the walkway towards the entrance. Within seconds, he was amazed to see they belonged to Professor Duncan Forbes, one of the most senior surgeons at the Infirmary. Bell had never known Forbes – or any other surgeon for that matter – leave the main building to visit him in his place of work.

"Doctor Bell," said Forbes who, despite trying to retain some form of composure, was clearly flustered and out of breath after his impromptu exercise.

"Mr. Forbes, what are you doing here?"

Forbes was straining to look past Bell into the morgue, "I heard of the tragedy on London Road. I think I know the victim – or at least I know her father."

"Really? Sanderson is the name I believe."

"Yes, that's right," said Forbes, "Edward Sanderson, he is a friend of mine. I heard about his daughter and was looking out for you bringing her back. Do you have any details yet?"

"No, it's too early to tell," replied the bemused pathologist, "how did you get to know about this so quickly?"

"Oh, you know how word gets about in a small place like this," replied the surgeon cryptically. "Would you keep me informed of any developments?"

"Developments?" repeated Bell, slightly put out by the presumptuous comment, "I'll be carrying out a post mortem and reporting my findings appropriately."

The orderlies meanwhile, having removed the body from the stretcher and laid it on the porcelain autopsy table, under the supervision of Doctor Bell's assistant, Murray, were waiting to get past the two medical men and back to their ambulance.

"Yes, yes, of course, of course," blustered Forbes, standing aside to let the two men by. "I would be just interested in the matter given my friendship with the girl's father. I will leave you to your work."

With that Forbes took his leave, leaving James Bell standing there wondering what the exchange was all about.

The same thought struck Bell's assistant, "It's unusual to see one of the great and good lower themselves to visit us," said Murray who had joined the pathologist at the door.

"Yes," Bell drew out his response as he watched Professor Forbes hurry back up towards the main building.

The two men entered their place of work and closed the door behind them. The stark, functional room had a low ceiling, a stone floor and was painted throughout with a drab monotonous whitewash. Against one wall was a large porcelain sink, beside which was a tall glass fronted cabinet that contained a wide range of surgical instruments; beside the cabinet was a short bench on which stood half a dozen specimen jars. Opposite was over a dozen chambers containing various corpses, either awaiting identification or autopsy, or awaiting their removal for burial. The harsh winter had taken its toll on the poor, destitute and elderly of the city and the mortuary was virtually full to capacity. The purpose of the room was aided by its naturally cool temperature, something that Bell and Murray had become used to over the years.

The corpse of Ester Sanderson lay on the autopsy table in the middle of the room.

Bell removed his hat and coat, put on his apron and began rolling up his shirt sleeves, "We'll remove the clothing and I'll carry out an initial examination," he told his assistant, "I won't have time to complete the post mortem today but it will be good to see if there are any obvious external features."

He and Murray removed the shoes and cut through the dress and petticoats of the deceased to reveal a corset and underwear. The body was in a severe state of rigor mortis which, along with the lividity marks, confirmed Bell's initial thoughts at the house that death must have occurred around midnight.

"Make a note of that, John please," he said to his assistant.

Murray was so familiar with the pathologist's methods and routine that he already had paper and pen at the ready.

As the naked corpse lay on the slab, Bell again inspected the marks on the victim's neck in more detail, before studying the deceased's arms – there were bruises around the biceps and wrists. Taking a lens he inspected them more closely.

"Umm, this young woman has been manhandled," said Doctor Bell, almost to himself, and then turning again to his assistant, "pass me a measuring tape please John."

Murray went over to the glass fronted cabinet and retrieved a tape from the lower draw and gave it to his superior, who measured the marks on the victim's arms and then compared them to her own fingers and thumbs. It was visually obvious that the victim could not have inflicted the bruising on herself but Bell wanted to document as much detail as he could.

"There is an eighth of an inch difference in size between the marks on her arms and her own digits," – Murray dutifully noted down what the pathologist had announced – "I'm sure Inspector Armstrong will be very interested in learning that."

"Should I asked George Taylor to join us for the post mortem, sir?" asked Murray.

Bell and Murray had worked together for so long, each knew instinctively what was required and when – this was another example of one knowing what the other was thinking.

"I think we should," replied the pathologist, looking at his assistant, gravely.

George Taylor was a photographer who had his own premises on Warwick Road. Taylor not only carried out portrait work at his studio, he had an interest in capturing people going about the daily business in a natural, unrehearsed state. For this he used his Facile camera, which to all intents and purposes looked like a basic wooden box with a hole for the lens in front. He would carry it around unobtrusively under his arm, capturing images when the subjects may not even have been aware of it. He was introduced to James Bell two years earlier by a mutual acquaintance and this gave Bell the idea of having Taylor take photographs of post mortem subjects if he felt there was some suspicious circumstance; his belief was that the photographs could be associated with his report and referred to in future as possible evidence.

Bell was delighted when he discovered that Taylor's constitution was as strong as his own and that of his assistant Murray – the gory sight of some poor soul's insides in no way put the photographer off; on the contrary, Taylor was fascinated by the images and never passed up an opportunity to attend one of Bell's autopsies.

At the appointed hour, after receiving Doctor Bell's invitation three days earlier, Taylor joined Bell and Murray at the Cumberland Infirmary. In the intervening period, Bell had carried out four other examinations that did not need the assistance of the photographer; now it was the turn of Ester Sanderson, the young woman whose passing had caused so much distress and interest.

"I want you to begin with some external pictures," said the pathologist to the photographer, "not only round the neck but see these marks on the victim's arms?" He pointed to the bruising on the upper arms and around the wrist."

George Taylor looked at the horrible marks on the neck of the cadaver, "Poor thing," he mumbled. As Bell and Murray helped to lift the body onto its side, Taylor took photographs from every angle.

"They certainly look like thumb and finger marks," said the photographer after studying them through the lens.

"We agree," said Bell, "and they are not her own either."

Some of the redness had gone out of the marks on the woman's neck but Taylor knew that once developed, the photographs would show the injuries in graphic detail. Each turn and manoeuvre of the body was closely followed by flash bulb and a woof from the photographer's camera. Throughout the examination, Murray noted Bell's comments.

The three men worked for most of the morning before the final revelation prompted James Bell to announce, "I need to take my findings to Inspector Armstrong immediately."

He took his own notes – those taken at the Sandersons' home earlier in the week – and those of his assistant during the examinations at the mortuary, and placed them in a large brown envelope.

"I am going to deliver these personally to Inspector Armstrong, John." Then turning to the photographer, "I think the police will need those photographs urgently, George."

"I'll sort them out as quick as I can, doctor," said Taylor, packing up his equipment.

Doctor Bell took an omnibus into the city. Finally, there appeared to be signs of a thaw in the seemingly never-ending winter; the snow had started to soften and slush had begun to appear in the gutters, not that anyone's journey – whether by horse-drawn vehicle or by foot – became any less treacherous. It took him over half an hour to get from the infirmary to the police station on West Walls.

"Would it be possible to speak with Inspector Armstrong?" Bell enquired of Desk Sergeant Bill Townsend upon his arrival.

"Doctor Bell, isn't it, sir?" said Townsend.

"That's right, it's quite urgent that I speak with him."

"He is in a meeting with the chief constable at the moment, sir, but he shouldn't be too long."

Since speaking briefly with Doctor Bell at the home of the Sandersons earlier in the week, Cornelius Armstrong had been drawn into other matters: the burglaries that had plagued the business community throughout the city, the recent drug problems that showed no signs of decreasing, and most recently the blackmail threat made to one of the leading breweries in the area. All of this combined, had consigned the tragic events of London Road earlier in the week, to the memory banks of the inspector. That was about to change with his imminent meeting with James Bell.

Armstrong came out of Henry Baker's office not long after Bell's arrival. Before he could enter his own, Sergeant Townsend intercepted him.

"Sir, Doctor Bell's here to see you."

Cornelius looked past Townsend and saw Bell waiting in the front reception area.

"James," he called, "what brings you here? Come on through. Thank you, Bill, could you get the doctor a brew please?"

"Certainly, sir," said Townsend.

Bell followed Armstrong into his office. "I've come about the post mortem I carried out this morning on Ester Sanderson," he said, as Armstrong helped him out of his heavy coat.

"The young woman we found hanging earlier in the week?" Armstrong recalled the dreadful scene.

"Yes that's right," replied Bell, opening the envelope containing details of the case. "Death will have taken place around midnight and it was caused by strangulation as suspected, but it wasn't that which I was concerned about. She had bruising on her arms and wrists consisted with someone grabbing her tightly."

Cornelius took the pathologist's notes from him and started leafing through them as the doctor spoke. "Did you take any photographs?" he asked.

"Yes," confirmed Bell, "George Taylor is working on them as we speak. I've asked him to make them his top priority in the circumstances, because there was also something else," – Cornelius looked up from the notes as the doctor paused – "The young woman was pregnant."

NINE

Five days had passed between Cornelius Armstrong and James Bell discussing the death of Ester Sanderson, first at the home of the deceased and now at the station following her post mortem. As far as Armstrong was concerned, the time in between had been taken up with other matters.

After his clandestine meeting with Reuben Hanks, the detective had briefly returned to the station to inform Sergeant Townsend that he was visiting the house on Robert Street where Hanks believed there may be some activity regarding the handling of drugs.

"Will you need some assistance, sir?" asked the desk sergeant, "I can locate a couple of the lads and have them meet you down there."

"No, that won't be necessary Bill," replied Armstrong, "I think I'll just go and keep an eye out, to see if there is anything untoward going on. We'll take it from there after that."

"Very good, sir."

Cornelius made the relatively short walk – less than half a mile – to the area of the city known as Wapping, another working class area with rows and rows of terraced houses and tenements, interspersed with the odd shop and pub. Half way down James Street was a public bathing facility and a Turkish Bath – something that Cornelius enjoyed occasionally by way of relaxing – and not far away on Currock Street was Iredale's Brewery, the biggest employer in the area and the subject of the apparent blackmail attempt.

First things first, thought Cornelius as he walked down James Street towards the junction at the bottom end. As he rounded the corner onto Robert Street, he jumped back behind the wall as he saw someone he thought he recognised on the other side of the street. The man was carrying a large canvass sack slung over his shoulder and was walking with some purpose until he reached number seven. Rapping on the door, it quickly opened and he entered swiftly without any pleasantries with the person who opened it – someone Armstrong couldn't see from the angle of his vantage point.

The policeman stood for a while deciding on the best course of action. It niggled him that he recognised the man but couldn't place him; he was in no doubt that it was in his professional capacity that he had encountered him but exactly when and in what context?

Cornelius always believed that one way of associating such villains with any misdemeanours was the first think of local pubs: gambling, brawling, hawking would usually take place in or around some tavern or other. He then thought of the *Goliah*, a particularly rough establishment, only a few yards around the corner from where he was standing.

That's it! The cockfight of a year or two back! We ended up arresting a load of them but I'm sure he was the organiser. But what was his name again?

As Cornelius was recalling the encounter, the door of number seven opened again and the man came out without the sack. Instead of approaching the house, Armstrong decided to follow the courier to see what he got up to. Keeping out of sight and at a discreet distance, he watched the man as he walked through Wapping, into Shaddongate and then into Caldewgate, where Armstrong's investigations had begun earlier that morning when he met with Reuben Hanks.

Paddy's Market was starting to wind down after another morning's busy trade, despite the inclement weather. There were still dozens of people and plenty of livestock on Bridge Street however, and Cornelius was therefore keen never to let his quarry get more than thirty yards or so in front of him.

As Armstrong passed a wooden pen full of pigs, the farmer responsible for them started to load them onto his cart. The pigs squealed raucously, causing a flock of chickens in a neighbouring pen to jump and flap with excitement – a commotion attracted the attention of everyone in the close proximity. The man up ahead also turned around in the crowd to see what the commotion was. Armstrong saw him turn and feared that he would be seen, but a combination of the instant realisation on everyone's part that the disturbance was nothing more than a group of animals being herded around against their will, and the policeman quickly turning his head away to feign interest in an adjacent stall, caused the incident to pass quickly and enabled the man to walk on unhindered. It also allowed the detective to resume his pursuit, unsuspected.

He followed the man around the back of Blue Lugs pub and down the streets he knew so well, until he saw him reach a tenement in a tiny court at the bottom of Byron Street. He watched him climb the steps and go inside. Looking at the door from a distance he racked his brain for a name before deciding to head back to the station.

"Any luck, sir?" asked Sergeant Townsend as the inspector walked in.

"I'm not sure, Bill," replied Cornelius who had wrestled with the identity of the man with the sack all the way back from Caldewgate. "I saw someone I know is up to no good but I can't put a name on him. Can you remember that carry on a year or two back when there was the cockfight at the *Goliah*?"

"Vaguely," replied Townsend.

"It descended into a nasty brawl – quite a few people got injured and we rounded up two or three of the wastrels that organised it."

"Oh, yes sir, now you mention it I think I do."

"Can you remember who they were?"

Townsend thought for a while, "Not off the top of my head, sir, but I can have a look through the records and find out."

"If you would, Bill, that would be really useful, thank you."

Armstrong had barely been in his office ten minutes when Townsend knocked and entered.

"Here you go sir; it was eighteen months ago. There were actually four of them that we pulled in," he handed the file to the inspector who looked at the names on the charge sheet.

"Kyle, Jenkins, Jones and Grant – Grant, that's him! Freddie Grant," he looked up from the file. "What was he up to I wonder?"

"Sir?"

Armstrong appraised Townsend of the morning's events, "I want someone to watch that house on Robert Street, Bill. I would like to know the comings and goings over the next couple of days."

"I'll get two or three of the lads to do a turn each," said the sergeant, "do you want anything done about Grant, sir?"

"No, I think we'll leave him for the moment," replied Armstrong thoughtfully, "let's see what our observations of the house bring first."

After putting plans in place to monitor one suspicious character, Armstrong turned his attention back to another. He paid a second visit to William Whitlock in light of the information gleaned from victims of the previous burglaries. At the end of his previous visit he told Whitlock that he would return at a convenient time; what he failed to establish was who it would be convenient for. His arrival at the solicitor's offices on Fisher Street was therefore greeted with indifference at best.

"I could have done with a little notice," snapped Whitlock as his clerk showed the inspector into his office.

"Good afternoon Mr. Whitlock," replied Armstrong, as if to emphasise Whitlock's curtness, "I'm afraid I can't regulate how and when evidence comes to my attention. It is important I follow information up as and when it comes in."

"Evidence?" asked the solicitor, "what evidence? I thought you were returning with the necessary paperwork."

"Ah yes, the necessary paperwork," repeated the policeman, being deliberately obtuse, "that would be the police report that would allow you to progress with your insurance claim. No, I'm afraid that is not quite ready yet, but it is on a similar theme that I want to ask you few questions.

"I visited other premises that were burgled over the past few months," – Armstrong took out his notebook and flipped it open – "you told me when we spoke last that you didn't know much about the other thefts. Yet it came to my attention that you acted as a broker for all of the victims as far as their insurance was concerned. I believe they were insured with Lloyds of London?"

Whitlock paused momentarily, taken aback by Armstrong's knowledge, "I didn't..." he stammered, "...I obviously didn't make myself clear when we met, inspector. I was in quite a state of shock as I'm sure you could imagine."

"Of course," accepted Armstrong noting that Whitlock's superior air had abated somewhat. "Can I ask who the insurance companies were?"

"Ugh, what?" – Whitlock suddenly seemed miles away – "oh yes, I'll have my clerk…" He rang a bell that sat on his desk and the clerk who showed Cornelius in reappeared. The solicitor scribbled down the list of clients and handed it to him, "Bring the list of Lloyd's syndicates for those clients, will you?" he said, handing the clerk the note.

"Very good, sir."

Whitlock then again turned to Armstrong as his clerk left, "Lloyd's do not operate as an insurance company, or even a group of companies," he explained, "instead groups of financiers join together in syndicates to share the risk."

"I see," said the inspector, "so how do you know who to pay the insurance premiums to?"

"There would be a lead broker locally who would administer the transaction."

"Sounds quite complicated," observed Cornelius.

"It's like everything else inspector," replied the solicitor, "easy when you know how."

Just then the clerk returned with the list requested by his employer. Whitlock read out the list, "Cuthbert Wilson, Winston Roby, Edinburgh Mutual, Yorkshire Mutual, Gilbert Brown, Thomas Webster, Bath Affiliates."

"And which syndicate are you yourselves insured with?" asked the policeman.

"We are with a syndicate called the Waterloo Veterans."

"Do you have any details of how I can contact these syndicates?"

"Why would you want to do that," asked Whitlock, back to his haughty self.

"Oh, just to learn a little more about how it all works," said Armstrong vaguely, "it might help starting at the wrong end of the investigation and working backwards, you never know."

Without necessarily understanding the comment – something Armstrong intended – Whitlock shrugged and again, called back his clerk.

"Can you check the ledger and see who our contact is for each of these syndicates?"

"Certainly sir," said the man, seemingly oblivious to his employer's rudeness.

Armstrong interjected, "I think once I have those details Mr. Whitlock, I will have no further need to trouble you this afternoon. Could I suggest I accompany…?"

"Baines, sir," said the clerk.

"…Mr. Baines, and then I can leave you to your work?"

Whitlock's whiskers bristled as he pursed his lips – it was clear he was not used to others making suggestions and setting parameters.

"Very well," he mumbled with a dismissive wave, "and I expect the appropriate paperwork the next time you visit."

"Very good, sir, thank you again for your time," said Armstrong.

The policeman accompanied the clerk to an office down the corridor adjacent to the strong room. He had the relevant papers laid out on his desk, having copied down the names of the syndicates a few minutes earlier.

"We have names and addresses of each financial body involved in the syndicate, sir," explained Baines, "most of them…" – he leafed through the pile of documents – "…do seem to have individual names attached to them."

"Good," said Cornelius, "I know it's a lot of work Mr. Baines, but could I ask you to copy out those details for me?"

"That is not a problem sir, in fact our Will Writer had already made copies in case we need duplicates."

Like every other room and office Armstrong had seen, this one had floor-to-ceiling shelves containing books and files. Despite the overwhelming amount of information, the policeman was left with the impression that Baines knew what everything was, and where it was. He asked Cornelius to step to one side as he wheeled a set of steps along to a specific spot; climbing the steps to the top shelf he returned with copies of the files that were laid out on his desk.

"You can take these, sir," he said, "if you promise to return them."

"That's excellent, Mr. Baines, thank you," said the detective, "I'll have them back with you within the next few days. One more thing," he added. "Who would make contact with these syndicates and lodge a claim – would it be yourself?"

"Oh no, sir," replied Baines, "that would always be one of the partners."

"Thank you again, Mr. Baines, you've been most helpful."

Inspector Armstrong spent most of the following twenty-four hours contacting various men who were involved in the different syndicates. The police station was one of the first buildings in the city to have a telephone installed three years earlier and – as uncomfortable as it was, situated behind the front desk in full view of anyone who entered the station – Cornelius virtually monopolised its use as he continually harried the operator to connect him with the various financiers at Lloyd's. To those he failed to speak with personally, he sent off telegrams, asking for an immediate return.

By the following day, the hitherto vague picture regarding the spate of burglaries was slowly developing a clearer image. The recollection from each of the syndicates' representatives were almost identical: they had received a relatively small insurance claim from Morley, Freeman and Whitlock in Carlisle, Cumberland, with regards to a burglary that the police had attended. In each case, as the claim was for such a moderately small amount by Lloyd's standards – in one case it was actually less than one thousand pounds – the claim was settled without cause for further investigation. In each case, the syndicates concerned had dealt with a Mr. Gerald Whitlock.

The detective sat in his office studying the information and twisting the horns of his moustache. As he did so, three constables – Jimmy Hall, Bobby Green and Sam Watts – appeared in his doorway. PC Hall knocked on the door frame; Armstrong looked up at the men, all of whom were out of uniform.

"We've got some information about that house on Robert Street, sir," said Hall.

It took Cornelius a moment to register the information, "Ah yes, were you the lads Sergeant Townsend sent down there on my behalf?"

"Yes sir," replied Hall, "we've been watching it over the last twenty-four hours."

"Have you just come back?"

"Yes we've been doing an hour or two about," said Bobby Green.

"You must be freezing!" said the superior officer, "Get yourselves a brew and I'll see you in the meeting room in five minutes."

The room between Armstrong's office and that of Godfrey Parker's was used by anyone as a meeting or interview room. As his men got some refreshment, he tidied up the papers on his desk and went next door to stoke up the stove that stood in the corner of the room. The constables joined the inspector a few minutes later.

"I brought you one in, sir," said PC Watts, handing Armstrong a mug.

"Thank you, Sam. Now sit yourselves down and tell me what you saw."

The men proceeded to tell the inspector of the numerous comings and goings that had occurred at all hours during their observations. Half a dozen young boys arriving empty handed and departing the house a few minutes later with small packages. The same boys would then turn up again sometime later and the process would be repeated. On two occasions, different blokes arrived at, and entered the house.

"Did you recognise either of them?" asked Armstrong.

"Yes, I recognised one," replied Bobby Green, "it was a bloke from Caldewgate who's a bit of a scallywag."

"Freddie Grant," stated Armstrong.

"That's right, sir," said Green, "How'd you know that?"

"Because I saw him myself yesterday. What about the other bloke?"

Green looked at PC Watts, "It was Sam who clocked him, sir."

"Yes, that's right," said Watts, "it was around ten o'clock last night when the bloke arrived. He went in and never came out again. A real rough looking character he was, not one of our regulars that's for sure."

Armstrong considered the information before bringing the meeting to close, "Thanks very much lads, that's some really good work. I'm due to brief the chief constable tomorrow and I'll make sure he hears about it. You stay in here and get yourselves warmed up and I'll go back next door."

"Thank you, sir," the men said as one.

The following morning Cornelius was sitting in *his* superior's office updating Henry Baker on the developments in each case.

"I think this house on Robert Street is being used as some sort of hub, sir," Armstrong told Baker. "Green, Hall and Watts had done some sterling work over the past couple of days. We've witnessed bags and packages being taken in and out; I have a feeling that this is where the opium is being handled and then distributed around the city."

"What do you propose to do about it," asked the chief constable.

"Well, if I'm right, that's just one end of the operation. We don't yet know where the drugs are coming from and who is bringing them in. There is one interesting local character who I've got my eye on. With your permission, I would like to keep tabs on him and see if he leads us elsewhere. I don't think he's got the brains or the means to run such an operation on his own, I'd like to know who he is working for."

"Very well, Cornelius," said Baker, "but make sure you keep a tight tether on him, I don't want us to let go too much, especially if we suspect children are involved."

"I agree, sir. At the first hint of any problems we'll move in. I'll brief the men to that effect."

"Good," said Baker, suitably reassured. "Now, what about the other matters?"

"The spate of burglaries is another interesting one, sir," said the inspector, "each of the victims has Morley, Freeman and Whitlock as their solicitors-"

"Weren't they burgled themselves?" interrupted Baker.

"That's right, only this week. They arrange the insurance cover for their clients and therefore organised for them to be compensated through the various claims."

"Coincidence?" questioned the senior officer.

"I'm not sure at this stage, sir," said Cornelius, "I'm not a great believer in coincidences."

Henry Baker smiled, "That's why I consider you my best man, Cornelius."

"When I contacted the insurance people, I found out that each claim was quite small and it was lodged with different companies, or syndicates as they are called."

"Why do you think that is significant?"

"Well, if there were several claims made against the same company, that might arouse suspicion. There is also something about this chap Whitlock that I'm not sure of; he doesn't seem very helpful if I'm honest."

"What about the other partners?"

"Morley and Freeman are no longer in the business, it's just Whitlock and his son who I haven't met as yet. It was the son who dealt with all of the claims apparently."

"That *is* interesting, Cornelius," said Baker, "keep me updated and thank the men for me.

"Thank you, sir."

Cornelius left Henry Baker's office satisfied that he was making good progress and pleased that he had the endorsement of his superior. His good mood was to be short lived however when, minutes later, he found himself sitting in his office talking to Doctor James Bell who was informing him that Ester Sanderson had signs of bruising and was pregnant.

TEN

Within half an hour of him leaving Henry Baker's office, Inspector Armstrong was knocking on the chief constable's door once more.

"Sir, there's something else."

"Already?" said Baker.

"No, it's regarding another matter. The young woman who was found hanged earlier this week. I've just had Doctor Bell in my office and he's told me that there were marks on her arms and her wrists. She was also pregnant."

"Unmarried?" asked the senior officer.

"Yes, sir, she lived at home with her parents – only child. From what I could gather the other day it seems as though she led quite a cosseted lifestyle."

The two men paused, not wanting to ask the inevitable question. Finally, Baker broke the silence.

"Is it likely that the poor girl was attacked and molested? That could be why she took her own life."

"We would certainly have to consider that as a possibility. Although recent bruising would not necessarily be consistent with a possible attack that occurred some weeks ago. In light of this information I will need to do some further investigation, perhaps first by re-visiting the parents."

"Add it to the list, Cornelius," said Henry Baker with a sigh, "and let me know how you get on."

Armstrong returned to his office as he had done less than half an hour earlier in a far less contented mood. Not only had his workload increased considerably, the thought of having to visit the bereaved parents again filled him with dread – it was always the worst task he had to undertake.

After recreating the journey he had taken some days earlier, a woman Armstrong did not recognise answered the door to the

Sandersons' home. Wearing a long black dress, she was early middle-age and demonstrated an air that suggested she belonged in the house.

"Good morning," said the detective touching the brim of his hat, "my name is Cornelius Armstrong, I'm a policeman. May I ask if Mr. and Mrs. Sanderson are at home?"

"Yes, sir," said the woman, "please come in. My name is Mary Ann Carver, I am Mrs. Sanderson's maid."

Cornelius entered the hall familiar to him from his previous visit; he recalled the same silence that was disturbed only by the ticking grandfather clock that graced the elegant entrance.

"I'm sorry Miss Carver," said Armstrong, "but I didn't know Mrs. Sanderson had a maid. I didn't see you here the other day."

"No sir," said Mary Ann, "when Mrs. Sanderson discovered poor Miss Ester, Mr. Sanderson sent me home. We were all shocked by what happened and I was particularly worried about Mrs. Sanderson, but when Mr. Sanderson's friend turned up shortly after, Mr. Sanderson asked me to leave for the day."

"His friend?" questioned Cornelius and then remembered, "ah, that would be Mr. Underwood."

"Yes, I think that was his name, sir. Mr. Sanderson did refer to him as Herbert."

"Hmm," Armstrong thought for a moment, "and how are Ester's parents?" he knew it was a stupid question but he needed to prepare for what was to be an impossibly difficult meeting.

"Mrs. Sanderson is terrible sir, as you might imagine. She and Miss Ester were very close..." the lump in Mary Ann's throat caught, causing her to pull a handkerchief from her sleeve and bury her face into it.

"I'm sorry," said the inspector, helping the maid into one of the Queen Ann chairs that sat either side of the grandfather clock, "I know my questioning must be upsetting, but I'm afraid it is unavoidable."

Mary Ann took a moment to compose herself, "I understand, sir."

"I'm afraid I need to speak with Ester's parents again," said Armstrong.

89

The maid looked up at the policeman in desperation. She got up from her seat, "I had better announce you, sir," she said.

"I think it would be useful if you could stay close by," said Cornelius, "I'm concerned as to how Mrs. Sanderson especially, might react."

Mary Ann knocked and entered the sitting room in which Armstrong had met Edward and Edith Sanderson a few days earlier; she closed the door behind her. Moments later she opened the door and invited Cornelius to enter.

"Hello Mr. Sanderson, Mrs. Sanderson, I've come to speak with you following Ester's post mortem."

The policeman sat down and fiddled with the brim of his hat nervously. Edward and Edith Sanderson sat opposite him perched, as they had been, on the same sofa when he had met them on the previous occasion. It was as though they had sat there, frozen in time, since their unimaginable loss. Neither made eye contact with the policeman until he announced.

"I can't imagine the pain you are going through at the moment but I'm afraid I have some more disturbing news, I felt it only right you were the first to hear about it."

The two looked up to face the inspector for the first time. Mrs. Sanderson in particular looked dreadful: she had the pallor of a ghost, while her eyes looked painful; crying and sleep deprivation gave the impression that they were sinking back into her face.

Armstrong knew there was no other way, "I'm afraid there was bruising on Ester's arms suggesting that she had been manhandled recently" – the Sandersons looked at Armstrong blankly, seemingly unable to comprehend what he was saying – "and there was another thing…Ester was pregnant."

A guttural noise came from Edward Sanderson. After a few seconds, his wife collapsed unconscious. Sanderson stared straight ahead, oblivious to Edith falling beside him.

Cornelius sprang from his seat, "Mary Ann!" he called.

The maid rushed in after hearing the call and the two helped Mrs. Sanderson back onto the sofa.

"I think she has just fainted," said Mary Ann, "but we need to get her up to her room."

"Yes," agreed Sanderson, snapping out of his stupor, "you help her up there and I will fetch for the doctor."

"Perhaps I could lift her," suggested Armstrong; following the silent consent from the maid and the husband, he picked her up in his arms and followed Mary Ann upstairs where he lay Mrs. Sanderson gently on her bed. "Is there anything else I can do?" he asked.

"I don't think so, sir," replied Mary Ann, "I just hope the doctor is gentle with her."

Cornelius thought this was an unusual comment but knew it was neither the time nor the place to pose further questions. He took his leave of the maid and went back down to speak with Edward Sanderson.

"I need to speak with you further, sir," said the policeman, "but I appreciate this is not the best time. Perhaps I could call again tomorrow?"

Sanderson's mind was obviously racing as he barely heard what Armstrong was saying, "Ugh?... What?... Oh yes that will be fine," he said at last.

"Could I be of any more assistance?" asked Cornelius, "perhaps I could wait with you until the doctor arrives?"

"No, that won't be necessary," said Sanderson, still looking at the floor, trying to come to terms with what was happening.

Armstrong left, feeling desperately sorry for the couple and the unavoidable part he had played in this latest development.

*

When he returned the following morning, Cornelius was surprised to see Edward Sanderson himself answering the door.

"Good morning, Mr. Sanderson, may I come in?"

Sanderson answered with a nod and stood aside, "You know the way to the sitting room," he said pointing.

91

"How is Mrs. Sanderson this morning," asked the policeman as his host closed the door behind him.

"The doctor came and suggested it was best to arrange for some convalescence to try and deal with the shock."

Armstrong was surprised at such radical action, "I hope it was nothing more than a fainting fit?" he asked.

"Edith has been suffering a lot lately with her nerves," mumbled Sanderson, "what has happened now has brought the whole thing to a head."

"I understand," said the policeman, uncomfortably. After a brief pause, he added "I know it must be desperately painful for you Mr. Sanderson but I need to ask you some questions about Ester."

Sanderson gave the same silent nod he had offered at the front door.

"Did Ester often go out on her own?"

"No," replied her father, "I did not allow it. I mean I sought to discourage it, the streets are not a good place for a young woman."

"Did she have a lot of friends?"

"Not that I'm aware of. There was a young girl who lives not far from here – they were close having grown up together. Apart from that, I'm not sure. She was closer to her mother who would probably know more."

"And I believe she was courting a young gentleman?"

Sanderson paused, as if trying to formulate an answer. "Yes," he said at last, "the son of a colleague of mine."

"A colleague – may I ask what you do Mr. Sanderson?"

"I'm retired, when I say a colleague, I mean he and I are members of the same club."

"What is the young man's name?"

"Whitlock, Gerald Whitlock."

"Whitlock?" exclaimed Armstrong, "as in the solicitors Whitlock?"

"Yes, that's right," said Sanderson, "his father has an office on Fisher Street. Do you know him?" Sanderson's tone changed somewhat to one of curiosity.

"I have had some dealings with Mr. Whitlock senior over the recently."

"What sort of dealings?" asked Sanderson.

"He had cause to call the police over something," said Armstrong being deliberately vague."

"I see," said Sanderson.

Armstrong was surprised at Sanderson's interest in the matter, especially considering his own loss.

"It is a difficult question to ask Mr. Sanderson, but I must ask if you believe Gerald Whitlock would be capable of…forcing himself on Ester."

"I don't know," said Sanderson, "the thought is monstrous."

"Did he ever visit Ester here?"

"No, they were always chaperoned in public, although he did visit here earlier this week to express his condolences."

"I will be very interested in speaking with Mr. Whitlock," said Armstrong, believing Sanderson could tell him no more at this stage. "Could I ask to see Ester's room again while I'm here?"

"Yes, I suppose so," said Sanderson, sounding like a broken man, "help yourself," he added gesturing towards the door.

"Thank you."

The detective found Ester's room virtually as it had been left following the discovery of her body. Even the heavy silken rope that was used to fashion a makeshift noose still lay on the bed where his police constable would have left it after taking her down. As uncomfortable as he felt in inspecting the bedroom, especially with Ester's father in the house, he was interested in the journal Matilda Chambers told him about – Ester's 'companion'. If he had access to it, and with it, access to her inner most thoughts, it would reveal what only she knew, and would help in giving him direction in his enquiries.

Cornelius looked through the drawers in the dressing table; he then checked the two large drawers at the bottom of each wardrobe; he checked any pockets in the clothes that hung in the wardrobes themselves; he opened the lid of the large ottoman that had been used as a makeshift scaffold. There was no sign of what he was looking for.

He re-joined Sanderson, who had remained sitting staring blankly at the wall; Armstrong had the impression he had been like this since his daughter had been discovered. It must have been worse still for Mrs. Sanderson who actually discovered the body.

"Thank you, Mr. Sanderson," said Cornelius as he entered the sitting room, "could I ask if you are aware of a journal Ester apparently kept?"

The man looked up from his stupor: his face was ashen and his eyes blank; it was as though he neither recognised Armstrong nor comprehended what was being said.

"Journal?" he repeated at last, "no, I don't know anything anymore."

The inspector thought this was a strange comment but just then he heard the front door open, followed quickly by the door leading from the vestibule into the hall. Standing near the doorway of the sitting room, he leaned out into the hallway to see Mrs. Sanderson's maid enter.

"Mary Ann, I didn't think you would be here this morning."

"Oh, good morning Mr. Armstrong," said the maid, surprised but seemingly pleased to see the policeman, "I've just come for some of Mrs. Sanderson's things. I was going to take them up to the hospital." She then lowered her tone to a whisper and pointed towards the sitting room, "Is Mr. Sanderson in there?"

Armstrong nodded and the maid entered.

"Morning Mr. Sanderson, I've just come to collect some of your wife's things to take them to the hospital."

Sanderson looked up and offered Mary Ann the same expression as Cornelius had received minutes earlier. As she re-entered the hallway, she said, "Could I have a word, sir before you leave?"

"Certainly," said Armstrong, "there was actually something I wanted to ask you too. I will wait outside."

As the maid went upstairs, Armstrong went into the sitting room, "I will leave now sir, although I may have to re-visit." Much to his discomfort there was no response; he let himself out and waited on the path.

A few minutes later Mary Ann appeared carrying a small bag.

"I wanted to fetch some of Mrs. Sanderson's own night clothes and personal things," she explained, "they've taken her up to the Garlands. Didn't even let her take anything with her."

"Who are 'they'?" asked Cornelius.

"That doctor friend of Mr. Sanderson's."

That meant nothing to Armstrong, "When was this?" he asked instead.

"Just yesterday. The doctor came down from the infirmary and within an hour, the poor woman was being taken away like a lunatic. Not right if you ask me."

"Will she be in any fit state to answer some questions?" asked Cornelius and, without waiting for an answer, "Can I come with you to see her?"

"Yes, certainly," replied Mary Ann, "but I don't know what we'll get out of her. I went up there last night and she was just dozing in the chair."

The two walked down the front path. Outside was a man sitting patiently at the reins of a horse-drawn cart.

"This is my husband, Geoffrey," said Mary Ann, "he's a carter, so he comes in useful at times."

"Pleased to meet you Geoffrey," said the detective offering a hand, "I'm Cornelius Armstrong, I'm a policeman. Do you mind if I tag along up to the Garlands?"

"Not at all, sir," said Geoffrey, rolling his eyes at his wife's putdown, "climb aboard."

"I'm impressed by your stoicism, Geoffrey, sitting out here in the cold," said Cornelius, first allowing Mary Ann to take the seat beside her husband and then climbing up alongside her.

"He's all right," said Mary Ann before he could respond.

"I'm all right," repeated Geoffrey flashing Cornelius a sly glance.

The Garlands Hospital was an isolated building in parkland, five miles south of the city. Its long driveway led to the dark-brick building whose front doors appeared tiny from afar, due to them being set back behind eight imposing columns. It was a facility for anyone out of the ordinary, from those poor unfortunates categorised as being insane to someone suffering from epilepsy. It was also known to accommodate a disproportionate number of women, from those of a certain standing suffering from exhaustion to younger women allegedly suffering from depression following the birth of an illegitimate child.

As the cart drew up, Mary Ann gave her husband a kiss and said, "You go back, luv, I don't know how long I'll be."

"What about you, sir?" he asked Cornelius.

"Likewise, Geoffrey, I'll find my own way back. Thank you for the lift."

With a slap of the left rein, Geoffrey turned the cart round and set it back within the tramlines he had made in the snow on his way up to the building.

Cornelius and Mary Ann meanwhile entered the building – the temperature inside the cavernous hallway was almost as cold as it was outside. The two stood for some minutes before a member of staff just happened by.

"Excuse me," said Mary Ann, "we are here to visit someone."

The man looked at the two blankly, "Do you know where they are?" he asked.

"I did visit last night, she was in a ward at the bottom of that corridor," Mary Ann pointed down one of the long wide corridors that led from the entrance hall.

"Oh, well she wouldn't have been moved," said the man, "just sign in the book and help yourselves." He pointed to a book that was perched on a lectern against one wall and carried on his way.

Cornelius had the impression that the whole of the hospital was the same: large, white, cold and hollow. Noises from patients – groans, shouts and screams – echoing through the corridors appeared to be the normal sound of everyday life.

96

He followed Mary Ann until they came to a series of wards.

"It was one of these, I'm sure," said Mary Ann, looking through the doorway of the first two.

Not only were there no actual doors to separate the wards from the corridors but the door frames were lined with cork and India-rubber; the walls of the third ward they came to was lined from floor to ceiling in the same materials.

"Ah, here we are," said Mary Ann looking into the next ward.

Sitting in a chair beside a bed was Edith Sanderson. Cornelius barely recognised her from their uncomfortable encounter the previous day. She was in a room with six other women, all differing in ages and all in various states of drowsiness; some were completely unconscious in bed, others like Mrs. Sanderson sat nodding in the chair.

Above each patient was a small blackboard with details of their names, condition, the doctor responsible and their medication. Various conditions included, *palsy, convulsive fits, lately with child.* What Cornelius noticed was that all of their medication was same: they were all administered paraldehyde.

Edith Sanderson's board also stated that she was suffering from *nervous exhaustion* and that she had been admitted by Professor Duncan Forbes. The policeman jotted a few notes down, as Mary Ann roused Mrs. Sanderson.

"Hello Edith," she said, placing her hand on her arm.

Cornelius could see the concern shown by Mary Ann and it was clear to him that the two were as much friends as employer and employee. It reminded him of his own relationship with that of his superior Henry Baker.

Edith looked up and attempted to smile through her drowsiness, "Hello, Mary Ann, have you come to see me, have you?"

"Yes, I brought some of your things from home," replied the maid, indicating towards the bag. She was disgusted that Edith was wearing the same clothes as she wore when she was admitted yesterday and when she went to visit her last night. "I've also brought someone else to see you," she added, standing aside to reveal Armstrong.

97

"Hello, Mrs. Sanderson," he said, "I'm the policeman who came to see you yesterday.

"Oh yes," said Edith without elaborating.

The inspector felt uncomfortable questioning the woman in this state but he had made the journey and knew he had to find out as much as he could, regardless of circumstance.

"Mrs. Sanderson, I need to ask you about Ester."

"Ah, my darling Ester," said Edith, her gaze wandering off into the middle distance.

"Did she confide in you at any point about problems she was having?"

Edith Sanderson didn't answer but continued to look at nothing in particular with a half-smile on her face.

"In particular," continued Armstrong, "I believe she filled in a journal – would you know anything about that?"

Again nothing. Mary Ann was unpacking Edith's bag, laying out clean nightwear and washing materials on the bed. Armstrong felt he was both wasting his own time and intruding on the women's privacy.

"I should leave Mary Ann; this is not good."

"Very well, sir," she agreed with a nod, "if she says anything, I will let you know."

"Thank you, and I'll make some enquiries as to how we can get her back home. This is not doing her any good."

"If you could do anything, sir we would be most grateful."

Armstrong left and was halfway down the corridor when he heard his name being shouted above the noise of the cries that permeated. He turned to see Mary Ann running after him.

"Mr. Armstrong! Mr. Armstrong!" as she got closer, he saw she was carrying a book, "I found this in the bottom of Edith's bag, I think it must be Ester's journal."

Cornelius took it from her and glanced through it, struggling to suppress his satisfaction at the find, "Yes, I think you are right Mary Ann. Where did you get Mrs. Sanderson's bag from?"

"It was in the bottom of her wardrobe in her room. I didn't look in it, I just filled it with items that I thought she would need."

"Ester must have put it there before..." he stopped himself from stating the obvious. "I need to take this away Mary Ann; it could prove very useful."

"Yes, take it," said the maid, "I'll tell Mrs. Sanderson – she won't miss it."

ELEVEN

Cornelius dared not start reading Ester's journal immediately for fear of getting too engrossed; he wouldn't get anything else done as a result. He decided that that would be his night-time reading in the confines of his own rooms. Instead, his first call was to be back at the station to pick up the police report he had promised William Whitlock before visiting the offices of Morley, Freeman and Whitlock once again. This time however, he was not necessarily interested in speaking with Whitlock senior, but with his son, the mysterious Gerald who was becoming a more interesting character as the days went on.

Armstrong's walk from the hospital to the terminus was long and the tram ride back into town was even longer. He was cold and hungry by the time the tram pulled up at the top of Botchergate. He bought a sandwich at Doyle's on the corner of the Crescent and arrived back at the station shortly after one o'clock. Doctor James Bell had arrived just a few minutes before him.

"Inspector," he said as Cornelius entered, "I have the photographs I promised from the post mortem."

"That's good, Doctor, thank you for bringing them down. Come through and we can go through them, if you don't mind me eating my sandwich that is."

"Not at all. I assume, like me you have a strong stomach – some of the images don't necessarily go hand in hand with mealtime viewing."

"I'm sure it will be fine," said Armstrong, and then turning to Sergeant Townsend, "Bill, can you get us both a cup of tea please."

"Will do, sir," replied the desk sergeant with a nod.

Cornelius levered himself out of his coat, went over to the little stove in the corner of his office and opened the iron door with some tongs. Lobbing a couple of small logs into the chamber; he closed the door, opened the vents of the stove and gave a contented rub of his hands as it roared into life.

100

"Now then James," he said unwrapping his sandwich, "what do you have?"

Before the pathologist could answer, Sergeant Townsend knocked and entered with two mugs.

"Thank you, Bill," said Armstrong.

The door closed and Townsend left them to it.

"As I was saying yesterday," said the doctor, taking the photographs out of a large brown envelope, "I believe the marks on the girl's arms are the most significant aspect." He laid the images on the inspector's desk, "Some of the internal pictures are a bit grainy; the lighting and conditions in the morgue are not the best, even for the professional photographer. But you see here," he pointed to the bruising on the upper arms and the wrists.

Armstrong studied the pictures closely while munching on his sandwich. Despite Bell's assertion that some of the internal images were a little grainy, they left nothing to the imagination. The torso had been opened up and the ribs cut and parted to reveal the young woman's glistening organs that could now clearly be seen following the pathologist and the photographer shining a light into the raw, empty cavity.

Cornelius wiped the corners of his mouth with a handkerchief and twisted the horns of his moustache. He took a gulp of tea.

"Is there any chance that bruising could have occurred after death?" he asked, "when she was being taken down from the ceiling for example."

The pathologist shook his head, "No, the body wouldn't bruise after death. Bruising, bleeding, tearing – they are all caused by the blood being pumped around the body; once the heart has stopped beating, it stops pumping blood. It's difficult to be accurate but I would suggest these injuries would have been sustained a day or two before she died."

The inspector didn't want to broach the most difficult of subjects but he knew he had to. "Given that she was pregnant – other than these marks on the upper body – were there any signs on the lower half of the body that would indicate molestation."

"There weren't actually," – there was surprise in Bell's voice – "I must confess, I half expected as much but no. I must say however that this is not necessarily an indicator that intercourse was consensual. I have heard of victims who put up no resistance whatsoever once the initial struggle is lost, for fear of an even worse outcome."

"If that were possible," said Armstrong to himself in sombre tones with a nod. "Well there's certainly plenty to think about here James, thank you for that."

"If I can be of any further assistance Cornelius, let me know."

Something suddenly occurred to the policeman, "Actually, there may be. Have you ever heard of a doctor called…" he referred to his notebook "…Duncan Forbes?"

"Yes – Professor actually – Professor Duncan Forbes. He's a surgeon at the infirmary. Why do you ask?"

"A surgeon?" repeated Cornelius. He explained, "I visited Ester's parents this morning to update them on developments and to inform them about Ester's condition at the time of her death. I found that *Professor* Forbes had committed Mrs. Sanderson to the Garlands Hospital for recuperation. It seemed a bit extreme to me so I went up to see her. She seemed drugged up and unable to comprehend what was happening."

"That is strange," agreed Bell. "Now you come to mention it, Forbes came down to see me at the morgue the day we brought the young woman in. Claimed he was a friend of the family and wanted me to keep him informed as to how things would develop."

"I wouldn't have thought it would be his job to refer anyone to the Garlands?" asked Armstrong.

"No, I wouldn't think so either," agreed Bell, "but in my experience – as in yours no doubt, Inspector – normal rules don't usually apply to some people."

"Which reminds me," said the policeman, "there is someone else I have to visit this afternoon who seems to be cut from the same cloth. Thank you again for your help with this, James. I have a feeling we haven't heard the last of it."

"No problem, Cornelius, let me know if I can do anything more."

The two shook hands and Bell left Armstrong to finish his sandwich.

The detective knew that his next meeting would be considerably less amicable. In visiting William Whitlock, and despite his efforts to solve the burglary experienced by the solicitor, he had encountered nothing but obstruction and contempt. He had no reason to believe today's meeting would be anything different, especially given that he was now aware information pertaining to Whitlock's mysterious son Gerald was being withheld from him. Whether that was deliberate or not, Armstrong was intent on finding out.

Once again, William Whitlock made no attempt to hide his displeasure when his secretary Mr. Baines announced Inspector Armstrong's arrival.

"What is it this time?" Whitlock mumbled under his whiskers.

Armstrong was waiting respectfully in the hallway for Baines to invite him in; after hearing the solicitor's comment through the open door, he decided to dispense with the feigning of any courtesy and entered.

"I have come with the police report you asked for Mr. Whitlock," he announced without any pleasantries.

"Ah, I should think so too," replied Whitlock, haughtily rising from his chair and thrusting out a hand, "that will be all Baines."

"Very good, sir" replied the secretary, a man whose stoicism Armstrong admired in the face of such rudeness.

Whitlock's arm was still outstretched and he gestured impatiently with his hand towards the file that the policeman held. Armstrong didn't flinch.

"I've actually come to give the file to your son," he said

"What?" snapped Whitlock.

"Your son, Gerald. After all, he has been dealing with the claims of the other victims' claims, hasn't he? What's more, I want to speak with him about another matter."

103

Whitlock was clearly wrongfooted by the policeman, "What other matter?" he said, finally lowering his arm believing that he was not going to be handed the file.

"Where is he?" Armstrong ignored the solicitor's question.

"He is away on business."

"Away on business?" repeated the inspector, "where? What business?"

Whitlock, clearly affronted by the policeman's tone, squared his shoulders in an effort to create a pose of superiority. "The affairs of this firm are nothing to do with you and I resent you coming in here demanding-"

Cornelius didn't wait for Whitlock to finish his protestation, "I am interested in the unusual pattern of insurance claims that your son is making with different companies on behalf of clients you represent. Furthermore, I learned only this morning that he was the fiancé of Ester Sanderson who was found hanged earlier this week. It is on those two subjects I wish to speak with your son about, Mr. Whitlock."

The solicitor's shoulders resumed their natural position, a sign that he was starting to lose control of the verbal joust. His gaze wandered from the policeman into no-man's-land.

"Where is your son, Mr. Whitlock?" asked Armstrong, lowering his tone and regaining the lawyer's attention.

"Erm, London," he replied after a pause.

"London!" repeated Armstrong, "what's he doing in London at a time like this?"

"A time like what?" blustered Whitlock.

"His premises have been burgled and his fiancée has died in suspicious circumstances. What is he doing going to London?"

One word jumped out at Whitlock, "Suspicious? How do you mean suspicious?"

Again, Armstrong ignored the enquiry, "What has he gone to London for and how long will he be?"

"Erm, I think he went to meet with the insurers about the theft."

"Did he go in person to meet them about the other thefts?"

"Erm, no I don't think so."

"You don't think so," repeated Armstrong, "so why did he particularly travel all that way, during this week of all weeks, to discuss this one theft."

The questions were coming thick and fast and Whitlock was struggling to keep up, "I'm not sure, he felt it would just be better. Besides I think he was meeting some friends as well."

This was another mistake on Whitlock's part.

"Meeting friends?" said Armstrong, "his fiancée has just been found dead and the first thing he does is go to meet some friends in London? Does that strike you as normal behaviour Mr. Whitlock?"

"Erm, no I suppose not seeing as you put it like that."

"Put it like that," repeated Armstrong who was now in total control, "tell me, how long have your son and Miss Sanderson been engaged?"

"I'm not sure, several months now, I think. I am a member of the same club as her father and it seemed a perfect match."

"And when were they due to be married?"

"I'm not sure of that either, my wife and Miss Sanderson's mother would be arranging that I expect."

"Well, they won't be arranging it anymore I'm afraid," Armstrong was now in full flow. "Why didn't you tell me where Gerald was when we met earlier in the week?"

"I think I did," said Whitlock.

"No you didn't, you said that he had been called away but you didn't say where. I then told you that I wanted to speak with him upon his return and instead he has run off to London."

"Run off?" protested Whitlock, "hardly run off."

"I disagree," said Armstrong calmly before delivering his final thrust in the exchange, "you probably don't know but Miss Sanderson was pregnant. What's more, there was some unexplained bruising on her body at the time of her death."

Whitlock's jaw dropped open and the redness that had built up in his face during the heated exchanged instantly drained away; his knees gave way and he fell backwards, fortunately landing in his chair.

"Ah, you weren't aware of that then."

Such was his state of shock following the revelation, Whitlock was now oblivious to the detective's presence, let alone able to hear what he was saying. Cornelius just looked at him: the solicitor's face was a blank mask. Unlike his feelings for Ester's parents, Armstrong had no sympathy for this man.

"You might see now why I am so keen to speak with your son," he said at last. "Anyway, I'll leave you to your contemplation," – he turned to leave and then checked himself – "oh, I nearly forgot…here is your police report."

He tossed the file on Whitlock's desk and left, informing Mr. Baines that his employer may need his assistance, on his way out.

Armstrong spent the remainder of the late afternoon in his office, reviewing the tasks he needed to do regarding the various cases he was dealing with. He finally realised he was getting tired when his insecure streak started to focus on the volume and severity of the cases, to the point where he was feeling a little overwhelmed.

"Trust yourself, Corny lad," he said to himself sitting back and closing his eyes for a moment.

He decided to call it a day, tidied his desk, gathered up the findings of Doctor Bell and put them into the brown envelope and added Ester's journal, obtained that morning by accident when he visited her mother.

Back in his own rooms, Cornelius freshened up and enjoyed his evening meal. Once Mrs. Wheeler had cleared away his dishes he took his long-stemmed cherrywood pipe and thumbed some tobacco into the bowl; pouring himself a glass of rum, he sat down in his leather-bound rocking chair beside the crackling fire and opened Ester's journal to see if the young woman could furnish him with any clues following her demise.

He was surprised that she had only started to complete it following her eighteenth birthday, a little over fifteen months earlier. In her first entry in late September 1899, she made no attempt to hide her excitement and enthusiasm as to what lay ahead:

I am here, adulthood! I wonder what awaits us all as we sit here on the eve of a new century. Whatever awaits, I will be part of it, no longer seen-and-not-heard. I can't wait to experience what lies ahead.

During her September and October entries, certain passages conveyed a similar enthusiasm. The young woman also demonstrated a mature, balanced knowledge of current affairs, particularly regarding the ongoing struggle for women's equality and her concerns about the increasing tensions in South Africa that would ultimately lead to war a few weeks later.

Cornelius was particularly struck by two entries in November 1899 that appeared to substantiate something Matilda Chambers had told him about Ester. First was an entry that contained a paragraph about an event at her father's club:

So excited! Father is taking mother and me to an event as his club. I love the term 'Ladies' Night' – it's so nineteenth century!

The following day however, she appeared to write with a sense of anti-climax:

I didn't enjoy last night at all. A room full of odious, boorish men, with their cigars and feeling of superiority. I was concerned that father was pairing me with the son of an associate of his. I took to neither him – Gerald – nor his friend.

Cornelius noticed that the word Gerald was entered with slightly darker shade of ink, as though Ester had been pressing extra hard with her pen as she wrote the name. He pictured her anger as she wrote his name for the first time. Thereafter, the entries became more and more melancholy. Throughout November and during the lead up to Christmas, she made several entries expressing her, 'concern'

107

regarding her father's intentions and her 'dislike' of his friends. This culminated in the New Year's Eve festivities. Her parents hosted a party where her father's friends and the wives attended. What should have been a once-in-a-lifetime celebration as one century transformed into another was a dreadful experience for the young woman. It appears as though Ester and Gerald Whitlock were the only single people there:

> *Is this what being an adult means? I can't remember a worse night throughout my whole childhood as that experienced last night. Father casually announced that he felt it appropriate that I should become engaged to G, much to the enthusiastic amusement of everyone present. The thought repulses me. I neither like the man nor have anything in common with him. I looked around the room at all of the women in their fine gowns, subservient to their loathsome husbands. Is this what awaits me?*

Cornelius noted that every entry following that night contemptuously referred to Gerald simply as 'G'. Throughout the remaining winter and spring months, Ester's notes sounded increasingly desperate. In January and February she was using words like 'sad' and 'disappointing'; by April and May they had been replaced with words like 'desperate' and 'angry'. In June, she confronted her father about how she was being treated:

> *Father is becoming intolerable. I have tried to speak to him about G several times but he either won't listen or is constantly at that wretched Book Club of his. I don't want this. I can't imagine living the rest of my life like my darling mother. Surely there is another way?*

A similar theme continued throughout the summer months until Cornelius came across a particularly peculiar entry in October:

Met WW today. It was the nicest thing that has happened in months.

"WW?" said Cornelius out loud. *Why would Ester Sanderson meet with William Whitlock and describe it as nice? Doesn't sound like the William Whitlock I know*, Armstrong thought to himself.

Several times in the remaining entries of 1900, Ester's abhorrence for G was clear, while her surprising affection for his father was equally demonstrated. The pages leading up to Christmas 1900 lamented the dullness of her mood and her father's refusal to buy her a pair of shoes she had seen in Gowan's Emporium.

Then intriguingly, Cornelius observed that the page for Christmas Eve had been ripped out of the journal. *What happened on Christmas Eve that caused her to do that?* Armstrong couldn't help feeling that was important but equally he knew the chances of finding the missing page were extremely remote.

The early days of the New Year provided the final entries in Ester's journal. The final cheerful notes were taken the day before and the day of Ester's shopping trip with her childhood friend Matilda Chambers. She also made no attempt to disguise her delight at buying the shoes she had coveted for so long. But any happiness the young woman felt was short-lived as her final entry – presumably written only hours before she died – read:

To my darling mother, you are the gentlest creature on this cruel earth. I cannot begin to tell you how sorry I am for what I am about to put you through. I can only hope that in time you can forgive me. I simply cannot stand this anymore. I am so dreadfully sad. The thought of a life of unhappiness is just too much for me. Please believe me when I say my actions are no reflection on the love and kindness you have always shown me throughout my short life. I hope I am going to a better place and that one day we will be together again. Although my body will be gone, please believe that my spirit and love for you will never die. Your loving yet weak and unworthy daughter, Ester.

TWELVE

Billy Grant sat in the tenement flat he shared with his brother in Caldewgate staring at the clinkers in the grate that had for some time ceased giving off any semblance of heat. He hadn't moved for days; he just sat there contemplating the situation he and his brother had gotten themselves into. The curtains were permanently drawn against the winter cold; the only sound was from the soft hiss of the gas lights. Billy didn't want to move. He suddenly tensed as he heard someone climbing the stone steps outside towards their front door.

"You still sittin' there?" said his brother as he entered, his face ruddy and chilled with the cold.

Billy relaxed in his seat.

"What's wrong with you?" asked Freddie.

"I don't know Fred, I'm just not happy with what's going on."

"Whaddya mean?"

"All this business with Roberts, it's gettin' out of hand?"

"Gettin' out of hand?" repeated Freddie, "it's too late for that Billy, lad. You can't make the money we've been making and get y'sel' high as a bird on that stuff in Whitehaven and then have no price to pay."

"He had me going collecting the rent – I didn't get it all. People can't afford what he's asking and when they don't pay, he goes and knocks seven bells out of them."

"It's not him that's putting the rent up is it?"

"No but I bet it's him that's suggesting it."

"We don't know that."

"But Freddie," Billy pleaded, "he killed a bloke! We don't even know who he was. And we were involved."

Just then, the brothers' attention was taken by the sound of footsteps on the stairs outside.

"Listen," said Freddie to his brother, "just calm down, keep your nose clean and things will be all right."

111

There was a knock at the door. Freddie opened it and the doorway was filled with the intimidating figure of Jack Roberts.

"Hello boys," said the villain as he entered without being invited.

Billy tensed at the sight of the man he had become terrified of.

"Jack, have a seat, do you want a cup of tea?" Freddie was trying to calm the situation.

"No, it's not a social call," said Roberts looking around the modest room and making no effort to disguise his contempt, "it's pay day!"

"I've got the money here Jack," said Billy taking out a box that was under the table, "I've taken my share."

"Probably smoked it away by now on that rubbish I send you to Whitehaven for eh?" said Roberts with an evil smirk.

Billy played along with a hollow laugh.

"Speaking of which," continued Roberts, "I was thinking about increasing the shipments – how do you feel about making a few more trips to the seaside?"

Billy knew he didn't have much say in the matter; what's more if it got him away from Roberts for a few extra days and earned him a bit more money, it could only be a good thing. As long as he stayed away from the *Albion,* he should be all right.

"Yes, that will be fine," he mumbled.

"I knew you would have no objections. I'll make some arrangements – every Wednesday from next week," Roberts leant into Billy's face and lowered his tone to that of a menacing threat, "straight home afterwards, mind you."

He gave that distinctive evil smirk as the terrified Billy swallowed hard. He didn't offer any verbal reply as both men knew that any future delays were highly unlikely.

"And what about you?" asked Roberts turning to Freddie, "did you take your wages out of the rent money?"

"No I haven't had mine yet," replied the elder brother.

"Here you go then." Roberts peeled off a few notes from a bundle of money he already had in his pocket. Neither brother dared ask where such an amount had come from.

"Thanks," said Freddie.

"Now," said Roberts changing the subject, "which one of you wrote that letter to the bloke in the brewery?"

"I did," said Freddie, "I put the deadline of the end of the month, just like you said."

"Right," said Roberts turning to Billy, "I want you to follow it up with another one telling him that the deadline's been extended by a couple of weeks. Just between the three of us there's been a bit of a hold up, but as far as I'm concerned, we'll still get the money out of him. Tell him it's ten thousand quid or his beer won't be fit for cleaning the floor by the middle of February."

Billy nodded.

"Right, I'm done here boys, I'm off to see that other idiot Jimmy Dunn to see how he's getting on. Keep up the good work." With that, Roberts left without further comment.

The two brothers stood in silence. Increasingly, they were surviving from day to day; all the while, they recognised that they had no influence, let alone control of whatever situations they were finding themselves in. Inwardly, Freddie felt the same way as his brother but was more prepared to put a brave face on. After a few minutes, a thought occurred to him.

"I thought you said you didn't get all the rent?"

"When did I say that?" countered Billy.

"Just before, when you were telling me that people couldn't afford to pay."

Billy's eyes dropped to the floor and he shrugged.

"Hang on a minute," said Freddie, "you went without, didn't you?" when there was no response from his brother, he continued, "you told Roberts it was all there and you had taken your share. But you didn't, did you? If you haven't collected what you should you couldn't have taken out your wages."

Again Billy didn't respond.

"Bloody hell, Billy!"

"It doesn't matter," said the younger brother, trying to ignore the humiliation he felt.

Jack Roberts left the two brothers to pay a similar visit to Jimmy Dunn at Robert Street. He had been introduced to Jimmy by Freddie Grant, not long after he arrived in Carlisle.

Freddie got to know Jimmy Dunn when they both did a bit of labouring on the railway. Like minds generally gravitate towards one another and it wasn't long before the two naturally lazy characters found the work too hard and the foreman too strict. They therefore didn't last long in their roles and both reverted to their previous vocation of ducking and diving. That was until Jimmy fell on his feet when he inherited a boarding house on Robert Street from his uncle; thereafter Freddie often wandered across to Wapping from Caldewgate to meet him for a beer in the *Goliah Inn* which was just around the corner. It was on one such night that Dunn left his pal slightly early and as Freddie was finishing his drink, he encountered Jack Roberts, who was on the lookout for recruits to help with his portfolio of villainy.

Once Freddie and his brother had been taken under Roberts's spell and the latter had proposed the opium trail should extend to Carlisle, Freddie suggested he could approach Jimmy whose premises could act as a hub for the drug to be moved around the city. Roberts liked the idea and left it to Freddie to organise. When Freddie mentioned the idea to his mate, Dunn had no hesitation, as he recognised the venture would bring in a lot of money and would involve him putting very little effort into earning it.

The final piece in the puzzle was for Jimmy to arrange distribution of the opium from his house around the city to the pubs and hawkers who he knew would be interested in the scheme. For this, he used the best possible vehicle; something – or someone – that will always be seen, ignored and never heard: children.

There was one young lad who wandered round the streets of Wapping begging and trying to sell anything he had come by the previous day. Jimmy Dunn would threaten to show him the back of his hand when he came knocking on his door, but when Freddie Grant put the idea to him about getting involved in trafficking drugs around the city, Jimmy did an about turn and took the young lad in, putting his own proposal to him.

Like his many contemporaries, the boy endured a hard life: when he wasn't sleeping rough, the best he could hope for was a bed at the workhouse. Jimmy put it to the lad that he could round up half a dozen other boys from the workhouse and bring them to him, where they could all earn a few pennies. The only stipulation was that they must not speak to anyone about what they were doing. The young lad's eyes lit up and the following day, Jimmy Dunn was entertaining half a dozen urchins, all keen to earn some money.

The Cumberland leg of the vast drug trafficking network was therefore complete: opium that had been grown in India, sold to China, exported to Britain, shipped around the country, picked up in Whitehaven, transported to Carlisle, carried by foot to a small house in Wapping, and then carried out by children, ended its journey by being consumed by the weak and vulnerable of the city. As they did so, every hand that had touched the narcotics were being financially rewarded – from the young runners earning their pennies to the masterminds of the organisation who were making tens of thousands.

And while the police and the authorities saw the problems the drug was causing at the end of this long chain, with those addicted increasingly breaking the law whilst under the influence, they had no way of identifying the route the drugs were taking to get here or who was responsible for their import.

Like Freddie Grant, any initial wariness Jimmy Dunn had about the scheme, or of this strange bloke from Manchester, was trumped by the promise of easy money – and lots of it. It wasn't long before he was making a tidy profit. Also, like his friend, Jimmy was no shrinking violet but similarly, his wariness of Jack Roberts had developed into a fear: this bloke from Manchester just seemed to turn up one day and yet appeared to have his finger in many pies; and when things didn't turn out the way he wanted, those same fingers would form a fist that needed to be avoided. And finally – just like the Grant brothers – Jimmy Dunn realised he was now in too deep; he had made a pact with the devil and he had to get on with it.

Roberts even had a distinctive knock on the door – not so much a knock as a hammer – that prompted Jimmy to know exactly who it was. This particular morning was no exception. Jimmy was in the back when he heard the front door being battered with the side of a fist; he looked up in nervous realisation.

"Hello Jimmy, boy," said Roberts as he pushed past Dunn in to the shabby hallway, "it's money day. A lot for me, and if you behave yourself, some for you."

"All right, Jack," replied the despondent Dunn closing the door behind him, "go into the back kitchen and we'll sort things out."

Three or four of the young boys Jimmy used as couriers were playing in the house, running in and out of the back yard giddily chasing each other – a rare glimpse of a normal childhood for these street-hardened ragamuffins. Since he had commissioned their services, his boarding house had become a bit of a second home for them; when there were vacant rooms, one or two would even stay there preferring it to the workhouse.

"Can I get you a brew?" Jimmy asked Roberts, keen to keep on his good side.

"Why not," said Jack, "I've got some business to sort out with you anyway."

"Oh, really?" asked Jimmy nervously.

"Awe it's nothing to fret about," Roberts was smiling at Dunn's discomfort, "I'm looking to increase the shipments to Whitehaven. I should be able to manage something every Wednesday from now on. Is that all right with you?"

Dunn knew that it was a ridiculous question, given that he wouldn't have any say in the matter, "Yes, I don't see why not." He poured the tea into two tin mugs and retrieved a tea caddy from a high shelf from which he produced a wad of notes, "there is one thing though."

"What's that?" Roberts's avaricious eyes looked up from the money, not used to having any objections raised.

"It's these young lads."

"What about them?"

Just as Roberts asked, one of the boys entered the hall and yanked open the door to the cupboard under the stairs. *"Gotcha!"* he cried as another boy was discovered in his hiding spot. "Your turn," he said to the second lad, "count to a hundred."

"Oi lads!" shouted Jimmy through the kitchen door that opened onto the hall, "take your carry on outside."

The two boys sniggered and ran off into the yard.

"As I was saying," resumed Jimmy turning to Roberts, "the demand for this bloody opium is taking over-"

"That's why I'm gonna bring more in," interrupted Roberts.

"I'm just a bit concerned about the safety of these young kids who are carrying this stuff about. It won't be long before somebody has a mind to mug them on their way to where they are going."

"Ah, they'll be all right," dismissed Roberts with a wave, "they all get paid anyway. Now, where do you shift the drugs to?"

Jimmy was disturbed by Jack's lack of interest in the boys' safety but knew there was no use pursuing the argument. "There's a list of pubs and doss houses around the town," he said.

"Well that's your homework for this week, Jimmy boy. Increase the list and make arrangements for more runners if you have to." With that, the villain peeled off some notes from the wad and threw them on the kitchen table, "I'll see myself out."

Jimmy Dunn was left sitting in his kitchen, looking at the money on the table. There would be more to come but the risks and dangers were increasing.

His concerns about the boys' safety would prove prophetic. One morning in late January, PC Sam Watts was on his beat in Shaddongate. Although it was still bitterly cold, the weather was finally relenting and there was a slight thaw underway. It only served however to make some of the pavements even more treacherous underfoot, as the well-trodden pathways were turning into a skating track.

Watts was waddling along Kendal Street when he heard a whimpering sound in a lane opposite Byer's Yard. Peering down the lane he saw a young boy lying in a crumpled heap, sobbing.

Watts scurried down the lane and crouched down, "What's happened here, son?"

The lad looked up; beneath the tears, his face was marked and his nose bloodied.

"Bloody hell, lad," said Sam when he saw his face, "what happened? Who did this?"

The young lad – probably no more than ten or eleven – just looked at the policeman and shook his head. Sam sensed that he didn't want to talk to anyone about what had happened, but equally, he didn't want to leave the boy in this state on such a day as this.

"Where do you live?" he asked.

Finally the young lad spoke, "I usually stay at the workhouse."

"Well let's get you back there. At least you'll have a roof and some food."

"No, no," said the boy, his voice rising in concern, "I don't want to go back there. Not now."

"Why not? I can't leave you here." Sam was keen not to distress the boy further. After a few seconds he made another suggestion. "How about the infirmary then?"

"No, I'm all right."

Watts made a final plea, "Listen, I'm not leaving you here like this. You're not in any trouble, but I can take you back to the police station, we can get you cleaned up and get you a hot meal and something to drink. Whaddya say?"

Much to Sam's surprise, the young lad agreed with a nod and the policeman helped him to his feet. The lad was freezing.

"Have you been here all night?" asked Watts taking off his top coat and wrapping it round the lad – it almost trailed on the ground.

Again, the lad gave a pitiful nod.

"What's your name?"

"Denis, sir. Denis Brown but they all call me Denny."

"Well then Denny, let's go and get you warmed up."

The two picked their way back up Charlotte Street and over the viaduct to West Walls. Watts told Sergeant Bill Townsend of his find

118

and the two set Denny up in the interview room by the stove and wrapped him in a blanket.

"Now you get yourself warmed up, young Denny and I'll get you something to eat," said Sam. He came back five minutes later with a bowl of broth and a thick slice of bread. "There you go young fella; the lads won't miss this from the back kitchen."

"Thank you, sir," said Denny, his mood clearly improving.

While Denny tucked in, Sam didn't want an assault on a child to go without some form of investigation.

"So take me through what happened," he asked.

Again Denny's head dropped; he was clearly reluctant to say any more than he had to. He took out an old rag he obviously used as a handkerchief and wiped his runny nose. As he did so, Sam noticed some brownish powder on the rag and a similar substance around the lining of the lad's trouser pocket.

"What's that?" he asked.

Denny saw what the policeman was looking at and burst into tears.

Suddenly, everything made sense to PC Watts: Denny was one of the young drug runners from the house in Robert Street.

"Calm down, Denny, you're not in any trouble. But this is a very serious matter. I think you have been attacked because you were taking packets of opium from Wapping. Am I right?" Denny's silence confirmed that he was, "I'm going to introduce you to another policeman who needs to look into this all right? There's nothing for you to worry about, you're not in any trouble, but this is very important. Do you understand?"

Denny nodded.

"Now you finish your broth and I'll be back in a few minutes."

THIRTEEN

Inspector Armstrong was sitting at his desk twisting the horns of his moustache as he flicked through Ester Sanderson's journal, reminding himself of what he had read the previous evening. There was a knock on the door and PC Sam Watts entered.

"Sir, I think you should come next door, there's someone I think you should meet."

Armstrong followed Watts to the interview room where Denny Brown was cleaning the last vestiges of broth from his bowl with his thumb and forefinger. He looked up when the two policemen entered.

"Denny, this is Inspector Armstrong," and then turning to his superior officer, "sir, I found Denny here a bit knocked about in Shaddongate this morning. He's been robbed of the opium he was carrying; he's one of the young runners who takes it from Robert Street."

Armstrong switched his mind from Ester Sanderson to the increased drug problem the city was experiencing. He had experienced an increase of crime as a result of opium: fighting in the street, vagrancy, petty theft – not to mention three suicides due to opium overdoses – now he could add beating up children to the list. He was appalled at the thought and pulled up a chair and sat beside the boy.

"Hello Denny. Let me say first of all that you are not in any trouble, but it is important that you answer some of my questions because I am trying to stop this sort of behaviour. Do you think you'll be able to do that?"

Denny looked at PC Watts for assurance; once it was given with a kind expression, he nodded his head.

"Where do you live?" started the policeman.

"I stay at the Workhouse, sir," replied the lad. "I don't have any mam or dad."

"St Mary's?" – the boy nodded – "Is it right that you know the people in the house on Robert Street?"

"Yes, sir," said the lad and then added, "well, it's just Jimmy who stays there. The other men come and go."

"How did you first get involved in what goes on there?"

"One of the boys from the workhouse came back one day and said a few of us could earn a few pennies if we wanted. All we needed to do was to deliver a few packets. It was easy."

"Did you know what was in the packets?"

"No, not at first. We all wondered what it was. Then, when Jimmy was upstairs one day, Mark Ridley said it was something that made people happy and we should see what the stuff was like. It's this brown stuff," – Denny showed the inspector the residue in his pocket where the package had split after being snatched from him – "we all dipped our finger in the bag and tasted it. *Cforr! It was 'orrible!"* I don't know how anyone can eat that or smoke it or whatever they do with it. After that I just took it to where I was told. The only thing was Jimmy told us that we couldn't say anything to anyone about what we were doing."

"And where did you take the packages?"

Denny hesitated. He knew that he was doing exactly what Jimmy Dunn had told him and the other boys not to do. Moreover he was telling it to the police. Armstrong sensed the lad's fear and moved to re-assure him.

"Denny, do you have any family at all in Carlisle?"

"No, sir."

"Well I could arrange for you to move to a new home in Brampton, which is a little town a few miles away from Carlisle. There is a home for lads just like yourself where you can get proper schooling and get well looked after – I believe they even have a farm where you can get to work with the animals. I know Mr. Fletcher at St. Mary's Workhouse and I can go and have a word with him – I don't think he would have any objection. It would mean that you can get away from all of this and you will be safe from anyone who might want to hurt you."

This was a lot for the young boy to take in and his mind was racing: he had already been beaten up and robbed; he would have to face Jimmy and the other boys – not to mention that other bloke – when they found out he had lost the packet; and he knew if he lost the money he earned from the running, he would go without. Without anything or anyone else to keep him in Carlisle he eventually nodded at Cornelius's suggestion. Anything would be better than the life he had here.

"Good lad," said Armstrong delighted that he was gaining his trust. He was starting to sense that this young lad could inadvertently uncover the whole local network. "So, I was asking where you took the packages of powder?"

"We took them all over, sir. I had two calls, a place on Newcastle Street and the *Jovial Sailor*. Other boys took theirs to Brook Street, Currock, a place in Botcherby, Mark even took his over the river to somewhere in Etterby."

Armstrong was struck by the diverse areas in terms of wealth that were being corrupted by the narcotic. This was certainly consistent with the rise in petty crime in all parts of the city during the previous eighteen months.

"Are there any other adults at the house apart from Jimmy?" he asked.

"There are another couple of blokes who come and go. One of them brings a big bag and he and Jimmy split it up to small packets for us. There's another bloke who comes – I think he is the boss 'coz Jimmy seems frightened of him."

"Do you know what their names are?"

"The bloke who brings the bags is called Freddie and the I think the other one is called Jack. I don't know where they live though."

Cornelius was pleased he had gained the boy's trust, who was talking freely now, as if relieved to get the secret off his chest.

"How often does Freddie bring the bags?"

"I think it's every few weeks because that's when Jimmy tells us to be there." Before the policeman could ask his next question, Denny added, "But that is going to change."

"How's that?"

122

"I was playing hide-and-seek the other day with the other boys at Jimmy's house when Jack was there. I was hiding in the cubby-hole under the stairs and I heard them talking in the kitchen. Jack told Jimmy that he was going to get the packets every Wednesday."

"Do you know where Freddie gets the powder from?"

"Jack said something about ships at White…White-" Denny looked into his lap as he struggled to recall the name of the place he had heard the two men talking about.

"Whitehaven?" suggested Inspector Armstrong.

"Yes, Whitehaven!" exclaimed Denny triumphantly, "that's what they said."

"That's interesting," said Armstrong, as much to himself as to the boy and his uniformed colleague. After a short pause he shared his plans.

"All right Denny, this is what we are going to do. I'm going to arrange for you to stay here this morning. I will go and speak with Mr. Fletcher and we'll make arrangements to take you to Brampton."

He then turned to Sam, "PC Watts I want you to change into your civvies and deliver a note for me. See me in my office in five minutes and ask Sergeant Townsend to come in here."

"Will do, sir," said Watts with a half salute.

Moments later Bill Townsend appeared.

"Ah, Sergeant," said the inspector, "this is Denny Brown."

"Yes, PC Watts brought him in earlier, sir," said Townsend, "how are you getting on young fella? Have you warmed up any?"

Denny nodded silently, still overwhelmed by the situation he found himself in.

"I want you to look after Denny, this morning Sergeant, while I arrange for him to be taken to a new home in Brampton." Armstrong turned to the boy, "You'll be in safe hands with Sergeant Townsend, Denny. I'll be back later around lunchtime to see you again – is that all right?"

"Yes, sir," said the boy quietly.

Townsend took the seat vacated by his superior officer who left the two and went to his own office. He took a piece of paper from his desk drawer and wrote a note. As he was placing it in an envelope, PC Watts appeared again in the doorway. Following his inspector's instruction, he had simply covered his tunic with his civilian overcoat.

"The master of disguise," said Armstrong looking up, "it'll have to do I suppose. I want you to deliver this note to this address," – he gave Watts the envelope – "and then I want you to spend an hour or two near Freddie Grant's tenement to see if there are any comings and goings." He wrote down a second address and handed it over.

"Very good, sir," said the constable.

"If I can make arrangements through the Workhouse, you can accompany the young lad through to Brampton later this afternoon."

"Will do, sir," replied the enthusiastic constable.

Armstrong himself made his way to the imposing St Mary's Workhouse. The policeman banged on the large, double doors which housed a smaller single access point. After a while the Gatekeeper appeared at the door-within-a-door. Cornelius saw that the man wore a tired expression, not surprising given the nature of his work; the number of desperate creatures he would have let in and out of these gates could not be guessed at.

"Good morning," said the detective, "my name is Cornelius Armstrong, I am a policeman. I would like to speak with the Warden, Mr. Fletcher."

The man invited Cornelius to step over the large timber lip with a gesture, "Certainly sir, I'll take to you his office."

The two men walked across the slippery cobbled courtyard to the office of Peter Fletcher who had worked as warden for over ten years. The Gatekeeper, knocked and entered,

"Excuse me Mr. Fletcher but there is a policeman here to see you." He stood aside to allow Cornelius to enter.

Fletcher was a middle-aged man who – despite his challenging profession – maintained an eager expression and a welcoming manner.

"Good morning," he said, getting up from his desk and offering a hand, "Inspector Armstrong isn't it? I remember you came to see me a few years ago about another matter."

"That's right Mr. Fletcher," said Cornelius shaking his hand, "it's nice to see you. I'm sorry to drop in on you unannounced but there is a delicate matter I need to speak with you about."

"Certainly, have a seat, can I offer you a cup of tea?"

"No thank you," said the policeman, "I'll try not to take up too much of your time."

"Thank you, John," Fletcher said to the Gatekeeper who had politely waited at the door in case refreshment was needed.

"Very good, sir," he saluted and closed the door behind him.

"It's about a group of boys who reside here," started Armstrong, "and one in particular."

He proceeded to inform Fletcher of how the boys were being exploited as part of the criminal activity being run from Robert Street. His narrative culminated in his proposal to re-locate Denny Brown to the home in Brampton for his own safety. Fletcher bowed his head, feeling as though he had failed in his duties to care for the boys.

"I had no idea this sort of thing was going on Inspector," he said. "Many of our residents are free to leave each day once their work and schooling is done. In most if not all cases, I don't know where they go or what they get up to."

"Don't distress yourself Mr. Fletcher," said the policeman in an effort to placate the warden, "no one could possibly blame you for the cruelty of others. The purpose of me telling you this was to ask for your help in re-housing the young lad Denny, and to be aware that we are looking to protect the other boys from similar treatment."

Fletcher nodded, "Yes, yes, I understand."

"It is important that you don't talk to the boys about this," warned Cornelius, "just tell them he has gone to stay with a long-lost aunt or something. I intend to catch the people responsible for this activity and it is important for the time being that they carry on thinking there is nothing untoward.

"Now, do you think you can help with the boys' home at Brampton? I would like to move him out there today."

125

"Yes, I'm sure we can arrange that," replied the warden, "I have a good relationship with all of the facilities in the area. If you will just bear with me."

Fletcher went to the corner of his office behind his desk where a candlestick telephone stood. Holding the earpiece in the heel of his hand, he tapped the receiver cradle that protruded from the top of the stick with his forefinger to attract the attention of the operator.

"Hello, Brampton 472 please," he said into the mouthpiece. There was a brief pause until he continued, "Good morning Edward it is Peter Fletcher at St. Mary's."

Without divulging the reason, Fletcher proceeded to tell the manager at Brampton about the young boy they were proposing to move over to him. After some minutes of jovial conversation, he hung up the ear piece on the hook of the phone.

"That's all sorted then Inspector," he announced, "they will be expecting young Denny this afternoon."

"Thank you for your help and your time Mr. Fletcher, it's much appreciated."

"You're very welcome sir," said the warden, "to be honest we could do with the extra bed, we've had so many people in during these last few months."

"Really?" questioned Armstrong, "why would that be?"

"Many of them have been complaining about the increase in rent," replied Fletcher, "they just can't afford to live up here."

"That's concerning," said the policeman, who was unaware the rent increases were a major issue until that point. "Anyway, I have another appointment so I must be off. Thank you again for your help."

The two shook hands and the inspector thanked John on his way back out onto the street.

He headed back towards the city centre through Caldewgate; his destination was a little coffee shop at the bottom of West Walls close to the Irish Gate. It was a twenty-minute walk and by the time he got there, the person he was hoping to meet was already waiting for him with his faithful dog resting at his feet.

Cornelius walked over to the corner table and sat down opposite Reuben Hanks. It was one of their regular meeting places: relatively close by for each party but discreet enough to keep away from potentially suspicious eyes.

"I got your note, sir," said Reuben, as Armstrong ordered a pot of coffee.

"Thanks for seeing me at such short notice," said the policeman.

"No problem, sir." Reuben was always keen to stay on Armstrong's good side.

"When we spoke the other day you told me about a house on Robert Street."

"That's right, sir, I've heard a few people talking about it."

"Well, it turns out you were right," said Cornelius, "it's being used as a hub to move opium around the city."

Reuben's expression never changed and Armstrong wondered if he knew this already. Regardless, he continued.

"I came across a bloke a while back – Freddie Grant – it turns out he is somehow involved. Do you know much about him?"

"He's a scallywag, no doubt about it," said Reuben, raking his nicotine-stained fingers through his tousled hair, "but I'm surprised to hear he would be involved in something like that. Seems a bit too organised for him."

"Hmm, that's what I thought," amused at the kettle calling the pan black, "I learnt only this morning that he is getting the drugs from Whitehaven where they are shipped in."

"So you think he collects them?" asked Hanks.

"Well if it's not him then somebody does," said the detective, "it seems there is a shipment into Whitehaven on Wednesdays that finds its way to here."

"Well it can't be him who collects it," said Reuben, "coz he goes to the same place as me on a Wednesday – I often see him."

Cornelius decided not to enquire where this place was and in what context Reuben was there. Instead he concentrated on Grant.

"Well he has certainly been seen taking the stuff to Robert Street so he must be involved somehow. You don't know anyone he associates with, do you?"

"Not really, Mr. Armstrong. There's just him and his brother who live in a tenement down our way. Funnily enough it's the brother Billy who has been attracting attention lately."

"Oh, how?"

"Well, he collects the rent and I've heard a lot of people complaining about him putting it up."

"You're the second person within the last hour who's mentioned rents going up. Who does he collect it for?"

"I don't know, sir, but you're right in what you're suggesting – it won't be him that's putting it up, he just collects it. Besides, he's a bit of a soft lad, he wouldn't cause trouble when he didn't have to."

"Thanks Reuben, you've given me a bit more to think about. If you hear anything more about these brothers be sure and let me know, won't you?"

"I will do, sir," said Hanks.

The two men finished their coffee and Armstrong left first, allowing Reuben to leave alone and blend back into the Caldewgate crowd on the other side of the Irish Gate.

Back in the station, Inspector Armstrong looked in on Denny Brown and informed him that arrangements were in place for PC Watts to take him to Brampton that afternoon.

"You'll be safe there," said Cornelius, "hopefully it will be a fresh start for you."

"Thank you, sir," said Denny, clearly relieved at being taken out of the circle of violence and deceit.

Just then, Sam Watts appeared from his morning's tasks, "I delivered the message, sir," he said.

"Yes, thank you Sam, the man I wanted to see got the message, I've just come from meeting him. How did you get on round at Freddie Grant's place?"

128

"It was pretty quiet, sir. There was only one other young bloke who came in and out. I heard the next-door neighbour shout over to him, calling him Billy.

"Yes, I've been hearing a bit about him, he's the brother." Armstrong was quiet for a while, "I've just had a thought. We've learned this morning from young Denny that the opium comes into Whitehaven on Wednesdays. I know that Freddie Grant isn't available to collect on a Wednesday but we know it ends up with him. Therefore, I wonder if it is his brother who collects it for him?"

"It's as good a theory as any, sir," agreed Watts.

"I think we will follow this little feeling on Wednesday, Constable. Leave this with me and I'll speak to you later. In the meantime, I made arrangements for Denny to be taken in at Brampton. Perhaps you can take him out there."

"Will do sir."

FOURTEEN

Since reporting the blackmail letter to Chief Constable Baker, Benjamin Woodward had been unable to sleep for fear of his beer being contaminated and his company ruined as a result – not that the previous months had been much better for a man who was of a naturally nervous disposition.

The beer industry in Lancashire had been rocked eight months earlier by the mysterious disease in the Manchester area that was characterised by muscle paralysis and loss of skin pigmentation. At first it was put down to chronic alcohol use but when it was discovered that only moderate drinkers were also displaying the same symptoms, tests revealed that victims were suffering from arsenic poisoning caused by contaminated beer. The disease quickly spread west to Liverpool and threatened to creep north to Preston.

Like everyone else in the industry, Woodward was keeping a close eye on developments; continually monitoring the number of newly reported cases of illness and seeking advice from the regulatory authorities. Both tasks were futile: he was powerless to restrict the numbers affected – or the spread of the disease which by autumn was of epidemic proportions – and the authorities advice consisted mainly of reminders to keep equipment clean and well maintained, which was ridiculous advice to any respectable brewer who carried out such tasks on a regular basis without a second thought.

Much to the industry's relief, the problem had been brought under control by the end of the year, although it was never established who was responsible for the contamination. Although Iredale's was never affected in the same way as those breweries in the Manchester area, Woodward struggled to contain his concern throughout the scare. It was on the approach to the holidays that he could begin to relax as the panic appeared to be over. A good Christmas and New Year followed and profits were on the up. Then the letter arrived only a week into the New Year. *That* letter – it may have been scrawled with an almost illegible hand but the message it conveyed sent the brewery owner into a state of near hysteria.

It was his wife who convinced him to approach the police and despite the threats, after a week Woodward relented. After meeting with Chief Constable Baker and his inspector, the brewery owner felt better for having relieved himself of the burden that was weighing heavy on his mind. On one level, their advice to remain vigilant seemed as inane as that issued by the regulators months earlier, but the two policemen somehow inspired confidence in Woodward and he left feeling that he had strong support. Then the second letter arrived.

Woodward could see that it was written in a different hand but the message was enough to confine the man to his bed, such was his state of distress.

It was left to his dear wife therefore to take it upon herself to report the matter of the second correspondence to the police.

"Could I speak with Chief Constable Baker please?" she said to the desk sergeant.

"Can I ask what it is concerning, madam?" Part of Bill Townsend's job was to sift the wheat from the chaff when it came to visitors' requests. Every individual who passed through the doors of the station believed their issue was of the utmost importance; Townsend had quickly learned that, in many cases, spending a little time simply listening to the complainant talk about their lost watch or the noise coming from next door, was enough to placate the individual and send them on their way, convinced that the police were now dealing with the matter but without troubling one of the senior officers. His role made him a good reader of people and something told him that this lady was not about to be placed in the time-wasters category.

"I am here on behalf of my husband who previously visited Mr. Baker," she explained. "He is Benjamin Woodward who owns Iredale's Brewery. I'm afraid he has been receiving threatening letters."

"I'm sorry to hear that, Mrs. Woodward."

Townsend did not enquire as to why Woodward had not appeared in person; instead he asked the lady to take a seat in the front area, "I'll see if the Chief Constable is available."

Teresa Woodward sat down on one of the wooden benches in the entrance of the police station – an unusual figure in such an environment with her elegant clothes and fine bearing – and waited patiently for the sergeant to return. As she did so, she observed an official-looking man moving between the offices that could be seen from the waiting area. He was smartly dressed in a waistcoat and matching trousers, and a uniformed officer – who continually addressed the man as 'sir' – also appeared and disappeared, apparently dealing with the same matter.

After several minutes of the two men going back and forward, the uniformed officer re-appeared from one of the rooms with a small child.

The plain clothed officer came to the doorway of his office and spoke to the boy as they passed.

"Good luck, Denny," Mrs. Woodward heard the man say, "I'm sure you will be very happy in your new home."

"Thank you, sir," replied the boy.

With a nod from the superior officer, the constable and the boy left. Mrs. Woodward's reverie was broken by Sergeant Townsend who re-appeared from down the corridor which led to the chief constable's office.

"Mr. Baker can see you now, ma'am," he said.

Townsend escorted Mrs. Woodward back down the corridor and past the rooms and offices in which the scene she had witnessed a few moments earlier had taken place. The sergeant knocked on the last door and entered.

"Mrs. Woodward, sir," he announced.

Henry Baker rose from behind his desk to greet his visitor, "Mrs. Woodward, please come in and take a seat. Can I get you some tea?"

"No thank you, Chief Constable," she said, shaking his outstretched hand.

"That will be all Sergeant, thank you," said Baker dismissing Townsend who left with a nod. Then turning back to his visitor, "Now Mrs. Woodward, tell me what brings you here."

"You will recall my husband brought to your attention the blackmail letter he received a few weeks ago?"

"Yes."

"Well another has arrived." She handed the note to Baker.

"Could I ask where your husband is?"

"I'm afraid he has been confined to his bed Chief Constable. He is a man with a delicate constitution to start with and this has affected him very badly."

Chief Constable Baker read the note, "If you just wait here one moment Mrs. Woodward, I will ask one of my men to join us."

He left momentarily and returned with the man Mrs. Woodward had seen earlier with the uniformed officer and the young boy.

"This is Inspector Cornelius Armstrong," said Baker, "your husband spoke to us both on this subject.

"Hello Mrs. Woodward," said Armstrong, "I'm sorry to hear about this latest development. I'm sorry also that we haven't been able to dedicate as much time to the problem as I would have hoped."

Armstrong was conscious that he had not had a chance to visit the brewery as he suggested he would. Rather than make pathetic excuses, he always believed it was best to admit to his mistake and seek to rectify the problem.

"Can I see the letter, sir?" he asked of his superior officer.

Baker handed it over and Armstrong took some minutes to study it.

"Do you still have the other one?" he asked the brewery owner's wife.

"Yes I have it here," she said unclipping the clasp on a small bag she was carrying.

Cornelius took the letter she offered and compared the two. Both had a raggy edge, presumably a result of being ripped from a book; the writing on both was in pencil; the paper was coarse, a dull grey colour with grubby finger marks.

133

"They are written by different people but the pieces of paper look the same, as if they are taken from the same pad or notebook."

"Yes," agreed Mrs. Woodward, "I noted that the spelling in the second letter is particularly poor."

Armstrong nodded his agreement as he read silently:

...so make shure you have ten thowsand pound ready by the middle of Febuary of they'll be trouble.

"Why would a blackmailer extend a deadline?" he asked the room. After a while, he turned his attention back to the Chief Constable and Mrs. Woodward, "I think this is a bluff."

"A bluff?" repeated the brewery owner's wife.

Armstrong explained his line of thinking, "These are not educated men, Mrs. Woodward. I wouldn't be surprised if they have seen an opportunity to frighten your husband into paying out in light of the contamination scandal last year. My understanding is that the industry has tightened up its systems and protocols, as well as developing greater regulation in its supply chain. I also read in the newspaper the other day that a Royal Commission has been set up to prevent any recurrence in the future.

If these notes had been received last year, I would have been far more worried," he concluded.

"Maybe the villains are taking advantage of such a view, Inspector," replied Mrs. Woodward, "relying on a sense of complacency, now that the searchlight has moved elsewhere, so to speak."

"That could be the case," conceded the detective, "but I would wager that these men are working class opportunists."

"So what are you proposing to do?" asked Mrs. Woodward showing a slight inflection in her voice for the first time.

"With your permission, sir," said Armstrong turning to Baker, "I would like to deploy a couple of officers at the brewery for the next few days, just as a presence and a deterrent," – and then to them both – "if you note, there is no detail of where or to whom the money should be delivered. Therefore, if they are serious, with the middle of the month only days away, it follows that there should be a further visit."

Mrs. Woodward seemed placated by the inspector's logic and assuredness.

"That does sound reasonable," she said after some thought.

"If we are satisfied with that approach then," said the chief constable, "let us call an end to this meeting. Perhaps you could give your husband our regards, Mrs. Woodward."

"And tell him that I will visit him at the brewery within the next few days to check that everything is all right," added Cornelius.

"Thank you both," said Mrs. Woodward, "I feel much better for having raised the issue."

Henry Baker showed his visitor out and returned to his officer to find Cornelius still there.

"I'll organise that, sir," said Armstrong.

"Yes," said Baker, "I must say, I think the wife has a bit more about her than the husband."

"Do you know them?" asked Armstrong.

"Not really," replied Baker, "that's the first time I've met Mrs. Woodward, but I had met her husband some time before he came to see us a few weeks ago."

Armstrong didn't ask his superior officer to elaborate on the comment but Baker chose to anyway, "He is an acquaintance of Herbert Underwood who asked to meet us both at his club about twelve months ago. It turned out that Underwood was offering us both a chance to join the Masons. I wasn't interested – funny lot if you ask me – but I believe Woodward took him up on his offer."

"Speaking of Mr. Underwood, I'm surprised we haven't heard more from him over the past few weeks."

The Chairman of the Watch Committee had a reputation for being zealous in his duties and was never reluctant to press Henry Baker, or his inspectors on whatever the latest concern was. Although rarely seen at the station, Baker regularly informed Armstrong that he had been summoned to the committee to explain whatever was current at the time. This hadn't appeared to have been the case recently.

"No, I was thinking that myself actually," replied Baker, "not that I have any intention of encouraging him. Maybe it's his New Year's Resolution to bother us a little less."

There was little conviction in Baker's last comment and both men knew that the irony was that there had been more crime committed in the previous twelve months than in the previous four years, due mainly to this increase in drug-related activity. If ever there was a time for the Watch Committee to be regularly meeting with the City Force it would be now. But given the strange, arm's-length relationship tolerated by both parties, neither Baker nor Armstrong had the time or the appetite to change the current situation. Instead, Armstrong brought the conversation back the subject of Mr. and Mrs. Woodward.

"His wife certainly seemed the stronger willed of the two," suggested Armstrong.

"Yes. Anyway, was there anything else, Cornelius?" The chief constable re-took his seat behind the desk.

Inspector Armstrong proceeded to inform Baker of his investigations over the previous forty-eight hours: the concerns about the insurance claims, the discovery that Whitlock's son was engaged to Ester Sanderson, and most significant of all, the breakthrough in revealing the route of the drugs into Carlisle, mainly because of the misfortune that befell young Denny Brown.

"What do you propose? Asked Baker.

"Well, I now know the opium is being shipped into Whitehaven. I also know that it finds its way to the tenement of Freddie Grant in Caldewgate who then takes it to the hub in Robert Street from where it is distributed around the City. I have also learned that Freddie Grant can't be the one who collects the stuff from Whitehaven, so by process of elimination, I reckon it's his younger brother Billy who is the courier. We know the shipment comes in on Wednesdays, so I would like to follow the younger brother's movements this week to see what he gets up to."

"It's a logical theory, Cornelius but I can ill-afford to have you travelling around Cumberland on what might prove a fool's errand," said Baker with some concern.

"I don't propose to go myself, Henry," replied Armstrong with just a hint of a mischievous glint in his eye, "I have someone else in mind."

As he said it, and without moving his head, he darted his eyes to his right. Baker, who was sitting opposite immediately understood what he was getting at. He got up from his desk and left his office for a moment. Cornelius heard his superior officer knock on the door of the adjacent office and enter. Muffled voices and a few seconds later, Henry Baker returned with Inspector Godfrey Parker just behind him.

"Hello, Godfrey," said Armstrong.

Although he worked just down the corridor from the more senior man, Parker had a reputation amongst his colleagues for shutting himself away in his office, while no one knew exactly what he was doing. As the office of Inspector Armstrong was the first one beyond the front desk and was permanently open – and when he didn't have people coming in and out of his office with problems, he would be out on enquiries – Cornelius could go for days on end without ever seeing his colleague.

"Oh hello, Cornelius," replied the old man, and then as he sat down added, "how are you getting on with the burglaries?"

Cornelius smiled to himself; had the question come from anyone else, he would have been offended by the effrontery of the man – after all, it was *Parker's* case not *his*. But he knew that there was never any malice in anything Godfrey did or said, just thoughtlessness. He took the question at face value therefore.

"Yes, we are making progress Godfrey, I'm pleased to say."

Henry Baker noted Armstrong's generous use of the word *we* and brought the pleasantries to an end.

"Cornelius, why don't you fill Godfrey in on your proposal."

"Certainly, sir." Armstrong turned to his colleague, "Godfrey, I am convinced that if we can put an end to this influx of opium to the city, we can greatly reduce the number of petty crimes and deaths being caused by the damn stuff."

Parker looked at Cornelius blankly and it crossed Armstrong's mind for a moment that Godfrey wasn't even aware of the opium problem. That couldn't be, surely? Anyway, he pressed on informing his colleague of his investigations over the last few days: The Grant brothers, Robert Street, the runners and finally Denny Brown.

"Good heavens!" said Godfrey with all sincerity, "a child!"

"It's a wicked world out there, Godfrey," said Cornelius. "Now, here is what I want you to do. The young man I suspect brings the drugs into Carlisle is Billy Grant. I think he picks them up from Whitehaven, somewhere at the docks. I want you to follow to see if we can confirm that this is the case."

Parker looked visibly shocked by this proposal. He was barely used to carrying out overt enquiries, never mind covert investigations. Armstrong sensed his concern.

"Don't worry about anything, I'll have young PC Watts follow him from his tenement in Caldewgate. If he does what I think he will do, he will catch the early train to Whitehaven where he must meet someone from the ship. You can take over from Watts at the station and get on the train and follow him to Whitehaven to see what he gets up to."

"What do you want me to do if I see him pick up the bag?" Parker was clearly nervous about the whole thing.

"I don't want you to do anything, Godfrey," reassured Armstrong, "all I want you to do is to observe his movements, from the time he gets on the train in Carlisle, to his arriving in Whitehaven. See what he gets up to down there and follow him back to Carlisle."

"Well, I've never been given such a task before," said Godfrey, "but I will try my best."

After Parker left the two contemplating this unusual instruction, Baker turned back to Armstrong.

"Do you think this is wise, Cornelius?"

"Oh, I think so Henry," replied Armstrong, "if it is as I suspect, this could be an important piece of the puzzle and will help us solve the opium trafficking once and for all. And let's be honest," he added, "even if Grant does see Godfrey, he would never take him for a policeman."

FIFTEEN

William Whitlock sat quietly in his study, contemplating the events of the last few days. The visits of Inspector Armstrong had acted like an epiphany – he had spent restless nights and troubled days. He was now wondering what the next days would bring and how his son would answer some of the questions the policeman had in store for him.

Gerald Whitlock had been born into a privileged life. His father was already a partner in his firm of solicitors, while his mother was the daughter of a wealthy financier. The best schooling, the finest clothing, a beautiful home in the most affluent part of the city, Gerald enjoyed a childhood most could only dream about. Not that the boy enjoyed anything very much; being an only child, he was spoilt to the point where everything he desired came to him easily.

When he came of a certain age his father – by now the sole owner of Morley, Freeman and Whitlock, having bought out George Freeman and following the death of Josiah Morley – welcomed him into his firm. But adulthood did nothing to develop any sort of humility in Gerald who wasted little time in ordering staff around, treating clients with contempt and continually disobeying his father's instructions.

Much to William's exasperation, his son becoming qualified – despite his modest exam performances – did little to arrest the pattern of behaviour and attitude that was threatening to become reckless. It wasn't until Inspector Armstrong had visited William Whitlock that the solicitor had given much thought to the fact that it was all of Gerald's clients who had been victims of burglaries. And once he had spent some time thinking about it, he realised that Gerald himself seemed quite relaxed, almost matter-of-fact about something that he himself had never witnessed in over thirty years of practice. And even when his own premises were broken into, Gerald seemed to demonstrate a sanguine attitude.

"Never mind," he told his father, "I don't suppose we should be exempt from such villainy. Leave it to me and I'll deal with Lloyds."

Then there was this business with the Sanderson girl. Found hanged. And pregnant. The fool.

Whitlock hadn't yet told Gerald's mother about the revelation; he didn't know how to. But it would come out sooner or later. He wondered how she would react; and what about other members of the club? And how could he face Sanderson, the poor chap having lost his daughter? What a mess.

William had managed to contact Gerald following Armstrong's last visit and was furious when the hotel on Park Lane, where he was staying, informed him that his son was out for the evening. When Whitlock did finally make contact, he ordered him to return home immediately to help with the police enquiries. Even then, William could not bring himself to broach the subject of the girl's pregnancy.

Realising the severity in his father's tone in referring to the local police force– not to mention the thought of possibly being arrested by Scotland Yard – Gerald agreed to return immediately and caught the sleeper north, that night.

On the morning that Ester's body was discovered hanging in her bedroom, Gerald had been informed of his fiancée's demise and had visited the Sanderson residence immediately. The following day, he set off for London, to visit Lloyds and deal with the insurance issues surrounding the firm and that of their clients. He had been there ever since.

Lying in his bunk on the journey back to Carlisle, he had plenty of time to think about the events of the previous few days and decided he was confident he could deal with any questions posed by some small-town policeman. That was until his father met him off the train, hurried him to the office and informed him about Ester Sanderson's condition. The younger Whitlock reached for a chair.

"What were you thinking, you bloody idiot?" shouted his father.

Gerald never answered but just looked blankly in front of him, unaware of his surroundings or his father's fury.

"You better get yourself round to see this Armstrong fellow, before it looks even worse, if that were possible."

After some minutes of sitting in his father's office trying to compose himself, Gerald got up and left.

Less than twenty minutes later, Sergeant Bill Townsend stood in the doorway of Inspector Armstrong's office.

"There's someone here to see you, sir. A Mr. Gerald Whitlock. Says it's urgent."

Armstrong looked up, surprised by the announcement, "That's interesting," he said quietly, "show him in, Bill."

Moments later, the sergeant returned with a young man in his early twenties, thin with a sallow complexion and collar-length black hair that was slicked back and shiny. Armstrong suspected that he would normally carry himself with an arrogant air but, in light of the current circumstances, there was more an appearance of uncertainty, even wariness. Cornelius rose from behind his desk.

"I believe you want to see me, Inspector…"

"Armstrong," – the detective was in no mood for pleasantries and got straight to the point – "Yes, I do. I want to ask you about the insurance claims you have been lodging with Lloyds on behalf of your clients, and the condition of your late fiancée."

"Do you mind if I take a seat?" asked Whitlock.

Armstrong, who was still standing himself, acquiesced with a gesture and sat back down.

"The insurance claims all followed a spate of burglaries that befell a group of clients of ours, Inspector," said Whitlock, trying to gain some traction as he anticipated a difficult conversation ahead.

"I know that," snapped Armstrong, "I am interested in the pattern of burglaries: in every case, the thieves knew exactly where to look; relatively small amounts were taken; the fact that each shop or company's business was underwritten by different syndicates who would not necessarily suspect any wrongdoing as they made a one-off payment, without any knowledge of similar pay-outs."

Whitlock was taken aback by the policeman's knowledge; he had clearly underestimated his opponent and began to wonder what else the man knew. He felt his eyes start to sting with sleep deprivation from his late nights in London and a restive night on the train.

"Surely you don't suspect me of any wrongdoing," he blustered unconvincingly, "after all, we ourselves were victims."

"Don't you find it strangely coincidental that this pattern should occur out of nowhere over the past six or eight months."

"Well, coincidences do happen Inspector," said Whitlock, feigning confidence.

"I don't believe in them, Mr. Whitlock, especially when there is a common denominator."

"Call me Gerald, please Inspector. Common denominator?"

"You, *Mr.* Whitlock. You are the common denominator. Not only is your firm responsible for the legal transactions of the companies involved, but you personally brokered deals on their behalf."

"I…I–"

"Why did you go to London, Mr. Whitlock?" interrupted Armstrong.

"In order to resolve some of the issues regarding the burglaries." Whitlock himself was now beginning to hear the lack of conviction in his voice.

"Had you been to London prior to this regarding any of the other burglaries?"

"No."

"Well why now, all of a sudden?" Armstrong didn't wait for Whitlock to answer, "Did you visit the home of your fiancée before you left?"

"Erm…"

"Miss Ester Sanderson," Armstrong was in full flow now, "surely you remember her, she was found hanging from a light fitting in her bedroom?"

"Yes, of course," said Whitlock, "there is no need to be so sarcastic and obvious."

"Well I think there probably is, Mr. Whitlock because like your father, I get the impression from you that your objective is to share as little information as possible, regarding some of the recent events. When did you find out about Miss Sanderson's death?"

Whitlock thought for a few seconds before responding, "On the morning she was discovered."

"And how did you find out?"

"I was contacted by Mr. Underwood."

"Who?" Armstrong was incredulous.

"Mr. Herbert Underwood, he is the Chairman of the Watch Committee I believe. We are in the same club, as is Ester's father."

For the first time, Whitlock felt he had wrong-footed Armstrong, who seemed to hesitate.

"I'm sure Mr. Underwood can confirm this," said Whitlock, unconcerned as to whether Armstrong took this as a threat or merely as name-dropping arrogance.

"And what did you do about it?" asked Armstrong, ignoring the comment.

"I went to see if I could be of any assistance."

"Assistance?" repeated Armstrong, "your fiancée has just been found dead and you want to see if you can be of any assistance?" Again, Armstrong never waited for an answer, "and were you?"

"I'm sorry?"

"Were you of any assistance?"

"Well nothing could be done, I'm afraid. It was felt that Ester had been dead for some hours."

"So you decided the best thing to do was to run off to London, out of the way?"

"Well it wasn't quite like that," said Whitlock, defensively.

"Why don't you tell me what it was like then?"

"Well, there was nothing I could do," Whitlock repeated pathetically, "and I had business in London."

Armstrong lowered his tone a little but remained pointed in his questioning, "See, the thing is Mr. Whitlock, I am asking myself what sort of person discovers that their fiancée has died suddenly, possibly even in suspicious circumstances," – a comment which caused

Whitlock to look up sharply from his lap – "and leaves the scene of the tragedy without a second thought."

Armstrong let his thought hang in the air for a few moments before continuing.

"When is the last time you saw Miss Sanderson, Mr. Whitlock?"

The young solicitor thought for a while, trying to unscramble his thoughts, "It would probably have been New Year's Eve. Her father held a party at the house and invited several friends."

"And how did Miss Sanderson seem to you that night?"

"I can't say I really noticed anything different. The ladies usually keep their own company on such gatherings."

"Whenever you met Miss Sanderson, were you on your own or were you chaperoned?"

Whitlock was now growing particularly nervous as he knew what the policeman was getting at.

"We were chaperoned."

"Always?"

"Yes," he lied.

Armstrong suspected that Whitlock – like his father before him – was being economical with the truth. Whereas he wanted to probe further, he didn't want to rush anything and compromise his investigation. His mind was made up for him when there was a knock on his door and Sergeant Bill Townsend entered.

"I'm sorry to disturb you sir, but you better come quick. The body of a young man has been discovered down by the river. Gibson and Stokes are down there now and I've sent for Doctor Bell to attend. Wilkins and Hall can accompany you, sir."

Cornelius' shoulders slumped and head bowed at this latest revelation; he could do without yet another major inquiry.

"Very well," he said rising from his chair and reaching for his hat and coat, "we will pick up this interview at a later date Mr. Whitlock."

By now he was fastening his coat and was walking out of his office. He turned to see the back of Whitlock's head – he was still sitting in his chair.

145

"Mr. Whitlock?"

He didn't notice that Whitlock hadn't moved since Townsend disturbed them.

"Oh yes," said the solicitor breaking out of his reverie, "contact me when you are ready."

"There is one thing you can help with before you go," said Armstrong, "Sergeant Townend here would like to take some imprints of your hands and fingers."

Townsend looked as surprised as Whitlock at his superior's comment.

"You don't have any objection, do you?" added Armstrong.

Whitlock knew it was an impossible choice: refusal would simply raise suspicion against him, but going ahead with the exercise could further raise suspicion against him. After a pause, he conceded.

"Certainly," he said with a forced smile, "anything to help."

"Very good, and thank you for coming to see me." Armstrong was genuine in his thanks, "I will be in touch again in due course – don't leave the city."

With that, he left on foot with two constables who were to show him the site of the latest discovery. Sam Wilkins was carrying a bag, while Jimmy Hall had a rope and tackle slung over his shoulder. Inspector Armstrong looked at them both, by way of an enquiry.

"This is a few pairs of overalls, sir," said PC Wilkins holding the bag open for his superior officer to see, "apparently the body is at the bottom of a steep bank. I imagine it'll be a bit clarty down there."

"And we'll probably need the rope to get down there, sir and retrieve the body," added Hall.

By the time the three policemen reached the bottom of West Walls, coincidence had it that Doctor James Bell was climbing off an omnibus at the Irish Gate, having started its journey at the infirmary. He saw the three policemen approaching and waited to join them.

"Good morning, Doctor," called Cornelius, "fancy meeting you here!"

"Gentlemen. Yes, it appears as though our meetings are becoming ever more frequent."

146

From Bell's tone, Armstrong assumed his reaction was similar to that of his own when he received the call about the latest body.

The four men strode down Devonshire Walk, with terraced houses on one side and the giant castle on the other; past the abattoir and into the parkland at the back of the castle. After a few hundred yards, two uniformed sentinels could be seen up ahead near the river, talking to a third man.

As the four men approached, the two police constables straightened their shoulders,

"Morning, sir," said Harry Stokes to Armstrong.

"What do we have?" asked the detective.

"There's a man's body, sir, down this bank," – Stokes indicated behind him – "it's pretty difficult to get to."

Both Armstrong and Bell held on to an overhanging tree and leaned over the precipice of the steep bank to see the supine figure down below staring back at them.

The last few days had seen a thaw; after three months of desperate temperatures, falling snow had gradually turned to sleet, which in turn had become drizzle. The wooded area and river banks had therefore become a patchwork of melting snow, slush and mud. Armstrong now understood his officers' decision to bring the overalls and rope – this was going to be a messy exercise.

"Presumably, the body has been covered with snow these last few days?" Armstrong said to no one in particular.

"I would think so, sir," agreed Stokes who had joined the inspector and the doctor, "revealed when most of the snow melted. The body was then discovered by the gentleman back there," – he indicated with his thumb to the man who was still standing on the path with PC Gibson.

"How did he discover that?" questioned Armstrong, given that the body was in such an awkward position.

"He saw it from the other side. Apparently, he came down to check if the river had melted so that he and his friends could go swimming."

"Swimming!" exclaimed Armstrong, snapping his head back to look at Stokes.

"Yes, apparently they are a swimming club who swim in lakes and rivers all year round. Silly sods, if you ask me."

Cornelius smiled at his constable's assessment.

The three men stepped back from the edge and joined the uniformed officers on the path with Mr. Martin. After appropriate introductions

Martin told Armstrong that he had spotted the body about two hours earlier, when he raised the alarm. There wasn't much else to tell.

"Very well, Mr. Martin, thank you for your help. I'm afraid we'll have to take you back to the station to take a formal statement from you but hopefully it shouldn't take very long. PC Gibson here will accompany you. And thanks again."

As the two men walked away, the inspector turned to James Bell, "Well I suppose, Doctor it is our job to scramble down that bank to see what happened to that poor chap."

Bell gave a resigned smile and took a pair of the overalls offered to him by PC Wilkins and traded them for his hat and coat; Armstrong did the same. Meanwhile, PCs Stokes and Hall set about lashing the lengths of rope to two of the trees that were near the edge of the bank. Once the inspector and the doctor had levered themselves into their overalls, they tied the other end of the ropes around their waist and prepared to lower themselves down the bank.

The constables took up the slack as the two men went over the edge. Although it was only a fifteen-foot drop to the water's edge where the body lay, it was steep and slippery; Armstrong and Bell gradually made their way down, losing their footing on a few occasions but managing to keep their balance. Once at the bottom, the bank flattened out; the man's body had come to rest with his arm on the very edge of the water.

The two men crouched down to inspect the corpse. It was fully clothed; a young man around his late twenties or early thirties; he had a full head of thick black hair and matching beard, both of which had been rendered almost completely white having been subjected to the ice and snow for some time. The length of time could not be fully determined but the corpse's skin was a horrible grey colour which suggested it had been many days, if not weeks.

There was a sickening, gaping wound at the front of the man's head that ran to the middle of his forehead; the blood caused by the wound had long since dried and hardened black, over the man's face and clothing. His eyes were wide open, staring out in a mixture of surprise and defiance.

Cornelius pointed to the wound and made the obvious point, "Presumably the cause of death?"

"I would have thought so," agreed Bell. "It's difficult to say whether it happened as a consequence of him falling, or if it was inflicted on him prior to him finding himself here. I'll know more when we get him back to the morgue."

Armstrong glanced around the immediate vicinity of the body, "There doesn't appear to be the remnants of any blood down here, so my guess would be that it was inflicted elsewhere and he was thrown down here."

The detective went through the man's pockets to see if there was anything that could identify him. He found nothing. Although rigor mortis had long since left the body, it was frozen stiff having been exposed to the freezing temperatures for some time.

"It's difficult to say how long he has been here," said the pathologist.

"Almost impossible," agreed the inspector, "the body has obviously been covered by the snow," – he looked up the bank down which they had scrambled and could just see the heads of his uniformed officers peeping over the top – "and no one could see him from the path above. It was obviously only when the snow melted that the body was revealed to the chap on the other side of the river."

Both men stood up, having completed their initial observations.

"Is there anything more you want to do here, James?" asked Cornelius.

"No, I don't think so," replied Bell, "I need to get him back to the morgue."

"I'll get a couple of these lads down here to move the body." Armstrong looked up, "Harry! Pull me up, will you?!"

Harry Stokes looked over the edge, "Will do, sir!" he shouted.

He and Jimmy Hall heaved their inspector up the bank, while Armstrong's undignified climb was visible only to Doctor Bell and the staring corpse below.

"Thanks," said Cornelius getting up from his hands and knees – Sam Wilkins gave him a rag to wipe his hands – "Have you got anymore overalls?" asked Armstrong.

"Yes, sir," replied PC Wilkins, "I brought a couple more pairs, just in case."

"Good," said Armstrong extricating himself from his own muddy protective-wear, "because these can't be used again in a hurry."

"I need a couple of you lads to go down there and help Doctor Bell get the body back up. In the meantime, I'll go back to the station and get Sergeant Townsend to send a wagon down to move him up to the morgue. Once you are done here, get yourselves cleaned up and I want some door-knocking done in Devonshire Walk to see if anyone remembers seeing anything. Look in on the slaughter house as well, to see if any of their staff are missing."

The three constables acknowledged their superior's instructions and – as Inspector Armstrong walked away – set about looking at one other to see who would be the unfortunate ones tasked with scrambling down the bank to haul the body up.

"Senior man!" declared Harry Stokes, straightening.

His two younger colleagues gave a resigned shrug and reached for the overalls.

Unaware of the discussion above him, Doctor Bell's voice could be heard from below, "When you are ready gentlemen!"

In the hours and days that followed, the police came no nearer to identifying who the unfortunate man was. There were no identification papers on the body; the door to door exercise turned up nothing; the abattoir didn't have any staff absent; and no one had reported any missing persons. It got to the stage where Inspector Armstrong had no choice but to release the story to the local newspapers in the hope that someone would know something.

Armstrong had a natural suspicion of the press; approaching them for help was something he didn't particularly relish – very much a last resort. But needs must and with a deep breath, he prepared to contact the *Carlisle Journal.*

SIXTEEN

Billy Grant had calmed down a little in the few days since his crisis of confidence regarding the extent to which he and his brother had become embroiled in the crimes and schemes conceived by Jack Roberts. He had managed to cut down on his opium consumption, he had reduced his drinking to the point where he would go the odd day where he wouldn't have anything at all, and he had listened to his brother's advice to keep his head down, do as he was told and collect his wages.

The blackmail letter for the bloke at Iredale's Brewery had been delivered safely under the cover of darkness and now he was due on the morning train to Whitehaven to pick up the latest shipment of drugs from McVey. It was the first of what would now become a weekly visit to the western port but no matter, it got him away from Roberts and out of harm's way for the day, so it was no bad thing. The only thing he had to remember was to keep away from *The Albion*. It was Freddie's final instruction to his brother as Billy left their digs.

"I know, I know," said Billy, "I've learned my lesson."

"You better have," said Freddie, "coz we'll both pay the price if you haven't."

With a contrite nod, Billy left his brother, "I'll see you later."

It was shortly after seven o'clock; his train was due to leave at half past and the younger Grant had no idea that this journey would be different – different in that every move he was to make would be observed.

PC Sam Watts was dressed in civvies with a scarf wrapped tightly and his cap pulled down. He had been waiting for over an hour in the shadows of a little alleyway at the bottom of Byron Street from where he could see the Grant's tenement flat in Duggan's Court opposite. Despite the continuing thaw, the temperature was desperate and it was taking all of Sam's concentration not stamp his feet or breath too heavily, for fear that any noise or the sight of his crystallised breath would betray his hiding place and arouse suspicion.

Acting on the information inadvertently supplied by young Denny Brown, and under instruction from Inspector Armstrong, it was Watt's job to track the movements of Billy Grant. If the theory was correct, he would be heading for the station to catch the half past seven train to Whitehaven. Watts had picked out his hiding spot a couple of days earlier. Given the time of the train, he knew that even if Grant did not appear, he could abort his task shortly after half-past, so the task wasn't too onerous. He was however, starting to question the wisdom of taking up his position so early.

As he contemplated nipping further down the alley to relieve himself, his mind was instantly taken off his discomfort when a door opened in Duggan's Court and the purpose of his wait appeared descending the steps onto the cobbles. Sam Watts held his breath and leaned back further into the darkness as Billy Grant crossed Byron Street and passed within ten feet of where he was standing.

After a few seconds Watts appeared; he looked down the street and across to Duggan's Court to check if anyone was around to observe him emerging from his hide. Satisfied that no one was, Sam quickly left the alley and scurried along after Billy Grant, who by this time had made it onto Bridge Street and was heading towards the Irish Gate and the town centre.

Early-morning traders and street vendors created sufficient cover for the constable to follow his unsuspecting quarry at a distance of fifty paces without being detected along Annetwell Street, Castle Street, English Street and then finally into Court Square and to the entrance of the Citadel Station.

The station was its usual hive of activity: fruit and vegetable merchants had already unloaded their produce from the overnight goods train, while sleeper-passengers were just being aroused from their slumber after arriving into the station an hour earlier. The platform bustled with travellers who either waited patiently for their connections to all points, or killed time by keeping the newspaper sellers and coffee vendors in business.

As Billy Grant, queued at the ticket booth, Sam Watts had the tricky task of keeping an eye on him whilst looking out for the man he was to pass the petty criminal onto. Darting his head back and forward between the queue and crowd, Watts finally spotted Inspector Godfrey Parker above a couple of dozen heads. With a final check of the queue to ensure Grant had not seen him, he motioned for Parker to meet in the corner of the station entrance, where he could brief the inspector while still keeping an eye on their subject.

Godfrey had been up since five o'clock preparing for the big day ahead; he had never undertaken anything like this before and nerves and excitement threatened to overwhelm him.

"Good morning, Sam," he said meeting the constable at the spot indicated.

"Morning, Inspector," replied Watts, conscious of Parker's rank, but uncomfortable calling him 'sir' as he would naturally do when addressing Armstrong. His discomfort continued when he set about briefing the senior officer.

"See the man fourth in line at the ticket booth?"

Inspector Parker studied the line, "The one in the black coat and brown hat?"

Parker's comment could have described any number of people milling around the station but once Watts had satisfied himself that the inspector knew who he was talking about, he confirmed, "Yes, that's our man. Billy Grant. I think your task is to take him on from here, Inspector. We believe he will be heading for Whitehaven."

"Yes, Inspector Armstrong briefed me on what was required." There was no suggestion of offence taken by Parker from the police constable; if anything he was reassuring himself that he knew what was required of him. "I bought my own ticket earlier."

For once, Watts was impressed by Parker's forward thinking, "Excellent!" – he realised that his genuine comment may be mistaken as condescending, bordering insubordinate and quickly added, "sir."

One of Godfrey Parker's endearing qualities was that he never took offence at anything, "Thank you," he said.

"Well, I'll leave you to it, Inspector, good luck."

With that, the younger man left Parker to keep an eye on the man that was now next in line to purchase his ticket. A few minutes later, the man in the black coat and the brown hat turned away from the ticket booth and appeared for a moment to be struck by some sort of cataleptic fit; he stood stock still for almost a minute staring at the newspaper bill board that was adjacent to the platform entrance. His reverie was broken by a blast of a conductor's whistle somewhere on one of the platforms. He quickly showed his ticket at the platform gate and hurried through the crowd, away from the main southbound platform to the one at the far end of the station, heading west. Godfrey Parker bought a newspaper and followed Billy Grant's every move at a discreet distance.

For no particular reason other than habit, Billy walked past the first carriage and opened the door to the second. Climbing aboard he nestled down in the corner of the carriage and hunched himself up against the window. It was his regular routine.

As Godfrey Parker followed his man towards the westbound platform, crowds thinned from the scores waiting to travel south on the mainline, to a few dozen heading west on the smaller train. They were sufficient however, to give the elderly policeman cover in his covert operation. Parker saw Grant get on the train from about twenty paces behind and deliberately walked past the door through which he had boarded. Instead, he walked to the furthest point of the same carriage and boarded through the second door. That way, he could enter the carriage and walk back the way and see exactly where Grant was sitting. Godfrey, in turn, could pick his spot where he could observe his quarry throughout the journey.

As he walked backwards through the carriage, Parker saw Grant at the farthest point with his collar turned up and his cap pulled down. This, along with the dozen or so people who were inadvertently jostling each other in the aisle, either lifting luggage overhead or taking their seats, gave Parker sufficient cover to pick a backward-facing seat six rows away from Grant on the opposite side to which he was sitting. He settled down and opened his newspaper; holding it up, it hid his face but allowed him to intermittently peep over top to keep an eye on the young man in the corner of the carriage. With everyone seated, the train lurched into motion.

An uneventful half-hour passed with the train buffeting along seemingly on time. Billy sat with his eyes shut, drowsing in and out of semi-consciousness. Until recently he had always journeyed the previous day to indulge himself at *The Albion*. He wondered if he would encounter any new problems now that he was travelling on the day of the delivery. If he missed McVey, it would be thought that he was in the opium den again, which would mean a beating for him and Freddie. His fearful thoughts were disturbed by the opening of the carriage door to his side.

"All tickets please!" shouted the conductor.

Billy straightened up and reached into a pocket for his ticket, "Are we on time?" he asked.

"Yes," replied the conductor, "there shouldn't be any problems today, son."

As the official moved down the carriage, Billy looked at his fellow passengers: a group of men not much older than himself, who looked as though they would be boarding a merchant ship once they arrived at the port; an old man reading a newspaper; a young family, giddy with excitement, on holiday perhaps; and a stern looking lady dressed in black with two young girls who looked as though they were forbidden to speak lest they would feel her full rebuke.

Billy settled back down to his previous position and waited out the rest of the journey. The conductor was proved correct in his prediction – the train pulled in at the scheduled time, much to Billy's relief. He wasted no time darting off the train, as he had no luggage and was positioned nearest to the door.

This was something Godfrey Parker had not anticipated and he became flustered when he found himself caught up in the melee that was now taking place in the aisle, as passengers reached for luggage and hurried to get off themselves. The situation was compounded by impatient passengers trying to get on the train before those alighting had cleared the aisles. Between trying to pick his way between his fellow travellers, Parker would dip down to see if he could see Grant; he saw him walking through the people waiting to get on and heading towards the exit of the station. It was now his turn to have a crisis of confidence.

Oh dear, if I lose sight of him Cornelius will be so disappointed. I will ruin the whole plan! Spurred on by such thoughts, Godfrey elbowed his way through the crowd aided by several "excuse-me's" and "I-beg-your-pardon's", and made his way off the train and hurried towards the exit.

Once outside, he scrutinised the street for Grant; fortunately the crowd had thinned considerably and with most of the passengers who had disembarked the same train behind him, Godfrey had little difficulty spotting his man walking down the sweeping road towards the docks.

Knowing that Grant would soon be subsumed by the hustle and bustle of the quayside, and with Cornelius's words constantly on his mind – "Keep him close enough so you can see him at all times, Godfrey; but not too close that he might suspect he is being watched" – Parker quickened his pace in order to close the hundred-yard gap that had developed between him and Billy Grant. By the time the young man had reached the heart of the dockside, Parker was less than thirty paces behind.

The colour, noise and smells excited the senses. The sea air and constant squawking of gulls took Godfrey back to his own childhood when the church community used to organise trips to the seaside. He was transported back in time to when he and his sister Dolly and their parents would have a wonderful time. All the excitement of the Charabanc journey to Silloth, where there would be bands playing, carrousels whirling and treats for him and Dolly that made them giddy all day. His mind wandered toward his sister and the length of time it had been since he had visited her and her husband in the north-east.

"Oi! Old timer! Gir'out the way, will ye!"

Godfrey's reverie was broken by a man with a barrow loaded with hessian sacks who was struggling to pick his way through the crowd towards a clipper that was berthed a little way along the quayside.

"This thing weighs a bloody ton!" he added as he made his way past the old man who had been standing in the middle of the walkway daydreaming.

With a sudden feeling of horror, Godfrey realised that his mental wandering had distracted him from his primary task. He frantically looked round the crowd to find the man he had followed from Carlisle: men, women, different colours and ages, different languages – the noise was deafening – merchants, dock workers. *But no Billy Grant!*

Parker started to panic, he walked this way and that, and then back on himself again, spinning around trying desperately to see if he could spot Grant among the sea of faces.

Nothing.

He glanced idly around in futile desperation believing he had ruined everything; to the ships, to a pub – *The Duke of Cumberland* – to the dockside warehouses. Suddenly, his head snapped back to the tavern in a violent double-take. There in the window sat Billy Grant! Godfrey stood in relief, his heart beating almost out of his chest.

He waited several minutes in order to calm down before entering the pub himself. His entrance – ten minutes after his man – never raised any suspicion, either amongst Grant himself, or anyone else. Even though it was not yet lunchtime, the tavern was close to being full. Parker couldn't believe his good fortune in spotting Grant in the window, such was the mass of humanity both outside and now inside the pub. It had worked out perfectly for Parker, not that he ever intended to share his stroke of good fortune with his colleagues.

He ordered a cup of coffee and a sandwich, and indicated to the landlord that he would be sitting in the far corner of the pub – at the furthest point away from the oblivious Grant who was sitting looking eagerly out of the front window. Godfrey picked his way through a group of raucous sailors to the vacant part of a bench he had his eye on.

"Come and sit down here, old timer," said a man hitching over to make the space bigger. On his lap sat a young woman; on her head sat his seaman's cap. The two were clearly enjoying each other's

158

company. "I'm sure Lizzy here can find you a friend to keep you company if you like!"

The two giggled at the crudity of the man's suggestion. It happened to be lost on the innocent Parker.

"No thank you," he said taking the seat, much to their continued amusement.

After a few minutes a waitress brought over a tray with a pot of coffee and an appetising-looking ham sandwich. Godfrey was thankful for the refreshment, given the early hour of his departure. Thankfully the couple next to him carried on their business and left him to his. He concentrated hard on watching Billy Grant from across the pub, determined not to let him out of his sight again.

After around fifteen minutes he noticed that Grant had relaxed in his seat and for the first time, sat back from the window. It was as though he had seen what he was looking for and sure enough, seconds later, a man entered the pub carrying a seaman's bag and went straight over to Grant. The two sat for a while in private conversation – there was no way Parker could hear what they were saying given the distance between them and the noise level in the tavern – before the man got up and left, leaving Billy Grant with the bag.

Godfrey had a desire to follow the man but remembered Cornelius had instructed him to keep his eye on Grant the whole time. Furthermore, Armstrong had predicted that Grant would meet someone and collect a bag from him. It had played out exactly as his colleague had suggested, Parker felt the most prudent course of action would be simply to keep an eye on Grant the whole time.

Billy Grant looked up at the clock that hung behind the bar every five minutes; he had now been in the pub for almost two hours. It was shortly before one o'clock when he finally finished his drink, slapped the empty tankard back on the table, slung the bag over his shoulder and got up to leave. In the far corner – partially hidden by the bar – Parker saw his man shaping to move and followed suit.

"Not stopping, old fella?" said the man next to him, "Lizzie's friend hasn't arrived yet!" He and his companion laughed at the inuendo.

159

"No, I have to leave I'm afraid," said Godfrey, politely touching the brim of his hat.

His words and gesture made the two laugh all the more.

Parker hurried out of the *Duke of Cumberland* and saw Billy Grant heading back through the dock area towards the hill that led up towards the railway station. Having checked his timetable earlier, he knew that there was a Carlisle-bound train at half past one. Convinced that this is where Grant was heading, Godfrey held back a little, following him at a greater distance. Inspector Parker was extremely pleased with himself having almost completed the task set for him by his colleague.

"Cornelius will be delighted, I'm sure," he said out loud.

He glanced to his right to see a woman by a fruit stall looking at this man who was talking to himself. Godfrey touched the brim of his hat by way of an apology and walked on.

SEVENTEEN

As the black-clad figures stood at the cemetery gates at the top of Manor Road, Cornelius Armstrong – as discreetly as he could – observed them from his position across the street. There were between thirty and forty people: an eclectic mix of young women and men of varying ages, waiting for the hearse to arrive and the service to begin at St John's, adjacent to the graveyard.

The coroner had recorded a verdict of death by suicide. The backlog of funerals – mainly of poor and elderly due to the brutal winter – had been cleared and the body of Ester Sanderson had finally been released for burial.

As he assessed the crowd of mourners, Cornelius wondered how Godfrey Parker was getting on in his own observations of Billy Grant. He had briefed him the previous evening as to what he was expecting; there was a lot riding on Parker but it was impractical for Armstrong himself to undertake the task, and it was unfair to ask one of the junior officers. Having discussed the matter with Chief Constable Henry Baker, it was decided to entrust the normally hapless Parker with the duty. Armstrong tried not to think about his colleague making a mess of the task; after all, even if he did lose Grant or miss the anticipated pick-up, there was still the opportunity intercept Grant and his brother when Billy returned to Carlisle.

Armstrong's train of thought regarding the task of his colleague was broken and his own duty was brought back into sharp focus when a solitary figure appeared, turning the corner at the bottom of the street. The man's appearance caused the crowd of mourners to cease their desultory mumbling as they turned as one to see the funeral director – dressed in the customary black top hat and matching frock coat, and making exaggerated movements with a long walking cane – begin his march up the middle of the road.

Seconds later two black stallions appeared, drawing the hearse; the coffin clearly seen through the glass sides of the carriage. At the sight of the casket some of the young women who had been chattering amongst themselves moments earlier – apparently not having seen each other for some time – immediately burst into tears. Armstrong assumed them to be school-friends of Ester and it was as if the news of their friend's passing had only become a reality at this moment.

Behind the hearse was another horse-drawn carriage, this time closed and presumably containing Ester's parents. This was confirmed some minutes later when the cortege pulled up outside the church. Four pall bearers appeared from the church's entrance and removed the coffin from the hearse. Hoisting it onto their shoulders they paused as the door of the second carriage opened.

Mr. Sanderson was the first to appear and he turned to help his wife down. Cornelius was pleased to see she had been released from the Garlands Hospital – her admission being a measure he felt was excessive at the time. Sanderson then helped a much older woman out of the carriage; someone Armstrong later learned was Ester's great aunt. Finally, Mrs. Sanderson's trusted maid Mary Ann made up the grieving quartet and they formed up behind the pall bearers who had waited patiently for them. At a discreet distance the group of mourners dutifully filed into church, completing the sad procession. The policeman then waited a further few seconds before sidling through the porch and taking one of the vacant pews at the rear of the church.

Cornelius hated funerals. He saw them as a very private matter, reserved strictly for those closest to the deceased; yet the bereaved had to endure the humiliation of displaying their inner most feelings in full view of those in attendance, some of whom had perhaps never seen the deceased in years, yet – due to the expectations of society – felt compelled to attend in order to 'pay their respects.' He hated the hypocrisy and most of all, he hated attending himself.

From his position in church, he looked forward towards the back of the congregation and wondered how many of those in attendance wanted to be here because they genuinely cared about Ester; how many were in attendance because they felt they ought to be there; and how many had turned up simply to gawp at the family's anguish.

He himself was there as part of his duty; it was something he hated most of all: attending funerals in his official capacity. The purpose was predominantly to observe those in attendance in order to see if it could open up any further lines of enquiry. After all, in this case, although the coroner declared a verdict of suicide, there was still the further question of Ester being assaulted before her death and possibly being forced upon before that.

There were several empty benches in front of Cornelius – between him and the back of the congregation who filled half of the seating in church. The congregation appeared to be split into three distinct groups. First were Ester's parents, family members and those closest to her. From his observations as they filed into church, Armstrong saw that they all wore the same blank expression: they looked all cried out and were in the early stages of accepting their loss, however unbelievable in still seemed.

The second group consisted principally of younger adults, mainly women but not exclusively. The policeman assumed them to be friends of Ester's, children and schoolfriends she grew up with. Among their number was Matilda Chambers, Ester's dearest friend whom Cornelius had met on the morning of Ester's death. Matilda's arm was linked to that of a young man and Armstrong remembered Matilda and her mother referring to the young apprentice tailor from the Co-op. Mrs. Chambers was also in attendance.

Having been close to Ester and her family at the time of the tragedy, Matilda wore the same expression as that of her friend's parents: staring in unwilling acceptance. This was in contrast to the young people around her, who had obviously not been as close to Ester and until this point, had just been shocked at the news of her death. Seeing the coffin and Ester's parents, had triggered the realisation that this was for real. The horror of knowing that their friend really was dead proved too much for some of the young women present who – feeling a mixture of embarrassed self-consciousness and guilt at losing contact with their friend – were trying to suppress their open sobbing.

It was the third group of people that the detective was most interested in however. They were all men who made up the rear two rows of the congregation, about a dozen in all. Most were late middle-aged or elderly, the two exceptions being Gerald Whitlock, who Armstrong recognised from their previous meetings, and a man who stood beside him. He roughly looked the same age as the younger Whitlock but whereas Gerald was a thin, wiry character, his companion was a chubby individual.

Armstrong also recognised Whitlock's father William and also Herbert Underwood, Chair of the Watch Committee who had been at the Sandersons' house the day Ester was found. There was also another member of the Watch Committee who Cornelius recognised. Like Underwood, George Sowerby was a magistrate; like Whitlock, he was a solicitor.

Armstrong thought it strange that such a group of men should be in attendance. Having heard reference by Sanderson, Underwood and Whitlock in the past to *their club*, he assumed that they were all members and were there to support one of their number in his grief. He also found it interesting that Ester's fiancée Gerald Whitlock had chosen – or perhaps had been asked – to stand alongside them, instead of standing with the family in the front benches.

While he was here, it was Gerald Whitlock that Cornelius was particularly interested in speaking with. He had had to interrupt their first meeting, following the discovery of the body down by the Eden. Armstrong had then followed up this meeting with a further visit to the solicitor's offices on Fisher Street but found Whitlock as unforthcoming as his father had been before him.

When Whitlock was at the Police Station, Armstrong had asked his sergeant to take impressions of Whitlock's hands and fingers. Bill Townsend had done this with the aid of some plasticine pads. When Armstrong returned from the scene of the murder by the river, he compared Whitlock's prints with the photographs of Ester Sanderson's arms, taken at her post-mortem. He satisfied himself that the marks on Ester's arms did not match: Whitlock's fingers were long and bony, whereas the marks on the victims seems much larger and thicker. The policeman was satisfied therefore that Whitlock was not responsible for any violence perpetrated against Miss Sanderson, but there were questions relating to the insurance claims that he still had his suspicions about.

As the service drew to a close, Armstrong slipped out of the church and waited around the side of the building, out of sight. Minutes later the pall bearers appeared, carrying the coffin, followed by the chief mourners and the rest of the congregation. The dozen or so men who sat towards the rear were the last to file out, by which time, the front of the procession was a hundred yards or so, along the path and heading towards the burial site. Gerald Whitlock was the last to appear, along with his friend.

"Mr. Whitlock? Can I have a word?"

Whitlock looked round, startled by the voice that came from over his left shoulder. He was even more startled to see who the owner was.

"What are you doing here?" was the best response he could come up with in the circumstances.

"Oh, just paying my own respects," said Cornelius, secretly enjoying the solicitor's discomfort and pleasantly surprised that he hadn't been spotted by Whitlock or his colleagues before or during the service.

"It is hardly the time or the place." Whitlock was starting to regain some of his self-assuredness.

"Well, I have tried to speak with you on other occasions," said Armstrong.

"I seem to recall it was I who voluntarily presented myself at the Police Station."

"It was and I appreciate that, but when I subsequently tried to reconvene our meeting the following day, I was told you were not available. We still have matters to discuss, Mr. Whitlock."

"I never harmed Est…Miss Sanderson if that's what you are getting at."

"No it isn't," said the inspector, much to the solicitor's surprise, "but I am still investigating the break-ins and the insurance claims regarding your clients."

165

Whitlock hesitated, before blurting out, "Well you obviously haven't heard about the latest burglary that neither involved us or our clients."

It was Armstrong's turn to be wrong-footed. "What burglary?" he asked.

"Another solicitor was broken into yesterday."

"Which solicitor? I'm not aware of anything being reported."

Whitlock squared his shoulder and raised his chin haughtily, "It was Sowerby's – George Sowerby's."

Armstrong had seen Sowerby in the congregation and looked beyond Whitlock and his friend to the see the aforementioned solicitor filing along as part of the human train moving through the graveyard.

"Why wasn't this reported?" he asked.

"I have no idea, Inspector. The matter is nothing to do with our firm. George is simply a friend of ours and he mentioned it to us earlier, didn't he Baldwin?"

Whitlock's companion – who Armstrong noticed had been shifting his weight uncomfortably from side to side throughout his conversation with Whitlock – picked his head up from staring at the ground, "What?" he stumbled, "oh yes, that's right," he added unconvincingly.

"And you are sir?" asked Armstrong.

"Oh, I am sorry, Inspector," interrupted Whitlock, "this is a good friend of mine, Stephen Baldwin."

"How'd 'you do," mumbled Baldwin.

"And what is your connection with the deceased?" asked the policeman.

"Oh, I am just comforting Gerald at this difficult time," replied the rotund young man.

"Well, I'm pleased to see you are holding up well, Mr. Whitlock," said Armstrong, and then addressing them both, "I'll let you two gentlemen get back to your mourning and I will speak with Mr. Sowerby before making further enquiries."

The two men left the detective and hurried along to reach the rear of the line that was still moving towards the furthest point of the cemetery. Armstrong turned, as if to give the impression that he was leaving. Instead he walked around the back of the church from where he could once again, see the line of mourners without being seen himself. He was not surprised to observe Whitlock who, not only hurried to reach the end of the line, but overtake some of his colleagues until he reached George Sowerby. He placed a hand on his fellow-solicitor's arm and the two stopped, allowing those behind to pass. Whitlock then proceeded to talk to Sowerby, whose expression appeared to be a mixture of bemusement and anger. Cornelius smiled knowingly and left the church grounds.

Armstrong was aware that George Sowerby had his offices on English Street, near the court buildings. Instead of making his way back to the station, he decided to make his was to the solicitor's instead.

"Good afternoon, sir," said the clerk as the policeman entered, "can I help you?"

"Good afternoon. My name is Cornelius Armstrong, I am a policeman." He showed him his warrant card.

The man looked a little surprised by the announcement. "Are you here to see Mr. Sowerby, sir? I'm afraid he had to attend a funeral; we won't be expecting him back for a little while yet."

"Well yes, it is Mr. Sowerby I'm here to see," said the detective, "but perhaps you could help me before he returns, Mister...?"

"Crain, sir," said the clerk, "certainly, if I can."

"I am investigating a series of burglaries Mr. Crain and I am given to understand your offices were broken into the night before last?"

Crain looked at the policeman blankly.

"I think there must be some mistake, sir," he said, more than a little confused, "our offices haven't been disturbed."

"Oh really?" said Cornelius, "maybe I have been misinformed. Perhaps I could wait and speak with Mr. Sowerby in order to clear up the confusion."

"You are certainly welcome to stay, Mr. Armstrong, although I am not sure when he might return."

"Perhaps while I wait, you could show me where the strong room is?"

Crain hesitated at the request but saw no reason why he shouldn't acquiesce.

"I'm sure Mr. Sowerby wouldn't mind," he said, reaching in his desk drawer and pulling out a set of keys on a large ring.

He led the inspector along a corridor where he opened a door and descended a set of stone steps and along a short passageway to another door.

"This is the strong room, Inspector," said Crain, "would you like to see inside?"

"Have you been in there yourself recently Mr. Crain?"

"Yes, I check these doors every night and have cause to withdraw and deposit items on a daily basis."

"And have you noticed any disturbance over the past couple of days?"

"None," replied the clerk, evermore confused.

"Then I don't think there is a need for me to look inside," said Cornelius. "Does anyone else have keys for these doors?"

"No, only myself and Mr. Sowerby."

Just then a voice called from above.

"Crain! Crain?"

"That sounds like Mr. Sowerby now, sir," said Crain to Armstrong. Then calling back, "I'm down here Mr. Sowerby, I'll be up presently."

The clerk led the policeman back up the stairs where his employer was standing.

"What were you doing down ther-" Sowerby's face dropped when he saw Armstrong following his clerk up the steps. "Inspector," he said, fighting to regain some composure, "what are you doing here?"

"Hello Mr. Sowerby," said Cornelius nonchalantly, stepping back onto the ground floor, "I'm here because I was told you were the victim of a burglary the night before last."

168

"Oh...erm...yes..." stumbled the solicitor, embarrassed by his clerk's presence. "It was nothing."

"Nothing?" repeated the detective, "I wouldn't describe a break-in as nothing, sir. It appears to be the latest in a series that have taken place over the last several months. In fact yours is the second solicitors to have been broken into in the last few weeks."

"Yes, I'm aware that Whitlock's experienced a similar fate."

"Sir?" said Crain, "I'm not aware of any break-in and nothing seems to have been tak-".

"Yes, I'll deal with this, Crain," interrupted Sowerby, "you carry on and I will speak with Inspector Armstrong in my office."

The confused clerk obeyed his employer and went back to his desk, while his employer led the policeman into his office.

Inspector Armstrong had experienced run-ins with the Watch Committee in the past. Most notably it was Herbert Underwood who questioned Chief Constable Henry Baker's decision to appoint the young Cornelius Armstrong to Inspector six years earlier and despite Armstrong vindicating Baker's decision with some outstanding police work since then, he always sensed a feeling of grudging tolerance rather than respectful admiration from Underwood. Other members of the committee – George Sowerby among them – always appeared keen to fall in line behind the Chairman's views which led to a difficult relationship between the City Police Force and the body they were accountable to.

"So who discovered the break-in?" Cornelius didn't wait for the solicitor to close the door of his office behind him.

"Err...I did," replied Sowerby with some uncertainty.

"I inspected the door leading to the strong room and there was no sign of any damage."

"No, I don't think they actually got into the strong room because nothing was taken."

"So how do you know there was a break-in at all?"

"Well, I must have foolishly left one of the windows open the other night and there were footprints on the window sill where someone had clambered through and then out again."

Armstrong was playing to scene for all it was worth by writing down what Sowerby was saying in his notebook.

"So why didn't they attempt to break into the strong room and the safe?"

"Perhaps they were disturbed."

"Mmm," the policeman continued writing.

"And why didn't you report this attempted burglary Mr. Sowerby?"

"I…err…didn't have time," replied Sowerby, weakly.

"So just to re-cap then: you left the window open; you came in the following morning to find footprints on the sill; you checked the strong room and found that nothing was missing; you assumed the would-be burglars had been disturbed, although you don't know by whom; and you neither mentioned the sequence of events to your clerk nor reported the matter to the police." Armstrong looked up from his notebook to deliver his final blow, "This despite the fact that you are a member of the Watch Committee and a City Magistrate."

"By the time Crain arrived, the matter had gone clean out of my head," replied Sowerby, compounding his position, "we are extremely busy at the moment as our Senior Will Writer has disappeared, blasted fellow. It's all hands to the pump right now as we pick up the slack and try to deal with the work that is mounting up. By the time Crain arrived for work I was engrossed in something else.

"What's more, I knew when I had time, I would report the matter to Inspector Parker who I believe has been leading on the case."

"Yes, well I'm just helping him out, but I am due to speak with him this afternoon so I will apprise him of this latest development. I'll show myself out Mr. Sowerby and thank you for your time." As Armstrong turned to leave, he hesitated, "Oh, I nearly forgot – I don't suppose you are insured with one of the syndicates at Lloyds, are you?"

Sowerby couldn't hide his shocked expression, "Yes we are as a matter of fact, how did you know that?"

"Oh, no matter," said Cornelius dismissively, "thank you again."

The detective left the solicitor to contemplate his position by closing the door of his office. On his way out he paused at the desk of Mr. Crain and asked if it was usual practice for his employer to check the doors and windows before closing up the building. He also asked who was first to arrive each morning. The confused Crain gave him the answers he was expecting.

Cornelius glanced over his shoulder at the closed door to Sowerby's office and smiled to himself.

"Thank you, Mr. Crain, you've been most helpful," he said as he left.

EIGHTEEN

"This is excellent work, Godfrey!"

It was now shortly after four o'clock and Cornelius Armstrong was at his office, having returned to the station from Sowerby's office earlier in the afternoon. When Inspector Godfrey Parker arrived back himself, Cornelius was eager to hear of his day's work. That morning, PC Sam Watts had reported to Armstrong that he had followed Billy Grant from his home to the station where he had passed him over to Parker. As Armstrong had been distracted with the funeral and then his encounter with Whitlock and Sowerby, he hadn't given much thought to his colleague's exploits. Once he returned to his desk however, the importance of Parker's mission came back to him. He had been fearful twenty-four hours earlier that he was asking too much of his elderly colleague. His fears were assuaged when Parker briefed him on his adventure.

He told Armstrong how he had shadowed Grant on the train to Whitehaven and followed him down to the docks – he avoided telling him about the point where he lost him in the crowd and was fortunate to spot him in the window of the pub. Once in the tavern, Parker told his colleague of the appearance of the second man with the bag. Godfrey even had the foresight when returning to Carlisle –travelling once more in the same carriage as Grant while retaining a discreet distance – of following him back to the brothers' tenement in Caldewgate. From there, Parker returned to the station.

"I can't compliment you enough on this Godfrey," continued Armstrong, "this is exactly what I had hoped we would find."

"I was amazed to see everything unfold just as you had predicted Cornelius," replied the senior inspector, proud of his work.

"I think it is now time to increase the activity in this drugs matter."

"What do you have in mind?" asked Parker.

"Let us take this conversation into the Chief Constable's office."

The two walked along the corridor and knocked on the door of Henry Baker. Armstrong entered; Parker – who was not as familiar or confident when dealing with his superior officer – followed him in.

"Sir," said Armstrong, "there have been some significant developments in the drugs matter."

Baker gestured for the two to sit down and Armstrong updated him on the days' events.

"What do you propose?" asked the chief constable.

"We now have the supply route of the drugs, the distribution hub and the various destinations around the city. And we also know who the operatives are on the ground."

"But we don't know who is behind it all and who is benefiting from it?" questioned Baker.

"And we are not likely to," answered Armstrong, "these people are always far removed from getting their hands dirty. I suggest to get to them, we need to first bring the goffers in for questioning. I would like to raid the Grants' tenement tomorrow morning and seize the drugs. We could also do the same at the Robert Street premises. Let's see what effect that will all have on the operation."

Baker thought for a while and nodded slowly, "Very well, Cornelius, let us see what that brings."

"Thank you, sir," replied Armstrong, standing to leave, "I'll organise something for tomorrow morning. As an afterthought he added, "I also need to brief you on the thefts, sir. There was an interesting development today."

"Very well," repeated Baker, indicating that Armstrong should re-take his seat, "tell me now."

Inspector Parker had been sitting quietly throughout the exchange and looked to his superior officer for permission to leave.

"Yes, you can go," said Baker, "and thank you for some excellent work Godfrey."

"Thank you, sir," said Parker.

Neither party could ever remember such a compliment. The elderly inspector was delighted as he left the office.

"Credit where it is due," said Baker as the door closed, "I never thought he had the gumption."

"I agree," said Armstrong, "he's done and terrific job today."

"Now what about this other matter?"

Armstrong proceeded to tell the chief constable about his experience at the funeral, his encounter with Whitlock and the subsequent, ridiculous conversation with George Sowerby.

"Sowerby? He's a member of the Watch Committee." Baker was incredulous.

"And a magistrate," added Armstrong.

"What do you think is behind it?"

The inspector hesitated, knowing that what he was about to say could have serious complications.

"Not necessarily *what* but *who*," said Cornelius, "I believe the younger Whitlock – whether his father knows about it or not – is making fraudulent insurance claims. From what I witnessed earlier, either Sowerby is also involved or he is covering for Whitlock for some reason."

"These men you saw at the funeral," said Baker thoughtfully, "how many were there?"

"I would say about a dozen," replied Armstrong recalling the congregation. "I recognised the Whitlocks, George Sowerby and Herbert Underwood. The others I didn't know."

"Was Woodward from Iredale's there?"

"I didn't see him," said Armstrong looking quizzically at his superior.

"Umm, just a thought," said Baker by way of an explanation. "I just remember Underwood asking Woodward and myself to his club that time. I wonder if that is anything to do with it?"

"I don't know, Henry," – it was Armstrong's custom to be more familiar with his boss when they were alone and in slightly more relaxed mood – "maybe that is something to bear in mind. Come to think of it, I remember Sanderson, Whitlock *and* Underwood all mentioning something about being in the same club, at various times over the past few weeks. There could be something in that."

"I hope not, Cornelius because this could get very uncomfortable, very quickly. No matter, first things first. Let's deal with these scallywags and the drugs tomorrow and take it from there."

From the Chief Constable's office, Inspector Armstrong went to see Sergeant Townsend on the front desk and asked him to round up as many Bobbies who were either in the station or in the vicinity as possible, and meet him in the briefing room in fifteen minutes.

At the appointed time, PCs Brady, Stokes, Green, McIntyre, Kirk, Riggs, Hall and Gibson, followed Townsend into the room where Armstrong was waiting for them. A series of 'sirs' from each of the men was followed by the detective inviting them to sit down and proceeding to brief them on what was expected the following morning.

"Right lads, some of you have been involved in the drugs case before now. For those of you who haven't, you should know that we are going to bring in two brothers from Caldewgate, Freddie and Billy Grant. At the same time, we are going to lift Jimmy Dunn, the owner of a boarding house on Robert Street."

"What time are we going in, sir?" asked Bobby Green.

"Six o'clock sharp," replied the inspector, "we'll probably catch them asleep but either way, I want it to be quick and clean, with no time for them to raise the alarm."

He had contemplated asking Godfrey Parker to lead on the Robert Street raid but decided against it. He didn't want Parker to blot his copy book and undo all of the good work he had done earlier this day. Instead, he turned to PC Stokes who he had known since his own days as a constable.

"Harry, I want you to take a couple of lads with you to Robert Street bring in this bloke Dunn. Meanwhile, the rest of us will go down to Caldewgate and arrest the Grant brothers. Any questions?" After a few seconds' silence and glancing around the room, "Very well, let's meet back here at half past five tomorrow morning. Now go home and get some rest."

The last task Cornelius himself had to do was to contact Peter Fletcher at the workhouse and ask him to hold the boys in the following morning on some pretext of some sort of census concerning residents of the workhouse. He knew that ordinarily on a Thursday morning after a shipment, the boys would make their way to Robert Street in order to fulfil their duty of distributing bags of opium around the city. If everything went to plan, he and his men would have picked up the Grants and Jimmy Dunn before breakfast and the boys would not therefore be subjected to any risk.

Fletcher was obliging in his request and the policeman went home, exhausted after another busy day. His mind was in a constant whirl these days as he wrestled with the various issues thrown his way. He couldn't remember the last time he went out walking, or bird watching, both solitary past-times he enjoyed immensely. He glanced over at the piano in the corner of his sitting room and realised he had never even attempted that Beethoven manuscript he purchased from Michael Rattigan some weeks earlier.

Cornelius shook his head in tired resignation, knowing that he was in for another restive night. He did however, begin to finally feel an element of excitement – something he hadn't felt in a long time – as his instinct told him he was on the brink of making significant inroads into some of the numerous cases he found himself dealing with. He sensed his suspicions concerning the insurance fraud were gathering more and more traction and would come to a head soon, but it was the drugs scourge that he was focused on for the time being. He knew the following few days could prove pivotal in stopping the flow of opium into the city and with it, see a reduction in the petty crime that resulted from its presence.

Across town, the Grant brothers were also about to settle down for the night. It had been a routine day for the two. Billy had been up early to make what was now his weekly journey to Whitehaven. The boat had been on time, McVey had met him in the appointed place at the appointed hour and he had kept himself out of any trouble, returning the drugs home without incident.

Freddie meanwhile, had spent his usual Wednesday.

At the bottom of Byron Street was a timber merchant, behind which was a small vacant warehouse that had been commandeered by a handful of local rogues who had turned it into a gambling house. It was a decent distance away from the main road, Bridge Street, further away still from the Irish Gate which led into the city proper, and therefore out of the sight and the mind of the authorities who may look unfavourably on such an establishment.

Reuben Hanks was one of the rogues in question but it was in his interest to stay in the shadows. His relationship with Inspector Armstrong was not common knowledge and if it became so, he knew that his credibility amongst the local populace would be damaged beyond repair. That was never going to stop him however from organising sweeps, cards, dice and anything else that could satisfy his contemporaries' vices while relieving them of some of their money. And having the gambling house open on a quiet day in the middle of the week reduced the likelihood of discovery still further.

This had become Freddie Grant's regular destination every Wednesday morning since he had started earning a decent amount of money during the previous twelve months. He had even felt the odd pang of guilt at chastising his brother Billy for succumbing to the temptations of opium, while he was experiencing similar feelings every time he wandered towards the large wooded door and waited for the tiny hatch to open in response to his knocking. The lookout's face would fill the aperture and once he was satisfied it was one of the regulars who was seeking entrance, the little grate would be snapped shut and the larger door it protected would be opened and the patron hurried inside.

Freddie was one of thirty or so who attended that morning and enjoyed a reasonable return on the stakes he placed. From there he went to meet Jack Roberts who he was scheduled to reassure that the increase in the number of opium shipments was under control and the blackmail letter had been delivered to Iredale's Brewery as per his instruction.

"Yeah, regarding that," said Roberts when the two met in *The Globe* that lunchtime, "I think it's best if we just kept that one to ourselves."

"How d'ye mean?" asked Freddie.

"I've been warned off putting the frighteners on the bloke who owns it," replied Roberts cryptically.

Freddie Grant couldn't imagine anyone warning Jack Roberts off over anything.

The Manchester criminal added, "But I reckon we should continue and see if we can get something out of it," – he shook Freddie's cheek between his thumb and forefinger, and delivered a couple of light slaps – "it can act as a nice little sweetener for us lads, can't it Freddie, boy?"

With that, Roberts left Grant sitting at his table wondering what further scrapes he and Billy were going to get into through their connections with this dangerous man. He reflected on his morning, spent first with what could be best described as a group of loveable local rogues, and ending in conversation with a dangerous psychopath who seemed hell-bent on turning Carlisle upside down.

He took his reflections home with him and awaited his brother's arrival from Whitehaven with the latest consignment of opium.

"Everything all right?" he asked Billy as he returned around half past three.

"Yes, I got the drugs all right," replied the younger Grant, lifting the sack off his shoulder and setting it down in the corner of the room.

Freddie sensed there was something else, "But?"

"When I was at the station this morning, the newspaper said an unidentified body had been found by the river. I'm scared it might be that bloke Roberts done in."

Freddie was as shocked as Billy at the thought.

"It couldn't have been, surely," he said, trying to convince himself as much as his brother, "we tipped him over the edge."

"I know," said Billy, "but we never saw him go into the water, did we? And it was dark and snowing, and the river was icy. It maybe just laid there covered till the snow melted and it was discovered."

The older brother knew what Billy was saying sounded plausible. "Well Roberts can't know about it because I was with him at lunch-time. He would've said summut. Let's not think about it and I'll get my sailor's gear out again, ready for tomorrow."

Freddie was trying to make light of the possible implication of the body being their victim by taking Billy's mind off it and referring to his own job the following morning: taking the sack of opium across to Jimmy Dunn, who would then send the young lads out and about. For this task Freddie always wore an old thick jacket and Seaman's cap; with the sack slung over his shoulder, he found that no one looked twice at the sailor obviously home for a few days. It had worked a treat so far – there was no reason to believe it wouldn't continue to do so. Freddie looked at the canvas sack in the corner and gave a crooked smile to himself, knowing that the contents were giving them a good living.

The two brothers turned in that night, content that they had a good thing going. As long as they could find the balance between keeping on Jack Roberts's good side – if he had one, that is – while keeping out of his way as much as possible, nothing could go wrong.

The thought was to be short-lived.

It must have been around six o'clock the following morning when Freddie sensed something was wrong. He was in the dazed state between sleep and consciousness when he thought he heard something scraping or rustling outside. Putting it down to a hazy dream he turned over and continued his slumber.

In actual fact, his sixth sense had not betrayed him. Half an hour earlier, Inspector Armstrong had left the station with five uniformed constables in a horse-drawn police wagon, while three other officers had hung back, waiting to make the shorter journey to Jimmy Dunn's house in Wapping.

Caldewgate was quiet at that time of morning and Armstrong halted the vehicle halfway along Byron Street. He didn't want to take the wagon straight up to Duggan's Court where the brothers lived, for fear of the horse's hooves alerting them or their neighbours to the impending raid. He instructed Eddie Kirk, who was driving the vehicle to stay with it.

"When you hear us breaking in," Armstrong told Kirk in lowered tones, "you bring it forward and we'll get them in the back."

Kirk nodded and his colleagues descended and made their way quietly about a hundred yards along to the street towards the small lane. The dark February morning gave the police officers sufficient cover as they made their way up the steps towards the door of the brothers' flat.

The four uniforms waited for their superior officer to give the signal. Cornelius Armstrong peeled back his coat and his jacket and took out his watch from his waistcoat pocket. He pressed the tiny mechanism on the side and the top flipped open: it was two minutes past six.

"Now," he said calmly.

PC Riggs put his weight behind the sole of his boot as it hammered against the lock. His effort was followed up by Ben McIntyre and Jimmy Hall simultaneously barging their shoulders against the weakened door and crashing through into the modest dwelling. All four uniforms were inside within an instant with their inspector close behind.

"Not in here, sir," shouted Green.

"The other room!" Armstrong ordered.

The verbal instruction was unnecessary as his men never broke stride, rushing across to the one internal door.

"Police!" they yelled as they barged through.

Freddie Grant was just getting to his feet, having been given a rude awakening by the cacophony of noise seconds earlier. Billy had been sleeping soundly and was only starting to stir confusedly. Neither stood any chance of resisting the officers as two each apprehended them – Green and McIntyre throwing Freddie back down on his cot – handcuffed them and marched their groggy prisoners back through into the main room where Inspector Armstrong was waiting for them.

"Fredrick and William Grant, you are being arrested on a charge of smuggling and profiting from the sale of illegal opium."

The brothers were in no position to challenge the detective's assertion as he was standing beside the large sack which contained the contraband. Both sunk their head between their shoulders as their minds began to race, wondering what the wider implications of their arrest would be.

Outside, the clopping of the horse's hooves could be heard as PC Kirk manoeuvred his wagon around in the tight alleyway. Kirk himself appeared in the open doorway moments later.

"Ready when you are, sir," he said.

"Right," said Armstrong, "get these two and that bag back to the station – I'll hang around here for a bit and meet you back there."

Kirk grabbed the canvass sack while his colleagues manhandled their submissive prisoners down the steps and into the wagon, much to the curiosity of a few neighbours who had now appeared at their windows following the commotion. As the vehicle pulled away, Armstrong set about searching the tenement to see if there was anything else that might be of interest.

The dwelling was dark and spartan: a couple of unmatching seats on the stone floor pointed towards an old stove, while a table was propped against the wall under a small uncovered window – the only natural light in the flat. The bedroom was of a similar standard: roughly the same size it had two cots at either side of the room with a small unit against one wall on top of which was a battered porcelain washing bowl. In the corner of each of the two rooms was a hanging rail that had been fixed to the wall. Various items of clothing were draped over them. Armstrong went through the pockets of each item but found nothing of interest.

He was about leave when he saw the table under the window had two long drawers positioned under the top. He slid them open and found they were full of old and desultory items thrown in untidily: pieces of string, three or four stubby little pencils, a screwdriver and pair of plyers, bits of cloth with needle and thread, small pieces of litter that hadn't been cleaned out in months. Cornelius rummaged through the loose items with his hands and discovered a grubby looking writing pad with scribbled notes throughout. He picked the book up and started flicking through its pages. As he did so, something came to mind and when he picked out the words *shure* and *thowsand* among the scrawling, he realised what that something was.

NINETEEN

The previous day, everything had been fine. There was the slight worry about the reported discovery of a body by the river, but there was nothing that could implicate them with anything. Now however, just a few hours later, Freddie and Billy Grant were sitting in cells in the rear of the police station and it was beginning to dawn on them both that their world was about to come crashing down. Both were wondering how they could have been found out. Freddie inwardly cursed his stupid, unreliable brother – he probably did something that gave the game away. But then he thought about his own shortcomings and vices – if he was that concerned about Billy's inability to carry out the task, why didn't he do it himself. In his heart of hearts, he knew the answer.

For his part, Billy was thinking similar thoughts – what had he done this time that had betrayed his mission? He must have done *something* wrong although his conscience was clear – he wasn't aware of doing anything deliberately. He sat on his bench dejected, believing that he had let Freddie down; he himself was unaware of his brother's regular Wednesday activities, something that Freddie – sitting in the next cell – was now not particularly proud of.

As well as wrestling with their own inner demons, both of them had the same thought at the back of their minds: the black, terrifying cloud in the form of Jack Roberts hung over their arrest. Everything that they had become embroiled in had originated from Roberts. How could they avoid implicating him? And what would the consequences of doing so be?

The four cells in the rear of the station all had open bars. The occupants of each cell could therefore see forward and to the side. The two brothers sat in separate cells, while PC Bobby Green stood outside to ensure the prisoners did not speak to one another. The act was regulation but, in this case, unnecessary. Despite their close proximity, and despite the fact that the two could see each other, both sat in silence with their heads down. They did however look up simultaneously when there was movement outside the cells. The figure of Jimmy Dunn was being marched down the corridor towards them flanked by two uniform officers. One unlocked the handcuffs Jimmy was wearing and he was ushered into one of the vacant cell beside Freddie. The two exchanged glances of resignation and Jimmy sat down.

A few minutes later, a sergeant appeared in the corridor with a tray.

"Here's some breakfast for you lads," he announced as he walked towards them, "you probably haven't had time to get any."

One by one, PC Green opened each cell door and Sergeant Townsend invited each prisoner to take a plate containing a piece of buttered toast and a mug of tea.

"Inspector Armstrong will be back to question you later," he said as he left the last cell.

However welcome the gesture of breakfast was, this last comment forced the criminals' minds back into a whirl. What would he ask? What could they say? – they each looked at one another, obviously thinking the same thing – *can I rely on them to say the same thing as me?*

Armstrong returned an hour after the prisoners had been brought in. Bill Townsend also provided the detective with tea and toast. As he was finishing his breakfast, the chief constable arrived and popped his head into the inspector's office on the way to his own.

"How did it go, Cornelius?"

"Very good, sir," replied Armstrong, "went like clockwork with no hitches. The three of them are in the cells now."

"How do you propose questioning them?" asked Baker.

"I thought about having a short session with each one to build up the picture and see how their stories match up as we go along. There is another thing I found, sir."

Henry Baker's tufted eyebrows rose and his forehead creased in curiosity.

"I found a notepad at the Grants' place. The paper and the writing match the blackmail letters that were sent to Iredale's Brewery. This is something else I am going to pursue with them."

"Excellent work Cornelius," said Baker, with a smile, "keep me abreast of developments."

"Will do, sir." Armstrong wiped the corners of his mouth with a napkin and tweaked the horns of his moustache. Taking his mug and plate back to the kitchen area he addressed Sergeant Townsend, "Thanks for that Bill, it was just what the doctor ordered. Now, I think we'll have the first of our guests join me in the interview room."

"Very well, sir," replied Townsend, "which one do you want to see first?"

"I think I'll start with Freddie, bring him through in five minutes."

"Will do, sir."

Cornelius set himself up in the room between his own office and that of Godfrey Parker's, which was used for interviews, briefings and in the case of young Denny Brown the previous week, recovery.

Five minutes later Sergeant Townsend led Freddie Grant down the corridor towards the room. Behind the prisoner was PC McIntyre who followed him into the room and sat on the chair by the door, while Townsend left them to it.

Freddie had encountered the local police on a few occasions during his lifetime. Usually he had been pulled up by uniformed officers and warned about minor misdemeanours and on the three occasions he had actually been brought into the station, the first two saw him questioned by an old man – he couldn't remember his name – who was easily fobbed off. The final time however – about eighteen months ago – he had been arrested for organising an illegal cockfight in the back room at the *Goliah*. It was this man, Armstrong, who questioned him about it. Grant found him a completely different proposition to the other bloke. It resulted in him being locked up in the County Gaol for a month.

The inspector looked up as the procession entered, "Take a seat," he said casually to the prisoner who was in no position to refuse. Once

184

Townsend had closed the door behind him, Armstrong paused for effect before beginning.

"Now then Freddie, why don't you take me through how you came by these bags of opium."

"Whaddya mean bags, there's only one bag," replied the criminal.

"There may only be one bag today but this has been a regular thing for many a long month hasn't it?"

Grant shrugged, "I dunno, I just came by it."

Armstrong gave a crooked smile, "You just came by it?" he repeated, "you can do better than that surely?"

Grant remained silent.

"All right then, where did you come by it?"

"Some bloke in 'Blue Lugs' the other night. I didn't know what was in the bag at first."

"And how did you pay for it? What were you going to do with it? What was his name? Why did you take a bag from a bloke when you didn't know what was in it?" Armstrong didn't wait for any answers to his staccato questions. Instead he changed the subject.

He produced the blackmail letters written to Iredale's "Did you write one of these?" he asked.

"No," lied Grant.

Armstrong then lifted a file that was sitting in front of him to reveal the writing pad he found in Grant's flat, "How do you explain the matching paper and writing on this then? I found this in your drawer half an hour ago."

Silence.

"They were only supposed to be a joke." Freddie was grasping at any straw he could think of.

"A joke? It threatened Woodward's business and the people who work there; the man has taken to his bed with worry; and you think it was just a joke? So when he came up with the money, you were just going to give it back to him and explain it was just a joke?"

Grant couldn't say anything.

Armstrong didn't wait for him to, "I'm further charging you with attempted blackmail," – then, turning to PC McIntyre – "Take him away." The uniformed policeman and the prisoner were both surprised. He had only been there a quarter of an hour. "Bring Jimmy Dunn in," he added to the inspector.

McIntyre opened the door and indicated to Grant to get up. A bizarre feeling of relief came over the prisoner as the interview had not been as painful as he had expected and significantly, nothing had been mentioned about the body found recently near the river. This suggested that no connection had been made between it and him and Billy.

Jimmy Dunn and Billy Grant were sitting in their cells, heads bowed, when Freddie appeared in front of his police escort. They were equally amazed, believing that each of them would be questioned for an hour or more.

"Inspector Armstrong wants to see Dunn," said McIntyre to his colleague Bobby Green who was still standing guard outside the cells.

Green opened the cell and gestured to Dunn to follow his colleague. He also told Freddie to enter the vacated cell rather than resume his original position between it, and the one occupied by his brother. There was now an empty cell between Freddie and Billy, and just to emphasise the point PC Green announced, "No talking."

Freddie sat on the bench vacated by Jimmy and bowed his head. His brother watched him through the bars and wondered what had been said between him and Armstrong; he also wondered why the interview had been so short.

Their confederate meanwhile was now in the interview room.

"Jimmy Dunn," announced the detective, "take a seat and tell me what you know about the opium shipments."

"I don't know what you mean," offered Dunn, not really believing that that was going to do him any good.

"Yes you do," – Armstrong was not in the mood – "you own the boarding house on Robert Street where Freddie Grant brings you a bag of opium every Thursday morning after it has been picked up from Whitehaven the previous day. You then co-opt a group of children to distribute bags of the drugs around the city for a fee. Don't play games with me son – you are in it up to your neck and if you don't help me, it will be very long time before you see the light of day again."

What colour that was left in the face of Jimmy Dunn drained away upon hearing how much the policeman knew about the operation.

"I…I,"

"You, what?" pressed the policeman.

"You seem to know it all," – Dunn was talking to his lap – "I don't think there is much I can add."

"Oh, but there is isn't there? How did you become involved in the first place?"

Dunn assumed that what information the inspector was in possession of, had been gleaned from Freddie minutes earlier. He didn't see the point of denying anything further therefore.

"Freddie came to me a while back and said there was easy money to be made from the drugs that were coming in. He asked if I could hold it until he got it shifted. I told him I could do better than that and could get a few lads from the workhouse to take it out. Nobody would suspect kids."

"Somebody did," interrupted Armstrong, "one young lad was beaten up and robbed last week."

"I didn't know that," said Jimmy, quite shocked at the news.

"You didn't much care either I suppose," countered the policeman. "Who is behind all this then?"

This was the question all three villains were dreading.

"How do you mean?" asked Dunn pathetically.

"Well those two idiots haven't got the gumption or the connections to come up with a scheme like this have they? And you look like a bone-idle lump – so who was the brains behind it all?"

"I don't know," said Dunn unconvincingly, "Freddie just told me about it and I thought it was an easy way of making a few quid."

"So who pays you and the boys?"

"I pay the boys."

Armstrong paused having only heard half of the answer. "And who pays you?" he repeated politely.

"Erm, well I think Freddie gets the money and he gives me my share."

"And where does he get it from?"

"You'll have to ask him."

Armstrong turned to the letters and the pad, unsure as to whether Dunn was involved in the blackmail scam. "Do you know anything about these?"

Dunn leaned over the table to see what the policeman was referring to. For the first time, there was conviction in his voice when he replied, "No, I've never seen them before. I know nothing about them."

"Very well," – the inspector again addressed the constable – "take him away and bring the other one."

It had been another equally short interview but Armstrong knew they were just the pre-cursor to the main event: he sensed that Billy Grant was always going to be the weakest link in the gang and he would be unable to resist the pressure of questioning. He decided to add to Billy's discomfort.

"PC McIntyre," he called down the corridor as the uniformed officer was leading Jimmy Dunn back to his cell – McIntyre turned – "just give me a few minutes before you bring the other one through.

"Will do, sir," replied McIntyre and resumed his escort.

Such was the layout of the corridor and the cells; all three prisoners also heard the instruction. Armstrong intended them to. Billy Grant was now nearly beside himself with worry. *What did it all mean? Why had the copper conducted such short interviews with Freddie and Jimmy? What did they tell him? How long would he be in with him? What could he tell him?*

He sat back down after preparing himself to be led away; fidgeting in his seat he rubbed his head with both hands: itchy, nervous, withdrawal symptoms threatening to engulf him. Two cells along, Freddie sensed his brother's discomfort. He was also nervous about what he might say. Like Armstrong, Freddie knew that Billy was the weaker man and it was unlikely that he would be able to keep anything from the policeman.

Finally, after a further five minutes – a five minutes in which Armstrong didn't do anything, he just waited – PC Green unlocked Billy's cell.

His colleague McIntyre announced, "All right son, it's your turn."

Billy looked up and thought that this is how it must feel when someone is being taken to the gallows. He felt the tea and toast sitting uneasily in his stomach as he walked along the corridor behind the policeman. Freddie and Jimmy watched the procession helplessly; once the door closed behind them, they had to leave him to his fate.

Inside, Inspector Armstrong greeted him with the same courtesy as the others, "Hello Billy, take a seat."

The younger Grant sat down, already drained from the morning's experience.

"Now then," said the detective gently, "I want you to tell me about the sacks of opium."

Billy sat silently with his head bowed. Armstrong gave him a few moments.

"You are in trouble, Billy, there is no getting away from that. This is your chance to reduce that trouble and ensure that you and your brother don't take all of the responsibility for what's been going on."

"How do you mean?" It was the first time Billy had spoken.

"I mean that you and Freddie are just a couple of runners and I think there are bigger fish in this pond. I don't believe you organised these shipments yourself – I think someone else did it for you and that's who I'm more interested in."

Billy's mind was racing: *Freddie can't have told him about Jack Roberts or anyone else – why would he be asking me? Or is it a trick – he maybe knows everything else and he just wants me to confirm it.*

Armstrong resumed, "Yesterday you left your house just after seven o'clock; you walked to the Citadel Station where you caught the train to Whitehaven at half past. In Whitehaven you walked down to the docks and sat waiting in the *Duke of Cumberland* pub, where shortly afterwards you met a man who gave you the bag of opium. You then returned to your flat with it later that afternoon and we picked you up this morning before Freddie could deliver it to Jimmy Dunn's boarding house."

As the copper recited the series of events, Billy gradually looked up from his lap in amazement at his knowledge; by the end, he was staring open-mouthed at what he was hearing. He knew there was no point in denying it, such was the accuracy.

"How did you know all that?" he said through his astonishment.

"It doesn't matter how I know," replied the inspector, "I just do. Now what I want from you are the names of the people who put you up to it."

"Freddie just asked me to do it," he replied tamely.

Armstrong decided to explore another avenue. He produced the blackmail letter and the note book from under the file.

"Which one of these letters is yours?"

Again, the younger Grant was incredulous. He started to feel nauseous. Knowing it was pointless trying to deny any knowledge or involvement, he pointed to the second letter.

"Why did you extend the deadline for the money?" asked Armstrong.

"I don't know."

"What do you mean, you don't know? There must have been some reason for it. You were either going to blackmail the brewery or you weren't. Why wait from January to February?"

"We were told to." Billy was weakening by the second.

"Who by?"

"I mean, *I* was told to." He was sweating profusely by this point.

"Who by?" Armstrong repeated.

Silence.

The policeman let his prisoner sweat a little more as he turned his attention to the note book. There were scribbles and notes throughout in each brother's hand. He flicked through the pages and noticed a recurring name relating to meetings and apparent instructions.

"Who's Jack?" he asked as he skimmed over the pages, almost to himself. He then saw a later entry that included the individual's surname; his piercing blue eyes looked up from the book and stared at Billy Grant once more, "Jack Roberts?"

TWENTY

After a few seconds of hearing the name, Billy Grant starting sobbing; this developed into slight convulsions, which caused PC McIntyre to sit forward in his chair. Seconds later he and Armstrong were on their feet as the prisoner was having some sort of fit; the two were just in time to catch him before he fell to the floor. They laid him flat and moved the table and chairs out of the way – Billy was shaking and murmuring incoherently. At least he was conscious.

"We should take him up to the Infirmary," said Armstrong, "just in case. Go and get the wagon."

"Yes, sir," said McIntyre hurrying from the room while Cornelius stayed with the prisoner who was now the patient.

From down the corridor, PC Green and the two prisoners heard the commotion, as did Chief Constable Baker who emerged from his own office.

"*WHAT'S GOING ON?*" shouted Freddie concerned about his brother.

Baker went to find out for himself and returned a few seconds later to update the elder Grant, "Your brother has had some sort of fit, it would appear. It doesn't seem serious but we are taking him up to the infirmary just as a precaution. In the meantime, you men can't stay here – we will take you over to the County Goal where they have better facilities to hold you."

Freddie Grant had spent a little time in the Gaol and he would dispute the chief constable's last comment but that is not the reason he protested.

"*Wait!*" he shouted, "I need to speak with Inspector Armstrong again.

Baker was taken aback by the request, "Why?" he asked.

"There is some information I need to give him."

Freddie suspected that either Billy had told the detective about Jack Roberts, or the policeman had spotted his name in the notebook. Either way, he wouldn't be surprised if the sight of Roberts's name was the cause of Billy's condition. In the hour or so since his own short interview, Freddie had reflected on the situation and concluded there was no escape from Armstrong finding out about Roberts's involvement. Rather than put his vulnerable brother through anymore torment, he decided the best approach would be to come clean, regardless of the possible consequences.

"Very well," said Henry Baker, "I'll let him know."

As he walked back, two officers were helping Billy out of the office and heading towards the main entrance where, presumably, the vehicle was waiting to take him to hospital. Grant was actually on his feet, having seemingly recovered some composure but the two uniforms were keeping him upright. Cornelius was also in the small party.

"Inspector?" called Baker – Armstrong looked round – "how is he?"

"I think he'll be all right sir. It's almost as though he has had some sort of fright attack – if there is such a thing. I think it's best if we take him away and have him checked just in case."

"Very wise," agreed Baker. "The brother wants to speak to you again."

"Does he?" said Armstrong with a half-smile, looking beyond his superior officer in the direction of the cells, "what might that be about?"

"He just said he needed to give you some information."

"Very well, thank you sir, I'll take it from here."

Baker returned to his office.

Armstrong followed McIntyre and Sam Watts – who happened to be in the station at the time of the commotion – as they carried Billy Grant to the wagon.

"You two lads take it from here," he said, "I need to speak with one of the other prisoners."

"Very good sir," said Watts, as he climbed in the back with Grant.

As McIntyre slapped the reigns on the horse's rump to signal the start of their journey, Cornelius re-entered the building and headed straight back towards the cells. He nodded at PC Green who immediately reached for the keys and unlocked the cell containing Freddie Grant.

"You know the way," said Armstrong standing aside and falling in line behind the prisoner.

Once they were back in the interview room Freddie saw the open notebook on the table and read Jack Roberts's name upside down. He knew instantly that this is what would have terrified his brother.

"So," said Armstrong, retaking his seat, "what have you got to tell me?"

"How's Billy?" asked the concerned brother.

"I think he should be all right. He had some sort of attack but he was calming down by the time we moved him outside. I wanted to send him up to the infirmary anyway, just to make sure."

"Thank you." It wasn't very often that these words passed the lips of Freddie Grant.

"So what was it?" asked Cornelius again.

Grant looked at the note book on the table, "It's about him," he said with a nod.

Armstrong took a moment to realise what Freddie was talking about and then followed his gaze to the page in front of him. "Who, this Jack Roberts?"

"Yeah, he's the bloke you want. He's behind it all."

"Explain."

"I first met him about eighteen months ago. I'd been having a drink in the *Goliah* with Jimmy," – he thumbed over his shoulder indicating towards the cell containing his friend Jimmy Dunn – "when he just appeared. Normally, people like me know each other but I had never seen him before. It turns out he was from Manchester and he came over and asked if I wanted to get in on various plans he had going. 'A few quid in it for you' he said. It started off pretty low-level stuff."

"Started off?" questioned the detective.

"A couple of break-ins here and there; maybe strong-arming a few people who were late paying their debts," explained Grant.

"But then?"

"Bit by bit, things got more serious. First, the strong-armed tactics led to threatening tenants who were struggling to pay their rent; this led to demanding protection money from shops and pubs. Then he told us about how he used to get opium shipped into Manchester and how we could all get rich off the back of it.

All we had to do was find out who would be interested in buying it – once that was done, we would go and get the stuff off the ship in Whitehaven. Jimmy said he could get a load of young lads who were always hanging about to distribute it for us. We all just got into the routine of doing it; demand increased and the money started to roll in."

"And no doubt you weren't bothered about the consequences it was having in the city?" asked Armstrong, angry at the careless attitude shown by the villains. He knew now was not the time to preach morality however, there was more information to be had. "Go on."

"As the shipments continued, he seemed to get more and more powerful, until it has got to the stage now he is out of control. The latest thing was the blackmail letters. He told us recently that he had been warned off going ahead with the idea but we were going to do it anyway."

"Warned off?" asked Armstrong, "warned off by who?"

"I don't know, he must have connections somewhere but we just deal with him."

"Where does he stay, this Roberts?"

"I'm not sure of the number but I know he is somewhere in Broad Street, at the Warwick Road end."

Cornelius was a little surprised by the location – perhaps not the most affluent in the city but by no means an impoverished area like the one inhabited by Grant and his contemporaries.

"Why are you telling me this now?"

"I don't want Billy to suffer anymore," said Freddie, "he's not as strong as me and I bet you've already worn him down asking him a few questions. He'll be terrified of giving the game away so it's best I do it."

Grant's explanation was plausible but Cornelius sensed that there was more than an element of fear in Freddie's tone as well.

"And you?" he asked, "how do you feel about Roberts."

Freddie lifted his head and looked directly at Armstrong for the first time, "Yeah, I'm not ashamed to say I'm scared of him as well. But I would rather it be me that snitches on him as Billy," he thought for a while before adding, "not that it will make much difference I suppose."

Freddie sat uncomfortably in his chair and Armstrong sensed he was wrestling with a further issue.

"Is there something else?"

Freddie had lowered his head again and was looking at the floor, left and then right. He finally spoke.

"Yes."

Armstrong knew how to interview; he knew when to interject and when to remain silent; this was a time to remain silent and allow Freddie to articulate what was tormenting him. The prisoner continued.

"I saw in the newspaper a body had been discovered by the river," – he paused – "I think this is someone Roberts done in."

"How do you know?" asked the detective.

"Because if it's the bloke I'm thinking of, me and Billy were involved as well."

This revelation completely threw Armstrong and he had to take a moment to compose himself and take in what he had just been told. Without him asking anything, Freddie explained.

"It was one night a few weeks ago when Jack told us he wanted us to see him and help him with a job. We met in the *Irish Gate* and he told us to go and wait in the yard at the abattoir round the corner. He then turned up twenty minutes later half-carrying this bloke – they looked like a couple of drunks from a distance."

"Who was the other man?"

"That's the thing, we don't know. Roberts never told us, but he took out a club and cracked the bloke's skull right in front of us."

"So what happened then?"

There was further shameful silence before Grant added, "He told us to get rid of the body. He told us to throw it in the river, so we wheeled it down through the trees and tipped it over the edge. From where we were standing, we couldn't see if it had gone in the water – in any case it was dark.

"I don't know if that was the same body that was discovered the other day but it could've been. It was snowing heavily that night and if it didn't roll into the river, it would've got covered in snow."

Armstrong sat back in his chair, trying to take in what he had just heard.

"And you don't know the name of the victim?" he asked.

"No, we'd never seen him before."

"What did he look like?"

"He was a youngish bloke with thick black hair and a full beard."

That's him, Armstrong thought to himself.

"Is there anything else?"

"No," Grant seemed relieved that the ordeal was over for now having unburdened himself.

"Right," said Armstrong, "we'll arrange to have you and Dunn taken over to the Gaol. I'll check on Billy later and if he is all right, he will join you; if not, he'll spend the night in hospital and be transferred tomorrow. In the meantime, I'll go and see if I can find this Jack Roberts character."

"If you don't mind me saying," said Freddie, "you need to be careful dealing with this bloke."

It was an unusual helpful warning offered by a villain to a policeman and its significance was not lost on the inspector.

"Yes, I will."

Cornelius escorted Freddie back to his cell and asked Sergeant Townsend to make arrangements to have him and Jimmy Dunn taken across to the County Goal on English Street. In the meantime, he went to brief Chief Constable Henry Baker on the productive morning.

"That is excellent work Cornelius!" said Baker, "to solve the drug marketing and the blackmail letters in one go will take a tremendous weight off us."

"Thank you, Henry, but we're not out of the woods yet," replied the inspector. "We have this Roberts character to contend with and we still don't know the identity of the murder victim; we don't even know for sure if it is the same man that Grant was talking about."

"Yes," mused Baker, sitting back in his chair, rubbing his chin, "this Roberts sounds like a very dangerous fellow."

"And I still haven't got to the bottom of the Whitlock affair, regarding insurance claims."

"Nevertheless Cornelius, we've made great strides in the past few days; and breaking this opium ring will save an enormous number of man-hours clearing up all of this petty crime we've been dealing with these past months."

"I agree," said Armstrong, "I'm arranging to have these two sent over to the Gaol. I'm going to see if I can find this Roberts on Broad Street."

"On your own?" Baker was alarmed at the suggestion.

"For the time being, yes," confirmed the inspector, "I don't even know exactly where he is; it's more of a reconnaissance visit."

"Well, regardless of that Cornelius, be careful."

"I will," said the detective with a smile as he reached for the door.

It was now late morning as he began his walk through the city centre and down Warwick Road towards Broad Street. The temperature was far more pleasant than it had been of late and this had brought more people out of their houses along the tree-lined road: some were tending to their gardens that were finally indicating some early signs of spring, while others were just enjoying a walk in the watery sun.

Half a mile or so down Warwick Road, on the right, was Broad Street, an equally elegant avenue which had the distinctive feature of the cobbled street having been set around the matured trees as opposed to the trees rising from the pavement.

As the policeman rounded the corner onto Broad Street, the only activity was that of a man further down the street loading some furniture on to a horse drawn cart. Cornelius looked at the houses on both sides of the street, not sure which one – if any – Freddie Grant was referring to when he pointed him in this direction. The thought he had earlier about it being an unusual location for a villain such as described by Grant, re-occurred to him. These were town houses, not tenements; there seemed a strange paradox in Roberts living here. He wandered slowly along one side of the street looking at each of the first twenty houses to see if there were any signs of life. There weren't any. He therefore crossed the street and did the same on the other side, with the same result, noticing that some of the houses were actually unoccupied.

Armstrong resolved to walk further along and disturb the man who was loading the cart.

"Excuse me," he said as he approached – the man stopped and glanced over his shoulder – "I'm sorry to disturb you but do you live here yourself?"

The man looked piqued by the question, "Well, I did until today," he replied grudgingly.

"Oh, sorry to hear that," said Armstrong, unsure if that was the correct response to the man's comment.

"We're having to move because of the constant, blasted rent rises," continued the man unprompted.

Cornelius noted the man's attire and his clean hands – not a working-class labourer; more like an office clerk.

As the two men were talking, a woman appeared at the door of the house the man was removing his furniture from, holding an infant in her arms.

"Will there be room for the little one's cot in this load George?" she asked.

"Yes, there should be, my dear," replied the man.

Cornelius touched the brim of his hat when the woman saw him. She scowled.

"Have they sent you to see that we move out on time?" she said.

The inspector realised her confusion and how his appearance could be mis-interpreted in the couple's circumstance.

"No, no, I do apologise for the confusion," he said, "I'm nothing to do with your landlord. My name is Armstrong, I'm a policeman" – the expression of the couple changed instantly to one of surprise – "I am looking for someone who I believe may live along this street. I don't suppose you know a man called Roberts…Jack Roberts."

The two looked at each other doubtfully.

"I don't think so," said the man.

"I don't think he has lived here very long, probably just a few months," prompted Cornelius.

"There have been a lot of comings and goings over the past twelve months or so. A lot of these houses are empty now because people can't keep up with the rent. We've been here three years," the man continued in full flow, "the first two were fine and then the houses were bought by those rogues who have gradually squeezed the life out of the tenants. It's finally caught up with us. I don't understand what they are thinking; surely it's best to have some income than have houses standing empty."

"So the landlord owns all of these houses?" asked the detective, pointing back down the street.

"The majority of them along this side," confirmed the man. "You could identify them by the ones that have received a threatening letter," – as he spoke he took a folded piece of paper from his inside pocket and threw it down in disgust – "I believe some tenants have even had the pleasure of a visit from some thug on the landlord's behalf. I wasn't going to let it get to that stage, so we are off."

Cornelius looked at the letter that had unfolded as it passed through the air and landed on the back of the cart. The headed paper caught his eye. The letter was from Morley, Freeman and Whitlock.

"Are they the solicitor's acting for your landlord?" asked Armstrong, staggered that the same name would crop up yet again.

"They *are* the landlords," said the man bitterly. "I don't know who this other man is you are looking for sir, but if you ask me, it's that gang of rogues who should be arrested."

Armstrong nodded knowingly, "Yes, I think that day is coming," he said, half to himself, and then, touching the brim of his hat, "I'm really sorry to have bothered you both. Good luck."

TWENTY-ONE

Gerald Whitlock and Freddie Grant were not acquainted; they had never met or even heard of one other. They did however have one mutual acquaintance: Jack Roberts. And something else Gerald shared with Freddie was the thought that the unidentified body found by the River Eden was a product of Roberts's handiwork.

Whitlock learned of the discovery when he read the story in the *Carlisle Journal*. He did not inform his father or anyone else of his suspicions but his instinct told him that he knew who the man was; and if it *was* who he suspected; he knew that he personally was an accessory to the man's demise. Not for the first time, he was beginning to wonder if he had got in too deep with the villain from Manchester.

Whitlock had met Jack Roberts when he came to the city eighteen months earlier. His arrival coincided with the younger Whitlock becoming a partner in his father's business and with the extra standing and responsibility Whitlock enjoyed, came an arrogance that would ultimately lead to recklessness.

The meeting came about when a favour was asked of his father: to provide accommodation for 'a friend of a friend' who was supposedly staying in the city for a few weeks before moving on. William Whitlock passed the matter to his son to arrange, as Gerald had been successful recently in purchasing a few houses in various parts of the city.

Gerald therefore arranged to meet his new tenant in Currock Street, Wapping one rainy Thursday morning in April of 1900.

"Mr. Roberts?" he asked as he shook hands with the man outside the designated address, "I'm Gerald Whitlock, the landlord."

The man laughed at the comment but shook the younger man's hand anyway. He was a big, brutish looking fellow who reeked of stale tobacco smoke; he had a hard face and an intimidating stare. But there was something about him that would fascinate Whitlock: a sense of danger perhaps; something or someone that he could never be. For

Roberts's part, he would quickly see that the young man was someone who could be influenced to the point of manipulation.

"I believe you are not from the area?" asked Whitlock as they entered.

Roberts wasn't in the mood for small talk and ignored the question.

"You own these houses round here do you?" he wasn't particularly interested in being shown around either.

"A few, yes," said Whitlock.

"When's the last time you raised the rent?"

The question took Whitlock aback, "I don't really know; rents are on a fixed scale I suppose. We just take our lead from the Corporation."

Roberts snorted his derision, "Do you want to make money or not?"

"I'm sorry, I don't follow."

"Why follow someone else's rules when you can make your own? There aren't enough houses to go round so people don't have a choice, do they?"

"I suppose not," said Whitlock slowly grasping what Roberts was getting at.

"Well then, increase the rents on the houses you own. You get rich, you buy more houses, you get richer still."

Whitlock stood for a moment, wondering at the simplicity of it all.

"There are all sorts of ways of making money," continued Roberts, "do you know anybody who deals with the Corporation houses?"

"I do as a matter of fact; I am in the same club as a couple of the councillors."

"Well then, negotiate buying some of their houses off them at a knock down price. Give them a cut to keep them sweet; you continue to put the rents up. Everybody wins."

"How would I raise the capital in the first place?" asked Whitlock as a pupil would ask a teacher.

"I'd guess there will be a banker in this club of yours?"

"There is actually."

"There always is," said Roberts knowingly, "get him involved as well."

The two sat talking for over an hour. Roberts had instantly cast his spell on Whitlock. The younger man envied his confidence and his knowledge; his courage and his complete disregard for other people's views; his bravery; his presence. Roberts was someone he could never be. He had a magnetism Whitlock found irresistible and over the following few days and weeks, Gerald found himself increasingly drawn to this man.

The one thing he did have that Roberts didn't were the contacts and the influence to put some of the villain's ideas into practice. Armed with some of the initiatives, he set about convincing his colleagues of the merits.

When he had reached adulthood and started working for his father, William Whitlock introduced his son and his friend Stephen Baldwin to Free Masonry. The first time the two young men attended a lodge meeting, they sniggered between each other at the secret handshakes, the bizarre rituals and the secret code words. But the advantages of being in the Masons soon dawned on Gerald when he saw how various members moved up the hierarchical ladder as they gained experience and respect within the society. And he was soon to find that even within this complex hierarchy, there was a group of Masons who met secretly; secret even from their own colleagues.

The group were formed some decades earlier by a group of local businessmen who were intent on looking after one another: calling in favours of acquaintances to aid a colleague in his latest venture; what could be viewed as low-level machinations that gained them an advantage without actually punishing or penalising anyone in the process. It was decided they should never number any more than twelve at any one time. Upon the group's inception, they initially considered calling themselves something exotically sinister like 'The Disciples' or 'The Sons of the Brotherhood.' But after much discussion it was decided to go with something far less conspicuous:

The Book Club was born; an innocent name for a group of friends who would never be suspected of anything other than meeting to discuss their favourite works.

The members of the Book Club met in private – often at the residence of one of the members – to manipulate the local economy for their own ends and with it, increase their own power and influence in the process. As the years progressed and some of the founders passed away, the criteria of the membership with gradually broadened to include financiers, councillors, magistrates, solicitors and doctors; when any one member died, those remaining would identify a suitable replacement from the lodge's number. He had to be someone who could contribute to the group and once he had been secretly vetted and finally approached to discreetly enquire about his ambition and intentions, he would be invited to join the Book Club.

Six months before Gerald's meeting with Jack Roberts, the Book Club mourned the passing of one of its number. Isaiah Glassman was a Financial Accountant with his own business. Gerald's father wasted little time in taking the unprecedented step of nominating his son to fill the vacancy. His fellow members had never considered someone so young in the past, but after much debate – and given the fact that the usual due diligence checks could be avoided on this occasion because of his father's sponsorship – it was agreed to allow the young solicitor into the group.

Following his meeting with Roberts, Whitlock saw how he could meaningfully contribute to the group for the first time. He made an approach to Bert Andrews and Brian Page, two councillors on the Corporation Housing Committee who were also members of the Book Club. He put forward Roberts's suggestion about purchasing property belonging to the city. Andrews and Page were reluctant at first but when Whitlock appealed to their greed by pointing out the profits that could be made in the long term – selling houses to him at a reduced price which would allow him either to sell them on at a profit, or hike up the rents of the tenants – they began to see the benefits of such a scheme. With two of the elder members of the club on board, Whitlock had an easier task in getting unanimous approval.

This proved a watershed moment for the Book Club, who from that point on were actively involved in perpetrating and covering up criminal activity. Once the housing scheme was accepted, the die was cast – there was no going back.

Roberts followed it up by planting the seed of shipping opium into the city. He had seen the money it made in Manchester and convinced Gerald that he and his colleagues could reap similar rewards. Monies gained from the shipments could then be invested in seemingly legitimate businesses. Roberts was so convincing in his argument that Whitlock virtually repeated word for word what he had been told, to his fellow Book Club members. Seduced by the thought of rich rewards for very little risk, they gave permission for Whitlock to ask Roberts to arrange the shipments on a trial basis. The Manchester villain wasted no time in getting together a local network that could collect and distribute the opium.

Following the trial, the group unanimously agreed that it had been a success and openly complimented Gerald on his finding such a lucrative market through the intricate local network that had been set up. For his part, Whitlock was selective in sharing information with his colleagues, regarding the part he personally played in organising the shipment and distribution; they were all starting to reap the rewards and that is all anyone needed to know. When the money started to roll in, Denis Richards – a stockbroker who was currently enjoying enormous profits generated from investments made with dubious companies who were supplying arms and goods to both sides in the Boer War – invested the takings on behalf of the group. Income doubled and then tripled in no time.

"Who is this chap Jack Roberts anyway?" asked one of the Book Club members over brandy and cigars, when the villain's name started to regularly crop up.

"He came from Manchester," said the Chairman, "I agreed to do an old friend a favour by arranging some accommodation for him," – he nodded towards William Whitlock, acknowledging his assistance in the matter – "while some issues he had in Manchester were sorted out."

"Well in that case, thank goodness for old friends," guffawed another member as he raised a balloon glass and blew a cloud of cigar smoke upward towards the high ceiling, much to the amusement of those present.

It was at that same meeting that Edward Sanderson took William Whitlock to one side for a quiet word.

"Fine young man you've got there," he said, re-filling the solicitor's glass.

"Yes, he's coming along nicely," replied Whitlock, looking at his son proudly across the room.

Sanderson leant closer and lowered his voice still further.

"My daughter Ester is now of age and I think they would make a good match."

William's attention returned from his son to his friend and colleague.

"I never thought of that," he said, "but now you mention it, she's a fine-looking girl from good stock," – the two guffawed at the comment – "I think that's a splendid idea. I'll have a word with Gerald, I'm sure he'll be delighted."

"There is a little age difference between the two but that shouldn't cause any problems. I seem to recall we have the Ladies' Night coming up in a couple of months, don't we? Perhaps that would be an opportunity to bring Ester along and introduce the two."

"An excellent idea," said William Whitlock, glancing back over towards his son, who saw his father looking and raised his glass in acknowledgement.

With the successes of the house purchasing schemes and the opium shipments under his belt, Gerald's confidence in business increased and blended seamlessly with his youthful arrogance. When mixed with the dangerous activities of Jack Roberts it became a potent concoction that would almost certainly lead to disaster if left unchecked. As Roberts felt secure in his new surroundings, Whitlock was enjoying the adulation brought by his scheming, while fellow members of the Book Club were sitting back and enjoying the fruits of such activities. With each party comfortable in their respective roles, no one gave a thought to monitoring the impact or possible consequences of what was happening.

In what he saw as a reward for the work Roberts was doing, Whitlock proposed that he move the villain into one of his newly purchased houses on Broad Street.

"A slightly more salubrious area of the city to that of the modest working-class area of Wapping," said Gerald, as he opened the front door.

Roberts followed him inside and retained his regular expression: a mixture of distain and indifference. He wasn't particularly bothered about the status such a move might bring but he did see the advantages of keeping on the move.

"It'll do, I suppose."

It was during this period that Gerald started to come up with his own ideas as to how money could be had.

"We have many clients on our books who we not only represent, but for whom we also arrange accounts and insurance cover," he explained to Roberts. "I wonder how you would feel about another little ruse on the side?"

"I'm listening," replied the villain.

He explained to Roberts that each of the clients he had in mind all had strong rooms with safes.

"If we broke in and robbed the safe, it would just look like an ordinary burglary. I would then arrange for an insurance claim to be made, the client would be reimbursed as it were, and we would have a nice little income stream."

"Wouldn't the insurance company get suspicious?" asked Roberts.

"No," replied Whitlock confidently, "I have them insured with different syndicates and although the amounts would be a decent return for us, the syndicates themselves would view them as a relatively small sum. Given that for each claim it would be viewed as a one-off, I reckon they would just pay out, with no questions asked.

"Who are the clients you talk of?"

"A mixture; mainly shops. As long as we don't disturb anything and just concentrate on the money in the safe, I reckon it should be all right."

"You reckon, do you?" said Roberts, sensing that the young man was growing in confidence – something he wasn't too keen on. "And who's *we* exactly?"

Whitlock looked at Roberts's hard eyes and realised that he shouldn't push his new found self-assurance, "Well…you, if you didn't mind?"

Roberts thought for a while before agreeing, "Might as well," he said, "nothing else to do round here on a night."

"Excellent!" cried the young man, betraying the poise he liked to demonstrate these days, "I'll bring a list of the places I have in mind and the plans of each building."

As well as this, he briefed Roberts on the best times to commit the thefts: when the safe was full of takings or soon-to-be-paid wages. The villain's skills included house and safe breaking so he found no difficulty in accessing the money following the first break-in at Ismay's Wine and Spirit Merchant on Scotch Street. Nothing else had been disturbed during the burglary and with Whitlock making a successful insurance claim on the merchant's behalf, the robbery acted as a blueprint for those to follow.

At first, Gerald did not mention the initiative to his colleagues but upon reflection, he realised that the insurance claims would need to be lodged through the firm; he therefore informed his father of what he had instructed Roberts to do. Whitlock senior was at first furious at his son initiating such a scheme without his knowledge or permission.

"You had no right to do this," he yelled, "we should not be involving or risking the welfare of our own clients."

"It is working fine, father," said Gerald, "I've told Roberts that he should not disturb anything other than the money in the safe. The client will not lose out and we will benefit."

William thought for a while, before asking his son, "This Roberts fellow, he sounds a bit dangerous to me."

"He's fine," lied Gerald, "just a little rough round the edges I suppose."

"Well," said William, suitably assuaged, "if you have already started with the hair-brain scheme, I suppose there is nothing we can do about it."

He shared the information at the next Book Club meeting. There wasn't the same level of concern raised by the other members as any clients of theirs were not victims of the burglaries. However, there was one proposal made by the young man shortly after that was unceremoniously refused.

During one of their meetings when Whitlock and Roberts had been discussing possible scams, the Manchester man brought up the subject of the beer in his home town that had been contaminated with arsenic. He suggested to Whitlock that a blackmail campaign against the brewery up the road from where he first stayed in Wapping would deliver an easy return.

"That's a splendid idea," replied Gerald, who was by now becoming almost giddy with excitement at the seemingly endless possibilities that existed, when it came to fraudulent activities and extortion.

His excitement regarding this latest initiative was to be short-lived however. For the first time, he saw what the brotherhood of the Masons meant.

"Absolutely not!" cried the Chairman, as the other members of group frowned at the young man.

"Why not?" he asked.

"Benjamin Woodward is the owner of Iredale's," he was told in no uncertain terms by the Chairman, "he is a fellow Mason – it is out of the question."

It was apparent to Whitlock that Woodward was not a member of the Book Club; regardless of this, he received the message loud and clear that members of the brotherhood were clearly off-limits and relayed this to Roberts. The villain smiled to himself and shrugged at the refusal.

Gerald soon forgot about the aborted proposal and concentrated on the schemes that were up, running and delivering a hansom return. As the ill-gotten gains were being re-invested in other business ventures and the stock market, it became relatively easy for Whitlock and his colleagues to convince themselves it was all a legitimate concern.

The summer passed and William Whitlock informed his son of the proposal made by Edward Sanderson concerning his daughter. Gerald had been ambivalent about a serious relationship to that point but upon meeting the unsuspecting Ester at the Ladies' Night event, he found himself instantly attracted to the pretty young woman. His friend Stephen Baldwin was too and spent most of the evening making salacious comments about Ester, much to Gerald's amusement. He was gradually warming to the idea of having a regular female companion. At that point life just seemed to be getting better and better for Gerald Whitlock.

TWENTY-TWO

Whitlock, Whitlock, Whitlock! This blasted Whitlock is always the common denominator. As Cornelius Armstrong walked back up Warwick Road after learning that the solicitor owned the houses on Broad Street, he mulled over the involvement of the young solicitor in the strange sequence of events and crimes that had occurred in the city over the previous six months or more.

He decided not to return to the station but instead to head directly to Whitlock's offices on Fisher Street. He was to be both surprised and disappointed: he found the offices locked and the blinds turned down. No amount of knocking or pulling on the big heavy doors produced any meaningful result. He made his way down the lane to the side of the building to see if he could access through the rear door; he was to be frustrated however when he found the lock on the lane door – something that had been smashed on the night of the break-in – had been fully repaired. The whole building was secured and apparently empty.

Armstrong made his way back out on to Fisher Street. He looked at the front windows again and saw that one of the blinds was not fully pulled down; cupping his hands around his eyes, he pressed his face against the window and tried to peer through the tiny gap to see if he could see anything.

Nothing.

Directly opposite was a glass-fronted sandwich shop owned by a middle-aged couple, who provided a popular service for the offices and businesses in the vicinity. The policeman went over to ask if either had witnessed any unusual activity at the Whitlock offices over the past few days. The shop was busy as always and Cornelius conscientiously took his place in the queue.

"Yes, sir," asked the man, when it came to the policeman's turn, "what can I get you?"

During his waiting time, watching the customers being served, Cornelius felt his stomach rumbling. He realised he should kill two birds with one stone.

"I'll try a corned beef sandwich please," he said.

"Certainly sir," said the proprietor, wiping his hands on his apron.

"Also," asked Cornelius, "I was hoping to see Mr. Whitlock across the road today, but his offices seem to be shut. I don't suppose you would be aware of why they are closed?"

Before the man could answer, his wife – who was passing a packet across the counter to her customer in exchange for some coins – interrupted, "I noticed a bit of coming and going yesterday."

"Really?" asked Armstrong, as the man rolled his eyes and went about making the customer's sandwich.

"Yes, there seemed a be a flurry of activity yesterday around lunchtime. More people leaving than going in. There was a big fancy carriage there at one point. I then saw Mr. Baines there this morning; didn't stay long before he locked up and left as well."

"Thank you," said Cornelius, "that's useful." He turned back to the man who had his sandwich wrapped.

"Doesn't miss much, the wife," he said under his breath as he handed over the packet.

Armstrong smiled, paid the man and left. He wondered what the best course of action was to take and decided in the first instance, as it was a nice day, to sit and eat his sandwich on a bench outside the cathedral.

What had happened to the Whitlocks and why were the offices closed on a regular weekday? Could it be the case all of a sudden, that there was some connection between Whitlock and this villain Jack Roberts, or was that just a strange coincidence? Armstrong then remembered one of the conversations he had with Henry Baker after discovering all the burglary victims were clients of Whitlock's:

"Coincidence?" Baker had asked.

Cornelius recalled the answer he gave to his superior officer, *"I'm not a great believer in coincidences."*

"And definitely not where Gerald Whitlock is concerned," he said out loud, as he finished his sandwich and disposed of the wrapper in a bin that stood beside the bench.

He decided against returning to the station; instead, he would make the long journey up to Kingstown, north of the city where he knew the Whitlock's lived. The tram ride across the river and through Stanwix took an eternity and the detective's impatience wasn't eased any by a farmer on Kingstown Road who was driving his sheep from a field on one side of the road, into another further up on the other side. It was almost half past two in the afternoon by the time Cornelius climbed down from the tram at the Kingstown terminus.

Just a few hundred yards along the road was a beautiful pink-coloured villa that would not have been out of place in an eighteenth-century novel. It stood in its own grounds, while trees and shrubbery lined the high wall that protected it from the road outside; woodland to the side and rear enhanced its secluded location. The gates were tall but unlocked; Cornelius let himself through with a clank of the lever and walked up the long sweeping driveway towards the stunning double-fronted property with two Georgian-style windows either side of a large black door that was flanked by two columns. He climbed the few steps leading to the door and rapped the knocker that was fashioned in the shape of a lion's head. No reply. He knocked again, louder this time. Still nothing.

"Damn!" he cursed.

He looked up at the six windows of the upper floor but there was no sign of life. Undeterred, the policeman wandered around the perimeter of the house to see if there was a rear entrance, or perhaps someone working in the garden. Looking up at the windows as he went, there were no lights on in any of the rooms; neither were there any fires lit in the downstairs rooms. There was a vacant landau parked at the rear of the house but there was no sign of any horse or groom. Cornelius remembered the owner of the sandwich shop referring to a fancy carriage. After twenty minutes of wandering the grounds, Cornelius's instinct told him something was not right here but there was little he could do about it. He decided therefore to return to the station, believing he would have to cease his search for Gerald Whitlock for one day. He walked back along the drive and took one final look back at the house before opening the gate and letting himself out.

As he looked back, he was not quite in time to see a figure in one of the ground floor windows dart back out of sight behind a curtain. Gerald Whitlock had been in the house all along with his father. When he had heard the front gate open and the crunching of footsteps on the gravelled drive, Whitlock had peeped out from behind a curtain to see – much to his horror – that Inspector Armstrong was approaching the house. He may have been dismayed by the sight of the policeman but he was not altogether surprised after a stressful twenty-four hours.

The previous morning Gerald Whitlock believed that everything was beginning to settle down again: the shipments of opium were coming in unhindered and undetected, the police enquiries into the insurance claims had gone quiet, and poor Ester was now buried and unable to ask any questions of her own.

This feeling of growing relief dissipated however when Whitlock read the morning edition of the *Carlisle Journal*. The front page continued a story it broke the previous day – that of a man's body being found by the River Eden. It described him as being in his mid-twenties, with thick black hair and a matching full beard. Whitlock knew instantly it was Dominic James.

"I have to leave for an urgent appointment," he told Mr. Baines as he hurried out of his offices on Fisher Street.

He jumped in a hansom cab in front of the town hall and instructed the cabbie to take him to Broad Street as quickly as he could. Paying the driver before the cab even stopped, he leaped from the hansom as it pulled up outside number six. Whitlock banged on the door with the flat of his hand, until he heard a muffled voice approaching.

"A'right, a'right!"

The door opened to reveal a groggy-looking Jack Roberts who it seems had been roused from his bed. Gerald pushed passed him.

"What's going on?" asked Roberts, rubbing his eyes.

215

"What's going on?" repeated Whitlock, "what's going on? It's not what's *going* on but what's *gone* on that concerns me."

"What are you talking about?"

"This," said the young solicitor handing the villain the newspaper.

"What is it?" Roberts took it without having any intention of reading it.

"It's full of a body being found down by the river. It was covered in snow for weeks until its discovery a few days ago. The description matches that of Dominic James. What did you do with him?"

Roberts thought for a while and recalled his dealing with James that night outside the *Irish Gate*. He played through the events and remembered he told those two idiots to dispose of the body in the river.

"I suppose it could be," he said, half to himself after a while.

"You suppose it could be?" shouted Whitlock.

"Well you told me to sort him out," protested Roberts.

"I didn't tell you to kill him, you idiot; I thought you'd just frightened him off – that's why we hadn't seen him for weeks."

Roberts was fully awake now and he grabbed Whitlock by the lapels and lifted him up against the wall. His unshaven, greasy face was less than an inch from Gerald's – his halitosis was the least of Whitlock's concerns as the criminal's mouth contorted into a feral snarl.

"Who are you calling an idiot, sonny? It seems to me that I'm the best thing that's ever happened to you and your small-town wannabe friends, kidding yourselves on that you know what you're doing."

Gerald was terrified: it was at that very moment, as he was pinned against the wall, that he realised he was in way above his head. Moreover he had dragged his unsuspecting father and his friends – blinded as they all were by greed and power – into league with this psychopath.

"I'm sorry," he spluttered, unable to control the sputum that shot from his mouth in his fear.

That didn't bother the revolting Roberts and, somewhat calmed by the apology, he lowered the solicitor down from his tiptoes.

"You told me that he was not from round here," said Roberts, as he was starting to think straight.

"That's right," said Whitlock pulling down his waistcoat and straightening his jacket, "he came from somewhere in the Lakes I think."

"Well then, if no one knows him round here and there's no identification on him, then no one will ever know who he was will they? I'll go and talk to the two who helped me with him; we all keep our mouths shut, and no one need know."

Whitlock was eager to latch on to any scenario that would see them get through this. Roberts's suggestion was as good as anything he could come up with.

"I suppose so," he mumbled.

With that, the young solicitor left, deep in thought while Roberts fixed himself some breakfast before going to see the Grant brothers in Caldewgate.

It was late morning by the time he left. Warwick Road was bustling with a desultory mix of characters: elderly women with baskets returning from the city centre markets; a young mother pushing a pram; a postman darting in and out of gates with his morning delivery. Everyone going about their own business and paying no attention to Roberts as he went about his. As he walked up one side of the road, he noticed a man in a knee-length brown overcoat on the other side, walking in the opposite direction. The man had a black bowler hat and a horned moustache.

There's a copper if ever I saw one, Roberts thought to himself, *I can spot them a mile off.* He sunk his shoulders and turned his face away to ensure that – even if the man did notice him – he wouldn't get a good look at him.

Roberts may have been correct in assuming that the man he saw was a policeman; what he didn't realise is that the policeman was on his way to Broad Street in search of him.

217

Roberts therefore, unaware of his near-miss, carried on his half hour walk to see Freddie and Billy Grant. When he arrived at their tenement, he found it empty. He banged on the door but to no avail. An old lady from across the yard came out with a pile of washing she was intending to hang out on one of a series of lines that stretched across the lane.

"They're not there luv!" she called when she saw the man banging on the door, "they were lifted this morning."

"Whaddya mean?" asked the man, seeing that the woman was addressing him.

"The police were here – arrested the pair of them!" The woman was delighted she had a chance to recount her eye-witness account. "Ooh, it was a queer carry on! There must have been about a dozen of them. All over the place they were. They had the wagon backed up here and everything. I always thought they were a couple of wrong 'uns. Here's us good honest folk, trying to get some sleep…"

But Roberts wasn't listening to her random sentences and commentary on what had happened, he only focused on the words 'police' and 'arrested.' It was now that his mind began to race: What did it mean for him? How much do the police know? Would Freddie and Billy keep quiet about their relationship with him? *Of course they wouldn't!*

It dawned on him that he now had this snivelling Whitlock on one side and those two gibbering idiots on the other and he was stuck in the middle. He had to move and move fast. The woman was still babbling on about the neighbourhood when he hurried out of Duggan's Court and onto Byron Street.

What had they been arrested for? The opium? The murder? It couldn't have been the murder because the bloke hadn't been identified so there was nothing to tie them to him. As he walked back through the Irish Gate, he recalled the man he saw on Warwick Road less than an hour earlier. *If he was a copper, was he coming to look for me?*

On his way back to his lodgings, Roberts knew he had to be extra vigilant as – regardless of whether the man was the police or not

– it was only a matter of time before he would find himself being hunted. On his way back, he decided to detour to Fisher Street where the Whitlock offices were. They couldn't have known about the arrests as they didn't know the Grants, or their role in the network that Roberts had built up; they were just the fat cats who sat back and reaped the rewards.

Roberts paused and reflected on his own role: he had spent his whole life in and out of trouble, chased by the police, always on the run; and for what? He didn't have a great deal of money; he didn't own any property and he had no family to speak of. He concluded that the only reasons he did what he did was for the thrill of getting one over on someone, the violence and the intimidation. It was the Whitlocks of this world who benefited without ever getting their hands dirty. It was the same in Manchester; now here he was in Carlisle having to get out but probably without the same assistance. He looked along Fisher Street to Whitlock's' offices and saw a flurry of activity as people were leaving the building with bundles of papers and incongruously loading them into an elegant landau that stood outside.

What preceded the activity was an animated and extremely loud meeting in William Whitlock's office between father and son; much to the embarrassment of the staff outside who could hear most of what was being shouted.

Gerald had returned from his meeting with Roberts earlier that morning, troubled by the encounter.

"What is it?" asked his father upon his return.

Gerald had spent the whole of his journey back wondering whether he should tell his father or not. When he saw him as he entered the building, he decided the best course of action was to confide in him. It was a typically cowardly decision from the younger Whitlock who, all of his life, had sought to abdicate responsibility for his own actions. On this occasion, he told his father about the newspaper story and his meeting with Roberts.

"I think the body is that of Dominic James," he said at the conclusion of the narrative.

"James?" repeated William Whitlock incredulously, "the Will Writer? What has this all got to do with him?"

"Something happened and I may have mentioned to Roberts that he was in my bad books."

"What are you saying?" shouted his father, "something happened? Bad books? So are you telling me this Roberts animal has murdered him?"

"I think so."

Gerald was pathetic, William was incandescent with fury.

"So the man has been murdered because he discovered you were manipulating Wills for your own benefit."

William was referring to another one of Gerald's suggestions that he himself had indulged, against his own better judgement and much to his own shame. Gerald was about to speak when his father continued.

"We need to clear the office of any incriminating paperwork," – before the son could retort, he shouted – "get on with it!"

The younger Whitlock sent one of the junior clerks to get word to his groom who should bring the landau down from the house. Mr. Baines meanwhile would gather together all of the documentation from the last eight months for each client and prepare to remove it from the office.

"Every client, sir?" asked Baines disbelievingly.

"Yes, every one!" shouted Whitlock, "now get on with it."

They spent the next two hours clearing the office and taking the papers up to the house. There was just enough time to empty the carriage, stable the horse and dismiss the groom for the day, before Inspector Armstrong arrived. With him now gone, Gerald breathed a sigh of relief and went round the front of a wing-backed chair, behind which his father was hiding, to tell him the rest of his story.

TWENTY-THREE

"I know this man!" said photographer George Taylor when he saw the body of the unidentified murder victim lying on the slab in the morgue.

He had again been called in by Doctor James Bell to capture the images of the man following his post mortem. There had been an inordinate delay in carrying out the autopsy due to Doctor Bell himself being taken ill, following the recovery of the body from the frozen river bank. This caused the pathologist to be away from his duties for ten days and when he returned, he found there had been no let-up in the number of bodies that had entered his mortuary; this inevitably created a back-log of work and it was therefore almost three weeks between the body's discovery and the post mortem.

The revelation by Taylor caused the Doctor and his assistant Murray to look up in surprise.

"You know him?" repeated the pathologist.

"Yes," replied the photographer, "I'm sure he was the young bloke who was the hero in the omnibus accident last year."

"I don't recall that," said Bell.

George Taylor was in the most appropriate job imaginable for a man with his photographic memory: every subject he ever encountered, whether posed-for in his studio or spontaneously captured in the street, was instantly locked into his memory banks. The dead man that lay before him on the slab was figuratively logged under the latter category.

George had become interested in photography as a young boy and this interest gradually became his passion and ultimately, his profession. It was inevitable that in time, such an exponent of his craft would succeed in starting his own business and this in turn led to him owning his own studio at the top of Warwick Road opposite the main Post Office. In doing so, he became one of the most respected photographers in the area.

Always pushing the boundaries of his profession and exploring new equipment and new techniques, in '96 he purchased a portable Facile camera which allowed him to take his work out onto the street and capture images of unplanned incidents or simply snap pictures of people going about their daily business. It was one of the former that brought him into contact with the man who now lay deceased before him.

It was about twelve months earlier when Taylor took his mobile camera with him to take some pictures of characters coming in and out of the County Court on English Street. The Facile he carried was nicknamed the 'detective' in the photography profession as it contained a lens set into a small wooden box that could be carried by the operator inconspicuously under his arm and allow him to take pictures without the subject necessarily being aware they were being snapped. If George captured any interesting images that no one else could obtain, it allowed him to offer them to the local newspaper; by doing so, this provided him with extra income when his studio business was quiet.

It so happened on the day in question that not much of interest was occurring at the court buildings. Around eleven o'clock however there was an almighty bang, immediately followed by shouting and screaming coming from the direction of the viaduct around the corner. Like many others on English Street he rushed around and ran the hundred yards or so towards the grand Central Plaza Hotel, which stood proudly just before the bridge.

The origin of the commotion was a horse-drawn omnibus that lay on its side. Some people were lying injured on the road having been thrown from the open top, while the poor horse was thrashing about on the ground in a panic, apparently uninjured but unable to free itself from the harnesses that tied it to the bus. There was screaming and shouting coming from inside the bus as people outside hurried about trying to be of assistance.

As the incident played out, it became apparent that a young hansom fellow – apparently a passenger himself – was carrying people from the stricken vehicle and laying them by the roadside. Given the awkward position of the bus, he was the only person strong and fit enough to climb up the underneath of the bus to access the entrance that was now pointing skyward. He did this bravely on several occasions and rescued at least a dozen people from the fallen vehicle. By the time he had pulled the last of his fellow passengers from the bus, ambulances had arrived and were loading the most seriously injured aboard, while the less seriously injured were being tended to by a doctor who happened to be having morning coffee with his wife in the hotel when the accident happened.

To round off his heroics, the young man unharnessed the horse and managed to calm the skittery animal down as he raised it to its feet. A spontaneous round of applause broke out from a few dozen onlookers who saw the man in action throughout. Also present, by this time, was a reporter from the *Carlisle Journal* who was quick to take a statement from the hero of the hour and those around who witnessed the accident and the aftermath. For *his* part, George Taylor had some wonderful images.

"So what is his name?" asked Doctor Bell after Taylor had recited the tale.

"I can't remember to be honest," replied George, contorting his face as he searched his memory, "I'm good at faces – not so much at names."

"So we are no further forward then?"

"I can easily find out though." Taylor looked a little sheepish at this point and explained, "I have a terribly vain habit of saving the newspaper clips that I have contributed to. It started off as a novelty when my work first made it into the papers and it's a bit of an embarrassing habit ever since. I'll have the newspaper article back at the studio somewhere."

"Excellent!" said Bell, "so we finally have something substantial to present to Inspector Armstrong. I should complete my report this afternoon, could you be available to meet at the police station around three o'clock?"

"I think I know where the article will be, so I should be able to make it," said the photographer, delighted that he appeared to be significantly contributing to the mystery.

Bell then turned to his assistant, "John, could you get word to the inspector that we will be coming?"

Murray nodded his agreement and the three went about their respective tasks.

At the appointed hour Doctor Bell met George Taylor in the entrance hall of the police station.

"Any luck?" asked Bell, referring to the photographer's newspaper clipping.

"Yes," said Taylor, enthusiastically, "I've got him!"

At that moment, Inspector Armstrong appeared from his office, having been informed a few minutes earlier by Sergeant Townsend that his visitors had arrived.

"Good afternoon, James," he said, offering a hand to the pathologist, "you have some information on the body by the river?"

"Good afternoon, Cornelius. This is George Taylor, a photographer who I believe can unlock the problem for us."

The detective and the photographer exchanged greetings and shook hands.

"Well I think I can identify the man," clarified Taylor.

"Come on through," said Cornelius to both men, while catching the eye of Bill Townsend – the tried and tested signal to provide him and his guests with some tea.

Once inside his office, Armstrong invited the two men to share their information. Doctor Bell took his report out of a brown envelope.

"Death was caused by two violent blows to the head with a blunt instrument, probably some sort of club or cudgel judging by the shape and dimensions of the wounds; one to the side of the head and one on the top of the head near the front," – he indicated on his own skull specifically where the blows were received – "I would suggest the first blow to the side was to render the victim unconscious and this allowed the murderer to inflict the second blow which was probably fatal."

"Would that have been instantaneous?"

"It's difficult to say. Some victims would go into a coma, some would die instantly. I think in this poor chap's case, he wouldn't have felt very much as it appears he was hurled over the edge of the bank, presumably with the intention of being swept down the river. There were other marks on the body which confirm he was thrown from a height but in the grand scheme of things, these were fairly superficial. Due to a combination of the blows, the fall and the cold, I would suggest he didn't suffer much."

"So Mr. Taylor," said Cornelius, after taking in the doctor's narrative, "do we know who the man was?"

"I do, Inspector," said the photographer, producing a newspaper clipping from his pocket. "His name is Dominic James, a poet and calligrapher who has only been in Carlisle for a year or so."

"A poet?" repeated Armstrong, "why would someone go to the trouble of murdering a poet?"

"A random act after a pub brawl, perhaps?" suggested Bell.

"I don't think so. I take it there were no other marks on the body which indicated a fight?" – Bell confirmed Armstrong's assumption with a nod – "Besides, if it was something relatively innocent that got out of hand, why would someone go to the trouble of disposing of the body in such a way? No, I think there is more to this than meets the eye."

Taylor shared the story he narrated to James Bell earlier in the day, with Inspector Armstrong. He handed over the paper cutting at its conclusion that contained two of the photographs he took on the day of the accident. He provided the detective with several more unpublished pictures, taken at the time. Armstrong studied the images.

"It's been a few weeks since I saw the body," he said, pointing to the pictures of the hero of the accident, "are you sure this is the man?"

"I am," Taylor was adamant, "I had to remind myself of his name but I never forget a face."

Cornelius nodded, leant on the arm of his chair and subconsciously twisted one of the horns of his moustache. He read the newspaper piece, which confirmed what Taylor had told him already but didn't give any address for the man. Describing the man's actions, the article contained eye witness accounts and victims' statements:

'I saw the whole thing,' said Mrs. Florence Smith of Blackwell Road, 'the wheels of the omnibus caught in the tramlines and cockled over.'

'It was mayhem,' confirmed Harry Jones, a road sweeper who happened to be speaking to someone on the viaduct at the time.

'It was very frightening,' said Mrs. Ada Sowerby, wife of magistrate George Sowerby, who was among the passengers riding on the omnibus at the time, 'had it not been for that young man I don't know what we would have done.'

"George Sowerby?" Cornelius read out loud.

"Inspector?" asked Bell.

The detective looked up from the page, "Oh, it's just someone mentioned here in the piece who I have spoken to recently."

"That's a coincidence," offered the pathologist.

There's that word again, thought Armstrong.

"Mmm. Well gentlemen, that has been really useful. Thank you both for your help, especially you Mr. Taylor, this information has proved invaluable."

"Not at all, Inspector, I'm pleased I can be of assistance."

"Do you mind if I hold on to this paper cutting for the time being?"

"No, please do."

The two men left the detective to contemplate the latest information. He sat tweaking the horns of his moustache thinking first about Whitlock and then about Sowerby. He glanced at the clock above his door and saw that it was almost a quarter to five. He grabbed his hat and coat and hurried out.

"I'll see you tomorrow Bill," he told Sergeant Townsend on his way past.

"Will do, sir," said Townsend.

Conscious that he had no luck with locating Whitlock, Cornelius hurried round to George Sowerby's office on English Street to see if he knew anything about first, Whitlock's whereabouts, and secondly, if he could contribute anything the to the emerging picture regarding the dead man he now believed was Dominic James.

He was to be disappointed yet again however, as he found the offices locked up; no amount of rapping on the door brought any attention from inside. He took out his fob watch and flicked it open: it was only five minutes to five. He thought it strange that the office would be closed before the end of the business day but by this time, he felt himself start to flag: the events of a long and tiring day – the latest of too many recently – had caught up with him and he decided that five minutes to five was as good a time as any to put an end to it.

Back at his lodgings, Cornelius asked if Mrs. Wheeler minded making him a slightly earlier meal than normal, intent as he was on an early night. His landlady was as obliging as always and by eight o'clock, he found himself nodding over a book in front of the fire. When his tenuous hold of the volume relaxed completely, it fell from his lap and landed at his feet with a dull thud, lurching him from his slumber in the process. He smiled to himself and decided it was time for bed.

The following morning Cornelius felt invigorated again after a good ten hours or more. Gone were the feelings of self-doubt, the slight bitter feeling that he was being expected to do too much personally – if he was honest, perhaps it was him that was guilty of taking too much on – and he was ready for the day ahead, especially given that he sensed he was getting ever nearer to the heart of some of the current issues.

He washed, dressed, breakfasted and took the five-minute walk to the station shortly after eight, where he was greeted by the ever-present Sergeant Townsend. He tidied a few papers on his desk and prioritised the day's activities in his mind: visit Whitlock first and establish if there was any connection between him and this Roberts character, by all accounts a violent and dangerous character who needed to be apprehended as soon as possible. If there was time, Cornelius thought it would be useful to pay another visit to Sowerby to see if he knew anything about the dead poet.

Before he left, Chief Constable Baker arrived for work which gave Armstrong the opportunity of apprising the previous day's events.

"So where does this poet chap fit in?" asked Baker.

"I don't know, Henry, but what makes it interesting is that everything always seems to lead me back to Whitlock, from unusual insurance claims to house-ownership; now we have this dead man whose name is mentioned in the same newspaper piece as Sowerby's wife. Sowerby, in turn, is connected to Whitlock."

"That last one seems a little tenuous, probably just a coinci-" he stopped himself saying it.

"Possibly," said Cornelius, smiling at Baker's self-interruption.

"And what about the drugs?" resumed the chief constable, "there is no connection there beyond this Roberts figure."

"No, but I suspect Roberts must have some backer somewhere. We know about what happened with the Grant brothers etcetera, who worked as part of the network below him, but we don't know who was above him and ultimately benefitting from the scheme."

"Umm," contemplated Baker, "well I trust you, Cornelius, you've done some outstanding work so far, but don't undo it all by going in too enthusiastically without the evidence."

"Understood, sir."

Armstrong informed his superior of his intentions for that morning, did the same with Sergeant Townsend and left to visit the Whitlock offices once more.

And once more, he was to be frustrated. Locked, blinds drawn, they looked completely undisturbed from his observations the previous day. Recalling his encounter at the sandwich shop opposite, he went over to ask if the owners had seen anything this morning. The man was opening up while wrestling with an A-frame advertising board he intended to stand outside the shop, while his wife was giving the counter a final wipe over before making the bread. Cornelius waited politely until the man had made it outside onto the street.

"Good morning, I was in the shop yesterday and you and your wife helped me with my enquiry about the solicitors' opposite,"

Cornelius threw a thumb over his shoulder indicating the offices concerned.

The man stood racking his brains for a while before Cornelius prompted him, "I think it was actually your wife who had seen some activity."

"Oh, yes I remember now," said the man with a knowing smile. He held the door open behind him and called to his wife, "Mildred, gentleman's here about them lot opposite; have we seen anything today?"

The woman came to the door, intrigued by who wanted to know what.

"How'd'ya mean?" she asked, wiping her hands on her apron.

"I'm sorry," said the questioner, touching the brim of his hat, "I should have introduced myself properly. My name is Armstrong, I'm a policeman."

"A policeman!" repeated the woman, rubbing her hands even more vigorously on her apron.

"Yes, it's really important I find the whereabouts of Mr. Whitlock, the solicitor from the offices opposite. They are obviously not open this morning, neither were they open yesterday afternoon when I called. I wonder if you have seen anything, other than what you told me yesterday?"

The woman overlooked the policeman's question and focused instead on her own inquisitiveness, "Why, what have they been up to?"

"I'm afraid I can't go into much detail at the moment," said Armstrong, much to the wide-eyed woman's disappointment, "all I can say, it is extremely important that Mr. Whitlock is found."

"There are two, aren't they?" asked the man, seemingly a little more eager to help than pry.

"Yes, father and son," confirmed the detective, "it's preferably the son, Gerald Whitlock I am looking for, but certainly, I'm sure Mr. William Whitlock can probably also help."

"Well there hasn't been any sign of anybody today," said the woman, finally harnessing her own desire for gossip. "As I said previously, the day before yesterday it was a hive of activity with people throwing bundles of papers into a fancy carriage. It was then all locked up around lunchtime. Then yesterday, that nice Mr. Baines came down and opened up but he was only here for half an hour or so. I didn't see him leave."

"You were probably distracted by some of those people that sometimes come into the shop," said her husband, "what are they called again? Oh, yes, that's right – customers!"

The woman playfully slapped her husband's arm with the back of her hand in response to his teasing.

"Well if you do see anything further," said Cornelius, bringing the meeting to a close with a smile, I would appreciate it if you got word to me at the station on West Walls. I would also be interested in speaking with Mr. Baines if he returns. A reminder, my name is Armstrong, Cornelius Armstrong."

With that, he thanked the two and bid them a good morning. As he walked away, he was amused further, when he heard the woman comment to her husband how she knew "…that lot were up to no good!" as he shuffled her back into the shop.

It was the only thing that was amusing about the whole situation: there was still no Roberts and no Whitlock either, and all the time, he had this nagging doubt that they now knew he was after them, which meant that time was now extremely tight. As he wandered up Fisher Street he began to wonder if it was going to be a case of so near, but yet so far.

TWENTY-FOUR

In the continued absence of Whitlock and the unknown whereabouts of Roberts, Armstrong had little choice but to visit George Sowerby, someone he had originally hoped to see later that afternoon, after what he intended would be a busy morning. He walked through the city centre to the bottom of English Street to where Sowerby's office was, only to be thwarted yet again by a closed, locked door. *What on earth is going on*? he thought as he banged on the door in frustration, with no response.

The lower half of the two ground-level windows of the office were opaque with Sowerby's name and title embossed on them in gold lettering. This combination made it difficult to see inside but Armstrong cupped his hands around his face and peered in, in what he thought would be a futile attempt to see anyone. To his surprise he sensed some movement at the far end of the office – this was all the encouragement he needed to impatiently rap on the window.

"Open up!" he shouted, *"this is the police, open up!"* The figure appeared to stop, as if wondering what the best course of action would be. The detective sought to make up his mind for him, *"Open up, I say, this is the police!"*

After a further pause, the figure started to move and Cornelius was relieved to find it seemed to be moving towards the door. A few seconds later, he heard the distinctive sound of bolts being removed, top and bottom, followed by the turning of a key. Finally the door was levered open.

"Mr. Crain," said Armstrong as the solicitor's clerk stood before him.

"Inspector," said Crain in a strangely even tone.

"I'm here to see Mr. Sowerby."

"I'm afraid Mr. Sowerby isn't here."

"He didn't seem to be here yesterday afternoon either," said Armstrong, "where is he?"

Crain thought for a while, as if weighing up his options before opening the door wider, "I think you better come in."

As Crain closed the door behind him, another figure appeared from a room at the bottom end of the foyer area.

"Mr. Baines!" announced Armstrong incredulously, "what are you doing here?"

"Inspector," said Whitlock's clerk in acknowledgement.

"I think we should go through to the back," suggested Crain as he bolted the door again and led the way.

The three entered Crain's musty stationary room where it appeared as though he and Baines had been hiding away. Crain brought in a third seat and offered it to the policeman. Armstrong was almost at a loss as to which clerk he should address first.

"Can either of you tell me what is going on?" he asked instead.

The two men looked at one another, uncertain as to who should say what.

Armstrong asserted his authority, "Mr. Baines, I believe your employer has committed some serious offences that, if true, will see him arrested. If he is convicted, he will be almost certainly disbarred and sent to prison." He turned to the other clerk, "Mr. Crain, I'm not sure about the extent of *your* employer's involvement, but there is certainly an element of suspicion by association. Now, gentlemen, I want you to think about your own reputations; if you deliberately withhold information pertinent to my enquiries, you will be deemed accessories to whatever crimes that may have been committed."

The two looked warily at each other, almost daring the other to speak first: it was Baines that took the lead.

"I've suspected wrong-doing for some time, Inspector. Things have changed with the firm since Mr. Gerald became a partner."

"In what way?"

"The standards that were upheld previously were let slip; things became sloppy and seemed to culminate in this ridiculous series of insurance claims that he was behind."

"Why ridiculous?" asked Armstrong.

"Well, nothing like that had ever happened before," said Baines, "and for so many claims to be made in quick succession like that looked very suspicious to me. I raised my concerns with Mr. Whitlock senior but he just told me to leave it to his son. It was only when you came to the office that day to question Mr. Whitlock that my beliefs were confirmed in my own mind."

Cornelius turned to the other clerk, "And you Mr. Crain, did you have any similar suspicions about your employer?"

"No sir," said Crain, "the first I knew anything about such a scheme was when you visited our office. I thought Mr. Sowerby's behaviour that afternoon very strange. It was only this morning when Mr. Baines came to see me that I found out the true extent of what was going on. It seems that Mr. Whitlock had asked Mr. Sowerby to essentially cover for him by suggesting that our premises had been burgled also."

"Why were both offices closed?"

"Mr. Sowerby received a telegram yesterday afternoon that sent him into a real panic. He ordered me to lock up for the day. I didn't hear anything further from him and therefore turned in for work as usual. It was shortly after that Mr. Baines arrived."

"And Whitlock's office?" the inspector asked of Baines.

"Something happened the day before yesterday. Mr. Gerald left in the morning and returned later in quite a fluster. He immediately went in to speak with his father and we were all instructed to clear papers relating to Wills the firm had dealt with over the previous twelve months and documents relating to any of the properties owned by the firm."

"What have Wills got to do with any of this?"

"I remember some months ago our Will Writer brought to my attention the number of Wills that had the firm listed as executors," said Baines. "I agreed this seemed quite unusual but when we raised the matter with Mr. Gerald, we were both given short shrift and told in no uncertain terms to mind our business. The exchange was particularly embarrassing as I remember Mr. Whitlock's young lady was within earshot."

"Miss Sanderson?" asked Cornelius.

"Yes, that's right. I never raised the matter following that but after the events of the other day, I now suspect there was something untoward going on."

"I can assure you that nothing like that was happening here, Inspector," said Crain.

Armstrong thought for a while before resuming his questioning, "It was actually over another matter that brought me here."

"Oh?"

"I wondered if Mr. Sowerby had any dealings with a man called Dominic James."

Both clerks looked at one another in surprise and then back at the policeman.

"James?" repeated Crain, "that's our Will Writer; he's been missing for weeks. Have you found him?"

"Your Will Writer?" said the detective, "No, it can't be the same man – the man I am referring to was a poet apparently."

"Yes, that is the same man," explained Crain, "last year there was an accident where he helped Mrs. Sowerby. When his name appeared in the paper Mr. Sowerby invited him in to thank him personally for his efforts. If I remember rightly, the newspaper article referred to him as a poet and calligrapher and during the conversation with Mr. Sowerby, he told him that he had recently arrived in the city from somewhere in the Lake District and was looking for work. It so happened that we needed someone at the time to copy out Wills and other documentation, so Mr. Sowerby offered him a position."

As Crain was talking – rather than interrupt him – Cornelius took the newspaper cutting, given to him by George Taylor, from his inside pocket and unfolded it. When Crain paused, he showed him the cutting.

"Is this the man?"

"Yes, that's the very clipping I was referring to!" said the clerk.

"And you can confirm the man in the picture is Dominic James?"

"Yes," said Crain, a little confused, "do you know where he is?"

"I'm afraid he's dead," said the policeman. "His body was found down by the river about three weeks ago. We think it may have laid there covered by the snow for a further three or four weeks. It's taken this time to carry out a post mortem and identify the poor chap. He was murdered I'm afraid!"

"Murdered!" cried the clerks in unison.

Armstrong waited a few moments for the shock of the news to abate. "Do you know of anyone who would want to harm him? Did he have any enemies?"

Crain continued to look at the floor in surprise. Instead, it was Baines who answered, "He was a big fine looking fellow. He seemed a very private person, but he always had a smile on his face. I couldn't imagine anyone wanting to harm him like this."

It was Armstrong's turn to sound surprised, "You knew him too?" he asked Baines.

"Sorry, you shocked me Inspector," said Crain, rousing from his reverie, "I was about to say that James's work was so good I referred him to Whitlock's."

Baines completed the narrative, "Good copiers are so difficult to come by and we jumped at the chance of taking him on too. He worked for us both in a freelance capacity, presumably between pursuing his own activities. I must say his work was excellent."

"So when you referred to the Will Writer bringing the 'executor' question to Gerald Whitlock earlier, that was actually Dominic James?"

"Yes, that's right," – Baines looked at Crain – "I can't remember which one of us christened him 'the Will Writer' but the nom-de-plum stuck and he has always been known as that ever since."

Armstrong sighed heavily and reached for the horns of his moustache, while the two clerks looked from him to each other and back again. The awkward silence was disturbed by a loud banging on the front door. The three men simultaneously gave a start and Mr. Crain went to see what the commotion was.

A muffled exchanged was followed by a returning Crain with Sergeant Bill Townsend just behind.

"Sir," said the sergeant, "I received this urgent telegram for you not twenty minutes ago," – he held out the missive – "I tried Whitlock's offices first but there was no reply so I took a chance and came here."

Armstrong took the telegram and ripped it open:

INSPECTOR ARMSTRONG COME TO MY HOUSE AT ONCE STOP
URGENT STOP
EDWARD SANDERSON END

"Thank you, Bill," said the inspector to his sergeant, and then turning to the clerks, "Thank you gentlemen for your help. I must ask you to keep our conversation this morning in the strictest confidence," – both men nodded – "and don't tell anyone about the demise of Mr. James. There is one last thing: do either of you know where he lived."

Baines again took the lead, "Yes, he rented a little room above a poultry dealer halfway along Globe Lane. We both used to take documents to him there," he added looking at the nodding Crain.

"Thank you again."

Armstrong spent the whole of the journey up London Road marvelling at how this case – or should that be, series of cases – never failed to link together and cause surprise in the process. Not only had the body of the murdered man now been identified, but yet another link to Gerald Whitlock had been made. He wondered now what revelation Edward Sanderson was about to impart.

He was greeted at the door by Mrs. Sanderson's maid.

"Hello Mary Ann, it's nice to see you again."

"Good morning sir, please come in, I was told to expect you."

"How is Mrs. Sanderson?"

"A little better thank you sir. I was pleased to get her out of that wretched place where you saw us last."

"But it's not *Mrs.* Sanderson I'm here to see?" questioned the policeman.

"No sir," said Mary Ann, "Mr. Sanderson is waiting for you in his study.

She took the inspector's hat and coat and showed him through one of the four doors leading from the hallway. The room was as elegantly decorated as the hallway with its walls lined with oak panelled bookcases that were filled from floor to ceiling with volumes of various sizes. Behind the matching desk sat Edward Sanderson, staring into middle distance. He appeared not to hear the door opening or the maid and the policeman enter.

"Inspector Armstrong sir," announced Mary Ann.

"Ugh? Oh yes thank you, come in Inspector," mumbled Sanderson, breaking out of his daydream.

"I'll make some tea sir," said Mary Ann excusing herself.

"You asked to see me urgently sir," said Armstrong.

"Yes, I have to share some information with you," said Sanderson, indicating his guest to a chair opposite.

It was clear to Armstrong that Sanderson was a troubled man, and he suspected it wasn't just the tragic loss of his daughter that was causing him distress. After a long pause – during which Cornelius wondered if he had changed his mind – Sanderson spoke.

"Something has happened that I can't conceal any longer."

Armstrong remained silent, inviting his host to go on.

"I am a member of group who call ourselves The Book Club."

The name sounded vaguely familiar to Cornelius and then he remembered that Ester had referred to such a club a few times in her journal. "Yes?"

"The club is not as conventional or as innocent as it sounds," continued Sanderson. "I myself am a retired financial accountant; other members include solicitors, stockbrokers, city officials, doctors. The club was formed about thirty years ago and has existed since, for the benefit of its members. If we are honest," – Sanderson snorted lightly to himself at the word – "we would have to admit that we have all been guilty in the past of manipulating situations for our own ends." He looked down and levered at his collar with a finger. "But recently things have changed."

"Go on," prompted the policeman.

"Last year one of the members invited his son to join."

237

"Gerald Whitlock," stated Armstrong.

"Yes, that's right," said Sanderson, unsure as to how much the detective knew. "He introduced some new ideas that frankly, appealed to our greed. But then one thing led to another and over the past few months, things have gradually gotten out of hand."

"What sort of things?"

"What started off as – what one might describe as low-level profiteering – has led to drug smuggling, fraud and extortion."

"And are you saying that this was perpetrated in the main by Gerald Whitlock?"

"Well, it would be wrong to blame the boy totally. We were complicit through our laziness and avarice. Let children play unsupervised and what do you expect I suppose," mumbled Sanderson into his lap.

"Do you recognise the name Jack Roberts?" asked Armstrong.

Sanderson looked up, surprised at the question, "Yes, I do as a matter of fact. Never met the fellow personally but he seems to be central to the issue. He appeared on the scene a few months ago and appears to have had a hold over Whitlock ever since. I'm never quite sure what ideas are Roberts's and what are Whitlock's but as we all seem to profit, the rest of us are guilty of not asking too many questions."

Sanderson began to redden and he took out a handkerchief and mops some beads of sweat from his forehead. As he did so, there was a knock on the door and Mary Ann entered with a tray and some tea.

"Thank you," said Sanderson, "could you also bring me a glass of water please?"

"Certainly," said the maid.

She returned moments later with a full glass and put it on the tray, by which point, Cornelius had poured two cups of tea. Mary Ann exchanged smiles with him as she turned to leave and he sensed there was little more than a tolerant courtesy between maid and employer; it was clear to him that Mary Ann's loyalties were predominantly with her mistress.

"We were talking about Roberts," resumed the policeman, "where did he appear from?"

"Manchester, I think," replied Sanderson, "there was something about a favour being done for a colleague in the Manchester area and he suddenly appeared."

"A favour?"

"Well putting two and two together, I wouldn't be surprised if the scoundrel has committed some mis-demeanours down there and has had to get out."

"And he has been assisted by the Book Club?"

Sanderson's head dropped again, "Yes, it would appear so," he said quietly.

"So why are you confessing this now?" asked Armstrong.

"My daughter is dead, Inspector; my wife is a broken woman; and I am ill. The last weeks have afforded me time to contemplate my situation and to question my own integrity. The answers I came to only increased my discomfort. Yesterday was the straw that broke the camel's back as it were."

"What happened yesterday?"

Sanderson had a slight coughing fit before resuming, "There was an urgent meeting called of the Book Club at Whitlock's house."

"I went there yesterday afternoon, around two o'clock," said the inspector, "I didn't see anyone there."

"We didn't meet until after four, to give time for the business owners to close up for the day." Sanderson continued his narrative, "At the meeting Gerald admitted to some of the schemes he had involved himself in without our knowledge. I wasn't the only one who was angry with the boy, even his father sat there stone-faced throughout the meeting. It culminated in him saying something about someone who had been killed and intimated this fellow Roberts was somehow involved. *Murder for God's Sake!*" Sanderson again reached for his handkerchief and to mop not only his brow, but the back of his neck. He breathed heavily in an effort to calm down.

"Does the name Dominic James mean anything to you?" asked Armstrong.

"James," mumbled Sanderson, "no I don't think so."

"He was Whitlock's document copier, apparently they called him the Will Writer."

"Whitlock did mention something about discrepancies with Wills amongst his other misdemeanours but he didn't mention anyone's name in connection with it. Do you think this James is another conspirator that we don't know about?"

"No, Mr. Sanderson, Dominic James is dead and I believe that he was the victim Whitlock was referring to."

The sweat was now pouring freely from Sanderson's brow as he started to follow the policeman's train of thought. He gulped at the glass of water.

"So it could be that this unfortunate James fellow discovered some of Whitlock's fraudulent activity and Whitlock had him killed as a result.?"

"That is one possible theory," replied Cornelius before broaching a difficult subject. "Talking of theories Mr. Sanderson, could I ask if *you* have any theory as to why your daughter took her own life?"

Sanderson's eyes widened in horror as he suddenly realised what Armstrong was hinting at, "*Ester?*" he cried, "*My God!* you don't think she knew about some of this do you?"

"I don't know. I simply ask the question because I am aware that she and Whitlock were engaged."

Sanderson grasped at the glass again before Armstrong continued by reaching in his pocket for his notebook.

"I would like you to give me the names of the other members of the club."

"Ugh? Oh yes," said Sanderson, trying to regain some semblance of composure. He breathed deeply and began, "As well as myself, there was my former business partner, Robert Carney," – Sanderson broke off and coughed again uncomfortably before resuming – "then there was Brian Page and Bert Andrews, who are both Councillors; John Clough who is on the Corporation Planning Committee; Denis Richards, a Stockbroker on Lowther Street; Duncan Forbes, a surgeon at the infirmary; Peter MacLeod, a building developer who also has his offices on Lowther Street; George Sowerby, a solicitor-"

There was a pause until Cornelius heard a gurgling noise and looked up from his notebook to see Sanderson – eyes as big as billiard balls – clutching his left arm. Armstrong leapt from his chair just as Sanderson fell from his; by the time the policeman made it across the room, the man was lying dead at his feet.

TWENTY-FIVE

Three months before her death, on a beautiful autumnal morning, Ester Sanderson was preparing to spend another crushingly boring day, cossetted in her home with nothing to do and all day to do it in, when her father unexpectedly called her into his study.

"Ester, dear, I would like you to do me a favour," – he handed over an envelope – "I would like you to run into town and deliver this to that young man of yours, Gerald. It's actually for his father but I'm sure he can pass it on."

The instruction filled Ester with mixed feelings. First the reference to Gerald being her young man repulsed her as she continued to resent her father for arranging the match and then deluding himself that all was sweetness and light. Secondly, there was a slight feeling of ignominy at the thought of her now being reduced to the role of an errand-runner. But overriding all of this negativity was the thought that she was getting out of the house, alone; with permission! This had never happened before and she was not going to pass up the opportunity of spending a morning window shopping and breathing in some fresh air, away from this suffocating atmosphere.

"Certainly father," she said with some enthusiasm, taking the envelope from him.

Sanderson handed it over and immediately went about his other paperwork with a dismissive grunt. The envelope contained his costings offset against estimated income regarding the younger Whitlock's zealous rent-increases. Whitlock senior had asked the retired accountant to carry out the exercise following some tenants moving out of properties and leaving them empty. His paper was to be discussed at the next Book Club meeting and Sanderson wanted to get it to Whitlock in time for him to consider it beforehand.

Sanderson didn't tell his daughter what was in the envelope and she didn't ask. As far as Ester was concerned it was a legitimate reason for her to be out of the house. She had received her meagre allowance some days earlier and she wondered if she could time her journey to meet Matilda for lunch.

The fresh air on the top deck of the omnibus was heavenly as Ester enjoyed the sights and sounds of people going about their business. She alighted in front of the Courts on English Street and made her way to the City Bank to see if she could catch Matilda's eye. She was to be disappointed however when she found the bank packed with four lines of customers, waiting to be served at one of the booths. They were an amusing sight as they all leaned this way and that, impatiently comparing the reduction in each queue and wondering if they had selected the correct one.

Matilda was one of the four clerks serving and Ester strained on tiptoes to catch her eye above the crowd. Matilda finally looked up to see her friend waving and instantly knew that she wanted to meet. Almost as instantly, the stern-looking overseer appeared behind her.

"Is there a problem, Miss Chambers?" he asked peering over the top of a pair of gold pince-nez that hung precariously on the end of his nose.

"No sir," said Matilda, disappointedly.

She flashed a look of resignation to her friend and indicated to her next customer to come forward. Ester sank back down from her tiptoes and left in much discontent.

Wandering aimlessly north along English Street – as much to kill a little time and delay her errand, as anything else – Ester came to the window of Gowan's Emporium, her favourite store. It was then that she saw her shoes for the first time: black suede with a slight heel and buttoned up the outside above the ankle. They were gorgeous. She stood looking at them for several minutes wondering if she dare to go in and try them on, knowing all the while that it was highly unlikely she could afford them. Regardless, the temptation was too great and in she went.

"Oh, they look beautiful, Miss," said the assistant after she had retrieved them from the window and Ester paraded up and down in front of her.

"Yes, they are, aren't they?" she agreed as she lifted her skirts and admired them in a mirror.

She had ignored the price tag when the assistant handed them over to her but now, she couldn't avoid looking at the ticket as she carefully unbuttoned them: £2. 3s. 6d. She knew she could never afford to pay such a price; she also knew that the chances of her father advancing her sufficient allowance for such an extravagant purchase were slim-to-none.

"Should I wrap them for you Miss?" said the assistant, trying to secure the sale.

"Mmm, I need to think about it a little more if you don't mind," said Ester, somewhat embarrassed by a lie she was almost sure the assistant could see through.

"Very well Miss."

The assistant took them from her and left Ester standing there in her stocking feet, feeling a little pathetic. She quickly pulled on her own shoes and laced them up before hurrying out of the store. As she did so, she inadvertently caught the eye of the assistant who was struggling to replace the shoes without disturbing anything else in the window display. Ester gave an embarrassed smile, while the assistant returned it with a timewaster's glare and carried on her business. Ester meanwhile hurried on in the direction of Fisher Street.

It was shortly before twelve when she entered the Whitlock offices and waited at the entrance desk as there was no one around. There was usually a nice man called Baines sitting there; Ester had met him on her few previous visits to the office. She assumed he wouldn't be far away so she waited patiently.

Gradually she became aware of voices coming from one of the rooms to the rear of the entrance area. The voices gradually increased in volume to the point where Gerald appeared in Ester's view speaking with some animation, apparently towards someone still in the room.

"You are not paid to question the work!" he said sternly, seemingly wanting to end the exchange.

Two other men followed him out of the office, and appeared in Ester's view, just after Gerald had made the statement. One Ester recognised as Mr. Baines; the other was a far more striking figure. He was tall, with thick black hair and a full beard; he wore a long ulster and carried a wide-brimmed hat; slung over his shoulder was a leather satchel.

"But Mr. Whitlock," the stranger protested, "it leaves the firm open to criticism and suspicion if it is found that they have set themselves up as executors every time."

"I have to agree sir," said Baines.

Whitlock flashed at his clerk, "You will do as you are instructed Baines, or you'll find yourself looking for another position. As for you James," he continued, turning back to the other man, "how dare you suggest that something untoward is going on."

"Mr. Whitlock, I'm not suggesting anything. I am simply pointing out how things might look. In this day and age, perception is as important as the truth."

"And I perceive that you need our work more than we need yours. Go about your business and do not raise such a matter again!"

With that Gerald disappeared into another office and slammed the door behind him, leaving the two men standing looking at each other. After a few moments the two shook hands and the stranger left, apparently deep in thought as he did not seem to notice the young woman that was standing patiently at the front desk.

Baines went to resume his position and suddenly recognised Ester, "Why Miss Sanderson, I'm so sorry to have kept you waiting, I didn't realise it was you."

"No problem Mr. Baines, I could see you were busy."

Baines flushed slightly as he realised Miss Sanderson must have witnessed the heated exchange.

"I'm here with a document for Mr. Whitlock," she said quickly, in an effort to reduce whatever embarrassment the clerk felt.

"Which one?" he asked.

"I think it is for Mr. Whitlock senior but I'm sure either one will do."

"Well Mr. Whitlock senior is out of the office this morning Miss, so I will ask Mr. Gerald to come through."

With that, the clerk went towards the door through which Gerald had disappeared some minutes earlier. He knocked and entered.

"Yes, what is it now?"

Ester heard the impatient voice of Gerald from where she was standing and swallowed hard at the thought of having to face the man. Baines's soft, inaudible message drew her fiancée from his desk.

"Ester, what brings you here?" he asked emerging from his office. His tone was brusque and dismissive.

"My father asked me to bring a document he had been working on for you and your father. I think it is regarding your meeting next week."

Gerald seemed to know what the document pertained to, and judging by Ester's innocent manner, decided she did not. "I'll take it," he said snatching it from her.

"Would you like...?" Ester started the question without thinking what she was about to ask: lunch? to send a reply? anything at all? She tailed off the sentence and waited to be dismissed.

"What?" snapped Gerald.

"Nothing, I'll leave now."

"Very well," said Whitlock turning away, leaving his fiancée standing there.

"I'm very sorry Miss," said Baines quietly, embarrassed by what he had witnessed, "he hasn't been in a very good mood today, I'm afraid."

"Don't worry, Mr. Baines," replied Ester, "there is no need for you to apologise."

She wondered how often poor Baines had to seek forgiveness from people for his employer's behaviour. She bid him a good morning and left, considering her journey into town a complete disaster after looking forward with such anticipation to a change from her normal dull routine.

Fisher Street was crowded with people coming and going from the covered market and on the junction with St Mary's Gate, which

246

led up to the cathedral, was a street vendor selling cups of soup drawn from a large steaming urn. The queue that stood patiently waiting to be served – tin mugs in hand – gave testament to the quality of the soup. As Ester left the solicitor's office and wandered back up Fisher Street, she saw the distinctive figure who had been arguing with Gerald moments earlier, being served by the vendor. The man was engrossed in the transaction and this afforded Ester the opportunity to get a better look at him.

He was tall and seemed to have a presence about him that – along with his unusual attire and shoulder-length hair – set him aside from those around him. But there was no air of superiority with the man; he interacted kindly with the soup seller and exchanged polite glances and comments with other customers. Ester found him strikingly handsome and after watching him for a few minutes, had an overwhelming desire to meet him.

She hurried to where he was purchasing his soup and made as though she was just one of the many pedestrians passing by. She timed her exploit to perfection, for as he completed his purchase and went to turn away from the vendor, she arrived at his side, just in time to ensure that the two collided. He couldn't avoid spilling some of his soup on the arm of her coat, while most of the remaining contents ended up on the ground.

"Oh, I'm so sorry!" cried the man, mortified by what he thought was a dreadful accident. He looked up to see a beautiful young woman looking at him.

"Oops!" she said as genuinely as she could. "No matter, no harm done."

"But look at your coat!" said the man fumbling for a handkerchief, "may I?" he asked politely.

The young woman assented with a coquettish nod and the man wiped off the soup from her coat as best he could. As he did so, the two of them felt obliged to shuffle out of the way for the queue to allow them and the soup vendor to continue their various transactions unhindered.

"I'm afraid it has left a bit of a stain," said the man.

"Oh no matter, I'm sure it will clean when I get home," said the young woman, "it was my fault anyway, I wasn't watching where I was going. It is I who must apologise for ruining your lunch."

The man found the young woman extremely attractive and impulsively asked, "On the subject of lunch, could I make up for this inconvenience by asking you to join me for something – my treat?"

Ester's heart leapt and she struggled to make her reply sound care-free and matter-of-fact, "That would be lovely, thank you."

"Perhaps the correct thing to do would be to introduce myself properly, my name is Dominic James." He offered his hand.

"Hello Dominic James, I am Ester Sanderson."

The two smiled and found themselves instantly attracted to one another.

"Where would you like to go then, Miss Sanderson; I'm sorry it is Miss is it?"

"Yes, it is and please call me Ester."

"Only if you will call me Dominic."

"Very well Dominic. How about we go to Mrs. Morris's Coffee Shop, it's just around the corner."

"That sounds splendid," – Dominic looked at what remained in the bottom of his tin mug – "do you mind?" he asked before drinking the remnants and putting his mug in his bag.

The two picked their way through the busy throng, the short distance to the coffee shop, where they were lucky to find a vacant table in a booth towards the rear of the shop.

"Now then Ester, what would like?" asked Dominic once they were safely ensconced.

"I wonder if they do soup?" said Ester with a mischievous twinkle.

They both laughed before deciding a sandwich and a pot of tea would suffice. Ester was first to probe a little further into the background of her new companion.

"I have a confession to make," she said. "I actually noticed you first in the office of Whitlock Solicitors."

"That's right, I was there earlier" replied Dominic, surprised by the comment, "I'm sorry, do you work there? I didn't notice you."

"No I'm…just a client," lied Ester, "I happened to be there when you were talking to Gerald Whitlock. You seemed quite upset."

"Yes, wretched man," – Dominic put his hand to his mouth – "I'm sorry, that's so unprofessional, do you know him?"

"Not really," *in for a penny, in for a pound,* she thought. "Do you actually work there?"

"In a freelance capacity," he explained. "I copy documents for them and other solicitors. They dubbed me the Will Writer a while back and that is how I'm known."

"The Will Writer?" repeated Ester, "that has a nice ring to it. And what is your normal profession." She was surprising herself by how forward she was with the man but felt so comfortable in his presence.

He made no effort to hide anything from her in reply, "I'm actually a poet."

"A poet! How romantic!"

"It probably sounds like that but in reality, it is difficult finding regular work, dealing with publishers and advertising one's work. That's why I came to Carlisle to supplement my income."

"Where are you from?" she asked and then chastised herself, "Listen to me, interrogating you in this way! For all I know you may be happily married somewhere with a family to keep."

"No, there is nothing like that," he said with a smile, "I'm not married or lucky enough to have a young lady of my own, yet. I came here from Bowness simply because the opportunities in a small village are very few. I have a little loft in Globe Lane, which is handy for everywhere I need to be."

Ester noted the word '*Yet*' and smiled inwardly.

"And what about you Ester," asked the poet, "what is your story?"

"Oh, nothing much to tell really. I still live with my parents."

"You said were a client of Whitlock's?"

Ester thought fast, "Well, my father really, I was dropping something off for him?"

"And what does he do?" – Dominic didn't allow Ester to answer – "I do beg your pardon, I am as bad, interrogating you!"

Ester was pleased he gave her an escape route from talking about her own situation. The two chatted desultorily like old friends for almost two hours. They both felt so at ease in each other's company: for his part, he was surprised how relaxed he felt telling someone he had only just met his life story; for her part, she surprised herself how easily she found concealing her full situation from him.

"You must have things to do?" she asked finally, as the waitress cleared away their second pot of tea.

"One or two things to copy out," he replied, "nothing of any great importance.

Ester again surprised herself by asking, "Could we meet again do you think?"

"I would like that a lot, Ester. It's not every day a fellow spills his soup on such a pretty girl!" – the two laughed naturally again – "I have really enjoyed this afternoon."

"Where and when?" she asked, trying to control her impatience.

"How about the same time in the same place next week?"

Ester had a tinge of disappointment at the thought of waiting so long to see him again, but felt at the same time, that she would need a week to concoct a reason why she needed to leave the house.

"That would be lovely," she said as they rose to leave.

They both gave each other an uncomfortable look, unsure whether they should kiss or embrace; instead, they both smiled awkwardly and offered each other a hand.

"I'll look forward to seeing you again, Ester."

His words were music to her ears as she made her way back through English Street to catch the omnibus home. As she did so, she smiled to herself and thought perhaps it had not been such a bad day after all.

Her reverie was broken when she suddenly saw Mr. Baines amid the horde of people. A combination of the throng and the fact that it had started to snow again – forcing most people to concentrate on their footing – meant that fortunately, Baines did not see her. It occurred to her that it was imperative that she was not seen with Dominic. She thought about how she could avoid this on the journey home.

That night, as usual, Ester and her mother had to sit in silence over the dinner table while her father read his various papers. The grandfather clock ticked on laboriously, adding to the monotonous evening.

"I delivered your document today, father," said Ester as they finished their main course.

"Ugh?" grunted Sanderson without looking up from what he was reading, "oh yes, thank you dear."

"I quite enjoyed it actually," she added. "I could do it again if you like?"

"Ugh...oh yes...we'll see."

To emphasise the point, Ester took a deep breath and said as genuinely as she could, "Besides, it gave me a chance to see Gerald."

At last, he looked up and smiled at her. "Well, that's a good reason isn't it?"

Ester swallowed hard and smiled back.

Later that night she sat in her night gown, thinking of her encounter. She took out her journal and thought about how she could record it. She had gotten into the habit of referring to people simply by their initials and considered referring to the poet as DJ; as she put pen to paper however, she decided it would be even more romantic to use the sobriquet he told her about. She simply wrote:

Met WW today. It was the nicest thing that has happened in months.

TWENTY-SIX

Unknowingly, Gerald Whitlock actually aided his fiancée's deception over the following months. As his illegal schemes and activities increased during the autumn and early winter, so the need increased for members of the Book Club – predominantly Edward Sanderson – to assess the financial risks and rewards of getting involved. As the retired financial accountant did more paperwork, his daughter continually offered to act as courier, without ever knowing the contents of what she was carrying. The truth was, she wasn't interested – she had other priorities.

Following her first wonderful encounter with Dominic James, she spent the week thinking about him by day, dreaming about him by night. She was completely smitten by this exotic figure who seemed to combine physical strength with a thoughtful gentleness; something she had never seen amongst the men she had encountered since coming of age – certainly not in Gerald.

As the week between that first encounter and their second scheduled meeting progressed, Ester became increasingly nervous about Dominic meeting someone else in the meantime or forgetting about her entirely. She wondered if she should have suggested just a few days between them seeing each other again, rather than waiting a whole week. Then there was the fear of being seen; she had already had a close encounter with that nice Mr. Baines – what if someone else not only saw her, but saw the two of them together?

By the time the day of their scheduled liaison arrived, she had convinced herself that she had handled the situation poorly: Dominic won't be there; he will have found someone else; he will have forgotten about her as he went about his busy life.

She had already spoken with her father forty-eight hours earlier and established that there was a document he wished to be taken into town. She agreed, as a matter of course to take it for him, all the while convinced that her trip would ultimately end in disappointment.

Much to her delight, she was to be mistaken. After dropping her father's envelope off with Mr. Baines – without even asking to see Gerald – she hurried along to Mrs. Morris's Coffee Shop to find Dominic already there, waiting in the same secluded booth as they had occupied the previous week. She could barely contain her delight as she rushed over to him. His expression was a mirror image as he rose from the table the two instinctively embraced before realising the magnitude – many would say, inappropriateness – of the gesture.

"I'm so sorry, Ester," said Dominic, feeling obliged to explain his forwardness.

"Don't apologise," she replied, "it's lovely to see you again. I've been thinking about you all week."

"And I you, I must confess."

It suddenly dawned on Ester, the risk she was taking by greeting a strange man so impulsively in a public place. She glanced over her shoulder, concerned that someone may have seen them; satisfied that no one in the crowded establishment had taken any notice, she ushered Dominic back into his seat and took hers opposite, with her back against a screen that protected her from most of the other customers in the coffee house.

The two picked up where they had left off the previous week, almost as though they hadn't been interrupted by the days in between. They chatted like friends who had known each other for years; about upbringing, schooling, poetry and literature, work and ambitions. Ester sat staring at Dominic dreamily as he talked with such a gentle voice for such a physically big man. He, in turn, couldn't stop smiling at this pretty young woman with her self-assuredness and confident opinions on subjects as far ranging as politics to the latest fashion.

What he didn't know was that Ester was not being completely honest with him about her circumstances. She was well aware of this too and had no intention of divulging her engagement to Gerald Whitlock.

"Do you have to rush away?" asked Dominic as they finished their lunch.

"No," Ester replied, "what do you have in mind?"

He leaned out of the booth to see past the other patrons and through the front windows. It had started to snow again.

"Well ordinarily we could go for a walk in the park but it would be difficult in this weather."

"You could show me the little loft you were telling me about last week?"

Dominic resumed his seat and looked at Ester, not quite sure what she had in mind. She just smiled expectantly at him.

"If you would like to," he said tentatively.

They got up to leave. There was a middle-aged couple standing in the centre of the coffee shop waiting for a table; Ester and Dominic both heard the man say to his wife, "Here we go, Mable, that nice young couple are just leaving."

Dominic and Ester smiled at one another, both pleased with the man's assumption. They acknowledged the couple as they passed and stepped outside into the difficult conditions. The mass of pedestrians was waddling around the town hall, struggling to keep their footing, while trams and buses clanged their bells, as a reminder to those on foot to watch where they were going.

Ester was pleased about the distraction of the weather as it afforded her some cover against being seen with Dominic – people were too busy going about their own business to concern themselves with hers. He offered his arm; she looked up briefly and smiled before linking, putting her head down – partly to snuggle in, partly to hide away – and walked down Scotch Street towards Globe Lane.

The lane was one of a series of downtrodden alleyways, consisting of shabby tenements, similar to those in Caldewgate, Shaddongate and Wapping. The major difference with the lanes however was that they were in the heart of the city. Hundreds of families lived cheek by jowl in this impoverished territory that was completely incongruous with the Georgian elegance of Lowther Street at one end, and the business and retail hub of Scotch Street and the market at the other. Some of the buildings doubled as commercial premises.

Ester had never been through any of the lanes before. She was shocked at some of the living conditions; yet she remained unaware how fortunate she was that the freezing conditions had helped kill some of the foul odours which often became trapped in the narrow alleyways and hung over the enclave in the warmer weather.

They hurried along the slippery cobbles as quickly as they could until they came to a door squeezed between a poultry shop and what looked like a small warehouse. Ester was more than a little surprised at such a modest dwelling but followed Dominic inside regardless, pleased to be away from the bitter cold. The door opened on to a set of stairs that led directly to another door facing on the landing above. She followed him up and into a small loft room where Dominic obviously lived.

"It's not much I'm afraid," he said half-apologetically, as he immediately went over to light an iron stove that stood against a wall.

The loft was twenty paces square; as well as the stove, it had a few sticks of furniture and bed against the wall opposite; standing beside the bed was a tall wardrobe and a smaller chest of drawers. There was a porcelain sink beside a little bench, presumably used for preparing a meal. Dominic's writing desk sat beside the stove: on top of it stood piles of papers and books of poetry. The only natural light came from a skylight set into the sloping roof.

The little stove almost instantly roared into life, as if it were pleased to see its owner and the room was quickly heated as a result, giving it a more homely feel. In spite of the modesty of the dwelling, Ester sensed it suited its occupant perfectly and found herself warming to it, almost as quickly as she had to him.

"I think it is perfect," she said.

He took her coat and offered a seat by the fire, "Would you like anything to drink?" he asked.

"No I'm fine," she replied with a smile, looking and feeling comfortable in her new surroundings.

They resumed their lunchtime conversation as though there had been no interruption whatsoever. Both were initially surprised how comfortable they felt in each other's company; now – even though it was only their second meeting – it felt so natural and relaxed, to the point where they teased each other about their respective backgrounds, interests and ambitions.

It was approaching mid-afternoon when Ester reluctantly said, "I really must be going."

Dominic looked equally disappointed but agreed with a nod. He stood up and looked out of the skylight window – he was tall enough to see the rooftops in the opposite buildings.

"The snow seems to have eased a little although it will still be bitterly cold."

Ester was loathed to leave the cosy atmosphere of the loft but went and stood beside him; the top of her head was level with his shoulders and she could only see the white sky through the window.

He turned to her, "Can I kiss you?" he asked simply.

"Yes," she replied, her heart pounding as the handsome man towered above her.

It was another milestone moment; a moment from which there seemed no return. Although she had not lied to Dominic, she had not been entirely honest with him either. She now found herself in love with this kind, honest man; he was everything her loathsome fiancée was not.

"Let me escort you back to the terminus," he said.

"No!" she said quickly, concerned about being seen; then recovering the moment with a smile, "no, I have to run a little errand before I go home. You stay here by the fire."

"Can I see you again?" he asked.

"Of course," she said.

"When?"

"How about Friday?" Ester didn't know if her father would have any documents to be couriered on Friday but decided that, one way or another, she would find a way of being here.

"That would be lovely."

"Let's say ten o'clock. I'll come straight here."

Dominic was both surprised and impressed by her assertiveness. The two kissed again and he watched as she descended the stairs towards the front door and the lane outside.

The only errand Ester had to run was to walk past Gowan's in order to admire those shoes she tried on the previous week – they were still there. She smiled. She looked around at the people who were hurrying along, shielding their faces from the cold; she simply walked along with her head up and her lovely face beaming – it had been a wonderful day.

On the journey home, she wondered how she could get her father to acquiesce to another journey into town within a couple of days. She was still wondering when she let herself in and inadvertently met her father in the hall as he was walking across to his study.

"Ester my dear!" he said, taking out his watch and checking against the time of the grandfather clock, "you're late."

"Good afternoon father," she said, removing her hat and coat as nonchalantly as she could, "Yes I was waylaid somewhat, but I delivered your document without any problem."

Sanderson seemed in no mood to progress the conversation – Ester felt there was sometimes an advantage to his ambivalence towards her – and he grunted and turned again towards his study.

"Father?" called Ester, "Gerald said he wanted to have a word with me about something and asked if I could meet him on Friday morning. Will that be all right?"

Ester was aware that she was starting to play a dangerous game by not only deceiving Dominic but now lying to her father, especially when she knew that he was an acquaintance of Gerald and could – if he so wished – check her story. Such was her desire to see Dominic she was prepared to gamble that her father's interest in her business did not stretch to such an extreme.

Sanderson turned back to his daughter and smiled, "Perhaps to discuss the wedding eh?" he said in an unintended patronising tone.

Ester was sickened by the thought; she coughed and felt the bile in her throat, "Perhaps," she said through a forced smile.

It had been an uncomfortable exchange but a productive one. There was now no need to attempt sneaking out unnoticed, or involve her dear mother in the deception; or feel she was on some sort of time limit. She could count the hours until she would see WW again.

When the morning arrived, she opened her curtains to find the weather conditions reflected her mood: a beautifully fresh morning with an early-winter sun doing its best to keep the temperature above freezing. She breakfasted with her parents, trying to appear as matter-of-fact as she could and ensuring the desultory conversation led anywhere other than the subject of town or fiancée's.

Once in the city centre, she strode through English Street alone, content in the knowledge that even if she was seen by someone she knew, there could be no element of suspicion about her presence there. She smiled to herself as she paused in front of Gowan's – *after all, a girl always has time to look at shoes!* she thought.

The Market Cross was as busy as ever and Ester felt a sense of security among the crowds. Her feelings somewhat changed however as she walked down Scotch Street towards the entrance of Globe Lane. The contrast between the middle-class commercial environment and what some would describe as slum conditions of the lanes could not be more marked; and only a few yards from one another.

The town hall clock struck ten o'clock as she entered the lane and picked her way along the slippery cobbles towards Dominic's door. As she did so, she noticed the dichotomy of impoverished, unwashed children playing in the lane, with the occasional, smartly dressed businessman, who was using the alleyway as a short cut between Scotch Street and Lowther Street.

Ester came to the door next to the poultry shop; she glanced up and down the lane before knocking. Within seconds she could hear the sound of footsteps running down the staircase behind the door. It opened and she rushed in, closing it behind her with her foot. The two embraced and kissed passionately.

"I've been so looking forward to seeing you again," she said.

"As have I," said Dominic, "come upstairs."

The two stopped for a moment in contemplation of what he had said, before bursting into laughter at how the comment could be interpreted. However inadvertent the slip was, it would prove a portent of what was to follow. As the watery sun filtered through the sky light window, Dominic and Ester consummated their relationship that morning.

It was everything Ester had dreamed about in her excitement of reaching adulthood. All of the disappointments of the previous twelve months left her instantly as she was completely besotted by this beautiful and gentle man.

Dominic felt the same way: he had never experienced feelings like this for anyone in the past. Ester was beautiful, funny and mischievous. He couldn't remember feeling this happy. Their morning was incredible.

They lay still on the rumpled bed in silence, using the first few moments of the aftermath to assess both each other and themselves as lovers. It was typically Ester, who broke the uncertain tension.

"So all in all, are you pleased you came to Carlisle then?"

He grabbed and tickled her playfully as the two of them again burst into laughter.

They not only consummated their relationship, they confirmed their mutual belief that they loved each other – something they both suspected the first time they met. It seemed as though that meeting had taken place months ago, such was their bond and feeling of comfort in each other's company; in actual fact it had only been ten days before.

The morning set the tone and routine for the weeks that would follow; throughout November and December, Ester would find a reason to leave the house – sometimes more than once a week – and travel into town to visit the small loft that sat above the poultry shop on Globe Lane. The dwelling was as different from her own home as she could ever have imagined, but she loved it: the cosiness of it, the seclusion of it and above all else, it was the home of the man now adored.

But as her feelings for Dominic deepened, the risk in continuing the relationship increased, because she was fully aware that she was deceiving both of them; something she felt terribly guilty about. He never spoke of his own family and she didn't press him on the subject, knowing that it would almost inevitably lead to them talking about her own circumstance.

The weather also proved an ally of Ester's during those weeks of secrecy. Ordinarily, young couples would walk out together, in the park, or for a nice wander along the river. But in those, late autumn – early winter months, as the snows increased, there was nothing else to do but stay inside. Although some of her reasons for travelling into town were a little imaginative – even suggesting on occasion that she was simply travelling the short distance to visit her friend Matilda – the important thing as far as she was concerned was that once she was there, she and Dominic would be locked away out of sight.

The one painful conversation Ester had to endure was in mid-December when Dominic asked, "What are your plans for Christmas?"

Ester couldn't disguise her displeasure as her head dropped, "I will have to stay at home I'm afraid."

"That's disappointing," he said simply.

She felt obliged to ask, even though she knew the answer beforehand, "What about you?"

"I'll just be here," he said, "I don't have much of a family and those I have are spread far and wide."

There was an uncomfortable silence when they were both thinking the same thing. She knew he wasn't in a position to make the suggestion so she did.

"I would love to invite you to ours…"

"But?"

"I have a confession to make," she took a deep breath, "I haven't told my parents about you yet."

Much to her surprise, he neither looked offended or disappointed.

"Why not?" he asked simply.

"It's complicated," she started, "my father…"

"I understand," he said kindly, not wishing to put her through any unnecessary suffering.

She began to sob lightly, overwhelmed by his generosity towards her. He hugged her all-the-more tightly and kissed the top of her head.

"How about I come on Boxing Day?" she said recovering some composure. "I could tell my parents I am visiting my friend Matilda."

"That would be lovely," said the poet.

And so it was: Ester's disappointment on Christmas Day was lessened somewhat by the Gowan's voucher she received from her aunt; and the following day she made the journey into town and spent most of the day with Dominic.

"You seem to be spending a lot of time with Matilda lately dear," said her mother, when Ester lied to her about the reason for her leaving on Boxing Day.

"Yes," said Ester, hating herself for lying to her darling mother.

The truth was that she had arranged to meet Matilda to go shopping the following Saturday – the first time she would have seen her friend in almost six weeks.

In the days between visiting Dominic on Boxing Day and meeting Matilda for their shopping trip, Ester made another excuse to leave the house and made the journey to Globe Lane once more. It was to prove a fateful visit.

Gerald Whitlock's friend Stephen Baldwin, worked for Denis Richards, the Stockbroker on Lowther Street. By chance, on this particular day, he was cutting through Globe Lane as many businessmen did, to drop some papers off at Whitlock's offices. By chance, he glanced up and amid the crowded alleyway was surprised to see Ester coming out of the door beside the poultry shop, halfway along the lane. She never saw him and started walking in the same direction as he was heading, towards Scotch Street. His surprise turned to suspicion when he saw her glance upwards over her shoulder, smiling at the skylight window.

TWENTY-SEVEN

Cornelius Armstrong's mind was racing; Sanderson lay dead but he had furnished him with what the detective thought were the final pieces of this elaborate puzzle. This so-called Book Club had hired Roberts to carry out their various misdemeanours, usually at the suggestion of Gerald Whitlock. The other members – fuelled by their own folly and greed – had gone along with the various crimes until it had all gotten completely out of control, by which time, it was too late.

The problem he now had was apprehending the real criminals; he may already have had the Grant brothers and Jimmy Dunn in custody but he knew they were small players in this much larger game. There was a possibility that Gerald Whitlock and Roberts had both fled Carlisle; perhaps the best he could hope for was arresting the remaining members of the Book Club.

He desperately wanted to get on with the task but first, he had to deal with the member of the club who lay dead beneath him. He knew that, in all conscience, he couldn't leave Mary Ann and her sick mistress to deal with this latest tragedy. All the while however, the clock was ticking and the dozen or more criminals responsible for the city's decent into chaos over the past twelve months or more were still at large.

"*Mary Ann!*" yelled Armstrong.

The maid gasped in horror as she burst through the door and saw Sanderson lying dead.

"He had a heart attack right in front of me," said Armstrong getting back to his feet after kneeling over the man to see if anything could be done. The wide staring eyes of the corpse indicated there wasn't.

Mary Ann had her hand to her mouth in shock and it was clear that her first thought was for Mrs. Sanderson; she looked over her shoulder and then back again at Cornelius.

"What are we going to tell her?" she asked.

"Mary Ann," he started, walking over to her and shielding her from the sight of her deceased employer, "I need you to be very brave...yet again I'm afraid. Firstly, do you know where the nearest telephone is?"

The maid sought to clear her head, "Er, yes, they have had one recently installed at the Salvation Army shelter, down the road; Mrs. Sanderson often does some voluntary work there. I know it will be locked up right now but Mrs. Sanderson has a key."

"Good," said Armstrong, "here is what is going to happen. Get me the key; I must go there and telephone the station for assistance. I will then go on to deal with some other urgent matters that are related to this. Do you think you will be all right staying here with Mrs. Sanderson until help arrives?"

Mary Ann nodded, pulling herself upright and realising that her main concern was for the welfare of her mistress. "I'll get that key," she said stoically.

Minutes later Cornelius Armstrong was running down London Road as fast as he could, towards the shelter as indicated by Mary Ann. It was an uncomfortable half mile in a heavy coat, hat and boots; the detective arrived at the location and fought to control the adrenaline that raced through his veins as he fumbled with the key in the lock. Once inside, he scampered round the hall until he found the wall mounted telephone in the far corner. Unhooking the earpiece he wound the mechanism furiously to rouse the operator. He was relieved to be connected in seconds.

"Hello, connect me with the police station immediately please, it's an urgent matter."

"One moment please," crackled the voice on the other end.

Seconds later, Cornelius was relieved to hear the familiar sound of Sergeant Townsend.

"Bill, it's Armstrong!"

"Hello sir."

"We need to move very quickly. First, we need to make a series of arrests; round as many men as you can."

Armstrong read out the list of names and their likely locations, given to him less than half an hour earlier.

"Commandeer anyone you can; get Parker involved and even the Chief Constable himself if he's available. Tell him I'll take responsibility. I am going to Broad Street to see if I can catch this Roberts character; I'll also need a couple of constables down there as well. Finally, get someone up to the Sandersons' house on London Road and arrange for a doctor and an undertaker to accompany them. I can't explain right now."

"Leave it with me sir," said the unflappable Townsend, "but before you go, I have some good news for you. The lads picked up Gerald Whitlock at the station this morning. He was trying to get on the southbound train; I've got him locked in the cells right now."

"That is excellent news!" Armstrong was delighted with the work of his men and the assuredness of their sergeant. Another thought suddenly occurred to him, "I'm not sure which house on Broad Street Roberts stays at – go and ask Whitlock for me will you."

Armstrong listened to the crackling for what seemed like an eternity. Finally, he heard Townsend's voice again.

"Number six, sir."

"Excellent!" he repeated, "thanks Bill."

He hung the earpiece back up and locked the door behind him, feeling suddenly that his luck was starting to change. He resumed his run back towards the city until he saw a hansom cab dropping a fair at the junction with Cumwhinton Road. As the cabbie sought to turn his horse around, Cornelius whistled from a distance and managed to catch his attention. *My luck really is turning*, he thought to himself; he didn't brake stride as he leaped into the cab.

"The bottom of Broad Street, as fast as you can!" he instructed the cabbie.

"Very good sir," replied the driver, whipping his steed into a trot.

As Armstrong's cab sped back into the city, zig-zagging its way through the streets towards its destination, Sergeant Townsend was following the inspector's instructions.

After informing Gerald Whitlock that the game was finally up for him and his fellow conspirators, the young solicitor confirmed to the sergeant that his father was still at their home at Kingstown. Townsend duly dispatched PCs Watts and McIntyre – the two officers who apprehended Gerald at the station earlier – to the Whitlock home to complete the arrest of his father.

PCs Brady, Gibson and Boothman were sent to apprehend the stockbroker Denis Richards and the building developer Cyril MacLeod, both of whom had offices on Lowther Street, while Inspector Godfrey Parker was asked to go to the infirmary to find and arrest Professor Duncan Forbes. Townsend could see that Parker was panicking about the task ahead and instructed Harry Stokes and Bobby Green to accompany him.

"Keep an eye on him Harry," he said to the most senior constable in station who responded with a reassuring nod.

As Townsend was organising the rest of his available men, two smartly dressed elderly gentlemen entered the station and approached the front counter.

"My name is George Sowerby," said one "and this is a colleague of mine Robert Carney."

Townsend recognised the names and looked at the list he had taken from Armstrong earlier. He looked at the men again: both wore an expression that was a combination of resignation and humiliation.

"I spoke to my clerk earlier," continued Sowerby, "who informed me that your Inspector Armstrong had visited my offices this morning, no doubt in order to arrest me. After speaking to Mr. Carney here, we have both decided to save him the trouble and do the decent thing by giving ourselves up."

Only because you were like rats in a trap! Instead of articulating his thoughts, Townsend simply logged their details and said, "Follow me please."

He led them down the corridor to the cells at the rear of the station. As Sowerby and Carney approached, they saw Gerald Whitlock through the bars of one of the cells. He looked up and saw them but dropped his head again. There was nothing to say.

As he walked back to his desk, Townsend gave a sigh of relief as he was running out of constables; by giving themselves up, the two men had saved him at least one head-ache.

Chief Constable Henry Baker had been roused from his office during the hive of activity and was waiting for Townsend when he returned to his position. He stood shaking his head.

"Sowerby is actually a member of the Watch Committee," he growled, "the very body who are there to oversee our work!"

Baker had had many a run-in with the Watch Committee over the years, when their pedantry approach to their role often lapped over into one of interference. And even when the methods of Baker's force proved effective and productive – despite the committee's unnecessary scrutiny – there was rarely an acknowledgement of this from its members. Neither were lessons learned from their erroneous approach, as the frustrating cycle of interference continually repeated itself, despite Baker's protestations.

The Chief Constable's appointment of Cornelius Armstrong some years earlier was a typical example: the committee expressed reservations in the strongest possible terms at the thought of such a young officer being promoted; seniority had always been the tried and trusted mantra. Baker ignored the views of the committee and promoted his man who immediately started to deliver results: detection rates were increased, as were arrests, while the amount of crime committed in the city generally was reduced. At no time did the committee acknowledge the success of the appointment, putting the trend down to simple coincidence, much to Baker and Armstrong's annoyance.

The astute Sergeant Townsend sensed his chief constable's anger and inwardly shared it. "Yes sir," he said, simply.

"Who else have we got to pick up?"

"Just the two councillors, sir" – Townsend looked at his list – "Brian Page and Bert Andrews. Inspector Armstrong is on his way to Broad Street to see if he can catch this Roberts character; I sent PCs Kirk and Wilkins to assist him."

"And how many constables do we have left available?"

"Only two sir, Riggs and Hall," he indicated the two men who were waiting patiently for their instructions.

"Very well men," said Baker, addressing the two, "you come with me and we'll see if we can round these other two villains up."

If the uniformed officers were in any doubt as to the seriousness of the matter, those uncertainties were dispelled with their chief constable's instruction. They had never seen him in such a determined mood before and they had certainly never witnessed him making arrests, personally.

The hansom cab carrying Inspector Armstrong meanwhile was clattering over the cobbles to get to the bottom of Broad Street. It arrived almost simultaneously with the horse-drawn police wagon driven by PC Eddie Kirk. He and fellow constable Sam Wilkins climbed down and virtually met their inspector at the door of number six.

"Kick it in!" instructed Armstrong, not concerned about standing on ceremony.

His constables obliged and the soles of their boots hammered against the lock three times before the door crashed open. The three policemen rushed into the house.

All was silent. Armstrong sensed he was too late.

"Go and check upstairs," he ordered his men, "and be careful. The man we are looking for is extremely dangerous."

Kirk and Wilkins nodded and climbed the stairs carefully, while Armstrong inched around the ground floor. He entered the back room and looked through into the kitchen: nothing. Walking over to the window to make an initial observation of the back yard, he saw a piece of paper sitting on the window sill. On the paper was scrawled in pencil:

Too late copper. If it's any consolation, no one has ever got that close to me before. Better luck next time.

The note was written on the back of a telegram. Cornelius turned the paper over:

THE POLICE ARE COMING STOP
FLEE STOP
WHITLOCK END

Armstrong's disappointment at failing to apprehend Roberts was tempered by his satisfaction that Whitlock had incriminated himself with the telegram. It was irrefutable proof that he and Roberts were in league with one another. For his part, the Manchester villain had probably taken great delight in not only taunting the police, but also implicating the solicitor, with the one action.

"No one up there," said Eddie Kirk, as the two uniformed officers appeared at the foot of the stairs.

"No, he's gone," said Armstrong, half to himself.

Kirk and Wilkins stood in an uncomfortable silence for a few seconds before Wilkins asked, "Back to the station, sir?"

"Yes, there's nothing else here," answered Armstrong with some resignation.

The three climbed up onto the wagon and set off up Warwick Road.

Armstrong had endured a busy, stressful day so far and he knew it was not going to get any easier with a series of interviews ahead of him. As the wagon trundled back towards the city centre, it occurred to him that there was a loose end in the case, that he could do with exploring further before speaking with Whitlock and his conspirators.

"Drop me off on Lowther Street," he said to PC Kirk, "I need to visit a property in Globe Lane before going back to the station."

Kirk reigned the horse at the junction indicated and Armstrong walked the length of Lowther Street until he reached the lanes at the northern end.

He turned on to the noisy lane that bustled with activity. Children played with hoops and tops, while their mothers scrubbed at their front steps and beat the dust from the cork matting. Businessmen came and went and traders ran their modest businesses, cheek by jowl. He gave a wide birth to an open smithy's shop that belched heat out onto the lane and passed a stack of barrels, behind which a carter was loading some hessian sacks onto a wagonette. Finally he came to a small warehouse beside which was an even smaller shop with three chickens and a goose hanging up in the window. The detective entered the shop.

"Excuse me," he asked the man behind a makeshift counter, "my name is Cornelius Armstrong, I'm a policeman. Do you know a man called Dominic James?"

The man looked startled by the announcement.

"Yes," he said after a few moments, "he rents the loft above the shop."

"Are you the owner?"

"Yes," said the poultryman, a little bemused, "is he in some sort of trouble?"

"No, I'm afraid he's dead. I'm investigating his murder."

"*Stone me! Murdered?* Who would murder a lad like that? He's such a pleasant lad."

"When is the last time you saw him?"

"Well now you mention it, I haven't seen him for a while," said the man, "he paid his rent six months in advance, so unless I saw him in passing, we didn't really have much to do with each other."

"Can I see the loft, please?" asked Cornelius.

"Yes of course," said the shop owner, coming out from behind the counter.

He led Armstrong back out onto the lane and opened a little door immediately adjacent to the shop door.

"Would you like me to show you up?" he asked.

"No, I think I'll see myself up, if that's all right. If I need anything, I'll come back down and see you."

"Very well, sir," said the man re-entering his shop. "*Murdered,*" he mumbled to himself, "I don't know what this world is coming to."

Cornelius climbed the steps leading up to the loft and entered. He was greeted by a shaft of early spring sunlight that beamed through the roof-top window. Glancing around the modest room, he gravitated towards the poet's desk upon which sat papers and books that had lain undisturbed for weeks; they were thick with dust as a result.

The policeman found a cloth and wiped most of the dust away from the papers, the desk and the chair which sat in front. He then sat down to leaf through the documents, to see if there was anything of interest. Most were scribblings, apparently relating to the man's poetry; then there were a couple of legal-looking documents that he had apparently been in the process of copying. They were both titled *Morley, Freeman and Whitlock,* which confirmed – if confirmation were needed – that Dominic James was connected to Whitlock.

Cornelius opened the single draw to desk and found a bible, underneath which sat a hand-written page, ripped from a book. The writing – although neat – did not match that of the calligraphic style of the Will Writer.

The policeman glanced over the page, his eyes resting on the initials WW. It suddenly dawned on him what he was holding: it was the missing page – written on Christmas Eve – from Ester Sanderson's journal. Like the final entry in the journal, which was written as a letter to her mother hours before she died, this entry was also written as letter. The difference was that this was a love letter:

> *My darling WW, I am so desperately sad that I am unable to spend Christmas with you. It breaks my heart to think of you alone in our tiny loft. The few months since we met have been the happiest of my life. From the moment I saw you I knew you were the kind, considerate man you proved to be. In fact I have a confession to make regarding our meeting. Our fortunate accident was not an accident at all. I made sure you bumped into me and spilled your soup, knowing we would then have to go to lunch together! I know you will forgive me; I can picture you laughing as you read this.*
> *I can't wait for the holidays to be over and we can be together again. I am counting the days until then. All of my love, now and always, Ester.*

Cornelius sat looking at the page. He wondered if he was being too harsh on himself for not working it out sooner. He originally puzzled over why Ester wrote so affectionately about William Whitlock; he now realised it wasn't the elderly solicitor she was writing about. WW was her code for Will Writer; her lover Dominic James.

The detective began to see how the whole thing fit together. He took the relevant papers with him and informed the poultry seller that he had seen enough.

As he walked back through the doors of the police station, the entrance hall was filled with a combination of uniformed constables and well-dressed businessmen, none of whom Cornelius recognised but it was clear to him that they were members of this Book Club. No one met the inspector's eye as he walked past them to the front counter where Sergeant Townsend was processing the arrests.

"Have we got them all?" Armstrong asked.

"Yes sir. The Chief Constable brought the last of them in a few minutes ago," replied the sergeant, "he's in his office if you want to speak with him."

"Good work," said Armstrong, smiling at the thought of his superior officer getting his hands dirty.

On his way to speak with Henry Baker, Cornelius looked further down the corridor and saw the four cells at the back of the station. Days earlier, they had housed the Grant brothers and Jimmy Dunn; today sat Gerald Whitlock in one, his father in another, George Sowerby in a third and another man of similar age and bearing in a fourth.

"Afternoon sir," said Armstrong as he entered Baker's office.

"Excellent work Cornelius!" said Baker, "have we got them all now?"

"I'm afraid not, Henry. Roberts had flown the nest when we got round to Broad Street."

"That's unfortunate," said the chief constable, "are you going to start interviewing?"

"Yes, I intend to start with the younger Whitlock who seems to be at the heart of all this."

"Very good. In the meantime, I'll make arrangements with Governor Lyons at the County Gaol to take some of these villains. I'll then alert the Manchester force and Scotland Yard that Roberts is still on the run.

Armstrong nodded and left to start his series of interviews.

TWENTY-EIGHT

With all of his uniformed officers occupied, Inspector Armstrong got the keys to the cells himself and unlocked the cage that contained Gerald Whitlock.

"Come with me," he instructed; he was in no mood for courtesies. He led him to the much-used interview room. "Sit down."

There was a part of Armstrong that was prepared for Whitlock to adopt his usual arrogant persona; avoiding questions and making crass comments. The policeman's preparation was unnecessary, as the pathetic creature that sat before him looked for all the world like a little boy who was completely out of his depth.

The detective was tired and angry; he was in no mood to pussy-foot about and went straight to the heart of the issue.

"I know all about the Book Club. I know about the fraud, the extortion, the misery you have caused decent people. I also know that you are an accessory to murder and that you have aided and abetted the escape of an extremely dangerous man."

It was Armstrong's last sentence that forced Whitlock to look up from his lap. The policeman saw fear in his eyes and produced the telegram he found at the house in Broad Street.

"You sent this to Roberts." It was a statement rather than a question.

It was futile to deny his own stupidity and Whitlock simply nodded and dropped his head again.

"Where did he go?"

"I don't know," said the young solicitor, speaking for the first time since he had been arrested.

"The house in which he was staying," asked Armstrong, "do you own it?"

"Yes, it is one of many owned by the firm."

"So I can add *protecting a fugitive* to the charge sheet." The policeman was in no mood to show any mercy.

He continued by reverting to the subject of the murder. He didn't know the extent to which Whitlock was involved but pressed ahead with a confident assertion.

"Tell me how you became an accessory to the murder of Dominic James."

"I didn't know what Roberts had done," said Whitlock.

"But you were involved?"

"I had told him to threaten James and tell him to leave Carlisle."

"Why?"

"Something happened, shortly after the Christmas holidays," began the solicitor. "A friend of mine, Stephen Baldwin, saw my fiancée near the home of James, who did some work for our firm. A week or so later, both Miss Sanderson and Baldwin happened to be in our offices, albeit on different business."

Ester was running another errand for her father, while Baldwin was picking some papers up for his employer Denis Richards. As the two were both waiting, Mr. Baines invited them to wait in one of the offices as Gerald was momentarily delayed. While they were alone, Baldwin confronted Ester about his suspicions. She was horrified by his discovery and failed miserably to explain it away.

"Come, come, Ester," said the obsequious Baldwin, moving closer to her and pinning her into a corner, "it seemed to me that you were extremely comfortable in that wretched place. There must have been something, or should I say some*one* of interest to take you there."

"I don't know what you mean," said Ester, starting to panic.

"I know that is where the Will Writer lives isn't it?" – he didn't wait for her to answer – "If you enjoy other male company to that of Gerald, perhaps I could be of assistance."

He grabbed her arms and tried to pull her towards him; she resisted and managed to pull away, only for him to grab at her wrists.

Just then the door opened and Gerald entered; it was probably the only time during their relationship that Ester actually was pleased to see him.

"What's going on?" he asked.

Baldwin quickly let go, "Oh, we are just discussing a mutual acquaintance."

"Ester?" Whitlock asked.

Ester ignored the question; she was desperate to get away from them. She reached into her purse and produced the document her father had sent her with; she put in on the table and rushed out without saying a word.

Whitlock continued his narrative to the policeman.

"Baldwin told me what had happened and – knowing that James lived on Globe Lane – I assumed that he was the subject of Ester's interest. I later confronted her with it and she was very evasive which confirmed to me that the two had met."

"So what did you then do?" asked Armstrong.

"I arranged for Roberts to be near the offices on a morning that I knew the Will Writer would be there. I slipped out before he arrived and stood with Roberts. I pointed James out to him as he arrived and told him to warn him off."

"Warn him off?" shouted Armstrong, "he cleaved his head in and had him thrown in the river!"

"I didn't intend for that to happen. I just wanted him out of Carlisle and away from Ester. Once I had pointed James out to Roberts, I returned to the office and informed the Will Writer that someone had been in earlier and requested a meeting with him about a possible commission. They were to meet in the *Irish Gate Tavern*. As we never saw him again after that morning, I assumed that he had left. When I asked Roberts about it, he just told me it had been taken care of. I didn't know he had murdered the man."

"So what happened next?"

"A few days later, when I was satisfied that James was gone, I went to Ester's house to give her another opportunity to explain whatever relationship existed between the two. She was again evasive on the matter. I told her that it was academic now anyway because I had made sure James would not be bothering anyone anymore.

"'What do you mean?' she asked, with concern in her eyes. I saw at that moment that my suspicions had some foundation. 'I mean he is no longer around,' I said in my anger, 'he could be dead for all I care.'"

"When did this conversation take place?" asked Armstrong.

"It was the night before she took her own life," replied the solicitor apologetically.

"Yet you previously told me that the last time you saw Ester was on New Year's Eve." Armstrong's comment was moot, given all of the information he now had, but he wanted to remind Whitlock of it anyway. "Tell me," he asked, "did you ever consummate your relationship with Ester.

Whitlock started to sob and shook his head slowly, "No."

His humiliation was complete.

The two sat in silence for a while. Armstrong took out his notebook and looked at what he had written in Sanderson's study earlier that day; it was only a few hours ago that Sanderson had collapsed but so much had happened since, it seemed like days had ago. His eyes ran down the list of names listed and their occupations. It had been the first time he had read it properly.

When Sanderson had begun to tell him about the secret society, Armstrong had written at the top of the list 'Book Club, no more than twelve members.'

"Tell me about the Book Club," said Armstrong.

Whitlock looked up from his misery, "I'm not sure what there is to tell. They are a group of friends-"

"Who specialise in profiteering, extortion and murder," interrupted Armstrong.

"Well…"

"Well what? If they don't actually perpetrate the crimes themselves, they certainly sponsor them."

Whitlock was silent, unable to deny the accusation.

"How did you come to be involved?"

"My father encouraged me to join the Free Masons; that's where the group are drawn from. When a vacancy came, my father pushed his colleagues to allow me into the club. They had never had anyone so young before but I think they must have felt I could bring a new vigour to their activities..."

Whitlock tailed off his narrative realising how open he was leaving himself.

"You certainly did that," said the detective, taking the opportunity. "So how did this Roberts get involved?"

"Well, it was actually one of the members of the club who introduced him. He said that he was doing a favour for a friend in Manchester by taking Roberts in, who apparently had to lay low for a while. Knowing that we owned several properties, father and I were asked to put him up. That's how I got to know him."

"So the inference is then, that this character has committed further misdeeds in Manchester and you and your colleagues had aided and abetted the villain."

Whitlock again remained silent, unable to deny the statement.

"Are there similar Book Clubs elsewhere?"

"I don't know," said Whitlock, "I think the name was just conjured up because it sounds so innocent and unassuming."

"You said that one of the members effectively brought Roberts to Carlisle, who was that?"

Whitlock again dropped his head. Initially, Cornelius thought he didn't know but then sensed it was more a case of unwillingness, rather than ignorance. He referred to his notebook again.

"I have the list of members here, Sanderson and his partner Carney, the councillors Page and Andrews, Clough, Richards, MacLeod, Forbes the surgeon and Sowerby the solicitor."

He interrupted himself and looked at the list again. For the first time he saw that there were only actually nine names on the list – Sanderson never completed it before collapsing. He looked again and realised that neither Gerald Whitlock nor his father William were listed; this left one unknown member.

"There is one missing," he said out loud.

Whitlock never replied.

"Who is missing from this list?"

Again, there was no reply.

"Look at me," Armstrong demanded.

His prisoner slowly looked up.

"There are only nine names on this list; you and your father make eleven, which means there is still one missing. Who is it?"

"It's the Chairman," said Whitlock resignedly.

"The Chairman?"

"Yes, he is the one that brought Roberts from Manchester. He said he was doing an old friend a favour."

"Well who is he, this Chairman?"

Whitlock's answer caused Armstrong to slump back in his seat. He drew the interview to a close and called William Whitlock and then George Sowerby in to see him. He simply asked them each one question: who was the Chairman of the Book Club? After some reluctance, independently of one another, they both corroborated Gerald Whitlock's answer. Inspector Armstrong put them back in their cells and knocked on the door of the chief constable.

"Just when you think you've heard it all," he said as he entered.

Henry Baker's forehead creased as he looked up expectedly.

"I think you need to prepare yourself for a shock, Henry," said the inspector, keen to forewarn his superior, "I've already had one man die on me with a heart attack today, I don't want another."

"What is it?" asked Baker.

"I've just questioned these lot," – he threw a thumb over his shoulder in the general direction of the cells, unable to hide his contempt for the prisoners – "and I've just found out who the chairman of this secret society – this so-called Book Club – was. It is none other than Herbert Underwood."

It took a few seconds for Baker to register what Armstrong had said.

"*Underwood!*" he shouted at last and immediately had to calm himself, "the Chairman of the Watch Committee?"

It was a ridiculous point of clarification, but one which Baker asked anyway.

"The very same," said Cornelius.

Baker sat back in his chair in disbelief, "So all the while, for all these years, these bloody people have been on our backs, and at the same time, they've been fiddling and conniving behind the scenes!"

"Well, I'm not sure about the rest of them but Underwood and Sowerby certainly have," corrected Armstrong.

"The rest are a bunch of bloody sheep anyway," retorted Baker, indiscreetly. It was testament to his relationship with his most trusted inspector that allowed him to make such a comment.

"Come to think of it," he continued, "through all of the last twelve months, I've often thought they have been conspicuous by their absence. They've even cancelled the odd monthly backside-kicking meeting! Now I know the reason why."

"It also explains why Underwood was at the house of Sanderson, the morning his daughter Ester was found hanged. It was no doubt an attempt to mitigate the damage her death would cause for them all. It was the poor girl's passing that set the chain of events in motion that has led us to this point."

"And if memory serves," added Baker, "Underwood asked for Godfrey Parker to attend that morning, no doubt confident that he could bamboozle the old duffer and lead him away from his own wrongdoing."

"In fairness to Godfrey," said Armstrong, "he and all the lads have done a super job over the last few months."

"None more than you, Cornelius," said his superior officer, "I don't know where I would be without you tying it all together."

Baker thought back to his appointment of Armstrong five years earlier and how Underwood and his cronies objected to the appointment. *No bloody wonder! h*e thought, *he could probably see the writing on the wall.*

Cornelius had rarely seen Henry Baker so angry; normally a light-hearted, gentle man, he was incandescent with fury at the betrayal and injustice of Underwood in particular; and the rest of these city businessmen in general. Together they had brought pain and misery to the city and caused him and his men headache after headache.

"I don't know how they put their head on the pillow at night," said Baker, almost to himself.

"I need to go and see if I can find Underwood," said Cornelius.

Baker looked at his office clock, it was approaching four o'clock.

"You're right. It's been a long day, Cornelius but it's not quite over yet. I will come with you."

Armstrong was surprised by the chief constable's announcement. If he needed any confirmation of Baker's strength of feeling regarding the matter, it was dispelled with the news that his superior was keen to be involved in his third arrest of the day.

"Do we know where he is?" asked Baker.

"Sowerby reckons he'll be at his house in Dalston," replied the detective.

"Very well, let's go."

Baker reached for his hat and coat and followed his inspector out of the office. In the corridor he looked to his right to view the cells; he stared at Sowerby who raised his head when he heard the office door opening but then refused to hold Baker's gaze when he saw he was being looked at. He knew what Baker must have been thinking.

Armstrong retrieved his own hat and coat from his office and gave a further instruction to the ever-reliable Townsend.

"Bill, the Chief Constable and I are going out to Dalston to arrest Underwood," – any semblance of respect for the Chairman of the Watch Committee had disappeared between the policemen – "Can you send a couple of lads out there with a wagon to pick him up? We will go out there on the train, it'll be quicker. We'll obviously stay there until they arrive."

"Will do, sir," said Townsend.

Armstrong then met Baker at the door and set off the short distance to the railway station, knowing that there were regular trains to the west of the county, all of which passed through Dalston, a village about five miles away from the city centre. They arrived on the platform just in time to catch the half past four service.

"To think, that bugger wanted me to join the Masons not very long ago," Baker said to Armstrong, as the train started to pull away.

Cornelius could see that his superior was still riled by the betrayal of Underwood. Something told him that once Henry had calmed down, he was going to enjoy arresting the man that had been a thorn in the force's side for many a long year.

Like Gerald Whitlock, Herbert Underwood had started his professional life as a young solicitor but he was far more intelligent and measured than Whitlock, and a combination of his influential connections and his own cunning saw him rise to prominence steadily in his early career. He became partner in his firm by '65 and was appointed to the Magistrates' Bench at the turn of the decade – the youngest magistrate the city had ever seen. Around the same time he was appointed to the Watch Committee and within five years, became Chairman. With the inexorable rise on the social and professional ladder, Underwood did not hesitate to use his power and influence all over the county, which gradually led to him becoming a well-known figure throughout the north west of England.

If his professional persona was in the public domain, his private one was known only to a select few. The seventies had also seen a small group of Free Masons form a club designed to benefit themselves by any underhanded means possible. They named it the Book Club, an innocent name that would never attract any attention if it were to be mentioned in public. Underwood was one of its founding members and within seven years, he had also become chairman of that particular gathering as well.

His position of influence was now complete: Chairman of both the official Watch Committee and the unofficial Book Club, as well of being a magistrate, he was in a position of considerable control within the city.

Which is the reason why he opposed the appointment of Cornelius Armstrong to inspector in '95. Armstrong appeared young, enthusiastic and *competent*. He much preferred the old stagers like Godfrey Parker who could be easily fooled, used and ignored.

Henry Baker was the main problem for Underwood. Baker thought for himself and trusted his instinct, much as Armstrong would prove to do. As a result, Baker constantly found himself at loggerheads with the Watch Committee, who in reality were a committee of one. It was only in the last hour that it had dawned on the chief constable how quiet the committee had been in its scrutiny of the City Force during what had been one of the worst periods for crime in living memory. Now he knew the reason why.

The two policemen climbed down from the train at the modest Dalston station. There was a carter with a vehicle – it couldn't really be described as a hansom cab – who was waiting for the last train before calling it a day. Pleasantly surprised to get a fare so late in the day, his two passengers shared his feeling as the two policemen thought they would have to walk the twenty minutes or so from the station to Underwood's house that stood at the Bridge End side of the village.

The house itself was an imposing gothic-style property with turreted towers on each of its four corners. As the cart crunched along the driveway leading to the house, something caught the eye of both Armstrong and Baker in one of the first-floor windows: it was Underwood looking down, as if expecting the visit. As they climbed down from the vehicle, the figure turned away from the window.

The two policemen walked up the steps and rang the bell. A few seconds later, a man – clearly the butler – opened the door.

"I am Inspector Cornelius Armstrong and this is Chief Constable Henry Baker of the City Police Force," announced the detective. "We are here to see Herbert Underwood."

The butler opened his mouth to speak but before he could, there was a loud *bang!* Instinctively, Armstrong pushed passed the butler and raced for the stairs, taking them two at a time. Henry Baker followed him but there was no way he could keep pace with his inspector. Cornelius reached the landing and surveyed the doors: three were open; he ran to the one that was closed.

As soon as he opened the door, his nostrils were filled with the smell of gunpowder. He looked over and saw the pistol still smoking. It lay before the body of Herbert Underwood who was slumped forward across his desk; the tell-tale sign of a scorch mark on his forehead confirmed what both Armstrong and Baker knew as soon as they heard the sound. A dark slick was still creeping across the blotting paper when Baker arrived on the shoulder of Armstrong.

"It's over," said Cornelius.